I0678486

ENEMY
AGENTS

SHAUN TENNANT

DEDICATED
to the genre fiction writers
upon whose shoulders I stand.

PART ONE:
THIS TIME, IT'S PERSONAL

1

A man in a custom-tailored grey silk suit walked alone into the Russian embassy in London. The perfectly tailored silvery fabric had been sewn in Italy only three days before. The suit rested gently on his massive shoulders, making a large man even more imposing, and some expert tailoring minimized his sizeable belly. A uniformed English valet announced him as Vladimir Plunov (the notorious Russian billionaire) as he entered the gala. With a quick and careful scan of the room, the man in the grey suit noted which dignitaries turned to face him—and which ones didn't pay him any attention. He would remember both.

When he descended the three red-carpeted steps to the ballroom, there was already a salt-and-pepper haired English butler waiting with a tray of champagne in crystal flutes. '*Nothing like an English butler,*' thought the man in the grey suit, as he took a flute and nodded a polite, wordless thanks to the servant.

He made his way through the middle of the crowd, steering clear of the dance floor. A Frenchman and his trophy wife greeted him warmly, but the man in the grey suit wasn't interested in these charming yet meaningless people. A delegate from Kazakhstan gave him the stink-eye but held his tongue; no doubt bothered by some old slight Plunov had done to his country in the name of expanding his petroleum empire. The man in the suit even paused a few feet from the Kazakhstani, just to see if he'd dare to say something. Satisfied that this low-level functionary would never provoke the mighty Vladimir Plunov, the man in the suit walked away, gulping down most of his champagne.

The embassy was expansive, built decades earlier to display the wealth of Russia to the western world, and although governments and economic systems had changed in the Mother Country, it was maintained in pristine condition for much the same reason. There were four-hundred guests at the party, each of them a politician, government employee, or a millionaire. The man in the suit hated these events, but he was here with a purpose. In a manner that was hopefully less direct than a heat-seeking missile, the man in the suit searched the party for Plunov's partner. Alex Maslov was in here somewhere. The man in the suit knew this for a fact because the tracking tag in the seam of Maslov's jacket was transmitting from within twenty metres.

The man in the suit expected it would prove tricky to get Maslov alone, but held onto the hope that surprise and fear could make Maslov come quietly. There was just one problem—Maslov was the one person in the room who knew that Vladimir Plunov had been dead for almost a week. The sight of his old partner sipping champagne might make him skittish instead of pliable.

The man in the suit carried himself like a heavy man, although he was only one-hundred and seventy pounds. His shoes provided an extra five inches of height without looking like lifts. The shoulders of the fatsuit were built up to provide the illusion of Plunov's impressive frame. And then there was the face.

The man in the suit wore a false chin and nose, crafted out of various latex and silicone prosthetics. The appliances covered his cheeks, but in a very thin layer. The colour in the prosthetics faded to clear just before the incredibly thin edges of the latex, allowing the man's real skin to blend seamlessly into the false face. His eyebrows were glued on with spirit gum, his hair dyed with a grey colour that would withstand a soaking of water or sweat, but would wash out instantly with a specific shampoo.

The man in the grey suit had sculpted the face himself, by hand, based on 3D models produced in a computer by comparing hundreds of recent photos of Plunov. His fingerprints were Plunov's, his voice was a flawless recreation of not only Plunov's specific hometown dialect, but also of the speaking patterns and vocabulary that Plunov frequently used. The man in the suit had been Plunov once before—three weeks earlier when he stole some documents—but he had been studying his mark for two months. Maslov's assassination of his old partner was unfortunate, but it had been quiet. Since nobody knew Plunov was dead, the man in the suit was able to slip into Plunov's life with little effort.

"Vlad, you old dog!" called an Englishman. "I thought you were off yachting with what's-her-name. The Wimbledon girl."

"Chris-to-pher," said the man in the suit, recalling Plunov's traditional greeting for the English music producer. "I thought I'd come here and find out what fine piece of musical talent you have squeezed into a bikini for me this week," he said with a hearty chuckle.

"Oh no, not just one girl, I've got a girl group now," said the music producer. "And they're all mine!"

"Very good! Tennis players are more flexible anyway." With that, the man in the suit carried on, smiling at some of Plunov's associates and keeping an eye out for his target. He spotted Maslov on the dance floor, doing a tango with his latest secretary/mistress. Out in the open, Maslov would be forced to speak with Plunov or risk making a scene.

The man in the suit slipped out of the crowd, pausing to allow the tangoing couples to pass before walking angrily up to Maslov. Thankfully, Maslov's back was turned. His secretary spun, then snapped back to Maslov with her mouth open, leaning in to bite the rose from Maslov's mouth. When her eyes focused on Plunov standing only a few feet away, she let out a brief, involuntary yelp before cutting herself off. The dancers jolted to a stop and turned to look. The woman blushed.

Maslov turned to see what startled her. His face went white.

"Alex," said the man in Plunov's suit. "We need to talk."

Upstairs, in a quiet room on the fourth and highest floor, Alex Maslov stood by the window, surely hoping that if people could see him from the street, he couldn't be hurt. They were alone now. Maslov and the man who looked like Plunov were granted access to a private meeting room with the security cameras off, thanks to their considerable clout with the Russian ambassador. The room was simple: a large table with eight chairs, two windows, and a small side table set up with vodka and glasses.

"You're dead," said Maslov. "I saw you die."

"What did you really see?" asked not-Plunov. "You saw your man poison my drink. You saw me clutch my

4

chest and collapse. You saw a body thrown overboard. But did you feel my pulse yourself? What did you really see?"

"You couldn't have known, you couldn't have known," Alex was starting to babble. "My people are untouchable."

"And just who are your people? Who is it you really work for, Alex? Was my handing you a half a billion dollars not enough?" The man in the suit wanted to play with Maslov's emotions, get him off-guard, and then get him to talk.

Alex Maslov looked out the window. He smiled to himself, and spoke to the window, rather than face the man he had betrayed. "You could not comprehend who my people are," he said bitterly.

"Are they yours? Or are you theirs? Or are you their dog?" The man in the suit knew that Maslov was a cocky, arrogant man, and a challenge to his manhood might provoke him to brag about his position within the cell. But instead, he stayed calm.

"I have my place. Other people have theirs." Alex suppressed his smile as he stared out the window to watch the assassin scaling the outside wall. He flipped open the lock on the window and started to roam around the room as he spoke. "But you will not learn anything from me, old friend."

"Alex. The game is over. I am alive because I am always ahead of you. And soon, you will be handed over to the people who helped secure my empire long before you came along. The people I never told you about."

"No, the game is not over. You are still playing," said Maslov, pouring himself a drink from a bottle of vodka. He drank it in one long gulp, and slammed the glass against the table. "…and you are bluffing."

"What makes you say that?"

"Because you are not Vladimir Plunov…" Alex relished his moment as he slowly let the next word slip over his tongue: "American."

The man in the suit felt a cold rock drop inside his stomach. His cover was blown. He had walked into foreign soil, confidently removed himself from the crowd, and set up his own ambush.

Alex grinned, and poured himself a new shot of vodka. The American reached up the back of his suit, and drew a black air-powered ceramic handgun from the small of his back. Alex hadn't expected a gun inside the embassy. He set his drink down.

"Tell me who you work for or I shoot you right here," said the American, now in his native accent.

Alex looked to the window behind the American, the one he had just unlocked. "Help me," he said. The American felt a cool breeze as the window opened behind him.

The American fired a single, quiet shot and the non-metallic bullet left a small entry wound in Maslov's forehead. Before Maslov hit the floor, the American was diving to his right, rolling as he did, to face the window. It was open, but there was nobody there. The American regained his feet, and scanned the room from a crouch. There was no sign of the assassin. Behind him, there was a footstep. The American turned and fired. Again, there was nothing. The ceramic gun was only worth two shots, so he dropped it. Hooking the middle fingers of his right hand through holes in his belt buckle, the American drew the two-inch-long dagger that was hidden inside. He rose to his feet, in a fighting stance. If the assassin had a gun, he would have used it by now. They would have to fight it out. The American was unhappy about fighting in the Plunov fatsuit, where the padding restricted his movement, but he had no choice. He kicked off the heavy shoes, preferring to fight in socks rather than lifts.

The assassin appeared behind the American, grabbing for his head in an attempt to break his neck. The American used his left hand to block the assassin's arm from moving, and used the blade in his right to stab the assassin's leg. The assassin howled and released his grip. When the American turned to face his attacker, the assassin caught him with a haymaker to the jaw. The false chin was pounded out of place, tearing the glued-down latex from the American's cheeks. He stumbled, but stayed on his feet. The assassin went for a front kick, but the American deflected it and punched the base of his palm into the side of the man's knee. The assassin hurled himself forward with his one good leg, sending his large body into the American's chest. The American stumbled over Maslov's body, sprawling onto the boardroom table, still dizzy from the punch.

As the American rolled to his right to get off the table, the assassin picked up Maslov's bottle of vodka and splashed the American across the eyes with it. The man in the suit was blind, dizzy, hindered by the cumbersome costume. He swung the blade twice in front of him before the vodka bottle hammered into the side of his head. The bottle did not break, but his skull might have. The American collapsed backward against a wall, and slowly slid to the floor. He rubbed his eyes, regaining some of his vision. The assassin stood over him, taking the cap off a syringe. It was the first time the American got a good look at his attacker's face.

"My god," he said. "You?"

The assassin stayed stone-faced. "Me."

The assassin leaned in and placed his thumb on the plunger.

Ten minutes later, Russian officials discovered the body of Alex Maslov, along with that of an unidentifiable stranger in a fatsuit. The stranger's fatsuit and clothing were intact, but his head was gone. The killer, it seems, had taken his head when he escaped out the window.

And there was a symbol finger-painted on the wall, written in blood:

2

Chris Quarrel threw himself forward at a full sprint, stretched out in the air and hit the ground hard with his knees and chest. His face splashed with the thin, watery mud from one of the ubiquitous puddles that dotted the landscape. The cold water soaked into his shirt—chest and sleeves alike—but Quarrel didn't move to get out of the puddle; he was already soaking wet anyway. All that mattered was that he had kept his unwieldy rifle out of the water, and that he was still warm enough to keep his hands from shaking.

Two quiet *twip-twips* from his four o'clock made Quarrel forget about his discomfort. One shot impacted in a tree root two feet beside Quarrel's head. The other shot hit the ground a foot before the root. Quarrel needed to face the oncoming shooter to his right, so he rolled onto his left side, swinging his gun with both hands. He tapped at the trigger at practiced, metronome intervals—tapping at exactly the right pace to avoid a jam yet without wasting a moment.

Fifteen feet back, the attacker took three shots to the chest. He was Pete Hershey, who worked in Quarrel's office. They were the same age, but Hershey had started his career a little earlier. Quarrel was one of only two people who had to work beneath Hershey, and Quarrel grinned now as he realized he had just killed his smarmy superior. Hershey was in a higher pay grade than Quarrel, but not so high up that he had an office; this was one cubicle drone killing another. Hershey quietly wiped at the red paint that had sprayed his face, flipped Quarrel the middle finger, and laid down dead—which for

Hershey meant relaxing in a dry spot with his hands behind his head. Hershey managed a smirk as he lay down, as though being eliminated from the game somehow made him better than Quarrel. In fact, just about everything he ever did made Quarrel think him a smug, superior bastard, but this was pushing it.

Despite whatever spin Hershey would like to put on the situation, Quarrel would still relish the fact that Hershey had missed an open shot, and that Quarrel himself had taken out his rival.

Quarrel was crawling through a forest in northern Ontario in the middle of the spring. The snow was mostly gone, leaving behind freezing cold mud for Quarrel and the nine other trainees to crawl through (although Hershey's clothes had looked quite dry, as if he hadn't crawled on belly but instead confidently strolled through the woods). It was a simple attack-defend game: one team of five defends a small wooden deck in the middle of the forest while the other team attacks it. There is a flagpole on the deck, with a symbolic skull-and-crossed-rifles flag flying. The attacking team wins if they can lower the flag in less than ten minutes. The defensive team wins if they can withstand for the full ten minutes. Either team loses if all five of their team members are shot. Quarrel checked his watch. The game was half over. He needed to move.

Quarrel quite enjoyed the physical aspect of this sort of training: running, crawling, shooting (even it was just a paintball gun), but having to work with a randomly-chosen team seemed pointless. Quarrel worked for a clandestine intelligence service. Once you were out in the field, there were no team-ups, no games, just a man alone against the enemy. So what was the point of learning

Army hand-signals if his entire career was going to be spent working solo?

While this particular training site (one secret enough that the actual Army didn't know about it) was located in Canada, most of the trainees were Americans. Only three of the ten—Quarrel, Hershey, and Gibbons—were on their native soil. The trainer, a legend of the spy game, was an American. Jack Hall had one week to put the team through their paces. At the end of the week, no more than five of the ten would be given a certificate that they passed the program. Most years only had three graduates. Today was the final day of training.

Moving as quietly as possible, hoping that his camouflage was working, Quarrel advanced on the structure. He didn't have a plan. While the other four team members had huddled to hash out a strategy, Quarrel had ran off to the side of the field of play and began his crawl toward the deck alone. This game was only ten minutes and the defenders knew they were coming. There was no time to plan, only to act, and Quarrel intended to win this thing on his own and guarantee that he passed the program.

The deck was pretty basic: an elevated wooden platform, six by twelve, with a stairway in each corner. The walls of the deck were four feet high, easily enough to hide behind, so the attackers would be at a severe disadvantage as they climbed the stairs. The instructor, Jack, sat on a sort of lifeguard chair behind the flagpole, elevated higher than the rest of the deck. He said nothing at any point in the game, other than declaring victory for one team or the other. Hall's chair pivoted so he could see all directions, observing the field of play. Three other instructors, dressed in bright orange like hunters, supervised from the forest below.

Quarrel pulled himself along the forest floor, watching the stairways on the deck in case any guards were watching. He saw nothing. With fifteen feet to go he broke out in a run, sprinting not to the stairs but underneath the deck, where he hoped the guards wouldn't be able to see him. There was no sound of footstep above, which did *not* mean he hadn't been seen, only that the defenders were smart enough to stay quiet.

Two other attackers were already there, having apparently chosen this as a rally point. Erica Gibbons, from Quarrel's office, and a skinny American named Jones. Quarrel raised one finger to them. *I got one kill.* The others both shook their heads. So there might still be four defenders. He checked his watch. Six minutes fifty seconds. If any other attackers were alive, they'd have to show up now. No one came.

They spread out, each to a different staircase. The combination of their heavy boots and the wooden stairs would make a stealthy approach impossible. Their best bet would be to storm three sides at once, hoping to overwhelm the defence. As long as one attacker made it to the flagpole, their team would win. Dying didn't matter. The mission mattered. Nothing else.

Jones gave the *advance* signal and all three attackers pounded up their stairs, running hard and making tons of noise. Quarrel turned his body to the doorway before he reached the opening so that when he emerged, the defender was right in his sights.

Twip. The defender went down. Directly in front of Quarrel, a second defender shot Jones. Quarrel shot the man in the back. The defender gave an annoyed shrug and looked over his shoulder at Quarrel before he too lay down, wanting to know who had shot him. On the far side, Gibbons had taken out her target before he could shoot. That left the fourth corner, the stairway that nobody had taken. There was a defender here as well; apparently their plan had been to guard all entrances, with the extra man, Hershey, roving through the woods. The last defender turned around, surprised to find enemies behind him. For a split second his focus was split between Quarrel and Gibbons. He made his choice and lined up Quarrel, just as both attackers unleashed a barrage of red paint at him. He went down.

Finally, Quarrel was able to break silence. "That's it. We got all five. Game over."

Sitting on his elevated chair, Hall said nothing. Quarrel smiled as he walked over to the flagpole. All that was left was to lower the flag and he'd not only have won the game, he'd also be one of just two survivors. That had to help with getting one of those five certificates.

He never heard the shot, just felt the familiar sting of a paintball in the back. He turned, confused, and saw a defender through the opening at the northwest staircase. Someone was still out there, approaching fast. Maybe it was a twist on the game: an unknown surprise to test the team who thought they had won. Quarrel was confused, but he dropped facedown on the floor, making sure to turn himself so he could watch the stairs that he expected the enemy to enter from. He wanted to yell at Gibbons to hurry up and lower the flag, but the dead can't speak. Instead she took a defensive position by the doorway, waiting for the attacker to enter.

Only a few seconds later he heard another shot. It came from behind him, opposite where he was looking.

The new defender had somehow made it up the stairs in silence, and placed a paintball between Gibbons' shoulder blades. Above them, Jack Hall blew hard into a whistle.

"Fuck!" she shouted, turning around.

With the game over, Quarrel rolled over and sat up. The new defender was in sock feet—he'd removed his boots in order to slip up the stairs. Otherwise, he was the same Pete Hershey that Quarrel had shot five minutes earlier. But this time Hershey's chest showed no sign of paint.

"I thought you said you got him!" shouted Gibbons.

"I fucking did!" Speaking to Hershey now, he shouted "I shot you three times in the chest. You're done."

"This chest?" Hershey tugged on the thin camouflage jersey he wore—they had each been given one, in slightly different colours to make it easier to know friend from foe. "Because I don't see any paint."

"So where'd you steal the extra jersey from?"

By now the other two attackers and the three referees were filing into the structure, drawn by the whistle.

"Did you see this guy shoot me? Did you?" he demanded of the referees as they climbed the steps. "Didn't think so since it never happened." The judges shared a look between them, each shaking their head.

"Oh fuck off," said Quarrel, shoving Hershey.

"Enough!" shouted Hall, jumping down from his perch. "Did anyone see anything to suggest that this guy was ever killed?"

The judges hadn't seen it.

"Then defenders win."

"Horse shit," said Quarrel.

"The point of the exercise was teamwork. Who lives and dies was unimportant, only the mission. Your team never accomplished your goals, so you lose."

Quarrel walked away, shaking his head. Jack shouted at him. "Got something to prove? You're on defence this time. There are clean jerseys for the attackers back at the start, and new ones for the defenders under my chair. Get clean, reload, and the next game starts in ten."

#

Nineteen minutes later, Quarrel was alone on the deck, waiting for something to happen. Well, not quite alone. Jack was up on his high chair, watching and judging, his eyes revealing nothing to Quarrel.

Quarrel's team had opted for the opposite tactic to the one that Hershey's team had used. They sent four of their members out into the woods, hopefully to ambush the attackers. Quarrel was left alone at the base, the last line of defence if an attacker slipped by or if the defenders were all dead. He had drawn the stay-here-and-wait job mainly because the other defenders on his team resented him for costing them Round One.

An hour earlier, the forest had seemed quiet except for the sound of the wind. Now, Quarrel heard everything. Scurrying in the wet leaves, chittering of small rodents, and the ever-changing wind whipping the still-bare branches. There were no bird calls, as it was too early for them to be back up north.

And finally, footsteps.

Front side.

Quarrel backed up against the rear wall, so that he'd have both of the front stairs in sight. The attacker would see him from the stairs, but that was better than having his back turned to one of the potential entrances, especially after Hershey had just demonstrated how to get up the steps in silence.

Quarrel kept his gun raised, safety off, his eyes flicking back and forth to the two stairways. Finally, there was a shadow in the stairs to the left. He lined up his sights and waited. Inhaled. He'd fire on the exhale. A shoulder poked around the corner. A shoulder dressed in the green and brown camo of the defending team. Could be one of his own. Could be Hershey in another stolen jersey.

"Sing out!" shouted Quarrel.

"It's a trap." Gibbons' voice. "He's behind me."

Then she jerked forward and up the stairs, revealing her wrists tied together in front of her with a plastic cable tie. Hershey was behind her, using her as a human shield. He was just small enough that he was safely hidden behind the slim woman. He kept her in place with a hand gripping the back of her collar. He held a small paintball pistol that Quarrel hadn't seen before. It would be terrible at range but considering that Gibbons was only six inches from the muzzle, it would hurt like hell. Worst of all, Hershey had stripped Gibbons of her mask so her head was exposed. A paintball to the face would cause an injury, regardless of who fired, and in the wrong spot (the eye) that injury would be permanent.

"Just let me lower the flag and she's fine."

"Or I could just shoot her and have a clear line of fire at you."

"You'd have to shoot her in the head to make her drop that quick." He spoke to Gibbons, gloating, "You don't want Chrissy to shoot you in the face, do ya?"

"Fuck off," she muttered under her breath. She was clearly embarrassed to be in this position, but they were supposed to act like there were real guns in play.

"Walk to the flagpole. Slowly."

She took a step. Quarrel watched her face for any sign. He could see a few inches of Hershey's grinning face, but dared not fire. Paintball guns aren't as accurate as the real thing. A minuscule dip in air pressure could throw the ball off course and hit Erica in the face – break her orbital bone or nose, or one of those big brown eyes – no, he couldn't risk it just to beat Hershey in a game. He could feel himself sneering in frustration, *Hershey gets another feather in his cap at my expense*, but made effort to hide his seething.

They were at the flagpole now, and Hershey had a problem. He needed one hand to hold his human shield in place, and another to hold his gun. He couldn't lower the flag unless he grew a third hand. He jerked Gibbons' collar. "Lower it."

Gibbons nodded, but before reaching forward, she slipped her fingers under the jersey, fumbling at the waistband on her pants.

"Lower it, or I shoot Chris," Hershey sneered, turning his gun on Quarrel.

Erica seized the moment. Spinning hard out of Hershey's grip, she dropped her body while raising her hands, now holding a white object that registered only as a blur to Quarrel. She slashed her hands at Hershey's face and fell away, stumbling.

17

There was a bright red line slashed across Hershey's neck. She had slit his throat.

Above them, Hall blew the whistle. "Defenders win."

"What the fuck?" Hershey shouted, wiping at his neck and smudging the ink from Erica's Sharpie.

Jack jumped down from the elevated chair and smiled. "Now that was exciting. Usually it's the same-old, same-old. Hostage situation. Entertaining at least."

"No way does she win. There are no knives in paintball!" Hershey's voice went up an octave as he whined.

Hall patted Erica on the shoulder. "There are also no pistols in the attacking team's loadout. You changed the rules, so don't complain when she follows." Hershey gaped, but had no comeback. Whining to Jack Hall was one thing, but even Hershey knew not to piss him off.

The four of them waited for a few seconds, listening to the suddenly loud forest as the other players and referees came back to the platform. While they were still alone, Hall turned to Quarrel.

"You should have shot her."

"He took her mask off."

"This flagpole might represent a nuclear weapon. You can't let him get that close. In a real life situation you shoot the hostage in the head and don't stop firing until the hostage-taker is down. Only way to be sure."

"But he took her mask off. I mean, this is only a simulation."

"You think the real bad guys play fair? What if they take your wife—"

"—not married—"

"Ok, they take your adorable little niece or your grandma or something. You think she's worth more than New York City? Worth more than Winnipeg or wherever-the-hell you're from?"

"You want me to shoot my adorable imaginary niece in the head?" As he said that, Quarrel realized that the rest of the class had gathered behind him.

"Everyone," said Hall, "we just had ourselves an honest-to-God hostage taking in here. Thanks to some very impressive work by Miss Gibbons, the situation was averted, and the defending team won. In the first game the winning team had one survivor. In this game the winning team had two. So therefore Team Beta gets the win for this morning's exercise." The three other team members, the ones who had died in both rounds, grinned and circled Gibbons, giving pats on the back and celebratory fist-bumps. Quarrel, who had also technically survived the round, had to wait for them to notice him before they would congratulate him.

"Now if you'll all just wait about five minutes, I'm going to go tally up my marks for the week and see whether or not any of you pukes actually graduate from the program or not. Then I'll leave, and you can all have lunch and talk about how much you hate me." There was a small chuckle in the class. Hall headed down the stairs, waving one of the referees to join him.

Quarrel felt a hand on his shoulder. He turned, expecting Gibbons. It was Hershey. "Good job man, you survived defending. Just like I did in the first game."

Quarrel tried not to seem angry. He still had to work for this guy, so telling him off wasn't a good plan. "Sure man, good game," was all he could muster. They had been at this for six and a half days, and the idea that

19

Hall was currently writing names on certificates sent his stomach into a spin. He looked around the group. Everyone had the same expression of trying not to look nervous. Everyone except Hershey, who was trying to look at his own neck in the reflection on his watch. For a moment, Quarrel locked eyes with Gibbons. She bit her lip and shook her head, a nonverbal *I'm not gonna make it.*

Finally, Hall returned. He carried a manila folder so you couldn't see how many certificates he had with him.

"OK everybody. It's been a good week. You all made your agencies and branches proud, and I've already been in touch with each of your supervisors with good things to say. But this program has a high standard. That's why it exists. This isn't a vacation. It's a proving ground. Being good here isn't enough and you knew that before you came. You had to be the best. And when I reward only the best, it means that anything less goes home empty-handed. So let's get to it."

Quarrel exhaled through his mouth, waiting for the worst and hoping for the best.

"First up—Peter Hershey." There was a smattering of applause that Quarrel forced himself to join. Hershey smiled broadly and stepped forward to accept his certificate. He shook Hall's hand—the first time all week anyone had actually shaken hands with the grizzled, legendary operative.

"Next," Hall wasn't wasting time. "The Bushwacker." A military guy named Bush stepped forward, laughing at the name. Bush had excelled in the earlier challenges, although he had died quickly in the role-play. He took his place next to Hershey, who had presumptuously stayed on Hall's side of the platform.

Bush happily accepted his certificate and shook Hall's hand.

Hall looked down to his folder again. "Wouldn't you know it, another one of the Canadians." Quarrel's eyes shot up from the floor to Hall, then quickly to Gibbons, who was already returning the look.

"Erica Gibbons."

Quarrel felt his lungs deflate, but smiled and clapped for his co-worker, and stuck out his hand for a high-five as she walked by. She joined the other winners and soon everyone's attention was back on Hall, waiting to see the next name to be called. Hall looked into the folder once again. "There's one more certificate in here." He held it up, the blank back side facing the class. Quarrel tried not to stare a hole through it. Hall continued, " . . . and it's blank. Nobody else is graduating this week." He flipped the page over, showing the horizontal line where Quarrel had wanted his own name to be written.

"This blank certificate will be here next year. If you think you can honestly do better, it'll be waiting for you." As Hall finished his speech, he was looking straight at Quarrel. At least, Quarrel thought so. Hall finally turned his head to the three graduates. "Congrats. Enjoy the lunch, drive safe. And remember the lessons we learned this week. This training will save your life." With that, Hall walked to the back stairs and disappeared.

"Alright everyone, back to the barracks for burgers and beer," shouted one of the other supervisors.

As the students filed out, pulling off the jerseys and stretching their necks, Quarrel just stood there watching Gibbons and Hershey. Here, he was one of seven who didn't pass. But in a day it would only be the three of them, two who passed and one who failed. He knew they were going back to the same office in Ottawa, where he'd be the only one who didn't graduate. Carol was going to be disappointed.

After the beer and burgers and packing their bags, the three Canadians hit the road. It was a ten-hour drive back to Ottawa, and they had to get in at least most of it today. They checked into a roadside motel that night, three hours from home but too tired to continue. They booked three rooms, all in a row, and were pretty sure they were the only guests.

As Quarrel lay in bed, reflecting on his own failure and guessing how Carol would react, the rhythmic thumping of the headboard next door made him sick. *Goddamn Hershey, probably going to brag about that too.*

3

The saltwater spray hitting William Thorpe's face made him wince, both from the shock of the cold and the salt in his eyes. He had to close his eyes and shake his head to get the salt away from his eyes, but his hands never wavered—one hand shoving the boat's throttle forward and the other holding the steering wheel steady. He rocked as the boat bounced through the wake of the larger vessel, but Thorpe's little speedboat never wavered from its course.

Thorpe was chasing a one-hundred-and-ninety-seven foot yacht through the English Channel. The yacht had no hope of outrunning Thorpe's speedboat, but they also weren't about to stop and make it easier for Thorpe to board them. Now that he was within ten metres of the yacht's stern, he was starting to wonder why nobody was shooting at him yet. It wasn't as if his approach had been subtle. And they certainly knew he was coming, considering that he'd been kind enough to leave their men alive back in Dover.

He had woken in a damp room somewhere close enough to the Channel that he could hear the waves. His face was swollen on the right side from where he had been knocked out (he would later recall that he had been clubbed with a scuba diver's air tank, but at the moment he just knew that his face hurt.) When he woke up after the knockout, they had him lying on a damp cement floor, arms tied behind his back, beneath a dangling light bulb that provided a ten-foot island of light in a huge dark room. He could smell the faint lingering ghost of a woman's perfume.

There were four guards. One of them, Morris, was familiar. Morris was Anton Sidorov's wild dog in Western Europe. Thorpe had been trying to kill Morris before his face became intimate with some diving equipment. The other three were unfamiliar, but the look of them told Thorpe enough. Local criminals, the sort of guys known for their violent tendencies. The sort that your average smuggler or drug dealer would avoid because they were too violent, too likely to become reckless when the smuggling game requires stealth. The sort of men that Sidorov cultivated wherever he went. Thorpe only hoped they would be easy to provoke into foolish rage.

The men spoke when they saw Thorpe stirring. They all had similar accents: English, trashy and uneducated. Only Morris, who wore a nice suit in his official role as "head of security" spoke clearly and without lapsing into slang. The smallest thug was Caucasian, wore a black New York Yankees cap not quite straight on his head, and had tattoos of flames creeping up his neck. The medium-sized thug was dressed in a white 'wife-beater' tank top as if he didn't feel the cold. His whole body was tattooed, but the art was ugly and poorly drawn. Some might have been done in prison, but Thorpe guessed that many might have been inked onto the thug when the tattooist was drunk or high. The tallest of the thugs was dressed for warmth in a thick black leather jacket. His hands were in his pockets, and he stood very still. Morris was at the edge of the light, still dressed in the same blue pinstripe suit as earlier in the evening. His back was turned, and he talked quietly into a cell phone.

The two shorter thugs took turns mocking Thorpe, and Wife-Beater even stepped into the light long enough to kick Thorpe in the thigh, but Leather stood still, saying nothing.

Thorpe let them have their fun. He even smiled for them, and winked at the short one, just to prolong their taunts. He needed the time. Behind his back, he was jerking his wrists against the rope, at the cost of several layers of skin, in order to line up two things. He needed his right thumb to reach the face of his watch, and he needed the 12 on the watch to line up with the rope. When Wife-Beater kicked him, he exaggerated his flinch of pain enough to jerk his hands around beneath the rope. His thumb drew a letter R on the touch-screen face of the watch, and then he felt the heat of the rope burning as the top of the watch fired a small, invisible laser beam. This was a dangerous play, since the smell of burning rope would be obvious soon enough, but Thorpe had no hope at beating the four of them without his hands.

Once he felt the fibres starting to slack against his wrists, Thorpe decided it was time to lure in one of the thugs.

"Hey, boy, you know what that symbol on your shoulder means?" he said to Wife-Beater. It was a Chinese pictogram that Thorpe didn't know.

"It's Chinese for fury."

Thorpe snorted. "I bet the artist wasn't Chinese, was he? Because that's Korean for queer."

"Fuck you it is! My brother gave me that tat."

"So your brother's Chinese then? Or maybe he just knows what you like . . . "

"Old bastard callin' me a bloody queer . . . " Wife-Beater mumbled as he stepped back into the light. Morris was turning around, having just realized that Thorpe was baiting one of his thugs. He tried to shout an objection, but it was too late. Wife-Beater leaned down and grabbed Thorpe by the collar, cocking his right hand back in a fist. It left his neck wide open. Thorpe sprung his arms free from beneath himself and smashed the butt of his left hand into the younger man's Adam's apple, knocking his throat sideways hard enough to ensure he would not be getting back up.

Then he was springing to his feet. The other two thugs came at him straight away, with Leather Jacket pulling a knife from inside his pocket. Thorpe found his footing while in a crouch, and then threw himself at the Yankees fan. He got the kid to stumble back, creating just enough time to assess Leather coming in blade-first, going for a high arching stab at Thorpe's neck. Thorpe caught the knife hand between his palms and twisted the thug's wrist, freeing the knife. Thorpe grabbed it out of the air with his left hand. With the man's arm raised and momentum carrying the thug forward, Thorpe's instinct was to stab the knife into the attacker's armpit, pushing as deep as he could. The leather softened the attack, but the man still screamed as the blade found flesh, and Thorpe scanned the room for Yankee and Morris. He saw the flame-necked goon to his right and turned toward him. That was all the opening Morris needed.

The veteran assassin looped his favourite weapon—a steel guitar string—over Thorpe's head and in an instant Thorpe was choking. The garrotte was too tight to get a hand under. He flailed at Morris, but Morris had turned his back to Thorpe's and was using the leverage to yank on the wire with all his strength. The blood was cut off from Thorpe's brain, he knew, and that meant unconsciousness in seconds. Fortunately, Yankee was just as violent and reckless and Thorpe had assumed. The young thug pulled a knife of his own and ran at Thorpe. With his vision narrowing, Thorpe managed to catch this blade as well, but instead of stealing it, he redirected the thug's arm, guiding him to stab past Thorpe's left side, burying the blade in Morris's belly. The garrotte went slack and Thorpe fell to the floor, gasping. His eyes saw black and white static while his brain drank oxygen again, and he then realized that the thug still had the knife. All three thugs were recovering now, although Wife-Beater was breathing in harsh, rasping chokes and was in no condition to fight.

Yankee came at him first, and in his barely-conscious state, all Thorpe could muster to defend himself was his watch. The thug kept his knife in his left hand now, but opted to start in on Thorpe with a punch. As the thug landed a harder-than-expected right cross, Thorpe rolled with the punch and raised his hands. The thug had leaned in with the punch, really committing to it as he also prepared to follow-up with the blade, and Thorpe turned the watch laser on just as the young man's carotid artery passed by the 12 o'clock mark.

The thug screamed. The laser cut flesh like a scalpel, leaving a very narrow slash across the vein. The blood seeped at first, but once the Yankee fan put his hand to his neck and depressed the skin, the artery opened up and hot burgundy blood painted his hand. Thorpe caught a deep breath, his own neck still screaming at him from Morris's wire, and threw a shoulder into Leather Jacket's leg. The big man fell, his weight threatening to crush Thorpe, but Thorpe rolled Leather over his shoulder in a comfortable Judo move. The same instant the big man's head hit the concrete,

Thorpe threw a hard left elbow into his temple. The big man's eyes suddenly lost focus, then closed.

When Thorpe looked at Wife-Beater, the thug was doubled-over, still fighting to breathe through a damaged windpipe. Thorpe turned his back to the thug and looked for Morris, but all he found was a rectangle of light: an open door, heading outside. Walking slowly, still catching his breath, Thorpe headed toward the door.

The sound from behind Thorpe was one he had heard a thousand times and from many distances. It was a gun cocking. He turned in time to see that Wife-Beater had raised a semi-automatic handgun, held out sideways like in the movies. Thorpe faked to the right and the kid fired, missing by inches. Not one to waste an opportunity, Thorpe tackled the kid, pinning the gun between his own arm and body. Another shot went off, and the muzzle burned Thorpe's arm, but the bullet had no hope of hitting him. As he overpowered the younger man, Thorpe's lungs were burning. He could taste blood. He was getting old. Still, he took the thug, at least thirty years his junior, hard to the cement floor and landed a headbutt to the kid's nose. The nose broke with a crunch followed by a weeping of blood that soon became a torrent. Thorpe twisted the gun free and pistol-whipped the kid across the cheek, triggering another crunch as the cheekbone caved. This time he really would stay down.

Thorpe stumbled his way outside, only now discovering that he was at a warehouse on the waterfront a mile from the port. There was only one obvious way to go from the open door: to follow the string of lights that led to the water. He jogged at a slower pace than he would have in his younger days, but even taking it easy on himself he was still out of breath.

Morris was just untying the mooring ropes on the speedboat when Thorpe spotted him and fired four shots. Morris ducked at first, then as more shots came he dove into the frigid water. Thorpe would have liked to find him and finish him, but there was no time; the boat was more important.

Letting Morris swim away, Thorpe jumped into the speedboat, already running in neutral, and threw the throttle forward. He was in the open water within seconds, and heading south.

He had no doubt that Sidorov's yacht would have filled up at this warehouse, and he knew they were heading southeast toward France. It only took a few minutes before the yacht came into view.

He was close enough now to make out the yacht's name, *Democracy!*, painted in blue script along the stern. There was a small platform on the back of the yacht, barely above the water. That platform might have been used for sunbathing or launching scuba divers, but now it would make an obvious place to board. Thorpe jammed the throttle until he rammed the larger craft, then ran along his speedboat and jumped. He hit the platform gracefully, staying on his feet.

He kept his pistol cocked and raised as he worked his way along the deck. Much of the cabin was glass, with massive windows along almost every wall. But there was no sign of movement, inside or out. Working slowly and steadily along the massive boat, it took Thorpe a few minutes to reach the cockpit. He took a quick peek through a porthole and saw nothing inside. Taking a deep breath, he yanked the door open and stepped into the doorway, gun ready.

It was empty. There was nobody driving the boat. Thorpe paused just long enough to throttle down the engines before he headed below deck.

The lower level was the same as above. No drugs. No guns. No henchmen. No Sidorov. Anton Sidorov was the most notorious smuggler, murderer, kidnapper, and all-around villain in Europe. He had gone to such trouble to arrange this boat, this warehouse. Was there really nothing on it? Or was Thorpe too late? He hadn't seen a helicopter in the air, but maybe…

After a quick but not exhaustive search, Thorpe barged into the captain's cabin. The bed was made. Towels were neatly folded, sitting on a dresser. There was almost no sign that the boat had ever been lived in. Except for the obvious one lying on the floor at the foot of the bed.

The dead woman.

Black hair, a blue dress, olive skin. She was lying in a crimson puddle that would soon turn brown.

"Carmen," sighed Thorpe. He could still smell her perfume on himself. As he knelt next to her, gently brushing the hair from her face, he realized his mistake. Behind her body, a flashbang grenade went off, blinding and deafening Thorpe.

True to the nautical setting, he felt a fishing net drop on him, just before a group of men tackled him to the floor. By the time William Thorpe regained his senses, layers of rope wrapped the net around him, his ankles were tied, and his watch was gone. And as his eyes relearned how to focus, Thorpe saw his target enter the room.

Anton Sidorov, tall and gaunt, with oiled-back hair and thin lips, smiled at Thorpe and puffed on a cigar.

"Agent Triple-Eight of the British Secret Service." Sidorov said. "Pleased to finally meet you face-to-face."

"The pleasure is all mine," said Thorpe.

"I do admire you," the Russian spoke English, heavily accented. "I love the British. So many unique forms of torture. What do you like better," he asked, his eyes alight with pleasure, "tarred and feathered, or drawn and quartered?"

Thorpe had tracked Sidorov, and knew his reputation. He knew that Sidorov would actually do the things he threatened. Sidorov liked torture. It was his hobby, his passion. Thorpe stared his captor in the eyes and answered:

"Actually, our worst torture is a naked woman and a bottle of scotch. I'd be terrified if you tried that on me."

Sidorov smirked and nodded to a guard. The guard held a damp rag over Thorpe's mouth and nose, and the world faded away.

4

Chris Quarrel walked into the same post office he visited every Monday. He smiled at the woman behind the desk, who recognized him vaguely as a regular customer. Taking out his key ring—the one that featured a gaudy and memorable plastic figurine of Donald Duck—he easily selected the correct key and opened up a P.O. box. There were seven envelopes inside, addressed to four different people. He slipped the envelopes into his inside pocket, closed the box, and left after waving to the desk clerk.

It was snowing in Ottawa, possibly for the last time since it was now late April and all the snow on the ground was already gone. This was one last reminder of what frosted roads looked like before the rain took over and gave way to summer. Quarrel hadn't had time to change his tires yet, and he justified his procrastination by saying he needed snow tires for just such an occasion.

The office was on the third floor of a generic-looking office complex in the southwestern part of the city. The other floors were full of ordinary corporate offices: a P.R. firm, a gas station chain, an electronics importer. The office where Quarrel worked was signed as "Ocean Association, Inc.," and if asked in the elevator, Quarrel would tell people he analyzed temperature patterns in the world's waterways. This was, of course, not true.

CSIS-2 was the top-secret branch of the Canadian Security and Intelligence Service, and this was its central hub. There were agents around the world: surveilists, hackers, and in a few cases, operatives who could carry out the more dangerous missions. But the paperwork had to be filed from somewhere, and this was the place. It was a bustling office full of young, energetic people who always needed something *right now*.

Quarrel first stepped into the "coat room," where he hung the keys next to a dozen other key rings, took off his wet jacket, and allowed a guard dressed as a janitor to scan his retina. This was the entry procedure: hang up your coat, get blinded in one eye.

In the thirty feet between the door and his cubicle, Chris was stopped twice. First, Erica Gibbons stopped him by slapping a manila folder into his chest. The folder was bright yellow and sealed with a red sticker.

"Courier just came. This is for you."

Quarrel raised a questioning eyebrow.

"I don't know. They told me it was for Level 7 clearance."

Clearance worked like golf scores: lower was better. A seven was top secret, but not nearly important enough for any of the big shots to be bothered with. Since he had been with CSIS before joining CSIS-2, Quarrel had been cleared up to Level 7. This was a unique position, since everyone else in the office was cleared for higher or lower levels, but Chris was the only seven. So he got a lot to work on, but never the important files. Erica, despite being a year older than Quarrel, was only cleared for 'secret' files, not for anything with a clearance number. This one was probably an expense report, or rejection from a budget committee. Even that dick Pete Hershey would tell Quarrel he was too busy to bother with a Level 7, so Quarrel was stuck with it. Just more paperwork for the pile. Quarrel tucked the folder under his arm, thanked Erica, and continued on his way.

Ten steps later, Carol Kimura, the Director of Intelligence, flagged him over from her office door. She was holding a stack of papers, on top of which was a dog-eared copy of *The Strange Case of Dr. Jekyll and Mr. Hyde*—a beat-up old paperback with a yellow cover that looked to have been published in the sixties.

"I need this book scanned and in the system by this afternoon."

"I do correspondence on Mondays."

"Correspondence shouldn't take you all day. Do the book after."

Carol shoved the book into his hands, keeping the stack of papers to herself. Quarrel couldn't help but sneak a peek at the Director's papers. The things he saw in passing, the maps and computer screens and high-level documents were what kept him motivated. He wanted to be trusted with secrets, to have people trust his judgement, his input. He wanted to be more than he was now.

In this case, Carol was holding a few pieces of paper, but the top was a cover sheet so he couldn't see much. He saw the heading on a printout of an email, *RE:888* and on the corner of the page there was something about how something was *DEFINITELY NICE*, but he didn't stare. He took the yellow book and headed for his desk.

A book cipher is common old-school spycraft. Two people have the same obscure copy of a book, something not easily obtained, but not something so strange as to be obvious. Then they can exchange information using a series of numbers. The numbers can correspond to some combination of page, paragraph, line, and word. The variation, like the cipher book, would only be known to the two people exchanging the information. Once you receive the numbers, it's a simple matter of flipping through and finding the individual words that make up the message. If Carol had a book that needed scanning, it meant they had intercepted somebody's communication and wanted the book in the computer to decode the numbers.

Scanning was unusual because it was easier to simply flip through the book and search it by hand. Scanning the book meant that they expected to receive several future communications so that the higher-ups could just input the numbers and have the message spelled out instantly. It also meant that an unimportant office drone like Chris Quarrel would get to stand next to the scanner for an hour of flipping pages.

But first, there were the letters from the P.O. box. There were three different credit card bills for Number 13, under the names Sarah Johnson, Paulina Prostelovich, and Elena James. He recorded the expenses into Number 13's file and saved it.

Next was a letter from Number 87 detailing his three rent payments in Washington, DC. Number 87 was a surveilist, a set of eyes in DC. He never left his territory and lived in three different neighbourhoods under three identities. He had already charged the rent payments from his identities' checking accounts, but there was always the matter of keeping track of expenses. The letter, on the face of it, was directed to Marco Ermi, a fake accountant that Number 87 consistently mentioned when sending in his expenses. This month he had used the return address of Edwin Brown, who lived at 'Apartment 2' on the list of rent payments.

The next two envelopes were addressed from Alan Tigh, one of the aliases used by Number 37. Thirty-Seven, like Thirteen, was an intelligence officer. While Thirteen tended to re-use the same dozen or so identities, Thirty-Seven adopted a new alias for each mission. He had been Tigh for almost a year, except for two weeks when Tigh went on a cruise and 'Michael Steinman' did a quick job in Monaco. Chris Quarrel opened each envelope, each containing an invoice, and noted the expenses to be paid in Number 37's file.

Quarrel was a junior intelligence analyst. He'd started with monitoring world media and occasionally sorting through intel gathered by surveilists, and writing reports on whatever the brass deemed important. He'd been good enough to get moved from CSIS to CSIS-2. CSIS is as well known in Canada as the CIA is in the United States, but the existence of CSIS-2 had never leaked to the public. If you were to look up federal spending, you would find that no such entity exists.

Quarrel interpreted the move to CSIS-2 as a promotion, even though he was essentially doing more paperwork jobs in a slightly more expensive office. However, his three years at the Service had at least put him ahead of people like Erica, who had been hired by CSIS-2 directly, without prior work at the Service. It was nice to have a clearance level, but it meant that the secret-but-menial jobs like the ones he had today tended to pile up on his desk. And he really hated that desk.

Quarrel was training constantly to prepare for field work. He had studied languages, martial arts, and was in the Service's training programs for surveillance and intelligence gathering. He knew that sometime soon, he'd have a shot at being assigned a personnel number and disappearing into the field just like Alan Tigh and Elena James. He just worried about whether he would be able to get the job done.

Then there was the last envelope. It was addressed to T. Takahashi, a name that Quarrel didn't recognize. It wasn't a previously used alias for any of the agents Quarrel did accounting for. That in itself wasn't unusual, although Quarrel now scolded himself for not opening this letter first. The P.O. box was used only by CSIS-2 agents, either for billing or communications—and this was probably the latter. Maybe Thirty-Seven had moved into a new apartment.

Inside was a single piece of heavy paper, with rough edges and a pulpy feel. The paper might have been handmade. There was a single sentence written in an artful calligraphy, which to Quarrel's eye looked like it had been drawn with a fine paintbrush.

Have you noticed the Letter Six yet?

This was the sort of thing you showed to Carol.

#

Elsewhere in the same office, a double-agent nervously fished for a cell phone hidden at the bottom of a desk drawer. The double agent sent a short message, just a series of numbers and letters, to the only number programmed into that phone. What the double agent had seen at Quarrel's desk was troubling enough that it had to be reported to the double agent's handler.

A minute later, the phone lit up silently as a response arrived. It was also coded, but the meaning was clear to the double agent.

Get out immediately.

#

In the office of CSIS-2 Director of Intelligence Carol Kimura, Quarrel sat nervously while the DI inspected the note. Carol was in her early fifties, and recently she'd realized that her years inside the service outnumbered her years as a civilian. She was still in shape, but wasn't about to sprint a four-minute mile anymore. Her hair had streaks of grey and she ran the office with both the carrot and the stick—she used whatever means she had to in order to make her team produce results. Those who took the right kinds of risk received a reward, those whose risks turned into mistakes were made to see their errors. She had always been firm but kind toward Quarrel, although now she knew that she would have to show this young agent what the stick looks like.

"Have you shown this to anyone?" she asked.

"No. Came straight to you."

"Leave me everything. The letter, the envelope. I'll take it to the lab personally. And don't tell anyone a word about this."

"OK. Should I look up T. Takahashi?"

Carol shook her head, "No. It's not important."

"But—"

"I'm not going to dance around here, Chris. If you so much as type that name into a search window things will be very bad for you. Bad like you'd be grateful if all you got was fired. Ignore Takahashi. That's an order."

"Understood."

"And scan my goddamn book. Now."

Quarrel left the envelope and the letter and headed out, closing the door behind himself. Carol picked up the phone and dialled. While she waited to connect, she lit a match and held it to the address written on the envelope. Once the name and address had burned away, she blew out the small flame and fed the remains of the envelope into her shredder. The speakerphone made a familiar electronic tone, and then a man answered the phone.

"Harry Milton."

"Carol Kimura calling."

"Oh, Carol. What can the United States do for you today?"

"Having flashbacks, Harry. Someone just sent a letter to Theresa Takahashi care of a CSIS-2 post box."

"Well I'll be damned," said Harry, "you haven't been Theresa for a very long time."

#

Chris Quarrel stood by a scanner in the office's copy room. Every ten seconds, he turned a page and placed the book back down. This was going to take hours. Staring absent-mindedly toward the door, Chris saw Erica pass by. He called out to her.

"You think you could get me a coffee? I'm stuck here for like a hundred and fifty more pages."

"Sorry, Chris. I have a meeting with Jean. Enjoy your reading, though." She smirked and disappeared from the doorway, down the hallway toward a few offices devoted to the Middle East.

The scanner didn't just copy the pages, it also read each word and saved it as a text document that could be easily searched. Whenever Carol decided to read a communication from the book cipher, she'd only have to enter the number chain into the database and it would generate the coded sentences automatically. Basically, the system made Carol's life very easy in the future, and Chris's life very boring in the *right-now*. But that was life at CSIS-2; everyone else saved the world, Quarrel did the filing.

Half an hour later, the book was in the system. Bored and stiff, Chris decided to head out to the nearest coffee shop to get some caffeine. There was a Tim Horton's around the corner, and a large black coffee would work wonders. Quarrel grabbed his coat and told the coat room guard he'd be back in a few minutes, then headed for the stairs. It was still cold outside, and Chris dug into his pocket to find his gloves.

As he stepped out of the stairwell into the lobby, he ran into Pete Hershey, who was stepping out of the elevator.

"Quarrel, you got back from a break like an hour ago and you're taking another break already?"

"Before I was running out to get the correspondence. *This* is my break," said Quarrel, fighting back the urge to end with the word *asshole*.

"You just spent a week at a training mission. You need to play catch-up. Get back to the office."

"I'll stop taking coffee breaks when you cut out smoking, OK?" said Quarrel, pulling on his gloves. As he pulled the front door open, he felt Hershey slap his shoulder.

"And did you receive a Level Seven folder today?"

"On my desk."

"Next time tell me when you get something like that, alright?"

"Sure, Pete."

Finally, Quarrel was able to escape the office, leaving Hershey, who was just taking a smoke break, to loiter in front of the building. As he walked toward the coffee shop, Quarrel was thinking to himself: *The last three Level 7s that came along, he told me to buzz off. So when I finally don't tell him about one he uses it as a reason to dump on me.'* And also: *'God I wish I was a field agent and I didn't have to put up with this passive-aggressive office politics shit.'* And of course there was the constant refrain of Quarrel's inner monologue:

'I wish I worked alone.'

As he rounded the corner from the side street onto the main road, Quarrel scooped up a handful of half-melted snow from the roof of a parked car, balled it up in his hand, and threw it at a young maple tree in the boulevard. It was a perfect throw, nailing dead center on the two-inch-wide trunk. For just a moment, Quarrel felt a hint of pride at his hand-eye coordination.

Just as the snowball impacted, Quarrel's office exploded.

5

The breeze blowing through the air vent was cold. It wasn't strong enough to carry the dust to the filters, so the vents were covered in a thick layer of dry filth. Jessica Swift was covered in it. The dirt stuck to her clothes, to the sweat on her bare skin, and collected at the end of her ponytail whenever she turned a corner. She crawled along a route she had memorized from the blueprints before she entered the building. Tonight was a dress rehearsal. She needed to know that she could get in and out of the vents where she needed to. She scouted possible B- and C-exits in case her original escape was blocked somehow. Wherever it wouldn't be noticed, she replaced vent cover screws with wing screws that she could pull off quickly and without tools. She studied the views from each vent and where it would lead.

This was mostly an office building. It belonged to a major bank, and only the first two floors were open to the public. The rest of the building was just offices, desks, computers, and cubicles. She was disappointed by that. Given the reputation of Swiss banks, she had hoped to find a secret hidden room, or at least soundproof offices. Where did they do all the scheming with South American despots?

WBS was the fourth-largest bank in Switzerland, headquartered in Zurich. This building was decades old, and the exterior matched its neighbours to create a charming street view. A 2000s renovation had modernized the inside; knocked down some walls and opened it up a bit, but the bones were still very boring to crawl around in. The building was square, and from the third floor up, every floor was virtually identical except for the occasional oversized executive office. They had installed some new vents, bigger than they would have been originally (which she was grateful for since she had a few inches to spare between her slim shoulders and the sides of the vent) but they hadn't upgraded the ventilation enough to keep the air moving, hence the dirt.

Jessica had never been to Zurich before, and she had hoped the assignment would be in something more interesting than this. The assignments she got from Jupiter, her handler, always gave her the basics—an address, a target, a timeline—but never a sense of what the place was actually like. A centuries-old castle would be fun to sneak into, or some postmodern twisting absurdity of steel and glass might be interesting. Instead she was in an ordinary six-storey building that was probably identical to half the other buildings on the street, trapped in the dusty air vent. It was exactly like her training, and she had trained in a filthy abandoned warehouse.

Her target was on the ground floor, but she was currently on the third. She wanted to make sure that if she needed to, she could get out this way after she had robbed the bank.

It was after hours, but not very late. She had entered through the front door just before the bank closed at five, made her way into a vent without a single person or camera noticing, and began her work. It was past six when she crawled past an office and felt the air duct sag under her weight.

It creaked, loudly, the steel twisting away from the ceiling just a little.

She wasn't near a vent cover, so she couldn't see where she was exactly, but since she had just passed an

43

office, she assumed that she was currently sitting above a hallway. And underneath her, someone said, "Was war das für ein lärm?"

'What was that noise?'

There was someone in the hallway. She tentatively shifted backward, pushing with hands as she walked her knees back. The pressure of her hands made the vent groan again, louder.

The person spoke again. "Die decke." *The ceiling.*

Suddenly, there was a dull sound of movement, and she knew someone was moving the ceiling tiles. She crawled backward faster, and just as she moved away someone poked at the vent. The steel panel where she had just been kneeling rose up an inch as somebody tested it.

The Swiss person, who she now assumed was one of at least two security guards in the hallway, said something else in German, but she didn't know enough of the language to understand it. A second person asked a question, and the guard answered.

She made it back to the vent over the office, and looked out in time to see a security guard in a blue and white uniform enter the office. She continued easing backward, silent as a mouse now that she was held up by better-supported vents. She thought she could get out of this. But then all of a sudden the guard jumped on the desk and shoved the air vent upward.

Jessica was wearing goggles to protect her eyes from the dust. She also had a black headband on her forehead. It was sweaty and dusty, but she ignored the filth and pulled it down to cover her mouth. That would have to do as her disguise. It was another ten metres of backward crawling to the corner, and the guard would poke his head up and see her before then. Instead of retreat, she crawled forward, toward the grate the guard was fighting to shove upward.

"Hello," she called, quietly, in French, a language she spoke better than German.

"Who is that?" the guard asked, his French was flawless. Like so many Swiss, he was multilingual.

"I was trying to get to my boss's computer. You caught me. I'll come out now."

The guard lifted the grate and she moved it aside, then lowered herself down to the desk, feet first, trying to look as awkward as possible. She didn't want to look like a pro. She wanted to look like an idiot.

"What were you doing in there, girl?" he asked as she came down off the desk.

"I messed up very bad on this week. All my reports are shit. I wanted to change it in my boss's computer. It's stupid."

"Who is your boss? What floor do you work on?" He reached out to pull the headband off her face.

She sighed. There goes that plan.

She grabbed at the key ring on the guard's belt, snapping it away before he realized what was happening. Then she was headed for the door, but the guard was quick. He ran at her and shouted for his partner, and before Jessica could reach the hallway the guard tackled her hard into the wall. Her shoulder immediately started to throb from the impact.

"You think I'm stupid, bitch?" he spat the words in German now.

Everything flashed in front of Jessica. All the trauma that had brought her to this point in her life. The fire. The beatings. The warehouse. Everything that had scarred and shaped her piled up around her. This guy was nothing compared to them. That was why she wouldn't hurt him. Couldn't hurt him.

The guard grabbed a handful of her hair with his left hand while his right went to grab her wrist. She ducked and spun, grabbing at his left forearm with the keys still in her hand. The keys bit into his skin just enough to make him let go of the ponytail, and by then she had spun all the way around his body, stole the flashlight from his belt, and was out the door. She pulled it shut just as the guard tried to grab the knob. Before he could overpower her and pull the door open, she jammed a key into the lock and broke it off with the butt end of the heavy flashlight, locking the guard in the office.

The second guard was only a couple metres away. She ran at him, full-speed. He was a smallish man, and didn't fill up much of the wide hallway. Clicking on the flashlight, she shined it into his eyes and threw it at his face. He reflexively caught the light, only to realize that the girl had slipped right past him. Before Guard Number Two even knew what was happening, the filthy girl from the vents was in the stairwell.

She didn't run the stairs, she leapt over them to each landing. It was four big leaps to reach the ground floor, and then she just slipped out the fire exit and into the street. She had a backpack tucked under a bush on the corner. One minute after a girl in black tights passed a guard on the third floor, a completely different girl in red sweater and blue jeans walked down the Bahnhofstrasse listening to her iPod.

The Bahnhofstrasse is the expensive street in Europe. Immaculate and lined with young trees, it was home to every prestigious retail store in Europe. Jessica didn't notice the beauty of Zurich's buildings or expensive shops on the way back to her hotel. She was too busy thinking back on her own mistakes, and wondering what would happen if anyone ever really had her cornered. Scratching a dumbass guard's arm was one thing, but in her business things would only get worse. Someday, somehow, someone would get the drop on her and she'd have to fight for her life, and Jessica's hands shook as she wondered if she'd even be capable of defending herself. She silently swore that she'd be better than she had been today, that she'd never be caught; always slip in and out without confrontation. She had to be the best, or she'd be dead.

The hotel had a bar in the lobby and she lingered, looking in, tempted. Her hands clenched and she walked away.

In her room she ran a scalding bath, stripped out of her clothes and scratched out the third-floor escape plan on her blueprints. With the water still steaming she climbed into the tub, kneeled down, dunked her head under painfully hot water, and screamed until she was out of breath.

6

Chris Quarrel was sitting in an empty office in a government building on the other side of Ottawa. The walls were recently patched but not painted, so several spots of white putty blotted the pale violet walls. The desk was cheap chipboard and peeling veneer, and the filing cabinet had two locked drawers nobody could find the keys for. Not that it mattered. This wasn't Quarrel's office. It was more like a waiting room. Or a jail cell.

With his entire office dead, Quarrel had become both a witness and a liability. He had spent the Tuesday and Wednesday in interrogation rooms, being asked the same questions by a series of men and women. He had very little to tell them. There was a strange letter. "Have you noticed the Letter Six yet?" A report classified level seven, that Quarrel had never opened. Correspondence from several foreign employees, who Quarrel did not know by name. A copy of Jekyll and Hyde that Quarrel guessed was part of a book cipher. That was all he knew. The detail of whom the letter was addressed to—T. Takahashi—Chris kept to himself. Carol had been damned worried about that little detail and Chris wasn't about to break the last promise he had made to her.

With every new person who came to ask questions, Quarrel became more convinced that they all wished someone more important had survived. Someone who had real answers. Every few hours, for the entire week, someone new had come along to ask questions and left disappointed. The one thing everyone knew for sure was that a lowly functionary like Chris probably didn't have any clue about any information that would be worth blowing up a building to destroy. Most of these interrogations / interviews / grief counselling sessions included a middle-aged man with greying red hair named Mr. Thompson. Thompson was a clearance level 4, and as such he was a nice buffer between lowly Chris Quarrel and the higher-ups who answered to the politicians.

Nevertheless, the mere fact of surviving was enough to draw suspicion. Chris was neither a helpful witness nor a very likely bomber, but there were people in the service who saw him as both. Thompson was nice enough, and Quarrel was glad to see that Thompson at least seemed to believe Quarrel's eyewitness account was helpful. Because of this, instead of sitting him in the interrogation room each day, Quarrel was given this half-renovated office to sit in and while away his days whenever he wasn't being questioned. He was given freedom to leave at night (under surveillance so obvious Chris felt both insulted and disappointed), and was back to sitting in the waiting room on the Thursday, the third day after the bombing.

Bored and fed up with his status as a pariah, Quarrel headed out into the hallway and started to wander. He poked his head into offices, rounded corners where he'd never been. When he saw an unfamiliar face he tried to act like he belonged there, and when he saw someone who knew him he pretended that he was just getting some coffee.

"Twelve hours to the deadline and you still don't have it?" The voice came from inside an office on the third floor.

"It's an entire country. At this point any analysis would be more guesswork than science."

"I've got to give the Brits something. Triple-Eight won't last much longer. They expect an answer within a half hour."

Quarrel stood in the doorway and looked inside. The office was more like a classroom, with papers and maps stuck to bulletin boards along the walls. The center of the room was a large table covered in papers, laptops, and coffee cups. Three men, plainly bookworms, sat at the table, looking like they hadn't slept in days. All three wore rumpled clothing, and the room smelled like they'd been there too long. The demanding one wore glasses, the others didn't. All three had their backs to Quarrel, focused on a map pinned to the wall. It was a map of France, with pins stuck in three places. One was obviously Paris, one a little southeast was likely Lyon, and one on the Mediterranean coast might have been Cannes or even Monaco.

"What are you looking for?" Quarrel asked.

They turned. "Who the hell are you?" asked the one with glasses. Before Quarrel could answer, he continued with "This is restricted information. Stick to your security level."

But Quarrel was starting to remember that corner of paper Carol had been holding. What was the title? RE:888. And the man had just said something about triple-eight.

Quarrel ignored him, walked through the room and approached the map on the wall. He fought to remember the email he had seen in Carol's hand. He had gone through training for this sort of thing, speed-reading, visual recall, and so on. The pin on the Med coast wasn't stabbed in either Cannes or Monaco, but between them.

"How did you narrow the cities down?"

"Who the hell—" stammered Glasses.

"I work in an office that you don't know about, and never will because it blew up on Monday. Now tell me what the hell I'm looking at."

"These are the only French cities where Sidorov is known to control properties."

Quarrel had no idea who this Sidorov was, but Carol's email had been very clear about what to say next. Quarrel jabbed his hand at the pin on the Med.

"Nice. Definitely Nice."

"Because some random guy walks in—"

"Tell them CSIS-2 confirmed it. Definitely Nice."

Quarrel walked out, leaving the three men to gape at each other. When he was back out in the hallway, one of them shouted, "There's a CSIS *two*?"

#

William Thorpe had not slept in three days. He had spent all three of those days naked, tied to a chair in a warehouse. He could tell he was in France, but otherwise he didn't know where he was.

Sidorov liked torture. He lived for the prospect of maiming and killing his enemies. And Thorpe had been his enemy for a long time. However, they hadn't hurt him as much as he expected. Sidorov had a reputation for making tortures last up to a month, often resuscitating his victims so he could kill them again later.

What was it he had threatened? *"Tarred and feathered or drawn and quartered."* Thorpe expected that sometime soon, Sidorov would make good on that promise. While he had trained himself to resist any torture, to never let his spirit break, a small voice inside hoped that Sidorov

51

would at least leave his body somewhere his country could find it. He wanted to be buried in England, to spend eternity next to Julia.

No, said another part of him, a stronger part. *You're not dead yet, old man.*

Sidorov had tied him to a wooden chair and then simply did nothing to him. That was the torture. No standing or lying down, no bathroom breaks, and starvation. Sidorov's goons would let Thorpe drink as much water as he wanted, but food was strictly denied. It was now day three, and Thorpe's lower body was completely numb. His head throbbed constantly, his belly ached and distended, and every muscle he could still feel was in agony at the combination of starvation and discomfort.

So far, Thorpe had not screamed.

On this evening, he was only guarded by a single thug, a local hire who he didn't recognize as one of Sidorov's regulars. Thorpe knew that even if he could somehow get free of his bonds, his extreme weakness and exhaustion would ensure that this thug could take him. Sidorov didn't need to post more than one guard now, because Thorpe's body was wearing down.

When he first woke up, Sidorov had been there, and so had Morris, who was wrapped in bandages after an underworld doctor had cut Thorpe's bullet out of him. Morris was the one who had told them to take Thorpe's clothes, a lesson he learned after Thorpe's watch had freed him the first time. But now, both Morris and Sidorov only visited occasionally. Ignoring a prize as hated as Thorpe meant they were working on something big. Something that required a lot of attention.

There was s crash somewhere to the left, out of sight. It was Sidorov, kicking the door open. He entered slowly, hunched over, carrying a heavy, lidded bucket in each hand. Thorpe's eyes needed a moment to focus before he could read the labels on the buckets. Sidorov had brought two 17-litre containers of driveway sealer. Tar.

Following Sidorov was a second goon, one who had guarded Thorpe the day before. This one rolled an empty oil drum. Thorpe understood immediately. They probably had feather pillows somewhere too.

"So that's it, then?" he asked Sidorov.

The Russian grinned. "I'm looking forward to your death."

"I heard you could torture a man for weeks on end. Those stories must be rubbish if you can't even go four days before killing me."

Sidorov was already setting up a little ring of cinder blocks. He would want a fire under that barrel to get the tar nice and hot. He spoke casually, as if he didn't even feel the malice in his words. "Mr. Thorpe, if I could, I would make you my masterpiece. I would cut off pieces one-by-one, letting each heal before I took the next. I would leave you as a faceless, armless, legless beast. I would take one lung, one kidney, both eyes, and all your teeth. I would burn and freeze and bludgeon and stab you. I would deafen you with loud music and feed you your own organs. I would deliver your heart to your Queen. But I am a busy man and I don't have time to give you what you deserve. Tar and feathers shall do."

Thorpe didn't hesitate in his response, not wanting Sidorov to think, even for a moment, that this torture was working. "I don't see any feathers."

53

Sidorov started to say something, then stopped and his cheek twitched. He spoke to the Russian thug, and the Russian gave a nervous answer.

"It seems we forgot the feathers. Nevertheless. The tar will take time to warm up. By the time I get back, we'll have quite a show."

He barked orders at the two goons, and left the same way he had come. The two goons set about building a fire pit from the cinder blocks, placing the barrel on top of it, and pouring the thick black tar into the drum. The quiet inner voice once again thought of Julia.

And then there were two quiet sounds. Twip-twip.

And the goons dropped dead.

There had been no warning. No siren, no signal. They had entered and infiltrated in total silence, like fog creeping through an open window; a team of MI-6 agents coming in from every direction. They swarmed toward Thorpe, cutting him free while the old agent fought the urge to sigh in relief.

"Where's Sidorov?" one black-clad agent asked.

"Out buying pillows."

"Anything you need, Triple-Eight?"

"I'll start with my pants," Thorpe said, "then a bloody large martini."

7

A day later, still sequestered in the unfinished office, Quarrel was sitting with his feet up on the desk reading a magazine, when the phone rang. Quarrel was surprised the phone was even hooked up. It had never rung before, and he'd never had any reason to pick it up.

"Hello?"

"Speedy?"

Carol had assigned everyone at her CSIS-2 office both a number and a codename. The number was on file. While those in the field got low numbers, double-digits, Chris was number 4042. The names, however, were not on file. They were strictly in-house, memorized by those who needed to know. Chris had only known his own name and those of a few direct superiors, and Erica, the one person who worked under him. In a quirk that must have given her some private fun, Carol had named everyone for DC Comics superheroes. Carol herself was Wonder Woman, and others included Mr. Freeze and Black Canary. Chris had been named Speedy, after the sidekick of Green Arrow. He had been disappointed, after Wikipedia-ing the character, to find that modern-day Speedy was actually a girl. It suggested that Carol didn't give the slightest thought to personalizing a cool codename. But that concern was childish even back then, and was absurdly petty now that Carol was gone.

In fact, everyone who had known that name was dead, weren't they?

"This is Speedy."

"My Name is Harry Milton. I work for the CIA. You'll want to verify that, even though simply getting through to your phone is proof enough. So call your superior and ask about me. I'll call back in five minutes. And you might want to take this seriously if you intend to learn about Takahashi."

The man hung up. Chris did as he was told and called the head of the station. He asked about Harry Milton and if he was legitimate. The chief, a man called Brooks, was unhappy that he had to lower himself off his pedestal to talk to someone as useless as Chris, but the mention of Milton made him sigh loudly and confirm that Milton was for real. While he waited for Milton to call back, Quarrel tried not to focus on how much he hated dealing with his so-called colleagues and once again wished he could be deployed into a nice, faraway city somewhere. Somewhere alone. Man on a mission. None of this bureaucracy and politicking.

The phone rang again.

"Quarrel,"

"Speedy?" said the man on the phone.

"Yes. I checked you out."

"Good," said Milton. "I'm told that you're the last person who ever talked to Carol Kimura."

"Yes."

"Wrong. I was. After you spoke to her about the letter you opened, she called me. An hour later she was dead. And we both know why. Theresa Takahashi."

"I never told anybody th—"

"Never told a soul. I know. And that means you have good instincts. We have a leak, Quarrel. Someone's got high-level information and they're using it against us. Your co-workers were not the first to die. One of my deep-cover operatives was taken out the day before. Which means that you and I are the only people who know that something's fishy in the community. My people are already booking your transfer to Langley."

"Transfer, sir?" asked Chris.

"You've just been called up to the big leagues."

#

Chris Quarrel approached the customer service desk at a bank in suburban Virginia.

"How can I help you, sir?" asked the woman at the desk.

"I'd like a loan to buy a Jet Ski," said Quarrel.

"Do you have collateral?"

"Only my father's watch."

"Follow me."

The woman led Quarrel to an office at the back of the building, told him to sit, and left. She closed the door behind her, and Quarrel heard it lock. Quarrel looked around. It was a very boring office: An organized desk with a large blotter, a framed photo of a woman dressed in out-of-date fashions, and a motivational poster on the wall that said "Faith" with a picture of a man about to bungee jump. The blinds on the window were closed. Most of the brushed concrete floor was covered by a large, ugly area rug depicting a squiggle of blue lines on a background of brown squares. After a moment's hesitation, Quarrel followed the woman's instructions, and sat in the armchair in front of the banker's desk.

After about twenty seconds, there was a click and Quarrel started to lower into the floor. The busy tangle of lines on the rug had perfectly concealed the seams where the drop-away floor was outlined. Chris, the chair, and a four-by-six-foot section of the carpet steadily lowered into the floor until he was so deep underground that the bank office became a small square of light overhead.

Finally, the downward movement slowed, and light appeared in front of Chris's feet. The other three sides of the shaft were solid concrete, but in front of the chair the wall ended eight feet above the floor, creating an opening. Once the elevator reached the same level as the floor in front of him, Quarrel stood.

There was an old man waiting for him. Harry Milton was almost seventy, with sagging jowls and thin, grey hair. He wore a neatly pressed shirt tucked into rumpled pants, and his shoes were a new pair of sneakers.

"Quarrel," said Milton. "Good of you to join us."

"Sir," said Quarrel, shaking the elder's hand. "It's an honour."

"Nonsense. You wouldn't call me 'sir' if you knew the things I've done." Milton paused while they started to walk down the corridor. "But then again, you never will."

The office was four stories below ground, and made entirely of concrete. In a few spots the walls had been painted, but mostly this was a grey, ugly place with fluorescent lighting and no windows. Quarrel noticed a series of coloured lines on some of the walls, like you'd see in a hospital, but decided not to ask what they meant or where they led.

He also noticed the dozens of security cameras that were constantly watching him. They were out in the open, hanging from the ceilings, not hidden under plastic domes or behind mirrors. These were the ones they wanted you to see, and Quarrel immediately understood that the best cameras were undetectable. The hallway led

58

to a large office space, divided into cubicles. Along one wall was a bank of TVs, and there were several small rooms off to the left that looked like editing bays or some kind of video-dubbing rooms. They walked straight through the middle of the office, and the pathway led them directly into Milton's private office. Milton closed the door to provide some privacy, and Quarrel sat down.

"No cameras in here?" asked Quarrel.

"None that I approved of. Or that I can find. But probably, someone's watching." Milton sat behind his messy desk, littered with both intelligence reports and fast-food cartons. "Why, you paranoid already?"

"Someone did try to blow me up. Plus I've just never been to a CIA facility before."

"We're not CIA. That's just what I tell people on the phone. We're CIB. Counter-Intelligence Bureau. It's our job to screw with the guys who want to screw the CIA."

"Never heard of it."

"Wonder why." Milton smiled a little. "Think of CIB as Internal Affairs for the American spy world. CIA, DHS, DOD, yadda yadda. We protect American agents from assassination, and root out moles and turncoats. We protect the people who smuggle secrets for America and catch the ones who smuggle secrets for our enemies."

There was a natural pause in conversation where the old spymaster sized up the new recruit. It was interrupted when two other men entered the office. Both wore suits, although one man's clothing was much more expensive than the other. The man in the nice suit was grey-haired, tanned, with deep frown lines ingrained in his forehead. The man in the cheaper suit was very tall, with a barrel chest and gorilla hands. He had thick, black hair and looked to be about fifty. He must have been a soldier at one point, but years of inactivity had packed on the pounds. Quarrel did a double-take when they entered, then stood up and held out his hand to the older, well-dressed man.

"Senator Anderson. It's nice to meet you."

The senator shook his hand, eyebrows climbing up his forehead. "You know me?"

"Sure. Senior senator for Ohio. Fifth term. You sit on several funding committees who hold closed-door meetings people aren't supposed to know about, and more publicly on the Armed Services Committee. I'm not really surprised you'd be in a place like this."

The senator looked at Milton. "This kid's not bad."

Milton spoke up, "Kid, this is Mr. Hinkston of the Central Intelligence Agency, and I see you already know who the good senator is. Now sit down."

Hinkston shook Quarrel's hand, his massive fingers engulfing Quarrel's right hand, while he also slipped a business card into Quarrel's left. Quarrel sat down, but Anderson and Hinkston stayed on their feet. The card had a CIA logo on the back, and on the other side it simply said HINKSTON and a phone number. Milton picked up the conversation.

"So Carol liked you, which means you got something going for you. But I gotta be honest, kid, you don't look like much."

"A good spy should never look like much. Much is conspicuous."

Milton chuckled. "Damn right."

Milton pulled open a drawer and fished around. Quarrel noticed that the old man's computer monitor (a big old CRT monitor, not a modern flat screen like in the other offices) was turned off and covered in dust. Milton found what he was seeking and tossed a photo at Chris. It was a generic-looking man of about thirty. Short hair, brown eyes, clean shaven, Caucasian. It was just a headshot, so there was no way to judge his height or build. Milton waited for Chris to size the man up. Quarrel shrugged.

"What you are looking at is the least conspicuous man in America. His name was Matthew Crowe. He was the best." Quarrel had never heard the name. Milton continued, "Crowe was a master of disguise. He could become anyone. Young or old, any language, any level of fame or notoriety, Crowe could assume the identity so completely that not even the subject's own mother would know. And last week somebody killed him. Twelve hours later they hit your office."

"Did his identity get leaked?"

"Don't know if anyone knew his real name, but his cover was definitely broken. Crowe was in the middle of a deep-cover mission posing as a Russian businessman. Somebody knew. And they had him taken out."

"How do you know it wasn't just a hit on the Russian he was playing?"

"The killer left us a note. He drew a picture on the wall of the room where Crowe's body was found." Milton handed over another photo. It was a finger-painted letter F, written in blood.

"F. The sixth letter of the alphabet. Like in the letter to the CSIS-2 postbox that I opened."

"CIB has a specific mandate. We protect American agents from things like this. It's one thing for us to investigate a dead CIA agent, but it's exceedingly rare that one of our own ends up dead."

Hinkston spoke now, "We need to sort this thing out, Mr. Quarrel. I've been pushing for an agent from outside the CIB to take point on Crowe's murder."

"You've been pushing for one of your lackeys to take point on this," said Milton. "And I refuse to let them know the inner workings of my organization." He turned back to Quarrel. "But I agree, CIB is too small a family to let any of my guys run this investigation. I could easily wind up tasking the traitor to find himself. I need someone from outside, and someone *not* answerable to Mr. Hinkston here."

Hinkston snorted but said nothing.

Senator Anderson interjected. "I think you see the conundrum. CIB is supposed to root out corrupt CIA agents when the need arises. Can't exactly send CIA agents in here, but at the same time the CIB is clearly compromised. Son, we need someone, to put it bluntly, like you."

Quarrel nodded. "Who had access to Crowe's mission files?"

Milton answered, "Nobody but me. However, there are a number of highest-value agents who have above-top-secret clearance. Any one of them could theoretically have gotten into our files, either here in the building or on the server, without my knowledge. But we have no record of anyone accessing the records in either manner."

"How many agents are we talking about?"

"Seven. The seven best agents the CIB had ever employed. One of them is a traitor."

Quarrel nodded, thinking. "*At least* one. More than one of them could have turned."

"We've considered that," said Hinkston.

"OK," said Quarrel, "why me? No offence, I'm happy to be here, but why call in a junior analyst from Canada to look at a leak at the highest level of American intelligence?"

"Because you're nobody. Because you aren't from here, you don't know me, and my agents have absolutely no idea that you exist. If I'm going to find this bastard I need someone on whom I can rely, and unfortunately that doesn't include any agent within my office or the CIA. I need a total outsider. And because yesterday you pulled some intel out of thin air that saved one of those seven agents from a slow and painful death."

Definitely Nice. Quarrel took it in. "I really just remembered a location."

Anderson smiled. "Brilliant and humble. This is your big break, kid."

"Not until I know he's my man," said Milton. "Do you want the job or not?"

Quarrel hesitated.

Milton smiled. "If you're wondering, the answer is yes, they are all capable of killing you. If you take this job, you'll very likely die if the traitor thinks you figured him out."

Now Chris cracked a smile. "Actually, that's exactly what I was wondering." He paused, thought of Carol and Erica and the others, and looked Milton in the eyes. "I'm your man. Let's have a look at those files."

#

Milton's top seven agents were the legends of the intelligence business. Quarrel had heard of three of them before, but all seven had startlingly impressive resumes.

The three Chris had heard of were Samantha Boswell, William Thorpe, and Jack Hall. Boswell was the All-American girl: gorgeous, athletic, and brilliant. She had completed over two-hundred top-secret missions by the age of twenty-seven, before going into a lighter workload and a semi-retirement. Chris had heard her name during his time at a CSIS training camp a year earlier, where a particularly nimble backflip off a roof and into a window below was called a 'Boswell entry.'

Thorpe was an old-timer, now almost sixty. He was English, serving in MI-6 for decades. He had their American file, and spent more time in America than at home. His relationship with CIB had become so intimate that he was allowed into their archives on several occasions. He was the master of seduction, and several women Quarrel had met in his years at the Service had told stories about Thorpe. Never any detail—that would break confidentiality—but Quarrel had seen enough professional women blush at Thorpe's name to get the idea.

Quarrel now learned that Thorpe's codename was Triple-Eight. He had been captured on the English Channel and held in Nice, until Quarrel's information saved him. He had not been treated well by the captors, which led Quarrel to think he wasn't likely to be the mole.

Jack Hall was the same man who had operated the training camp where Quarrel failed to graduate only a week prior. Mid-forties. American, he was brought into the CIA/CIB after a distinguished career in the Navy SEALs. He was a master tactician and was able to apprehend even the best-guarded target. Quarrel doubted Hall would be the traitor, but then maybe that was because he was the only suspect Quarrel had actually met. Maybe he was still seeking Hall's approval. But when Quarrel thought about it a little more, an instructor at a course like Hall's would be able to influence a lot of young spies—and possibly turn that influence into something dangerous.

The other four were strangers to Quarrel; either by being so good at their jobs that they were not well known, or by being less flashy than the first three. Their names were Peter Scarret, Khalid Saleb, Jessica Swift, and one simply called "Mr. Smith." They all had their talents and their impressive lists of missions completed. The files also contained psych profiles outlining the myriad reasons why they were good agents, and in one case why they were not. Of course, those reasons led very directly to motives for betraying America.

Saleb, an Afghan by birth before immigrating to the USA at age eight, was now in federal custody. Six months earlier he had snapped and killed his partner. It was believed that Saleb was attempting to turn double. He had failed to escape because his partner managed to get a shot off before she died. She put the bullet in his brain. Saleb had gone into a coma for a month. He was now claiming amnesia—that he had no memory prior to waking up five months ago. Milton had ruled him out as the leak because he had been locked up long enough that he wouldn't possibly know about Crowe's mission. Still, Saleb could have leaked for years before his partner finally shut him down. Since he was already contained, Quarrel made Saleb a low priority. After all, this was the one suspect who definitely had nothing to do with the Ottawa bombing.

Jessica Swift was a cat burglar. Her file described "highest-level infiltration and safecracking." However, she was not a killer. Her profile listed her as "unlikely to be capable of killing," and "too empathetic for type-one jobs" while warning that exposing her to excessive violence would likely compromise her mental state. Quarrel put her to the bottom of the file as well.

Mr. Smith was a blank slate. He had no place of birth, no social security number, not even a next of kin. His psych record was on the same standard form as the others, but instead of a well-reasoned profile, it just said "as expected" in a man's handwriting and then had a date stamp. Chris looked up from the file and over to Milton, eyebrow raised in an exaggerated arch. "Was this guy, Smith, grown in a lab or something?" Milton smiled and nodded. Chris moved to the next file.

Peter Scarret, codenamed "Shark," was also a former SEAL. Unlike Hall, Shark Scarret had gone rogue twenty years ago and was captured by the CIB when he was trying to sell rocket propelled grenades to Iraqis militia. He was charged with treason, sentenced to death, and offered his role at CIB as an alternative to the firing squad. He spent the last twenty years serving dutifully in high-risk missions. He never betrayed CIB in all those years, likely because Milton had installed a small explosive charge in Shark's neck. If Shark went off-mission, Milton could blow his head clean off from anywhere in the world. Not exactly the best way to get a man's loyalty, but it seemed to have worked so far. Quarrel saw in Shark's profile someone who would be likely to hate both America and the CIB, but it was a very real question whether Shark would take the risk of getting his head blown off just to get back at Harry Milton.

Nevertheless, Chris lifted Shark's file and waved it through the air. "We have a winner. I'll want to talk to him first."

"I thought you would. I bought your plane ticket this morning."

8

Thorpe strolled into a small office near the top of a London high-rise. It still hurt a bit to walk, but he wouldn't let it show. He had to look invincible for the people here. He had to look like the man who always kept England safe.

The building was known as the London headquarters for a multinational bank, and was most definitely *not* known as the headquarters for a secret branch of Her Majesty's Secret Service.

Entering the reception room, Thorpe was glad to see that there was already a woman sitting in the waiting area. She was Kathy Cashmere, the coordinator for the ten Triple-Digit agents. Kathy was almost forty, with a soft, round face and a body that she worked hard to keep skinny. She wore a skirt suit as always, and immediately Thorpe wished she would one day abandon those long skirts for something shorter, with a slit up the thigh. Still, Kathy was warm and energetic, and would rescue Thorpe from having to be alone with the receptionist, Ms. Halstrom.

For almost thirty years, the Ringmaster's secretary had been a rather plump woman with hair that Thorpe thought resembled a bird's nest. Ms. Halstrom was joyless, followed every rule to the letter, and her scornful looks reminded Thorpe of the nuns from the orphanage where he'd grown up.

Ms. Cashmere grinned when Thorpe sat down next to her.

"Nice to see you again, Triple-Eight. You've lost weight."

"Likewise, Kath," he smiled his best cheeky smile, "although your weight loss was voluntary."

"Mmm-hmm."

"Have you seen him today? Has he seen my report?"

"Don't know. He sent a message asking me to accompany you but that's all he'd say."

"Likely not good then." Thorpe waved at Ms. Halstrom.

"Afternoon Ms. Halstrom. How is he today? Not particularly angry about everything that happened, I hope?"

Ms. Halstrom pushed her glasses up her nose and pursed her thin lips. She pulled out ear buds that Thorpe hadn't noticed at first, and for a moment he wondered if the old bat had been listening to music, before realizing how silly the very thought of it was. For a joyless creature such as Ms. Halstrom, music and the workplace must exist in separate universes.

"I'm a receptionist, not a psychologist, Triple-Eight. And I'd appreciate a little quiet while I transcribe Triple-Four's debriefing, if you don't mind." She gave him a condescending smile and put the buds back into her ears, turning her attention back to typing.

"Did you know that she was typing?" he whispered to Cashmere. "I had no idea. Just pulled those headphones out of nowhere."

Kathy grinned like a schoolgirl who'd just seen a classmate get caught passing notes, then pointed to the lights on the wall beside the Ringmaster's door.

"Let's get on then. Light's green."

"Oh it is, isn't it?" Thorpe stood, facing the two lights, one red and one green, which indicated whether the boss was available. "Guess we'll just go in then," he said loudly, turning toward Ms. Halstrom, "seeing how the light's green. Wouldn't want to trouble you to tell us when it turned green, since you're so busy."

The older woman scowled but said nothing, so Thorpe and Cashmere went into the old man's office.

The Ringmaster was in his sixties; a thick, stocky man in a finely tailored suit. Thorpe knew little of the man's life outside this room, but had long-ago deduced that Ringmaster never had any children with Mrs. Ringmaster, and therefore had much disposable income to spend on his exquisite wardrobe. Thorpe had complimented the old man's suit from time to time, and Ringmaster always sighed, saying that when one worked in a financial building, one had to dress the part.

His office was small, with a window looking out at the river and the huge London Eye Ferris wheel. The other walls were panelled in lightly coloured wood, and the old man's desk was a massive thing of black-stained oak. In such a bright office that desk was a black hole, and the eye was drawn toward it. Thorpe wondered sometimes if the man's authority was derived more from that desk than from his rank.

Once the door was shut, Ringmaster flipped a switch and the light above the door turned from green to red. There was a subtle sound of machinery near the door as it locked and sealed, making the room soundproof.

"So what have you got to say for yourself, Triple-Eight?"

"Well, sir, I was wondering how I could get Ms. Halstrom to type up my debriefs for me."

"Triple-Four lost two fingers last week. He's still working on his typing skills so I had him record his debrief on tape. So I suppose if you want to cut off a few fingers we could arrange something."

"Down to eight fingers? Well you do call me Triple-Eight. Might be fitting." Thorpe smirked, but Ringmaster was having none of it. "Tell Four I hope he gets better."

"Or perhaps you could tell me how you managed to get an informant killed, let Sidorov's shipment vanish and lose both Sidorov and Morris all in one night? Or perhaps explain how you managed to get captured and forced me to send a team into the Continent. Were you going for some kind of record for how many different ways you could botch the same mission?"

"That yacht should have been loaded. The girl gave me the details. Morris handling the whole thing himself…"

"You're off Sidorov."

Thorpe reddened. "Sir—"

"I said you're off it!" Ringmaster stood up behind his giant desk.

"He starved me for days, sir."

Ringmaster ignored Thorpe's insistence. "Ms. Cashmere, I'm putting Triple-Eight on the job you have Triple-Seven working. Give him the details."

Kathy hesitated, she was struggling to find the right words, and finally said, "Sir, isn't that a bit… well it's… a conflict of interest?"

"Do you think letting him go back after Sidorov after three days of torture would somehow be *less* a conflict of interest? Your job is to do what I tell you with my agents, not to second-guess me. Tell Thorpe what you know then go reel in Triple-Seven, got it?"

"Yes, sir." She turned to Thorpe, her behaviour was still strange, awkward. "William, it's Martin Mercier. He's back."

Thorpe froze up. Just the mention of Mercier's name made him tense. "Mercier? We finally got something on the bastard?" Thorpe wasn't sure if he was grinning or grimacing, but just the thought of running down Mercier made his heart beat a little faster. He'd gladly forget about Sidorov for a shot at Mercier. Sidorov had tortured him for days. Mercier had tormented him for decades.

Cashmere continued her debrief: "Not much, frankly. Triple-Seven was looking into the theft of information from one of our contractors. Globection Corp. We use them to communicate with bases in Afghanistan, and someone's been listening in. Triple-Seven picked up some stolen information. Some paperwork printed from Globection's secure servers. He ran fingerprints and…"

Ringmaster cut in, "Martin Mercier has his fingerprints all over stolen intelligence. Seems he's been digging into the satellites GX built for our Army comms. It's the first time his name has even come up in twenty years, and I need my best man on the job."

"He does mean his *best* man, William." said Cashmere. "Which means you'll have to keep a clear head about things."

"But you will send me." Thorpe was looking at Ringmaster with such intensity that he expected to be admonished for it. He wanted Ringmaster to know that even if he was removed from this assignment, he would be hunting down Mercier anyway.

"We'll send you. Mercier tore this agency apart for almost ten years before he disappeared. I don't intend to let him come back and do it again. I need someone to track him down and kill him, and that's where you come in," said Ringmaster. "And I'm right, aren't I?"

"Oh yes. I'll hunt him like a damned fox. And kill him like one."

"Good. We'll fly you into New York. Try to figure out who's stealing from GX, and follow them back to Mercier. Do not let this bastard slip away again, understood?"

"Yes, sir." Thorpe knew he shouldn't smile when given a kill order, but he couldn't help it.

#

It was almost seven at night when Thorpe got to St. Michael's. The receptionist recognized him and waved him in, smiling. It was a very sterile place, cold and full of echoes, but Thorpe was used to it now.

Julia was by the window, staring out at the rain. Thorpe knelt down beside her, put his hand in her hair, and kissed her lips. Her eyes widened and focused on him, and the left side of her face curled up into the warmest of half-smiles.

"It's been too long, I know. But I'm back for now before they send me to America."

His hand was still in her hair, gently cradling her head. His middle finger ran a soft circle around the bald spot on her scalp, the entry wound where the bullet had gone into her brain. Slipping the hand lower, he found the gold chain around her neck and fished it out from under her shirt, turning it until he found the clasp.

73

"They finally let me have what we wanted. They're sending me after Martin Mercier."

Thorpe let the gold ring slide off Julia's necklace and into his palm. He slipped the band over his left ring finger before re-clasping the necklace back around her neck. Her mouth opened, her half-smile showing those lovely, perfect teeth. She made a sound like a word, which was so rare it made him smile and his eyes well up. He took her hand in his, their wedding bands a perfect match and kissed the soft skin on the back of her hand.

"They're finally letting me go after the man that did this to you."

PART TWO:
THE SECRETIVE AGENTS

9

Quarrel was in the driver's seat of a GMC van on a hot day in Venezuela. His passenger was suspect #1, Peter "Shark" Scarret. Shark was in the back as Quarrel drove through an unfamiliar neighbourhood, in the space at the edge of San Cristobal where the houses were far apart but you weren't quite into the rougher Andes terrain. Quarrel could barely hear over the rock station blaring on the radio, but he noted the sound of something banging around, and the sound of zippers and buckles being fastened.

It was three in the afternoon on a sunny Wednesday, which Shark thought was a great time for an assassination. One of the major drug lords had recently moved his residence into this country, and was bribing local officials. The CIA wasn't happy about this kind of man making friends with the socialists. They much preferred drug lords confined to impoverished narco-states.

As they passed a walled and gated villa, Shark shouted from behind Quarrel.

"Pull over past the house," he said in a rough, but somewhat disinterested voice. Shark was more focused on listening to the music than talking to Quarrel.

Quarrel had been assigned to carry out this mission as a way to study and learn about Shark. The cover was that the CIB wanted someone to evaluate Shark's methods, which was flimsy and they both knew it. Shark was very aware that Quarrel was there to spy on him, but he had to put up with the situation. Like anything else the CIB told him to do, Shark had an easy choice—comply or die. The bomb in his neck made the decision pretty easy.

The van rolled to a stop a hundred yards past the villa, and Shark threw open the sliding side door. With a backpack thrown over his shoulder, he pulled the door shut and approached the passenger window.

"You sure you don't want to wait 'til dark?" asked Chris.

"Pff. Twice as many guards at night."

"You didn't tell me how you were going to get inside."

Shark smiled. Despite the ugly melted skin down the right side of his face, he was a handsome man. "Gettin' inside's easy. They'll take me in once they catch me."

Quarrel was dumbfounded. "Once they *catch* you?"

"Yeah," Shark said, raising a piece of equipment for Chris to see. "After I fire the grenade launcher."

"Grenade launcher?"

"Yeah. They're gonna be so pissed."

Shark rapped on the roof twice in lieu of a goodbye, and headed off toward the villa. He didn't turn back to look at his indignant "partner," but he did turn on the radio earpiece and test the signal. He wore many-pocketed black cargo pants and a matching vest. His long black hair was slicked back behind his ears, and he had a toothpick hanging from the corner of his mouth.

At the outside wall of the villa, Shark smiled for the security camera, then took a left to follow the wall down the side of the property. Once he found a tall tree, he shimmied up the trunk and settled on a branch that looked over the wall and into the property. It was beautiful and perfectly maintained, with green grass, bushy gardens, and bright trees that had as much pink as they did green. The house was a mansion, with smooth white stucco walls and arched windows. Birds were chirping, a limping old gardener trimmed the bushes, and the two guards patrolling the perimeter together were smiling and talking.

Quarrel watched from the van as Shark fired the grenade launcher into the yard, and a few seconds later the explosion sounded, and Quarrel felt the van shake. Quarrel counted three Mississippis before the alarm went off. These guys were slow.

Shark shimmied along his branch until he was over the ten-foot-high brick wall, then flipped upside down, hung on with one hand, and let his legs drop until he was standing on the wall. Walking along the wall, he watched the guards rushing past the windows inside the house, on the first floor. He looked ahead to where they were going and fired a grenade in front of them, but into a window on the floor above them. Quarrel couldn't tell if the floor caved in on the guards, but Shark seemed happy with himself.

The scar-faced agent aimed at something else in the courtyard, and fired. A huge orange fireball rose above the wall and Quarrel recognized it as a gasoline explosion.

"What was that?" Quarrel said aloud, mostly to himself.

"Lamborghini convertible. Musta had a full tank."
Shark said through his earpiece, "They might not like the
van sitting there. You should probably drive around back.

"There's no road around back," said Quarrel.

"You got tires, don't ya?"

Shark hopped down from the wall and Quarrel was
left alone. He put the van in gear and looked around.
Over the earpiece, he heard guards shout at Shark.

"Hands up," said the first guard in Spanish.
Quarrel knew a handful of languages, and thankfully
Spanish was one of them. He had been working toward a
job in the Americas, so his Spanish was much stronger
than his Mandarin, Japanese or his German. He knew
almost nothing of the Middle Eastern languages.

Shark must have complied with the guards since
there was no sound of gunfire or violence.

"Do we kill him?" asked Guard Numero Dos.

"No," said Numero Tres. "He blew up the
Lamborghini. The Boss wants him."

Another guard, likely Guard Numero Uno again,
spoke in stilted English. "You bad news, pal. Boss wants
you. Boss not happy."

Shark was almost laughing at these three. Whatever
they were doing—patting him down, tying him up, who
knows—he clearly thought it was amusing. "Yeah. I
heard. Stick to Spanish, your English sucks."

And then the three guards led him inside, which is
exactly where he wanted to go.

Quarrel pulled off the road and drove through
some brush on the south side of the villa, circling toward
the back, which was the farthest you could get from the
front gate. When he got there, he heard a new voice, this
one spoke English with almost no accent. Quarrel pulled

to a stop and listened as Shark was now in a room with his target.

"You blew up my car," said The Boss.

"Yup."

"You American?"

"Man can't help where he's born."

"Who do you work for?"

"People."

"I have a soundproof room in the basement and I employ five interrogators. Why not just tell me everything about the people who sent you now and we can get this over with." As The Boss spoke, Quarrel wondered if he should load a gun and try to help Shark.

Shark's voice: "Sure, I'll tell you whatever you want to know."

Quarrel spoke up, "You can't—"

Shark's earpiece volume went down, something you could only do if you were touching the earpiece itself. "It's fine, kid, I got this," he said in his now-quieter voice.

There were some surprised, confused voices in Spanish, and then Shark chuckled. "Yeah, sorry. Took those off. Chafing."

Quarrel heard The Boss scream at his men in Spanish.

"Here's the thing," said Shark. "I could tell you everything, but you'd really have no use for the information when you're dead."

The boss stammered but gave no commands to the men.

"Because your guards made four mistakes." Shark paused, and Quarrel imagined him raising four fingers to count. "They let me live. They kept me conscious. They brought me inside. And they left my belt on."

With the sound turned down, Quarrel couldn't tell what the metal clinking sound was, but it could have been a man unbuckling his belt. "Now you can surrender peacefully and I'll just arrest you, or you all die in about ten seconds."

The boss scoffed, and said "Fuego—"

There was a whip-crack sound and a gunshot, followed by a very fast rustling and two more shots. The sound of running footsteps, going away from Shark, and another shot.

"Roll over, fatty, or I'll shoot ya again." Shark was still alive, and that must have meant the guards were dead. Quarrel couldn't understand how he had done it. Cartel thugs were ex-military. How Shark could kill three of them while armed only with a belt seemed absurd.

Quarrel's smartphone lit up, showing a streaming video of The Boss's face. Shark was connected to both Quarrel and the CIA, filming the boss in close-up.

"Say your name."

The fat man spat at Shark.

"Say your name."

"Vete al infierno."

Shark reacted immediately with a hard pistol-whip to the boss's face, knocking him out and spraying blood on the camera phone. He grabbed the man's right hand, and pressed the phone's screen against the man's thumb. A moment later The Boss's name and photo appeared on Quarrel's screen.

"Positive ID," said Quarrel. "This is the guy."

Shark pointed the camera back at the boss's face and then the tip of a gun barrel appeared onscreen. Shark

80

fired at the man's face until the gun was empty. One shot would have been enough, but Shark kept shooting until the screen showed a horrifying mush instead of a face. Then he fiddled with the phone, and Quarrel realized he was sending the video to CIA to confirm the kill. Then Quarrel's camera feed cut off.

"Still with me, kid?" Shark asked over the earpiece.

"Yeah, where are you?" said Quarrel, trying to sound calm despite what must have been a near-overdose of adrenaline by now.

"Coming over the southeast corner of the wall."

Quarrel stepped on the gas and followed the wall around the house. He stopped at the corner and idled. Shark didn't appear. Quarrel was off-road in a bulky, twenty-year-old van, parked within five feet of the home of a very powerful man whom he had just watched die. It wasn't the sort of situation that led to a lot of patience. After a half-minute, Chris spoke to his earpiece.

"Where are you?"

He heard a crackle of static followed by silence.

Quarrel watched the clock count off two more minutes. There was nothing. Not even the sound of a gunshot from inside the compound. He put the van into drive.

There was a startling bang as something smashed into the roof. Quarrel looked over his shoulder and saw a three-pronged grappling hook impaled through the steel. A second later there was a thump as a man hit the roof, cut the line, and the hook fell to the floor behind Chris. A figure dropped past the passenger window and out of sight. Quarrel picked up his gun, but he was also ready to stomp on the gas pedal if the man outside was hostile.

Shark rose into view, opened the door, and tossed the heavy backpack onto Chris's lap.

"Let's go."

Quarrel dug into the pack. It was overflowing with cash in various currencies, mostly US dollars. "You took the drug money?"

"Better I have it than them."

Quarrel said something under his breath, tossed the pack behind him, and drove.

As they reached the road, Shark turned the radio up.

"What was that about your belt?" Quarrel asked, trying not to sound like a nerdy schoolboy.

"What?" Shark asked over the music.

"The bit with your belt. I counted three guards and their boss. You had a belt. Four on one and you only had a belt. How did that work?"

"Maybe if you weren't Mr. Stay-In-The-Van you'd know how to do things like that."

"I just can't figure it out."

Shark laughed a little. Quarrel heard the ringing sound of a blade being drawn, and then Shark stabbed a small dagger into the dashboard. This was a strange weapon. It had a two-inch blade and instead of a handle it had a small square of metal, just big enough to hook two fingers into. Quarrel realized the square was a belt buckle.

"I see."

Shark lit a cigarette, and turned up the music so loud it ended the conversation.

In Caracas, Shark got on a private flight to a destination he wouldn't tell Quarrel. He took the bag of money with him as a carry-on, and somehow the security guard didn't look inside. Chris got the feeling Shark was afforded that type of discretion on a regular basis.

He had spent almost twenty straight hours with Shark, mostly driving, and mostly in silence. And he had no idea if Peter Scarret was a mole or not. At the very least, he knew that he didn't like him. Altogether, his investigation had turned up absolutely nothing solid.

After Shark had disappeared on his private plane, Quarrel got on a commercial flight to Washington, to meet with the next suspect on his list.

10

Jessica Swift crawled through the ventilation ducts of WBS, but this time it was no reconnaissance mission. This time was for real. After her first visit, she knew how dirty the vents were, so tonight she wore grey instead of black. With her brown hair in a bun at the top of her neck and her belt covered in tools and pouches, there would be no mistaking her for anything other than a burglar, so she promised herself there would be no slip-ups this time.

It had been a long time since the woman codenamed Io had started stealing from people. As a teenager she was always shocked at how dumb the boys were—stealing things by smashing and grabbing, or robbing a place at gunpoint. It was much easier to just sneak into a place where nobody was looking and walk out with what you wanted. By the time she was seventeen, Jessica had hooked into the world of organized thievery, cracking safes for some very dangerous characters. It was decent work: four big, scary men would coerce and bribe any guards who needed to be absent, and Jessica would just have to walk into a place and open the safe. She was making an equal share to the rest of the gang—great money for any seventeen-year-old.

Of course, she wasn't aware that all the money was just a down payment for the burden she would have to carry for the rest of her life.

Inside the vent, Jessica weaved a strong fishing line through the slats in a grate below her face. Once she was sure the line would hold, Jessica tied off the ends of each fishing line attached to a frame that fit around the outside edges of the grate. The frame was magnetic, and wouldn't move once the line was holding the weight of the metal grate.

Now she inserted a J-shaped hand-cranked screwdriver through the vent, hooking back up to the first of the screws that held the vent in place. Cranking the handle, she removed the screw. Her steady hands kept the screw balanced on the tip of the bit, until she raised it back up and pocketed the screw. She did this for the other five screws in less than a minute. As the last screw came out, the grate dropped, dragging along the fishing line for an instant before it ran out of slack, and then swung open, the end tied by the wire acting as a hinge.

Dropping into the back room of the bank, she felt the same familiarity that hit her on every break-in. The same sense of almost being caught, the thrill of the trespass, the sickness in her gut. Sense memory of this feeling ruined it every time, corrupting the thrill into a flashback of the day that ruined her life.

After months of flawless robberies, Jessica's crew had set their sights on the office in the back of a strip club. Ricky, the crew's leader, insisted that the safe in there would be the biggest job they ever pulled. He was right. The building had no security aside from basic door locks, and the safe itself. Jessica cracked it in no time, and they found almost three-quarters of a million dollars inside. Ricky never told them whose money it was.

In Switzerland, Jessica was using a drill to access the inner working of the vault's keypad. She would first have to manipulate the time lock, which was connected to a physical timepiece inside the wall. Once the clock thought it was 8:47 a.m., opening time, she would be able to hack the keypad and open the vault. It was a three-minute window. Once the lock reached 8:50 a.m., a silent alarm went out to the security company, who would then call police.

Ten years earlier, she was tucking some of her cash into a getaway bag in a locker she rented from a fitness club. It was one of several stashes she used, just in case she had to leave town in a hurry. Even at seventeen, Swift had been thinking about contingencies. The radio station the gym piped in through overhead speakers gave the news every half hour.

'An update on the fire at Club Mystique strip club, authorities now say the fire was set deliberately; an act of arson meant to cover up that the people inside had been shot before the fire started. Police are calling it an act of organized crime, as the club's owner was a known associate of gangland kingpins.'

Jessica had stolen from the mob. And when the strip club owner tried to explain that he'd been ripped off, the mob bosses didn't believe him. He paid for that seven-hundred thousand dollars with his life, and the lives of his two best friends, his wife, and a stripper who had the bad luck to show up early. As the realization hit her—these people died because of me—Jessica had to run for the washroom. She didn't make it. She threw up in a bin of towels.

The vault opened at what it thought was 8:48 a.m., and Jessica found the safe deposit box easily. Number 191. She picked the lock with practiced ease, and pulled out the drawer. Inside was a thin folder. She grabbed it. There were also several bundles of cash, freshly counted and bound in paper bands. American dollars. Fifty grand. She took that too.

Normally, she would climb back into the vent, carefully remove her equipment, and leave the vent cover exactly as it had been. But after running into the guards during her scouting mission, she didn't trust the vents not to sag and squeak while she did so. So instead of bothering with all that, she pulled a thin fabric mask over her face, opened the deadbolts from the vault room and ran through the bank and out a fire door. She was sprinting from the second she touched the pavement. She was a mile away before she heard sirens. They would already have security footage of her from the first attempt at infiltrating WBS, so now they would have a little more: Footage of a masked, petite woman escaping with a small pack and a belt of tools. That was better than taking the risk of guards cornering her again.

"Io to Jupiter. I have the documents." She typed into a smart phone, while sitting on the bed in her hotel room. She waited almost five minutes before the phone lit up with a response.

"Confirm."

She used the phone's camera to take a picture of the file folder, and sent it back. The response was immediate:

"Burn them." That was all Jupiter had to say.

Shrugging, Jessica pulled the trash bin over to the side of the bed. Opening the folder, she started to crumple the pages and toss them into the basket, until something caught her eye.

There were several photographs inside the folder, showing a beautiful, well-dressed woman lying in a pool of blood. She had an entry wound in her forehead. It was the caption that got her attention, the one that started with her name: "Jessica . . . " Suddenly compelled to know more about this woman, Jessica began to read through the file.

At first, it seemed to describe a murder. A woman named Jessica Jordan had been killed in Paris. She was a suspected American spy. Then she started to read about the killer. Khalid Saleb, also a US spy. There were photocopies of a kill order. A type-one job, as they called it. One spy had killed another. Why would they do that? Then things got stranger.

There were other documents; a train ticket ordered online. From Paris to Lyon. The same night as the murder. What was going on? Was this proof of an escape? Evidence of Saleb's getaway? And why did the name Khalid Saleb sound so familiar?

Swift picked up her laptop and googled the man's name. It came up right away—the Afghan-American who killed a spy. Standing about ten feet away from each other, both Saleb and Jordan had simultaneously shot each other, like a wild west shootout. Jordan died, Saleb lived. It was a mess of extradition. Very public. If Saleb was really a spy, that kind of public spectacle shouldn't have happened. Not in an American ally like France. This guy, Saleb, was being hung out to dry.

It was the final page that put it all together. It was an email from one numbered address to another. No names.

Saleb has orders to be in Lyon. They will be apart. I'll take Saleb. You take Jordan. Leave a mess for the police to find.

Saleb hadn't killed her. They had orders that kept them apart, so that they would both be alone. Whoever was pulling the strings wanted them both dead, but when

88

Saleb survived a bullet to the head, the Powers That Be framed him for his partner's murder.

Suddenly Jessica flashed back to the morning news report. The black body bags on gurneys being wheeled out of the burnt husk of the strip club she had robbed three days earlier. Five people dead because of her greed.

Jessica Jordan was dead because of someone else. Khalid Saleb was locked up somewhere because of someone else. Five people were dead because Jessica Swift had acted in her own interest.

She knew she couldn't let it happen again. Saleb was up for treason and murder. It was a guaranteed death sentence. These papers exonerated Saleb for the murder he had taken the fall for. She was supposed to destroy them, and in doing so destroy any evidence that he was a victim, not a traitor. The people she worked for, even her handler Jupiter, wanted this man to die for a crime he didn't commit. She couldn't do it.

No one was going to die because Jessica Swift stole from the wrong people. Not again. She was going to have to find this man, Khalid Saleb. This spy who was under lock and key in some black site somewhere in the world. And she was going to set him free.

She tucked the documents into her carry-on bag, then tossed the folder they had come in into the trash can and set it on fire. Snapping a photo of the flames, she typed a message:

"Documents destroyed. Io out."

11

"So what did you get from Shark?" asked Milton. Chris Quarrel was driving a rental car into Connecticut. Milton's voice emanated, tinny and distant, from the car's speakers. Quarrel spoke loudly to make sure Milton could hear him through the shoddy hands-free system.

"He's reckless, unreliable, and he steals drug money."

"Yeah, but that was in his file. What's your gut tell you?"

"Honestly," said Quarrel, trying to listen to instincts that had never been tested in the field, "I still can't figure it out. Shark could be bitter and loyal, or he could be bitter and dangerous. No way to tell just yet. Honestly, I don't know if I have the instincts for this. I've trained to interrogate a suspect, but in a proper interrogation room, and I wasn't training against top-level agents. It was role-playing with other trainees."

There was a sound that might have been static from the speaker, or Milton grumbling on the other end of the line. "Kid, in this game you need two things: evidence and guts. If you only have a hunch you'll never prove it, and if you only have evidence you're walking into a trap. No elite agent is going to leave you a trail of breadcrumbs unless they're trying to play you. And if you only go on your gut you'll miss some key detail and blow an entire operation. The evidence is strongest against Shark, so now I need your gut. Give me an answer."

"Right now, I can't do that. Shark could be anything and I wouldn't be able to tell."

Milton grunted. "Disappointing, kid. Maybe you'll have better luck with Boswell." The line went quiet, and the little speaker spat static until Quarrel changed radio stations.

Samantha Boswell was a legend. For ten years, she had been the CIA's best (or, Chris Quarrel knew now, the CIB's best) operative. She could get into any location, kill any target, and escape unseen. For ten years, "Cipher" was a rumour, and her actual existence doubted by top members of the CIA, MI-6, and even her enemies weren't sure she was real. Her targets died, and somehow, eventually, those kills were all attributed to "Cipher."

There had been conjecture that "Cipher" was a team of assassins, not just one person. At one point, a Chinese official wrote a report guessing that a famous American spy who had been dead since 1985 was actually alive, and training as many as a dozen agents who were, collectively, Cipher. Her first mistake, in her eighth year of service, was to let a guard live. She hadn't seen him, because the guard had been cowering in a closet instead of protecting his asset. After that, word got out that Cipher was just one woman.

It was in her eleventh year of service that Cipher made her second mistake, and finally revealed herself to the small, secretive world of spies. This mistake involved bringing the wrong equipment. She had scanned for signals coming out of a target's home, but hadn't detected the tiny camera hidden inside a book on the shelf. That camera had filmed her shooting the target as he lay sleeping.

The woman on the video was the same one the guard had described. Suddenly, Cipher had a face. After that happened, Harry Milton had been forced to reveal that, yes, Cipher worked for him, and she was in fact a single person. Word of her exploits spread through the world of Western intelligence, and even though only a handful of people had ever seen her picture, and even fewer had met her, Samantha Boswell became a legend.

She was seen by many as the American equivalent of William Thorpe, the invincible British agent who had been so great during the Cold War. If you believed everything you heard, Thorpe might have single-handedly saved the free world on a daily basis from 1970 through to 1990. And now, according to the whisperers, Samantha Boswell had done much the same in the new millennium.

Quarrel knew it was mostly exaggerated, but after he had taken a good look at her file in Harry Milton's office, he realized that the scant details he had heard were nothing compared to the real files. Boswell had over 200 assassinations to her name, and never once botched a job. In fact, the rumour that she had never once fired a shot that missed its target seemed to be confirmed by the case reports.

Two hundred missions, thousands of rounds fired, and every single bullet struck where it was supposed to—whether that target was the tire on a moving car, or a person shot while jumping off a roof. That was the legend of Sam Boswell, and now Chris Quarrel, whose own legend began and ended at paintball, was on his way to investigate her. And then he'd have to decide whether or not to accuse the planet's deadliest woman of treason.

But first, a bake sale.

#

Chris walked into a fairly new elementary school in a subdivision outside Hartford, Connecticut. The doors were open, and he passed straight through the small lobby into the gymnasium, which was full of a mix of adults and kids as the school held its Spring Bake Sale to pay for the end-of-year field trip for the graduating class.

There were thirty-something moms everywhere, but Quarrel had seen a photo of Boswell, and hoped to spot her easily. He was wrong about that, since she flanked him before he could spot her. He was pretending to study some butter tarts on a red tray when someone tapped on his shoulder.

"Hi, Chris, glad you could make it."

He turned around and there she was. The hard-edged woman from the photo, the one who looked like she wanted to kill the camera for looking at her, was not the person he saw now. This woman was tanned, dressed in relaxed jeans and a pale green cardigan. She smiled, and it seemed genuine.

"Mrs. Boswell, how nice to see you again."

She hugged him lightly, and stepped back.

"How was the drive?"

"Lovely. How are you?"

She smiled again. "Busy, busy. You know how it is with kids. Always something." She led him through the crowd, to a corner of the gym where the tables were selling old toys and homemade art. They were less popular than the baked goods, so there was room to talk without anyone overhearing.

She continued. "You know, you think you've got your day all planned and then some kid comes along and messes everything up."

"Sorry about that," he said, his own smile a little sheepish.

"How's Harry?"

"He needs to hire someone to dust his office."

She laughed. It was fake, as was the entire conversation, but she played the part well. Another mom, behind a table of snowman sculptures that were surely leftovers from a Christmas bake sale four months ago, smiled at them and waved to Boswell.

"Old Harry never did know when to leave the office. Hi Bonnie!" She made no move to introduce her young friend, instead motioned Quarrel toward a set of metal doors that were on the gym's back wall, which were still closed. She pushed on one and Quarrel found that they were outside, behind the gym, and alone. The metal door squeaked as it swung shut.

Once it clicked into place, Boswell elbowed Chris in the solar plexus so hard he lost all the air in his lungs and collapsed to his knees. The fringes of his vision flashed black and the ground in front of him was dotted with white stars. Once when Chris was ten, he had fallen off a jungle gym and landed flat on his back. Nothing since then had knocked the wind out of him quite so hard, until he met Sam Boswell.

"Oh boy, Chris," she said, still playing the neighbourly mom, as she pulled him to his feet. He was still doubled over, hands on his knees, trying to make his lungs work, when she whispered in his ear.

"I know you're just following orders. I know you don't know any better. But if you ever bring business within ten miles of my kids again I'll shoot you in the face."

Unable to speak, Quarrel nodded.

"So what the hell does Milton want with me? He knows my deal. I go on the road six times a year. I don't do interviews with junior Canadians."

94

Wheezing, Quarrel managed to spit out "How did—"

"You have an accent. You might not hear it, but I do."

"I hafff . . . have to. Ask you—"

"Catch your breath, sport. I'm not going to hurt you."

The pain had spread through his torso, making his body feel like a massive bruise, but he didn't argue with her. "Have you ever heard of Digamma? Or the letter six?"

"Is digamma the triangle? No, that's delta. I was never a sorority girl."

"It's like an F but with a thingy on the bottom horizontal line." He drew one in the sand with his finger:

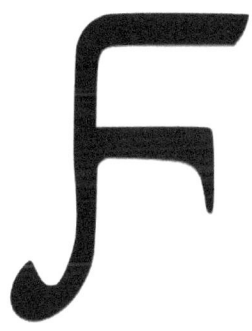

She shook her head. "Try a cryptologist. Can I get back to my cupcakes?"

"One more thing. When did you cut down from full time to six trips a year?"

"Few years back. After I had my girls."

"That's an eighth grade fundraiser. You had kids for years before you retired. So why?"

"The fact that you know my name is answer enough. I love my country, but not enough to bring its shit down on my kids. Once they got me on video, that was it for me. Can I go, or is Harry gonna send you back to bother me again?"

"One more question."

"The last one was one more." Now he saw the hateful woman from the photograph. In the school she was a helpful mom. Back here out of sight, she was like a cornered snake. Quarrel imagined that this was who she was when she was "on the road."

"Can you think of a single reason for terrorists to blow up an office building in Ottawa?"

Her eyes narrowed a bit, studying him. For the first time, he saw wrinkles at the corners of her eyes. "I would assume it wasn't just an office building, otherwise Harry wouldn't give a damn. But before that bomb went off, no. Honestly, I'm surprised your country still pretends to have spies. It's adorable."

Her condescension was insulting, but to Quarrel's not-very-proven bullshit detector, it seemed truthful enough. Boswell had no idea that CSIS-2 existed.

"I'm done," she said, pointing along the brick wall of the gymnasium. "You can walk around that way to get back out front. Don't come through the gym." She opened the door, and the sounds of the bake sale poured out; voices blending into a din, kids laughing and screaming. "It was so nice to see you again, Chris. Shame you can't visit again." She pulled the door shut behind herself, leaving him alone, out of breath, and even less sure of his investigative skills.

Driving back toward the District of Columbia, Quarrel called Milton again. "She damn near broke my ribs, but she seemed clueless about the big stuff."

"Just how much did you tell her?" Milton asked, his voice agitated.

"Enough that if she's your mole, she'll probably try to kill me."

"Well," Milton said, sounding pleased, "I guess that's progress. You might want to come in and sign out a gun."

12

Chris Quarrel and Harry Milton were in the underground bunker that was the CIB. This time, they were on the floor beneath Milton's office in an expansive concrete room where the walls were covered by two things: hooks for lab coats and racks of guns. Scattered throughout the lab were ten of CIB's scientists, working on assorted projects and experiments. The first counter they passed was flanked by two young men setting up a chemistry experiment. One of them was checking the temperature in a beaker that sat over a Bunsen burner flame, while the second was attaching a Kevlar vest to a gel torso. Once the vest was attached, they nodded to each other. The first chemist poured the blue liquid from the hot beaker into a larger beaker that was already half-full of clear liquid. The blue colour faded until it disappeared, and the resulting compound looked like water. Then the chemist picked up the beaker and threw the liquid at the vest, splashing it everywhere. Within a second, the Kevlar started melting into a thick, black slime. Milton made a questioning grunt to get their attention.

The second chemist looked at Milton. "We're looking for a way to remove body armour without killing the man underneath. If you can take away his sense of safety, he's more likely to surrender. It could prevent situations from escalating."

Milton nodded politely, said nothing to the eager young scientist, and kept walking. A few steps later, he leaned conspiratorially toward Quarrel. "Very bright minds here, but they don't realize that the people we employ would always make the headshot anyway."

At the next station, a woman stood facing a narrow hallway that extended out sideways from the main room. She shouted, "Fire in the hole!"

Quarrel realized it wasn't a hallway at all, but a long rifle range. The woman facing down the range was not holding a gun, but an umbrella. After shrugging her shoulders to loosen up, she held the umbrella straight out horizontally, holding it with both hands. With a click of her thumb on the handle, a two-inch long rocket-propelled grenade fired from the tip and down the range, exploding with a huge noise but very little vibration.

"There's an accelerometer inside of it. It only fires if you hold it steady and within three degrees of horizontal for three seconds first," the woman said, turning and removing her earplugs. "That way you don't accidentally blow up when you twirl it."

Milton offered the woman a handshake. "Chris Quarrel, this is Mcg. Meg's our fabrication specialist. Anything we can't buy, she builds."

Quarrel shook her hand as well. "What do you take in school to get that job?"

"Electrical engineering. But we've got everyone from nuclear physicists to auto mechanics. If you can build gadgets and gizmos, you can work here." Meg was surprisingly young, probably close to thirty but looked like a college student. She had short, spiky brown hair and a round, slightly pudgy face. She was skinny despite the baby fat on her face, so she was practically swimming in her big white lab coat.

Milton guided them toward the middlemost counter, which was covered in a variety of guns and knives. "Agent Quarrel has decided he needs a weapon. A good sidearm he can keep for a while, nothing '*special*'."

"Gig!" Shouted Meg. A lanky young man in a Ninja Turtles t-shirt emerged from an open door behind the counter.

"What ya want?" He said before he saw Milton. "Oh, hi, sir."

"New guy wants a gun," explained Meg.

"OK. I'm Gig. I'm the procurement specialist. I buy the stuff Meg can't build." She gave him an angry look.

"I can build anything, it's just faster to buy certain things."

Gig shrugged. "Mostly I'm the gun guy. You want a gun, I'm the guy."

Quarrel was amused by the pair of excitable young nerds in the heart of the secret underground bunker. He shook Gig's hand. "Gig and Meg?"

"Codenames, obviously. The network guy's called Kilo."

"I see."

Milton wasn't as amused. "Just a sidearm. Nothing special."

"Anyway," Gig said, "we have a lot of nothing special in stock, and even more standard issue. It's the special orders that keep me up at night." Gig gestured to the table of guns like a spokesmodel on the 'Price is Right.' "Take your pick and we'll sign it out."

Quarrel studied the guns. He had used about a dozen of these before but had never really thought about his own preference. And he was very intrigued by the variety of weapons he'd never even tried before.

Suddenly, the elevator at the end of the room dinged open, and a short blonde man with thick legs and large biceps sprinted out of it. Quarrel knew him; he was

Jack Hall from the training program. Hall didn't break stride until he reached Gig, but by then he was already barking out orders.

"Gig! M-two-forty-nine with a grenade launcher. H-E rounds and flashbangs!"

Gig disappeared back into the door beside the counter as the big man turned to Milton. "Harry, we have a big problem. A guarded CIA convoy just got hit about a half-hour outside of Langley."

"What the hell were they moving?"

"Control computers for American nuclear weapons."

"Control computers?"

"Outdated technology, not in use anymore. They tracked the missile's location and only armed the bomb when it was near the target so that you didn't have any nuclear accidents if the missile was shot down before it got to the target. There was a team dismantling old nukes at a site on the northeast coast. The actual bombs and fissionable materials are already secured and harmless. These computers were the last components to be dealt with. And there were six of them on the truck. Supposed to just go to a recycling plant and get ground into bits."

"What use is an old computer without the bomb it's attached to?"

"Don't know. I guess in theory if you happened to have a thirty-year-old nuke lying around, this thing could set it off but you'd think anyone with decent electrical skills could just hack it."

"So why steal them?"

"No idea. These things have a short-range tracker but they predate modern GPS. If they get away, we lose 'em for good."

101

"Jesus Christ. Take a chopper. You bring the computers back or destroy them, but don't let the hijackers keep the damned things!"

"That's why I need a nice big bang."

As if on cue, Gig emerged from the door with a machine gun and a black messenger bag. The blonde man took the bag first, and then the gun.

"I just attached that grenade launcher—I'm hoping it fires straight."

"I guess we'll find out."

The big man sprinted for the elevator. Staring at the table of weapons, Quarrel asked Gig a question: "These things loaded?"

"Yeah, why?"

Quarrel grabbed a handgun and a light machine gun and ran after Hall. "I'm going with him!"

The big man turned back, looking past Quarrel to Milton. "Who the hell is this guy?"

"Foreign exchange student. He's field trained."

Stepping into the elevator beside the big, intense American, Quarrel offered a handshake. "Chris Quarrel. You trained me."

The doors closed. "I remember now." He ignored Chris's hand. "You failed."

#

After twenty minutes, they were flying low over a highway in central Virginia. It was still just mid-morning, and the traffic was light. Jack sat next to the pilot, navigating from a small tablet computer that was tracking the signal from the control computers. Quarrel was in the back, trying not to look terrified.

Between talks with the pilot, Jack would speak to Chris through the headsets they wore to communicate over the drone of the engines. He had filled Chris in with the pertinent details. There had been a five-vehicle convoy. The front and back vehicles were armoured SUVs, and the three middle vehicles had been armoured trucks. The computers were in the last truck, a detail the thieves must have known in advance. As the convoy went through an intersection, a semi-trailer truck rammed the target truck at fifty miles an hour, rolling it over. A team of at least twelve men then emerged from the surrounding area with machine guns and hand grenades, to hold off the rest of the convoy. A team then cut into the rear of the armoured truck, killed the men inside, and took the computers. Then all of the attackers got into five high-end sports cars and took off at well over a hundred miles an hour. They made it far enough that all authorities on the ground had lost them—meaning they could have switched vehicles and might be driving anything.

Hall seemed to be unfazed by that. "As long as we have the tracking beacons within ten miles they can ride a goddamn rocket ship and I'll still find them."

Now they were within a mile of all six tracking signals, which were still lumped together on the radar. There were three vehicles in a pack ahead of the helicopter. "Bring me over top of that cube van," said Hall to the pilot.

They pulled over top of the van, and Hall nodded. "That's the one. They're right under us. Pull away a bit so I can see them."

Quarrel looked out the window to see the van, which was bunched closely between two other vehicles in the slow lane. In front was a luxury convertible with the top up, and behind was a minivan. "Are the other cars with 'em or civilian?"

"I don't know. Either way we want to isolate the van."

Suddenly, Jack threw open his door and leaned out of the moving helicopter. "Lower!" He raised the M249 and slid the safety off. Then he unleashed a barrage of bullets at the van, hitting the street first and then punching the driver's door with several shots. After the burst, he waited. The minivan behind the van slammed on its brakes, while the convertible and the van both sped up.

"Closer!"

Realizing that he could help, Quarrel climbed over next to Hall, trusting his restraint straps to hold him inside the chopper. He raised his own weapon and lined up the sights. Before he could fire, Chris realized that the convertible's top was opening. He readjusted to aim for the roof of the car. As soon as he saw a person, he fired. He missed. The man in the back of the car was holding something. There was a bright flash, and then a contrail of smoke shot past the chopper's tail rotor.

"Rockets!" shouted Hall to the pilot, who sped up to pull them ahead of the terrorist vehicles.

Hall loaded a flashbang grenade into the under-mounted launcher on his gun. He took aim again, this time at the car, and fired. The round hit the hood of the car and exploded in a bright flash. The driver stomped on the gas and launched the car well ahead of the cube van. A second later, Chris realized the driver was blind when the convertible kept going straight where the road curved, and it slammed into the guardrail. The rocket-man standing in the backseat was thrown fully across the two lanes on the other side of the guardrail, while the driver was smashed into his steering wheel so hard that even if he survived, he wouldn't be a threat. A second after that, the cube van passed the wreck without slowing.

"Aim for the tires?" asked Chris.

"Save your ammo. I got it."

Hall reloaded the launcher, this time with a high explosive round. He took his time aiming as the chopper swung around to keep up with the bending road. They pulled up alongside the van, about fifty feet from the ground. "Hold that speed!" shouted Hall. Instants later, he fired.

The grenade hit the road a few feet in front of the speeding van. The van was almost on top of it as it exploded, and the force was enough to throw the front end of the van into the air so it was only driving on the rear wheels for a second. When it slammed back onto the ground, both front tires exploded and the van started to slow, gradually rolling to a stop. Either the engine was dead, or the driver was.

"Bring us down in front!" shouted Hall when he saw that the van was stopping.

A hundred feet in front of the stopped van, the helicopter lowered to the ground. Hall was diving out about eight feet from the ground, while Chris waited for touchdown before he ran out into the road, ducking his head out of fear of the rotors.

Hall waved his hands in signals that Quarrel knew meant "Take the right, and take cover." Quarrel jumped the guardrail to the other side of the road. It wasn't busy, but he still felt uneasy about standing in the fast lane with

105

his back to the traffic; however, the guardrail was the only cover available to advance on the van. Meanwhile, Hall was charging down the paved shoulder, his weapon ready in case anyone in the van moved.

They got within thirty feet before the van's windshield exploded with handgun fire. Hall dove to his left, seeking shelter in a ditch. The bullets missed him by inches. Quarrel had never fired on a person before, but if he didn't provide some cover, Jack Hall would be killed. As the terrorist fired on Hall, Chris took aim from a kneeling position behind the guardrail and fired at the shooter. His shots rattled the driver's side door, where the window exploded. The terrorist stopped firing, and Quarrel indulged the thought—the fear?—that he'd killed the man, until he heard the bullets ricocheting off the guardrail. The driver was alive, and firing a machine gun back at Chris. Quarrel turtled behind the steel ribbons of the guardrail as bullets honed in on his position.

Hall poked up from the ditch to see that Quarrel had drawn the enemy's fire. He aimed quickly and shot a grenade straight into the van's open windshield. It hit the back wall of the cab with a thunk, and a split second later the cab exploded. A second after that, the gas tank went and a ten-metre-high gasoline explosion spat heat at Quarrel.

Quarrel watched the flames roll upward, thought of his mission with Shark, and wondered if giant fireballs were typical for CIB agents. Quarrel had fired on the thieves but knowing that Hall had killed them was somehow a relief. Killing a man was a step Quarrel hadn't been prepared for; a realization that only occurred to him now that he was face-to-face with it. While Quarrel was still awed by the fireball, Hall flanked around the back of the burning van and waited for the rear doors to open. They stayed shut. Quarrel joined Hall at the back of the burning van. After a minute of the fire heating the van, Hall shot out the locks and pulled open the doors. Black smoke poured out, but nobody attacked.

There were two men in the back, both lying face down.

"They weren't in there long enough to die from smoke inhalation," said Quarrel.

"The force of the grenade probably got them. It's like dynamite fishing."

Hall dug through the rubble of the van until he found a black steel case. There was one-half of a set of handcuffs still attached to the handle.

"Probably cut it off the guard with the same thing they used to break into the armoured truck." He gave the case to Quarrel. "Take it to the chopper. If any of them are following, you take off and leave me. I'm going to search these guys and see what they've got on them."

Quarrel nodded. He did as he was told. The pilot had already called in their location, so it was just a matter of waiting for the CIA to show up. The first responders were the state police, followed closely by field teams from both the FBI and CIA. The media were on-site within twenty minutes. As soon as Hall saw the first TV crew setting up, he climbed into the helicopter and ordered the pilot to take them home.

"We don't need to be on camera," he said through the headset.

"Shouldn't the CIB have a presence down there?" asked Quarrel.

"Who do think those FBI guys were?"

"Oh."

Five minutes later, Harry Milton messaged Hall with the code to open the case. The inside of the case was hard foam, with six slots cut into it to hold the six control computers. The computers looked like a combination of a remote control and an old stereo, with two connector wires hanging from one end. They were each the size of a 1980s cell phone, with a twelve-button pad and a rudimentary digital screen like on a graphing calculator. While there were six slots in the case, there were only five computers.

"They got one," said Hall. "The minivan."

"What good is a thirty-year-old tracking computer?"

"Don't know," said Jack Hall, staring at the sun-drenched landscape below. "We only know two things. The first is that whoever it is, they have highest-level intel on us. They knew when the components were moving, and they even knew which truck to hit."

"And the second thing?" Quarrel asked, knowing the answer already.

"The second thing is that they just stole something whose only purpose is to set off a nuclear bomb."

13

It was May 1st, a chilly night in the Arizona desert, where a long, white bungalow housed three federal agents and one amnesiac prisoner. Khalid Saleb, as usual, was watching TV. He had no access to a computer, but the agents who guarded him let him watch TV—which he kept tuned to the news channels. Maybe he was filling in the gaps in his memory, or hoping to see something that sparked a recollection.

Saleb's room looked like a normal bedroom inside the ranch house. He had a large window, with no metal bars to show that this was actually a prison cell. The window was actually shatter-resistant, bulletproof glass, with two three-quarter-inch panes providing redundant security. The walls, ordinary drywall painted a pale blue, covered cement-filled cinderblock. The fire-rated door was made of oak heavy enough that you wouldn't notice that it contained an inch of plate steel.

Jessica Swift knew all of this as she watched Saleb through that window. She had been watching them for two days now, at a distance, through a telescope.

Finding out where he was being held wasn't hard; she needed only to break into a field office of the United States Marshals Service, which was the agency assigning the guards who watched Saleb.

She had also located plans for the building itself, which was much more than a simple house. There were security cameras watching every direction outside the house, and every square foot of the inside. Cameras mounted on posts north and south of the house watched the road, which was usually empty in this barren piece of desert. This security video played in a room of the house, where one of the three guards-on-duty was always stationed. The other guards intermittently watched Saleb and took breaks. They rotated every two hours, until the end of the twelve-hour shift, when a new set of agents took over. The agents on the night crew were two women and a man. Whenever the man was on video duty, the women would sit down in the living room and play cards. Jessica was waiting for tonight's game to start.

She pulled out a piece of blank white paper and wrote on it in big letters, then flipped it over and wrote on the back. She folded the paper and tucked it into her pocket. Everything else she needed was on her tool belt, except for the bikes that were lying in a ditch, covered with a brown blanket for camouflage. She had come here on one of the bikes. The second—a folding bike—had been strapped to her back. It was already unfolded and ready to ride, under the blanket.

Through the eyepiece, she saw the guards pull out a card table, and she took a deep breath. She was about to commit to a course of action that could be called treason. She set the telescope down and started walking toward the house.

She knew the exact spot where she would become visible on the cameras. Dressed all in black, she crouched beside a large saguaro cactus and crawled toward the house, keeping herself hidden in the cactus's shadow. Once she ran out of shadow, she would be visible on the camera.

Jessica pulled out a small air-powered handgun and took aim at the one camera that could see her. She fired a small dart that stuck into the panelling an inch below the camera. The dart would give off magnetic pulses for eight seconds, causing interference with the camera signal, so there would be waves of static on the screen.

The moment she heard the dart hit and stick, she was sprinting for the house. It was a bungalow, so she was able to run up the wall, jump, and pull herself onto the roof without any tools to help. Once she was on the roof, it was easy. First, she waited to hear if the guard would come investigate the staticky camera. After a couple minutes, she decided she was in the clear and moved to Saleb's window. After tying off a rope on a pipe sticking out of the roof, she lowered herself down to the window and pressed her piece of paper against the glass. It took Saleb a moment to notice, but then he walked over.

The paper said: YOU WERE SET UP.

She turned the page over: I WILL GET YOU FREE.

After Saleb nodded a baffled 'OK,' she raised what looked like a large laser pointer or a small flashlight. It didn't make a sound, just clicked on and started shining a red light on the glass. As the light cut through the glass, she slowly and methodically shifted the beam in a two-foot-wide circle. With her other hand, she attached a heavy duty suction cup to the inside of the circle. Once the beam had gone all the way around, she flicked off the light, removed the large circle of glass, and gently dropped it to the ground. Then she set in on the second window, which was already scored by light that had gotten through the first pane. Half-way through cutting the second pane, she saw that the laser was leaving a brown circle on the opposite wall, and if she continued cutting, the beam would slice Saleb. She waved him to the side. He was confused until he saw the line on the wall, then got out of the way. Once she finished the second cut and removed the glass circle, Saleb's escape hatch was complete. Saleb moved to climb through, but she held up a hand to block him and waited a few seconds. After a while, she gently tapped the edge of the glass to see how hot it was, and then waved him through. It was awkward for him to climb through a hole that far off the floor, but he managed to pass through using the armchair as a step. For the first time in months, Saleb was outside.

Jessica held a finger to her lips. Amnesia erases personal memories, but not basics of communication. Even Saleb would understand she wanted him to be quiet.

Jessica held his hand and walked him along the wall toward the back corner of the house. She stopped there. She leaned in and whispered into Saleb's ear.

"We have to sprint. Hard and fast and don't stop until I do."

He nodded.

They both took a few deep breaths, and then she started to run.

They were fifty feet out before the male guard saw them on his screen and hit the panic button.

A quarter-mile away, at the spot where her telescope still lay on the ground, Jessica pointed to the blanket on the ground. She picked up her backpack and stuffed the telescope into it before swinging it onto her shoulders. Meanwhile, Saleb had pulled back the blanket to discover the pair of bicycles. Swift looked over her shoulder—there were flashlights outside the house. The Marshals were coming.

"Don't stop. Don't look back. Just follow me as fast as you can."

The guards would eventually find the tire tracks, but it would be too late to follow them. Five miles away, Jessica's rented Jeep was waiting.

#

In a small apartment that Swift had rented in Tucson, Swift handed Saleb a bottle of water before sitting down at the table. The furnishing was thrift-store: A table, two chairs, and two sleeping bags. But it wasn't a hotel because Swift was worried the authorities would be watching every hotel in the state.

"Who are you?" asked Saleb.

"My name's Jessica Swift. We're in the same line of work."

"Are we friends?"

"We've never met. Don't worry. You're not forgetting me."

"Then why would you come for me?"

"Because last week I was sent on a mission to destroy some files. Specifically your file. This file." She pushed the stack of pages across the table. "You were ordered to go to Lyon the night your partner was killed. They wanted you apart so you'd both be easier to kill."

Saleb stared at the documents, confused. "Who ordered . . . ?"

"I don't know. Someone above you. Above us. Probably the same person who ordered me to destroy the evidence. But someone in the CIB wanted her dead. They might have wanted you dead too, or maybe this frame was planned. But the point is: you did not murder Jessica Jordan."

"What's it to you?"

Swift sighed. "Let's just say I don't like having my strings pulled, either. If I did my job and burned this file, you would have been executed for murder and treason. I just can't be a part of that. I have a conscience, even if nobody else does."

"So what now?" Saleb was still so overwhelmed, he couldn't think.

"Now," she said, "you disappear. Go off and build a new life. Escape from this. And someday I'm going to find the assholes pulling our strings and I'm gonna get myself free, too."

"You just want me to walk away? You tell me that someone else killed Jessica, and framed me for it, and you expect me to just let it go?"

"Why not? You have amnesia, right? You probably don't even remember your Jessica. So why bother looking for revenge?" She reached across the table to put her small hand on Saleb's larger one. "I don't want all this effort I put into setting you free to go to waste. Just get out of here, Khalid. Live a happier life than me."

"I can't."

"Why not?"

"You don't know? About Jessica?"

"What about her?"

"Jessica Jordan wasn't just my partner. She was my wife."

Swift's shoulders dropped as her eyebrows spiked upwards. "She was your wife?"

"They've been telling me I killed her, but . . . "

"But you didn't."

"I know this is crazy. I don't remember her at all. But something always felt wrong about their version of events. Like a gut feeling I couldn't express. Like I could never . . . like I'm not even capable of . . . "

"Killing someone."

"Killing *her*. They tell me I killed other people and I believe them. But not my own wife. How could I possibly do that? It always felt wrong. I might not remember who I was, but I know myself, you know?"

"You were right."

"Someone did this to her, to us, and they got away with it. If I really loved this woman, if we were happy ..." Saleb was struggling to say whatever he was feeling. Swift couldn't imagine what the man was going through. It must be like having your entire love life on the tip of your tongue; like searching for loved ones in the dark and never finding them. "I owe her. I know that's stupid, and she's like a stranger to me now, but I can't walk away. I have to find out who did this."

Swift rubbed her face, momentarily hiding behind her hands. "My life is very . . . supervised. I'm kept on a leash. They won't let me disappear. If you hang around, they'll know I'm with you and then we're both on death row."

Saleb nodded. "I'm not asking you to—"

"I'm in," said Swift. "Your wife deserves justice. Let's bring the bastards down."

14

If it could be possible for one trait to tell you everything you need to know about a person, then Chris Quarrel knew Mr. Smith the moment he heard his voice. It was somehow simultaneously flat and cruel, emotionless yet spiteful, and always impatient. His voice was deep but not hoarse—he was certainly not a smoker—but had an unsettling hateful quality that immediately told Quarrel that there was not going to be any small talk.

Quarrel and his latest suspect, the mononymous Smith, met in the back of a taxicab in front of a reasonably priced New York City hotel. Smith was already in the cab when it pulled up for Quarrel. Milton had told Quarrel on the phone that they would meet at nine a.m., and Smith showed up exactly on time—9:00:15 on Quarrel's watch; not bad for the morning rush in Manhattan.

"Good morning," said Smith, in that deep, cold voice. He turned his head only briefly to look Quarrel in the eyes as he spoke, then turned forward again to speak to the driver.

"The second destination now."

The car pulled back into traffic, which was exceedingly slow. Quarrel was there under the guise that he was a new transfer to the CIB, and Smith had to act as his handler until someone else was named as a permanent handler. Quarrel decided it would be quite a challenge to get Smith talking and opted to try a barrage of questions to see if Smith would surprise him and have a conversation.

"Nice morning, isn't it?"

Smith turned his head a bit and gave a single nod.

"I've been to New York before, but I always took the subway. I figured the traffic would be miserable."

Smith said nothing. After an awkward pause, the driver chimed in. He was a grey-haired Indian man in his forties.

"Oh people always think that, but you know what? I get no complaints. So where are you from, mister?"

"I'm from an office in Toronto. They sent me down to meet with my American friend here to close a big deal this morning."

Considering that both Quarrel and Smith were dressed in navy blue tailored suits, the businessman story seemed appropriate. Smith seemed to tense at Quarrel's small talk, preferring to ride in total silence. Quarrel asked him a few times if he had been to this tourist trap or that landmark or if he had a favourite restaurant in the area—small talk that wouldn't seem suspicious to the cabbie—but Smith just ignored him, occasionally nodding. After about ten minutes, Smith pulled out a few twenty-dollar notes and held them up to the window behind the driver.

"Here is good," he said.

The driver took the money and Smith looked at Quarrel with eyes that said, "Get out." He did just that, and Smith followed him out the same door, waving a hand to the driver to tell him to keep the change.

Quarrel was vaguely disappointed by having to get out of the cab. He had actually never been to this city before, and he had hoped they would continue north far enough to cross into the Bronx so he could see Yankee Stadium. Instead they were in Manhattan somewhere east

117

of Central Park, but Quarrel didn't know the city, so he hardly knew where they were.

As the yellow cab blended back into the background, the impeccably dressed men, each with a leather briefcase, strolled down the busy sidewalk. It was just a bit chilly, the sun still low enough that the canyon of buildings blocked out the warming light. Still, the sky above was clear and the weather reports said it would be the first truly warm day of the year. Quarrel was glad for the changing seasons; Smith just marched forward, oblivious to his surroundings.

They walked for a long enough time that Quarrel started to wonder why they hadn't just stuck with the cab. Perhaps Smith was bothered by Quarrel making small talk with the cabbie. Or maybe he just didn't want anyone else to know their destination. After walking fifteen minutes at a comfortable pace, Smith pivoted to a set of glass doors without so much as nodding to Quarrel to say they'd arrived.

It was a coffee shop. A busy little independent operation on the ground floor of a low-rise office building. Quarrel tried to think like a spy—*where are the exits? Are any of these people dangerous?*—but mostly he followed Smith, who went to an empty table against the far left wall and sat down.

"Shouldn't we order something?"

Smith reached into his pocket and pulled out a five-dollar bill. "I'll have water in a sealed bottle."

Quarrel joined the line, trying not to stare at Smith, the emotionless robot in the black suit, who was sitting by himself and watching the door. Smith had black hair in a crew cut, short enough that it stood up in little spikes without any hair product. He probably buzzed his own head on a regular basis, possibly daily. Quarrel couldn't imagine Smith sitting down with a gabby hairdresser, but Smith standing in front of a bathroom mirror and methodically running a trimmer over his head? Yeah, Quarrel could picture Smith doing that.

Quarrel returned to the small table with two coffees in to-go cups and a bottle of water. "I figured I should buy one for whoever's going to join us," he said. Smith nodded, his gaze still on the door.

Smith drank half the water bottle in one long chug, then capped it and set it aside.

"So who are we meeting?" asked Quarrel.

"Intelligence asset."

"Oh. How long have you been working him? Her? Them."

"First meeting in person was one year ago. Sporadic communications since then. I don't meet people in person very often."

Quarrel nodded. He was surprised that Smith met with *anyone*. Still, gathering and pushing assets was a big part of the spy game, probably the biggest part in terms of pure information gathering. New York had a lot of embassies, corporate offices, and international visitors. This was a city where literally anyone could walk in the door. With Smith being so quiet, all Quarrel could do was sit quietly and stew on the possibilities.

Quarrel didn't like Smith. Out of all the possible suspects on the list, Smith was the most likely in Quarrel's mind. He had no personality and no history, and that was suspicious. In Quarrel's few years of training for a life in the service, he had encountered a wide range of people, but between them all there were only a handful of reasons to get into the game. Some did it for

119

patriotism, like Jack Hall. Others for thrills, or because their previous career in law enforcement or the military had prepared them for this line of work. But mostly, people became spies because it was a little exciting and because a government paycheck is always nice. None of those reasons seemed to fit Smith. Quarrel had studied the one-page file on Smith only once, which was enough to have it memorized. Codename: Smith. No real name given. No place of birth. No psych exams beyond the vague phrase "as expected". Not even a physical. The guy was just a codename and a passport photo, in which Smith looked and dressed exactly as he was now. The man might very well have been some sort of robot, or clone, or alien in disguise, but this wasn't a fantasy world of genetically engineered spies. It was the real world, where offices are blown up by fertilizer bombs and where even an enigma like Smith was still just a man with the right kind of training. Quarrel made up his mind to think of Smith's stoic lack of personality as a facade, something he did to try and cover up his real motives. Smith could damn well be the man who blew up the Ottawa office, or murdered Matthew Crowe, and if acting like a Spartan asshole was his form of cover, Quarrel wasn't going to buy it.

The idea of sipping a cuppa joe across from a man who might very well have blown up the CSIS-2 office in Ottawa made Quarrel's stomach turn. He thought of Carol, dead at her desk after surviving decades of field work, and of poor Erica, who hadn't even earned a clearance level before the job killed her. Even Hershey, smug bastard that he had been, was at his core a patriot and a hard worker, and his reward had been to die before he turned thirty. Quarrel didn't even know if any of his coworkers' bodies had been found in the remains of the building, but it had been two weeks since the bombing and they would have had funerals already. Quarrel was sure that if they did find bodies, they'd never find Hershey's. Hershey had been standing out front, having a smoke when the bomb went off in the parking lot in front of him, only feet away. He would have been vaporized.

Quarrel hadn't bothered to look up the memorial services. He had never planned on attending any of the funerals. He was too busy trying to catch the asshole that caused them. And the more Smith acted like an angry jerk, the more Quarrel hoped for a reason to vent some of his simmering rage in Smith's direction.

Quarrel was spinning these dark thoughts through his mind when Smith stood up. The younger agent also stood, and turned, somewhat flustered, toward the doorway. The woman coming toward them was young, about twenty-five, and was dressed in casual business clothes with a messenger bag over one shoulder.

"Hello again," she said, shaking Smith's hand.

"Hello again and again," said Smith. It must have been some kind of practiced greeting they had worked out to say the coast is clear, because Quarrel didn't expect Smith would try to be cutesy.

"And you are?" she asked.

Quarrel looked toward Smith for some guidance on how to proceed but got nothing from Smith's poker face.

"Chris. I'm a new transfer." They shook hands.

"Maggie Reville."

They sat back down, Smith on one side of the table, Chris and Maggie on the other. For a moment, they didn't speak.

"Don't get offended or anything," she said to Quarrel, "but can I see some ID?"

Quarrel nodded and fished into his inside pocket. He had been given a couple of government-issue IDs, since the existence of CIB was still a secret. He pulled out a CIA badge and passed it to Maggie. She studied it carefully for about five seconds before handing it back.

"OK. Just being careful." She was shy, uncomfortable. Her shoulders slumped and her voice was very quiet. She sheepishly looked to Smith. "Careful like you taught me."

Smith actually smiled for her, even if it was blatantly fake, more of a condescending pat on the head than a sign of real emotion. "So let's get down to it: why did you want to get together?"

Maggie was visibly uncomfortable, but Quarrel didn't know his role here. He wanted to put his hand on her shoulder and tell her to relax, instead he leaned on the wall and said nothing. She pulled the messenger bag into her lap and opened it, to pull out a thin manila folder.

"I used that program you sent me to get into the secure servers. I did it from a floor I almost never go to so it would be harder to trace. I found these."

She opened the folder to show several pages of blueprints, obviously printed by an office laser printer. They were almost too small to make out. "I have them on the thumb drive, too."

"What are we looking at?" asked Quarrel.

"The files only had numbers for names, but I looked at the electrical info and this thing needs more juice than most small towns. It's some kind of a high-energy science-y thing. But I thought it was weird enough to make a note of."

"You could have sent this without meeting in person," said Smith.

"I know—" Maggie was obviously very torn about all of this. After all, she was spying on someone—probably a corporation she worked for—and all so she could report to this emotionless jerk. Quarrel leaned in and put a hand on her knee.

"It's alright. Drink your coffee. If you wanted to talk in person, we're here for you. Your comfort is our job."

She took a sip and rolled her shoulders. Quarrel took his hand off her leg, thinking it might be inappropriate to leave it there.

"There are two other things. First . . . " she pointed to the corner of one page. " . . . these aren't Globection designs. They're scans of something that has a stamp on it . . . "

The name Globection jumped out immediately. Guess that's where she works. Guess that's who she spies on.

Quarrel read the image. "CIA? Globection has access to CIA schematics?"

"Exactly," she said. "We don't have any CIA contracts. This shouldn't exist on our servers. Someone's using Globection to host stolen information."

"You find any more like these?"

"No schematics like that, but," she was talking to Chris now, Smith just observing, "I did find something else that jumped out at me."

She pulled the last page from the file. It was a list. At the top was *'lastname_firstname:password'* under this was a list of over twenty names and passwords, organized alphabetically.

"I looked up the names. They don't work for GX. So I started googling them. Recognize anyone?"

Quarrel scanned the list but came up blank. He kept his own poker face this time, trying to look like he belongs on this case, then passed the list to Smith, hoping he'd see something Quarrel missed.

Smith gave his usual barely-perceptible nod. "Helen Prince, Daniel Chang . . . these people work for the CIA."

"Exactly. I tried a few. They work. Anyone with this list can get into your system. I mean, there are firewalls around the important stuff, but they have access. To the secure site." She leaned in and whispered. "Someone who works for GX is stealing information from the CIA. This is hard proof. You can bust them now. My job's done."

Smith nodded and put the pages back into the folder. "I'll need the thumb drive." She nodded and passed him a small USB stick.

"So what now?" she asked, turning her head to look at both of them.

"You go back to work. Live a normal life until the arrests come down, then quit the company. But for now, don't do anything to get noticed." Smith spoke in a voice that sounded less spiteful, a sort of practiced kindness that sounded entirely phoney. He was trying to reassure her, but his total lack of empathy made it hollow. "You've done a great job. Keep your head down and you'll be fine."

"So I just go back to work this afternoon?"

"Exactly."

She closed her bag and sipped her coffee. After a pause, she turned to Quarrel. "Are you going to be around for a while? Should I have your contact information?"

Smith interrupted. "Chris is just learning the ropes. I'm the agent in charge of your file."

"Oh."

"I'm going to use the restroom. Be right back." She stood up and walked off without hesitating, taking her bag with her.

She didn't come back. After ten minutes, Smith chugged the other half of his water, crushed the plastic in his fist, and tossed it onto the table. He cracked his knuckles. "I'm going to look for her. Stay here."

Quarrel waited while Smith investigated first the women's room, then the men's, then checked for a back exit. He came back after about a minute.

"There's a back door that leads into the building. She's gone." Smith took out a cell phone and dialed. He waited through several rings and hung up. He picked up his briefcase, packed away the manila folder and the thumb drive, and started to leave. He turned to Quarrel almost as an afterthought.

"This is not how it usually goes. She got spooked. I'll find her. It's what I do. I'll be in touch." With that, Mr. Smith slipped out the front doors and into the Manhattan morning, leaving Quarrel to find his way back to his hotel, or wherever he wanted to go.

Analyzing what had happened, he decided he still didn't like Smith, and still thought of him as a prime suspect.

Quarrel grabbed an abandoned newspaper from another table and read the local sports while finishing his coffee. One good thing about NYC: they have hockey coverage. Years in Ottawa had converted him to a Senators fan since there wasn't any other sports team in the area. The Sens were playing the Islanders that night. *God*, realized Quarrel, *I haven't even read this stuff since the bombing*. It took about ten minutes for the coffee to go down, at which point Quarrel realized that just about everything in the paper seemed so trivial compared to his mission. He decided to hail a cab and go back to his hotel to contact Milton and wait for Smith.

On the street, he flagged down a yellow cab and was one leg into the back seat when a woman called out.

"I'll split that with you."

Maggie Reville climbed into the cab beside Chris.

"What are you—"

"I'm going where you're going."

Quarrel gave the name of the hotel to the cabbie, and they rode in silence.

Back in Quarrel's second-floor hotel room, she finally opened up.

"You're new in town, right?"

"Just transferred in."

"To the CIA?"

Quarrel shrugged.

She was really working up some anger now, talking loud and fast. "And why exactly would the CIA transfer an agent to the FBI?"

Shit. Smith had been pretending he worked for the FBI, Quarrel had shown her the wrong ID, and now she was suspicious of the whole operation. Why couldn't Smith have been more talkative and filled in little details like what agency he was using as cover when dealing with the asset?

"I'm not at liberty to say."

"How long have you known him? Smith?"

"We met this morning." Quarrel was starting to realize where this was going.

"You trust him?"

"Do you?"

Maggie sighed. "I want witness protection. When I broke into the servers, the hacking program worked, but they detected the intrusion. GX knows I was poking around in their servers, and I cannot go back there."

"Why not tell Smith?"

"Because I just can't trust that guy. It's hard to pinpoint, but I get this vibe off him. It's like he hates me or something."

"I know what you mean, but—"

"The last two times I told him where I was getting information, the sources dried up. One was an old records room nobody really organized. I found a lot of questionable billing practices, thought they were ripping off the government. That was what got me started when I went to the FBI. But once I told Smith where the information was coming from, they removed all the files. The next source I found was a secretary who told me that the company was getting payments from some Swiss account, but without ever sending bills to anyone that would explain what the money was for. Once I told

Smith, the secretary was fired and I couldn't find any record of the payments. You see what I mean?"

"So you think Smith is trying to protect someone at GX who's stealing secrets. But why would Smith recruit you if he worked for GX?"

"He didn't. I spent the first month reporting to some guys at the Federal Building, and then Smith transferred in and took over my file. He never let me contact anyone else, until you showed up today. I thought maybe you were there to investigate him or something."

Quarrel fought back a smile. *Clever woman.*

"So you want me to get you to safety, and without Smith or the FBI knowing about it."

Maggie smiled. It was the first time Quarrel had seen her smile. Her sour, unhappy face suddenly became quite lovely. Her curly blonde hair bounced as she nodded.

"And I'd like it if you guys would get my stuff from my apartment. I haven't been back there since last night when I got caught with my hand in the cookie jar." She opened her messenger bag and pulled another file folder and another thumb drive. "I made backups of everything since I knew Smith would just bury it."

Quarrel waved his hand toward the drab hotel room. "Make yourself comfortable. I have to make a call."

Quarrel almost dialed Milton's number, but at the last second he changed his mind and decided that he'd rather throw a bone to Hinkston at the CIA. It might help if Hinkston owed him a favour. Quarrel dialed the number on Mr. Hinkston's business card. A female secretary answered. It took a while to get the agent on the phone. Once Quarrel could actually speak to the guy, it was pretty simple to arrange a pick-up for his first witness. Hinkston only had one condition.

"I want every last shred of information that woman has. If she's got stolen CIA material, you're turning it all over to me. Your investigation does not grant you access to CIA plans." Hinkston, as before, sounded bitter and angry. Quarrel agreed to hand over Maggie's files.

Quarrel wanted to know what those strange blueprints represented, but he knew he didn't have long to review them. He couldn't make copies since he knew Maggie would tell the CIA everything, and if he took her USB drive and made copies from it, they'd know. The last thing Quarrel needed was the CIA hunting him down in the middle of the investigation. After hanging up the phone and telling Maggie about the plan, he spent some time trying to decipher the strange, complex blueprints. He couldn't make sense of any of them. It wasn't really a building, although it seemed to be huge. It wasn't a schematic for a machine, although power lines ran everywhere. Whatever it was on these CIA plans, Quarrel couldn't piece it together.

Half an hour later, Maggie, the papers, and the USB drive were bundled into a van. She thanked him for his help, shook his hand, and disappeared into Manhattan traffic along with every piece of real evidence Quarrel had.

15

William Thorpe lay in a king-sized bed smoking a cigarette. Other than the silk sheets, he was nude. His clothes were scattered around the room, leaving a trail that outlined the passions between Thorpe and this night's conquest. The girl's black lingerie also littered the room. It was a sprawling, modernist penthouse at the top of an expensive hotel, lots of cold concrete and minimal furniture. The sound of the girl's shower echoed through the large bedroom from the half-open bathroom door. Between drags on his cigarette and sips of his champagne, Thorpe looked to the doorway. Wisps of steam that flowed out and faded into the bedroom's musky air.

The girl was the personal assistant to the head of the multinational corporation, Globection Corp. That man was Hugo Zoeli, the famous self-made man. Zoeli had started a small independent cellular phone business in the late 1980s, and now he was a worldwide communications leader and defence contractor.

Globection was everywhere. Twenty years ago they were a private infrastructure firm, setting up high-end communications in America and Europe, and water systems in South America. From launching their own satellites, they had gotten into aerospace development, which led naturally into weapons contracts with the United States and NATO allies. Soon, Globection was providing soldiers of fortune—"*private contractors*"—for Iraq and Afghanistan, as well providing as the internet, phone, and water services vital to the war effort. A soldier going to war in Iraq in 2005 would have flown there on a GX plane, ate GX food, drank GX water, and phoned home on a GX internet connection. And when his time in the army was over, that soldier would be offered a contractor job as a GX security envoy, doing the same job for triple the pay. There were many who felt that if GX were to cease to exist, so would the United States military.

Thorpe knew he had to figure out who was selling GX's information to Martin Mercier, but to do that he needed to know who had the access codes to the top-secret intelligence. And to know that, he needed an in. Seducing Zoeli's assistant was a good start.

She was very resourceful and had an intelligence that bothered him. He always felt like she was thinking three moves ahead whenever he spoke to her. But like so many young women in proximity to powerful men, she was gorgeous, and Thorpe was a man who appreciated gorgeous. Now that he had bedded her, it would be easier to gain her trust, and eventually to turn her to his side. It was an ugly truth of the spy game that you needed to turn an innocent into an ally. Thorpe was used to turning women into honeypots when needed, but he did feel a faint twinge of regret at knowing that she could suffer for his actions if Mercier suspected she was helping him. Women had been hurt and killed because of Thorpe's charm. More women than he liked to admit, but if this mission brought him the man who put a bullet in Julia's brain, that would help Thorpe sleep at night.

His cell phone rang. Answering it, Thorpe saw the face of the Ringmaster. They spoke over video chat, and Thorpe didn't care that he was talking to his boss while he was obviously naked in bed.

"Good evening, Triple Eight."

"Evening, sir."

"Hard at work as usual."

"Aren't I always?"

"Are we alone?"

"For the moment."

"Two things, Thorpe. The first is that Harry Milton wants to know your location. He won't tell us why, so we've held back the information. But you can call if you feel like it, since I know you and Harry go back quite a bit. The second thing is the woman you asked us to check into. We've run her name and her photo and it seems she's not who she claims. You've listed her as Diana Torrens, assistant to Hugo Zoeli of Globection. But she's not. Diana is almost fifty and at least a hundred pounds heavier than the girl you've met. She's playing you, Thorpe."

"Good to know, sir. I'll be in touch."

He hung up. The girl was still in the shower. Now things were interesting. If the girl wasn't with Zoeli, then why had Thorpe spotted her inside his office? Thorpe pondered whether it was possible he had shagged the very mole he was hunting without realizing it, and silently cursed himself for thinking with his libido instead of checking the girl out first.

Thorpe climbed out of bed and started to pull on some clothes, pulling pants over the bruises that lingered from being tied up in Nice. He seemed to take longer to heal now that he was older, but thought his body was still in fine shape otherwise. Once he had his pants on, he reached under the pillow and pulled out his Glock 19, and waited for the shower to shut off and let him know that the girl was coming back.

She had been in there for almost twenty minutes. Thorpe listened to the sound of the water. It was steady and constant. He realized that the sound was so uniform, there was no way a person was moving underneath the stream of water. Either she was standing dead-still under the water, or she wasn't in the shower at all.

Thorpe gently pushed the door open with his foot and entered the steamy bathroom gun-first. The fog was so thick he could barely see, and the heat hit him like he had opened an oven. Reaching the shower, he grabbed the curtain with his left hand, his right holding the gun. He jerked the curtain hard, intending to surprise the girl, but there was no one there. The tub was empty. The girl was gone.

Thorpe was struck by two questions: how had she gotten out, and what good was it to sleep with him and leave? If she had tried to kill him, that would at least make sense. Instead, she had simply vanished.

He studied the bathroom. There were no windows, but there was a large vent at the bottom of one wall. A sufficiently lithe young woman might have been able to fit in there. He pulled the plastic grate off easily—it was not screwed in place. Looking inside, the vent ran straight vertical. She could have gone up or down, no way to tell, but this was definitely her escape route. One question answered.

In the bedroom, Thorpe picked up her champagne glass and sprinkled it with fingerprint powder from his bag.

Once several prints were visible, he took a high-res scan of the prints and emailed them. Then he made another video call, this time to Ms. Cashmere, who handled a lot of different jobs for MI-7's ten 'Triple' agents.

"Kathy, I'm sending you prints. Top priority."

133

"OK. I've got them. Hold on a second." She waited for her computer to run the prints. "Oh, are you shirtless? Do pan down and let me have a peek."

"Oh, Kathy. You haven't the proper security clearance to view all of my secrets."

She grinned at him before her eyes flicked away, back to the computer. "No positive ident. But those prints have been suspected to belong to a cat burglar and assassin who goes by the name Fatale. Also known as Rochelle Noir, Sasha Black, and Inga Palme. Why, William, were you spending the night alone with Miss Palme?"

"That'll do, Kathy. Tell the Ringmaster that the woman in the photos is Fatale. We can at least put a face to her now. Talk to you in the morning."

Thorpe finished getting dressed, and tucked the gun into a holster under his left armpit. Beneath his tailored suit jacket, the gun was invisible. He left the bedroom and passed into the penthouse's Spartan living room. He hated minimalist living spaces, preferring European glitz and comfort over modernist urban-style spaces like this. When the girl had brought him here three hours prior, he was shocked at how empty and cold it felt.

Now he was shocked by another sight. Between the blocky, angular armchair and the equally blocky couch, a wide pool of red had spread across the polished concrete floor. There was a corpse lying face-down in the blood, a young man with a knife jutting from his blood-soaked back. The man was dressed in suit pants and a dress shirt, and looked to have been stabbed several times. There was no doubt that he was dead.

Thorpe was impressed by how fresh it all looked. Either Fatale had only just killed the man minutes before, or someone had staged it all while Fatale kept him occupied in the bedroom. It had been just over twenty minutes since Thorpe had seen the girl, and in that time she had vanished from the bathroom and, maybe, planted the body as well. She wasn't just skilled, she was borderline supernatural. Thorpe knew he had been set up as soon he saw the body. The pounding on the door only confirmed it.

"NYPD! Open the door!" shouted a man outside the door. Thorpe didn't answer. Instead, he grabbed his briefcase, went straight to the spacious balcony and started looking for an escape route. The walls were too flat to climb either up or down. As this was the penthouse, there was no neighbouring apartment he could jump to. He was stuck.

The police officer banged on the door, and Thorpe was sure they would break the door down within seconds. Desperate, he lifted his right foot and opened a compartment in the heel of his leather shoe. He pulled a thin string from inside the opening and set the foot back down, his feet together. He looped the string through a tiny, near imperceptible hook on the heel of his other shoe, then tied the end of the line to the railing.

As the door burst inward, the first police officers into the apartment saw the body, but didn't notice the fifty-year-old Englishman out on the balcony. In those brief seconds, Thorpe climbed onto the railing, extended his arms forward, and jumped. Thorpe fell freely for about twenty stories before the line started to tighten and his descent slowed. As the line stretched and Thorpe felt his champagne-filled stomach shift in his body, it occurred to him that he had never actually used this line before, even if it was rated to three hundred pounds. The best-case scenario was that the line and the knots held, and Thorpe was pulled quickly upward, where he would smash against a wall or a window. The worst-case scenario was a face-first trip to the sidewalk.

Looking to prevent both of those results from happening, he fired a small line from his watch, which dug into the floor of a balcony on the seventeenth floor. He pulled the line tight, just as he felt the bungee line try to jerk his ankles back up toward the penthouse. For a moment he dangled there, seventeen-and-a-half floors above the street, upside-down and hanging by his heels and one wrist. He tossed the briefcase onto the balcony, then he swung his legs around, angling his body toward the balcony below, and with a click of his toes, the line in his shoe released. It whipped away, springing back up toward the penthouse, and he expertly flipped feet-first to the balcony.

Detaching the line from his watch, Thorpe made a mental note to refill both of his escape lines. There was no way to pick the lock on the sliding glass balcony doors, so Thorpe was forced to swing his metal case through the glass. The sound of the shattering glass woke the couple who were staying there, and the husband jumped from the bed, flicking on his lamp, but before he could see anything the door to the hallway was closing and Thorpe was gone.

An hour later, in a 24-hour diner that served him tea and toast, Thorpe called CIB. Harry Milton, the man who seemed to never sleep, answered. Milton did not take video calls, so this was an ordinary phone call.

"Milton. Triple Eight. Please tell me that you were looking for me to warn me about the female operative who was slinking her way through New York."

"Not at all. What happened?"

"She disappeared out a room that only had one door, which I was watching, left me a fresh corpse and called the police."

"Tonight? How long ago?" Milton sounded more interested than usual.

"Just an hour ago. Why?"

"We had something similar happen. Some young woman hit one of our safe houses. Broke a fugitive right out from under us last night. She was only on the camera for a few seconds."

"Doubt this was the same girl. Mine's been in the GX office all day. What did you want to talk to me about, Milton?"

Harry paused. "Nevermind that now. You find your girl, I'll find mine."

16

Quarrel's next assignment was easy to find. It turned out that William Thorpe, the legendary British secret agent, was also in the USA, and also interested in Globection Corp. It was a no-brainer for Quarrel to spy on him next, using the excuse that the information he had heard from Maggie meant they were both after the same thing.

Thorpe was not what Quarrel had expected. Based on the file, Quarrel thought Thorpe would be the prototypical super-spy; all lean muscle, charm, and good looks. Instead, the Briton was carrying a bit of a spare tire under his rumpled dress shirt, his face was getting saggy, suggesting that if he worked out less he'd have jowls, and while he still had a thick head of hair it was mostly grey.

And the man drank like a fish.

Thorpe was staying in a hastily rented room in a high-rise tower across the street from GX's New York office. This was technically office space, but it was totally empty of furniture except for a box of fluorescent light bulb tubes and a stack of drywall. Thorpe was making due with a box of high-end surveillance equipment, a cot, and a folding table that served as a well-stocked bar. An open suitcase of clothes lay against the back wall.

When he opened the door for Quarrel, Thorpe wasn't angry at having to put up with a CIB sidekick the way the others had been, nor did he question Quarrel's true intentions. Instead, he offered a handshake and an introduction, pointed Quarrel to the bar, and went back to the telescope he used to study the GX building.

"Got any beer?"

"No refrigerator, no beer . . . but that ice bucket's full. Try the Irish whiskey."

"Did Milton tell you why I wanted to come in on this?"

"You think Globection is stealing secrets; I'm after a guy whose fingerprints are on secrets stolen from Globection . . . " The Brit looked over his shoulder at Chris, raised his martini, and smiled. "Good enough for me."

Quarrel poured himself two fingers of the Irish and added a single ice cube from the bucket. "To catching the bad guys," he toasted.

"God, you're young," scoffed Thorpe. Then he gulped down the remaining half of his martini. "But I'll drink to any toast." For a second there was silence between them, before Thorpe licked his lips and said, "I need a fresh martini."

Quarrel picked up one of the two cocktail shakers—the gold one—and offered to mix the martini. Thorpe quickly stopped him. "Not that shaker, my boy. I've been using the silver one all day and clearly this place doesn't have a dishwasher." As Quarrel handed over the gold shaker, Thorpe nodded to the telescope, binoculars, and cameras set up by the window.

"Take a look. See if you have better luck catching the bad guys than I do."

Quarrel was in no rush to peep in GX's windows, since ultimately his job was not to catch GX but to figure out whether or not Thorpe was the source of the leak. But Thorpe reeked of cigarettes so Quarrel moved toward the window just to get a few feet of space between himself and the smell of nicotine. He picked up the binoculars and took another sip of the whiskey.

139

Sense memory took him back to the last time he'd had a drink of straight whiskey. It had been almost six months earlier, at the Christmas party in his Ottawa office. It was a strange, awkward kind of a party, where the fun was half-hearted because many of the attendees were still clocked in, and everyone was a government employee. Still, there had been a case of beer in the fridge and a makeshift bar on the side counter (a bar that was actually smaller than the one Thorpe had set up for himself in this empty office space). It had been the first, and now only, party that Quarrel ever attended with his co-workers. He was new, but not as new as Erica, who had been around only a few weeks before the party.

Sexual relationships in the office were explicitly forbidden. Not only was it a bad idea in a workplace, but among top-secret agents, "sexpionage" was a constant threat. Even outsider relationships required a security check, and relationships with people from the inside always came with serious risk. While there had been some smiles and flirtations between Chris and Erica, nothing ever came out of it, due to both parties following their agreement to not have a relationship with a fellow agent.

But there had been that shot of whiskey.

Everyone at the Christmas party was having a drink, but nursing it slowly. Nobody wanted to look unprofessional, so it was a strange vibe as everyone made idle chit-chat about their families or about shows they followed in the few hours they got to watch TV. Chris recalled how it had been Erica who pulled him away from a conversation with Scott from archives and into the kitchen. She smiled at him, a naughty we're-gonna-be-bad grin that he could still see when he closed his eyes. For a second he thought she was going to push him against the wall and make out with him, but it wasn't nearly so risqué. She had just wanted someone to do a shot with.

"This job is my dream and all, but this party sucks," she had said. "And I'm the one they made go to the store to buy all this liquor that nobody's drinking."

Before Quarrel could object, she was pouring two shots of Jameson's. "I figure we're the new kids around here, so why not toast each other?" She handed him his shot glass.

"Have a merry Christmas," said Chris.

"And a happy new year," said Erica.

They drank.

A happy new year. She was dead by April.

They had put down the shot glasses, still facing each other, still standing close. The whiskey had given both of their faces a flush, and wincing from the whiskey had brought back a hint of Erica's beautifully wicked smile. There had been a moment . . . (had there?) . . . a moment where Chris felt a strong desire for her. A moment where his rank was his job and her position as his subordinate fell away and he wanted to grab her, to kiss her, and to sneak away from the office together. And the longer that moment went on, the more urgently he had felt the need to act on it, until they were interrupted.

Peter Hershey walked into the kitchen, looking for a paper towel to clean up something he had spilled in the other room. He spotted the whiskey, but didn't seem to notice Quarrel discretely taking a step away from Erica.

"Hey, at least someone's acting like this is a party!" It was a bit forced, coming from a smarmy, insincere climber like Hershey, but then he picked up a clean shot glass, refilled the other two glasses, and offered the shots to Quarrel and Erica without much of a question about

141

whether they wanted more. They drank the whiskey, grabbed a roll of paper towels for Hershey, and the three of them returned to the party. Somehow, Hershey had passed the paper towels back to Quarrel and he ended up wiping up Hershey's mess while Hershey and Erica blended into the party together.

The moment had passed. That was the only time Quarrel had come close to ignoring his common sense and hooking up with his beautiful co-worker. After that, it was a nice, slightly flirty working relationship. He had never once met Erica outside of office hours other than for the occasional field-training session. Of course Hershey and Erica had ended up breaking the no-sex rules together on at least one of those field-training missions, and looking back on it Quarrel was glad for them, finding something in each other before they died.

Quarrel set his glass of whiskey on the small table in front of the window and used the binoculars to study the front entrance to Globection headquarters. It was six at night, and people were filtering out of the building, one or two at a time.

"So what are you hoping to see—someone in a window, someone going in the front door . . . ?" he asked Thorpe.

"Either works. I'm after a girl."

"The one who, um, left you . . . "

"—naked with a dead body in that hotel, yes. That's the one. She's working with someone else. Someone worse. An old assassin from the Cold War days who I would very much like to speak with."

"So who is she?"

"Rochelle Noir, also known as Fatale. She`s a very expensive free agent. She was in the CEO's office poking around. I staged a meeting with her, and she told me she was his assistant, which lined up with what I had seen. So I took her to bed, thought everything was going smoothly, however . . . " Thorpe paused, pouring his martini into the glass, an unlit cigarette dangling from his lip.

Quarrel finished the sentence: " . . . She wasn't his assistant."

Thorpe nodded. "This was obviously the first time I'd met her, but her reputation is wonderfully twisted. A real black widow. Heard a story a few years back that Fatale escaped from a Turkish prison by seducing the warden. Got interrupted halfway through killing him. As the story goes, she ran three kilometres stark naked before she vanished into the Black Sea."

"And you're hoping she'll just walk in the front door of GX's office? Even after she knows you're poking around"

"If you know how to spot someone without a stakeout, enlighten me."

Quarrel shrugged, took a sip of his drink. "You got a photo?"

"Sure." Thorpe picked up a stack of papers from the seat of the chair, flipped through it, and handed Quarrel a photo of the girl who had framed him. She had dark brown hair, beautiful cheekbones, and big, dark eyes.

"Happy new year," said Quarrel.

"What?"

Quarrel shoved the photo into Thorpe's face. "You sure that's the one? This is the right photo? The girl from the other day?"

"I think I know her quite intim—"

143

"—Erica Gibbons." Quarrel chugged the rest of his drink, the ice cube clinking against the glass. "Her name is Erica Gibbons."

"You've met?"

"Yeah. Used to work together." And then, with a heartbreaking realization dawning on him, Quarrel continued, "She blew up my office."

#

Ten minutes later, Quarrel was on the phone with Milton. The idea that Erica was still alive—that Erica was the one who bombed CSIS-2—was still spinning wildly through his head. Thorpe had offered him another drink, and he'd taken it, but the world was spinning for entirely different reasons than alcohol.

Erica, who had worked in CSIS-2 for almost six months.

Erica, who had been good enough to walk into Jack Hall's training camp without raising Hall's suspicions.

Erica, who had lured the legendary Triple-Eight into a trap within weeks of "dying" in the Ottawa bombing.

Erica, at the office party with a grin on her face.

Erica, expertly defeating Hershey in a paintball game.

Erica, sleeping with a superior the night before the office blew up.

Erica, alive.

But she wasn't Erica Gibbons, traitor. She was Rochelle Noir, assassin.

And then his mind started to realize the immensity of the information. There was more going on than just a double agent in CIB; there was a deliberately placed professional who had made it within the very heart of CSIS-2. Suddenly, this investigation wasn't just about a leak; it was about a long-term, international conspiracy spanning different secret agencies at the very apex of the intelligence world. And with his mind firing off like a fireworks pinwheel, with his stomach burning from hard liquor, Chris Quarrel told Thorpe the real reason he was there. He told Thorpe about the mole, about the small list of suspects. And then Quarrel gave voice to a plan.

And William Thorpe smiled in agreement, and the plan started to form. It was simple, obvious, and wildly unpredictable. It was the tactical equivalent of throwing shit against the wall to see what would stick. But it was a plan.

Happy New Year.

"Sir, I don't think me tailing these guys is going to accomplish much. I have a better idea."

"Do you now?" said Milton with more than a little condescension in his voice.

"Yes, sir. We need to get you, me, and all of your suspects into a room. And we have to tell them that there's a traitor in our midst."

"Are you insane? You want to blow every single cover—"

"What I want is to catch the double. Sir. I can't do it alone. I need the best, and the best just so happen to be the same people on your suspect list."

"Quarrel, this is reckless. They'll tear each other apart. My entire operation—"

Quarrel was getting nervous now, but he needed this gambit to work. He pushed forward, his words coming faster and angrier than he had intended. "Mr. Milton, as a member of CIB with high-level access, you yourself are not above suspicion. And if you interfere with my method of cracking this case then I'll have no choice but to tell my suspicions about you to every single one of the contacts you've set me up with. How would Jack Hall take the news that you might be a terrorist? Or Agent Hinkston? Or Senator Anderson and the defence appropriations committee?"

Milton sighed loud enough for Quarrel to hear. "Kid, you were supposed to be easy to control." Quarrel could practically see Milton slumping back into his leather chair.

Now Quarrel dropped his trump card. "I already booked the meeting. I called the other agents first. You were the last to know. I only called because I need you to bring in Jessica Swift."

Milton let the silence between them linger for almost ten seconds, before he said, "Fine. I can't stop you. But you had better realize what you're doing. You're about to send the six deadliest people in the world out for each other's blood."

Quarrel stared at the Globection logo across the street, feeling more purpose and drive than he had in his entire life. "No, sir. I'm sending them after *mine*."

#

Jessica Swift was nibbling on a scone inside a lobby cafe in an expensive Zurich office building. Sitting alone at a small round table, she appeared to the rest of the world to be a shy woman waiting for her extra-hot coffee to cool.

In reality, she was casing the lobby security system. The Café was only a small section of the ground floor, and this building belonged to the Douxieme Banque Suisse. She still needed to know her way around the upstairs before she could break in, but she wasn't planning on going that far until she was sure she knew the easiest way in and safest way out. She wasn't sure she would find anything here; any records of exactly what had happened to Saleb and Jordan would have been in the file she already stole. But the contents of a box on the second floor of this building would likely point to a suspect, tell her who had shot Saleb and killed Jordan, and that was enough.

Swift and Saleb had come this far by hacking into the internal networks of several Zurich banks. It was relatively easy to hack a bank from outside now that everything ran on wireless networks. She was able to sit in a van parked nearby and run several encryption-breaking algorithms that had worked for her before, bypassing security and allowing her to login, undetected, as the bank manager.

The first bank they hacked was WBS, the same bank she had broken into before her little trip to pick up Saleb in the USA. Using information in the WBS system, she was able to identify the owner of the box she had robbed as Robert Roux. Further work showed that Robert Roux didn't really exist. He had existed long enough to set up an account, open the box, and add an authorized signature for a woman called Helena Roux, and after that Robert was no more.

They had hacked every major bank in Zurich searching for anything else Mr. and Mrs. Roux may have been up to, and that hunch paid off. On the same day that Mr. Roux rented the box from WBS, he also opened a box at Douxieme Banque Suisse, and again he added Mrs. Roux as a signature. At both banks, Mr. Roux paid the box rental up front for ten years. That meant that there was possibly something else here, stashed away in Box 222, that would indicate just who Mr. and Mrs. Roux really were. It was only a possibility, a very slim hope considering that Jupiter had already tried to destroy the contents of one box, but Swift was willing to break in to find out.

Her cell phone buzzed. She felt no need to fake a local cover, so she answered in English.

"Hello?"

"Io." It was the digitally-altered voice of her handler.

"Jupiter."

"There's a new situation. A problem within the community. We're bringing you in."

"You told me I had autonomy," she started to argue.

"And if you want to live you'll forgive my asking for one meeting."

"Meeting?" Io and Jupiter had never met. Her training and indoctrination had been done in a warehouse facility in Kansas called the Academy, where she once heard the name Jupiter. A week after she was let out into the free world, the calls and texts from Jupiter started. The prospect of actually meeting the man who pulled her strings—the same man who ordered her to burn Saleb's file—was enticing.

"When and where?"

"You'll get a text." Jupiter hung up.

Swift locked the government-issued smartphone, and put it into her purse. At the same time she withdrew a second phone, a cheap pre-paid disposable. She dialed a number from memory.

"Tony's fix it," said Khalid Saleb.

Swift rubbed her thumb across the receiver, creating a sound of rummaging. "Sorry, I dropped the phone." This had all been rehearsed before they parted; a simple series of responses to ensure that neither was under duress.

"I can hear you very clearly."

"I'm abandoning the Zurich job. Something's come up."

"What? You can't just walk away from the only—"

"Jupiter wants to meet me. In person."

Saleb barely paused. "When and where?"

PART THREE:
I DON'T APPROVE
OF YOUR METHODS

17

Jessica wore plain jeans and a long sleeve t-shirt to the bank in Virginia at ten in the morning on the day of the meeting. She went through the ceremony of code phrases and responses with the girl at the desk, and was treated to the bizarre elevator ride from a bank employee's office down to the depths of the Counter Intelligence Bureau. There was a soldier, or at least someone who looked, stood, and *vibed* like a soldier, waiting at the bottom. He was dressed in a black suit and tie, but Jessica knew right away that this guy was basically there to kill anyone who wasn't authorized. He scanned her right eyeball with a handheld device and told her to follow the yellow line.

The bunker under the bank was impressive in scale. It was grey and claustrophobic, but also awe-inspiring in a way. Jessica had always seen the espionage world from the grimy street level. She was recruited out of county jail, trained in a refurbished warehouse, and now worked day-in and day-out crawling through mud and dirt. The idea of a high-tech, ultra-secret underground lair was the stuff of science fiction for her. Yet here she was, following the yellow line through a bona fide underground spy base.

She didn't stray from the line. Sticking to the main corridors, she walked past rooms filled with computers and video monitors, and lingered in the doorway of a cavernous lab where young scientists were trying to melt a Kevlar vest, but seemed to be arguing over some details. At one intersection she noted a hum that was likely a massive air-mover to keep everyone in this place breathing. There was a room of nothing but guns, guarded by two more black-suited tough guys, and one room where people just watched the news on about twenty different news channels. She walked past a gun range that nobody was using, and a tech-support room where a tall computer technician was playing with the guts of a smartphone.

Finally, she ended up in a conference room. The room was round, with two doors exactly opposite each other. The one she had entered by following the yellow line was open, and the other door was closed. The entire room was dominated by the massive conference table, ring-shaped to match the round room. The ceiling was padded, likely to make it soundproof, and there were eight chairs around the table. At the far end, by the other door, there was a small lectern sitting on top of the table, and a white screen had been pulled down next to the other door.

Jessica was the first to arrive. She chose a chair on the left-hand side, not wanting to turn her back to either door. Some of the CIB workers passed by the open door, but nobody stopped to talk to her. Wherever Jupiter was, he didn't seem to care that Jessica Swift was in the building.

Eventually, a man showed up. He was tall, forty-ish, with stubble on one side of his face, and an ugly burn scar on the other. Like Swift, this new man hadn't brought anything with him to the office. He sat down

151

directly opposite Jessica, likely because he also didn't want his back to the door.

"Lovely sunny day out. Perfect if you're wasting it a hundred feet underground."

She wasn't sure what to make of him. "Are you Jupiter?"

The man squinted at her. "What? Like the planet?"

"Nevermind."

She shrunk a little smaller in her seat.

"My name's Shark. You?"

"I don't know if I'm allowed to say."

"Make something up."

"Io."

Shark smirked and started quietly singing with a country twang. "Old McDonald had a farm, E-I-E-I-O. You smoke, I-O?"

She shook her head. Shark grunted, fished a beat up, bent cigar out of one of his many pockets, and began patting his body in search of a lighter. Finally he found it in a side pocket on his cargo pants, and lit up the stogie.

"Is that allowed in here?" she asked.

"That damned lab blows shit up all day long. I'm sure if they can do that, I can do this." He blew a smoke ring, and another woman entered the room. This one was in her thirties, conservative, and carried herself very well. She seemed to be both solidly built and light on her feet. She'd be quicker than she looked, like a sleeping lioness. Swift realized she was sizing these people up, and then realized that even if one of them did try to hurt her, there was no escape inside this bunker. She continued sizing up each new entrant anyway.

"Sammy! Long-time-no-see, I heard you quit the biz." said Shark. The woman sat next to Swift.

"I'm Samantha. Ignore the ogre," she said, offering a handshake.

"Are you—" Swift started to ask, before Samantha cut her off.

"I'm just as in the dark about this meet as you are, kid. You'll get no answers from me."

"OK."

Shark snorted. "She was probably gonna ask if you were Venus."

"What?"

"Ask her."

Both of the older agents looked at Swift, and she tried to shrink even further. Was she actually blushing? She felt so out of her depth here, in this place and among these people, and Shark's cocky attitude was wearing her down. She reminded herself that she had a job to do. Someone here had betrayed Saleb and his wife. Someone was a killer and a traitor. She needed to find that person, and bring them down.

Next to enter was a British man in a dapper grey suit, who was carrying a leather briefcase. After nodding hellos to everyone, the Brit opened the case to reveal that it wasn't for paperwork, but was actually a travelling bar. He pulled out two bottles of booze, a pair of steel martini glasses, and a silver shaker. Swift noted that he also had a back-up martini shaker, which looked like solid gold.

"Anyone for a martini?" He asked, as if that was introduction enough.

"It's ten in the morning," said Samantha.

"Not in London, my dear."

"I'll have one, Limey. A double." Shark put his feet up on the desk.

The British man poured into the shaker, then shook it, then poured it out again into the glasses. As a finishing touch, he pulled a spoon and a jar of olives from the case, garnishing both drinks with a couple green orbs. It seemed Mr. British liked his drinks dirty.

He slid the double around the table to Shark. He spun the glass, putting some English on it, so it actually curved with the table on its way to Shark, slowing to stop an inch from Shark's boot.

"Thanks, man!" Shark said, scooping up the martini and drinking it, pinky in the air, in one gulp.

"William Thorpe, MI-7, at your service."

"Shark Scarret, not here at anybody's service."

Next to enter was a man in a black suit with a spiky crew cut, who didn't acknowledge the others at all. He simply entered, sat at the nearest empty chair, and stared forward. Swift didn't like him immediately, based on a gut feeling that there was something deeply wrong with him.

After that came another clean cut American man, this one in jeans and a t-shirt, rushing in as if he was late to the party. He had a gun strapped on his hip and gave an apologetic wave as he entered. "Sorry, I'm late," he said.

Once he was settled, the new man stared at the burned man and looked perplexed.

"Scarret?"

"Howdy Jack," said Shark.

"I thought you were dead."

"You ought to since you're the one who put me on death row," Shark sucked on the stogie and grinned. "But death row ain't permanent."

The new man, Jack, shouted with rage. Getting very loud and hostile, he jabbed a finger in the air toward Shark. "I don't know how you ended up here, you son of a bitch, but I—"

"He's here because I called him, Jack" said a voice from Swift's right. Someone had finally come through the other door. There was a young man—the one who had spoken—and another man who looked to be in his seventies.

"So this is about the nukes?" asked Jack. The very word 'nukes' made Swift a little bug-eyed. "Is Scarret here to testify?"

"No, no, no," said the old man, stepping up to the lectern while the younger one stepped to the side. "Jack, you did great work twenty years ago when you caught Scarret. But in those twenty years he has been a valuable asset for the CIB. Which is what all of you are, which is why you are here."

The old man went into a speech:

"Some of you know each other. Some of you don't. Almost all of you know me. I am Harry Milton, and I created this bureau for the purpose of hunting down the people who threaten Western intelligence agents. And today I'm here to tell you that we're facing a threat to our agents like we never have before."

The old man paused and the younger one put a messenger bag on the desk and started pulling out some files. In the moment of silence, Swift chimed in. "Did he say nukes?"

"That's not your case, Io." said the old man.

"Get back to 'facing a threat.' All that stuff," said Samantha.

"We are facing a threat that's more dangerous than CIB has ever faced. To be blunt, we're facing one of you."

For a few seconds, everyone looked around the room, as if the traitor would stand up and wave. After the awkward silence, the younger man spoke up. He clicked a remote, and a projector on the ceiling put a photo on the screen. It was a plain-looking man.

"This is Matthew Crowe, he was CIB's best deep-cover agent. Deep cover in this case meaning nobody even knew who he really was when he was out in the field. He completely assumed the identities of his marks, and Harry assures me he was the best in the world."

"And one of you killed him," added Harry. "The only records of his last mission were stored in this building right here, on the secure server and in my own files. For someone to know where he was, and what identity he was assuming, they would have needed access to either my office or the main server. The only people to have that kind of access are in this room right now."

The younger man started passing out the files. Each one had a name on it. The one for Jessica wasn't labeled Io, but said *Jessica Swift*. So much for codenames.

"This is the information on everyone here. We need to find the traitor, but we can't do that if we don't have our top agents in the field. And right now, our top agents just happen to be the suspects."

"So lock us up," said Swift.

"What?" asked Jack. Based on his file, his last name was Hall.

"If the worst traitor ever is in here, lock us all down until you sort it out."

"I don't think so," snapped Shark.

"That doesn't work," explained Harry Milton, "because this is a game of chess. I can't take five of my pieces off the board just to get one of theirs."

"Plus there are nuclear components running loose in this country, and wasting time on a mole hunt won't change that," said Jack.

While they were talking, Samantha Boswell had been reading through the files. "You gave them my address?" She screamed, out the blue. "I have kids living there, you little son of a bitch!" She was screaming at the young guy.

"They've been moved," said Harry in his calmest voice. "And nobody will know where they went until this is over. You can video-chat with them tonight."

Now Shark was reading the files, and while he didn't shout, his voice was tinged by undisguised rage. "You gave them everything. My service history, my criminal record, missions I went on, people I killed. Cartels don't forgive the kind of shit I do. If word gets out that certain deaths are on my hands, certain kill-squads would be sent for me. Maybe if you're trying to protect information, don't give everyone all my top secret shit, right?"

The young man answered, "All this does is even the playing field. Whoever's been digging around in the files already knows everything about you. Now the good guys know as much as the bad guys do. " The younger man was trying to sound confident in the plan, but his nerves were showing.

"So I guess I'm done chasing drug lords? All hands on deck to catch your leak?" asked Shark, his voice calming.

Swift raised her hand like a school kid. "Did you say bad guys? Plural?"

The younger man nodded. "There's no way to say for sure that there's only one traitor. We have *at least* one leak, maybe more."

Boswell sounded exasperated. "You just ruined my daughters' lives on the hunch that I can find whoever it is you're after? What if the moles outnumber the good guys? Ever think of that?"

The younger man, whose own information was not in the file he had given everyone, stared Samantha hard in the eyes for a moment, and nodded. He had no rebuttal, just hope that good outweighed bad. If there really were more traitors than loyal spies, this meeting could result in a massacre. With nothing left to say, the young man moved on with his briefing. He clicked his remote and the image changed to a blown-out shell of a building.

"This was the office park bombing in Ottawa a couple weeks back. What you may not know is that there was a secret Canadian Security Intelligence Service office inside. My office. And everyone I knew was killed. Before they blew it up, the office received some interesting pieces of a puzzle. One was this . . . " He clicked again, and the next slide was a strange letter F.

"It's a digamma. In numerology it corresponds to six. It's archaic, so it's no longer used in the Greek alphabet, but it's still used in higher math, in something called a digamma function. Not sure if that's significant or not."

He clicked to another picture. It was a fancy room, very old-world, lots of wood paneling. And on that wall, painted in blood, was the same funny F.

"This is the room where Matthew Crowe died. They cut his head off and wrote this letter on the wall. Note the way the lower horizontal line bends downward. It's not an F, it's a digamma. That was one day before my boss received a digamma in the mail, which was an hour before the building exploded. First they mail us a message, then they paint it in blood, then they try to blow up all traces. Doesn't make sense, but it's a start."

He changed the image again, showing a funny little retro electronic gadget. "This is a control computer from a 1980s-era nuclear warhead. One of these computers was stolen this week, but nobody tried to move on the actual bombs when they were taken apart last month. The thieves knew where and when the transport would be. They even knew which trucks were decoys."

After another click, the screen showed a beautiful woman. "This is the only other survivor from my office. She survived because she was a mole, planted in my office for unknown reasons. You've heard of the freelancer Fatale, AKA Rochelle Noir, AKA Sasha Black, well this is her. She worked in my office for six months and on the very day we got that letter, the office exploded. She is currently in the employ of an assassin named Martin Mercier, who has her poking around the executive offices at Globection Corporation. We don't know what they want to steal from GX, but Fatale going directly from the Ottawa bombing to undercover at GX headquarters tells us it's a priority. And every step of this scheme—Crowe's real identity, my office, the control computers—indicates that our terrorists have intel from the very top. From inside CIB."

Milton chimed in again. "And since I know I'm not the goddamn traitor it must be one of you, selling us all out. At least now that you've seen each other's faces, you know who to watch out for."

Hall leaned on his elbows. "We're completely compromised? Is there anyone we can trust?"

Harry shrugged as he answered. "Young Mr. Quarrel was called in from Canada just for this. He had no idea CIB existed until I told him. You can trust him with anything you turn up. And considering that Martin Mercier hates William Thorpe more than seven burning hells, and spent most of the 1980s trying to kill him, I'd say Thorpe's about fifty percent trustworthy."

"Thanks, old chap," said Thorpe, raising his martini.

Quarrel turned off the projector. "Any questions?"

Shark threw his metal martini glass back to Thorpe. "If this Mercier's so bad, how come I never heard of him?"

Milton answered. "Because he was the best. Left no traces. We only know of him from a few cases MI-7 investigated, but nobody has ever seen his face or even officially confirmed—"

"One person did. One person saw his face," interrupted Thorpe, looking into his drink.

Milton continued, "Plus, Mercier retired. Disappeared. I don't think we've even heard his name

160

since the Berlin Wall fell. But MI-7 tells me his prints turned up at the GX New York office on some stolen CIA information."

There was a heavy silence as everyone tried to figure out who among them best fit into this complicated situation. Swift felt that this might be her last chance to address them all, and forced herself to raise her hand.

The young man, Mr. Quarrel, nodded to her. "Yes, um, sorry we haven't met, you're Swift?"

"Yeah. I was wondering . . . who's Jupiter?"

Nobody answered. Jack Hall moved his mouth like he was thinking about saying something, but eventually they all looked at Milton.

"There is no Jupiter," Milton admitted.

"Of course there is. I talk to him on the phone. I've worked for him for years."

"I've been Jupiter from time to time," said Hall.

"Ditto," said Samantha.

"Me too," said the one called Smith, finally speaking.

Milton explained, "You see, it's just . . . he's not a person. Jupiter's a computer. Miss Swift, you have a set of skills nobody in this room can match. And sometimes, we need you to acquire things for us. When that happens, we call a computer system, which we call Jupiter. It modulates the caller's voice so you always hear the same voice on your end. It allows agents to use the best infiltrator in the service—you—without actually having to blow their covers to meet with you. As for today's meeting, I'm the Jupiter who called you, because I'm the one who put your name on the suspect list, because I know you've been in the mainframe and I know you're a lying thief and I know you're less trustworthy than any of

161

the other agents here today. Does that answer your question?"

Swift was floored. Not only was there no Jupiter, but Milton just told a room of deadly assassins that she might be the traitor. "Um . . . " she began.

"Quarrel didn't mention it, but Khalid Saleb was broken out of custody last week. By a woman. Any comment?" Milton asked.

"Don't look at me," was all she could think of. She wanted to tell them that Jupiter was evil and that Saleb was innocent, but what good would it do? The mole was in the room. Talking about Zurich would only make them cover their tracks.

"And why not look at you?" asked Samantha. Before this, Swift had been glad for the other woman's company, but now Samantha looked dangerous. She reminded Jessica, once again, of a hungry lioness. "If I didn't do it, and this Fatale didn't do it, who does that leave?"

"Break it up, ladies," said Quarrel. "We're done. The top priority for all of you is to investigate the leak, find proof, and bring it to me. We want the mole alive if possible."

With that, Milton and Quarrel filed out of the room, closing their private door behind them. Each of the other agents took their time, eyeing each other, wondering when to leave. *Was it safer to leave early, or did that look suspicious?* Thorpe mixed himself another drink. Boswell and Shark pored over the documents. Hall was the first to go, since he obviously couldn't stand to be in the same room as Shark, and he was followed quickly by Smith.

162

Shark put out his cigar on the table and then thumped off with noisy footsteps, and Thorpe packed his folder into the bar-case along with the bottles, glasses, and shakers before he departed. Watching them file out, one at a time, Swift realized that they were letting each other ride the elevator alone. Was that to avoid a fight, or to give each other a five minute head start?

Finally, it was down to Boswell and Swift, still sitting next to each other. Boswell had read every detail of the case, and Swift was still only half-way through.

"I know I didn't bust that traitor out of jail," Boswell said menacingly. "And if this Fatale character was in New York while someone else was in the desert, well there ain't many top-level female *infiltrators* left in the world, are there?" Boswell's fingers tapped loudly on the tabletop, before she scooped up her folder and headed for the door. She shouted back at Swift, without so much as turning around.

"I gotta call my kids. But I'll be seeing you real soon."

18

"This was foolish," shouted Harry Milton a half-second after leading Chris Quarrel back to Milton's office.

"It's a calculated risk."

"Calculated on what, exactly? Hope that they won't all kill each other, or that they will? For god's sake you can't just put Hall and Scarret in a room and hope it'll all work out."

"What I hope is that the good eggs outnumber the bad ones." Quarrel was surprised how calm he was now that the meeting was over. He had wanted this, he had initiated it. Now it was over and the real work could be done. "They're the best in the world. If we've got one loyal agent for each traitor, we come out on top."

"So that's it?" Milton was angry. Quarrel had never seen him this angry. Milton's default mode was to be curt, but right now he was fuming. The left side of his upper lip was twitching upward into an involuntary sneer. They both stood to the side of Milton's office, where a narrow counter ran between a filing cabinet and a shelving unit. "Your brilliant plan is hope that they *cancel each other out?*"

"Not at all," said Quarrel, "The real purpose of this meeting should happen within the next few hours."

Milton pulled the cork from a bottle of scotch and threw it against the wall. He swilled straight from the bottle. "If you don't stop dicking me around—"

"I know who bombed my office. It was Erica—*Fatale*." Quarrel picked up two of the glasses from the counter, flipped them right-side-up, and poured scotch from Milton's bottle. "And now the traitor knows that I know."

"So?" Milton's lips pursed shut and he cocked his head while slowly walking behind his desk. As he passed Quarrel, the young agent pushed a drink into his hand. Milton was calmer now, and Quarrel could see the gears turning behind the spymaster's eyes.

"You're using the mole to send a message," he thought out loud.

"I had to send up a flare. Let the leak run and tell Mercier that we know all about Fatale."

"That'll force them to go on the offensive to cover their asses. They'll want to kill you to protect whatever they've got planned. You're painting a target on your own back."

"After this morning every bad guy in this thing's going to be gunning for me. The mole, Mercier, Fatale; they'll all want me gone. And that's when the traitor will show himself. When they come for me."

"This is a terrible plan," said Milton. "They'll just kill you. Sniper round to the head. Poison in your sleep. Then we're back to square one."

"I realize that's a possibility," said Quarrel. "Like I said, I hope the good eggs outnumber the bad. As long as I have some allies in that room, I think I can do this. I know I can trust Thorpe. He showed me a photo of Fatale without realizing I know her. If he was on the inside, he would have been trying to keep me from making the connection." Quarrel sipped his drink, his hand was steady. "That's one ally. And I'm betting that not everyone's as corrupt as Erica."

Milton gulped his scotch. "I give you fifty-fifty"

"You think half of your guys are bad?"

165

"No. Fifty-fifty that you survive."

They clinked their glasses together and drank.

#

Senator Bill Anderson was dining at an expensive steakhouse in Washington D.C. A couple of lobbyists from the oil sector were buying him a very large steak and talking about offshore drilling. Anderson schmoozed like the talented politician he was, asking the occasional pointed question, laughing at jokes, and not committing to anything they wanted. After ordering a tea and a small slice of pie, the senator excused himself to the men's room.

There was a man in one of the stalls, but otherwise it was empty. Anderson used the urinal and by the time he was done the other man was washing his hands.

"Hey, aren't you the congressman from Ohio?" asked the man, looking at Anderson in the mirror.

"Senator, yeah. Bill Anderson," he said. "Anywhere else, I'd shake your hand," he joked while he waited for his turn at the sink.

"So you were the one who let that Canadian punk worm his way into the CIB?" The man was still rinsing the soap bubbles off his hands.

Senator Anderson turned pale. "Are you here to kill me?"

"No, sir. Just the distraction. She's here to kill you."

The Senator felt a pinprick at the back of his neck, and suddenly the world was blurry.

#

Quarrel was eating room service and digging through old case files when his cellphone rang.

"I was wrong." It was Milton, and his voice was shaky. It was the first time Quarrel had heard the old man sound like this. He was scared, or at least very sad.

"Milton?"

"I was wrong. When I told you that you were drawing a target on your own back. It wasn't you who should have been afraid." Quarrel realized that Milton sounded so strange because he was well on his way to being drunk.

"Harry, what happened?"

"You let the dogs loose, kid. You cornered a dangerous animal." He paused and Quarrel heard a gulp. "Turn on the news." Milton hung up.

Quarrel turned on the TV to one of the all-day news networks. The story was just breaking. Senator Anderson was dead of a heart attack in a restaurant bathroom.

19

It had only been twelve hours since Chris Quarrel had left the meeting with CIB's elite. After speaking to Milton, he booked a hotel in Washington and scheduled a meeting with the only suspect he had not spoken to—Jessica Swift. At the hotel, he received the news that Senator Anderson had died of a heart attack. Of course, Quarrel knew the truth. He had used the Senator's name to arrange the morning's meeting of elite-level killers. Someone in that room didn't like that Quarrel (and therefore Anderson) had changed their game plan, and now Anderson was dead. Quarrel was counting on them coming for him next.

He had put his own face out there for the enemy to see. There were now a half-dozen trained killers who may or may not have a reason to kill him. And now one of them had fired the opening shot. The murder served a double purpose; it removed Anderson as an ally of Quarrel's, and sent the message that these people can kill you and make it look like natural causes.

Having read each agent's file, he had seen stories of undetectable poisons, "accidental" car crashes, kill shots fired from three blocks away, car bombs; murders both spectacular and mundane. Thorpe once dropped a man from a blimp over Brussels. Boswell once smothered a woman with a pillow on a transatlantic flight. It was almost reassuring that the one suspect who Quarrel had to meet with today was also with the only suspect who did not have a confirmed kill. Somehow that made Swift safer than the rest, even if the odds were better than 50-50 that she was the traitor who was helping Saleb. Safecracker, computer hacker, infiltrator, and possible leak. She was all of those. But Quarrel believed the psych report that said she would never be capable of murder.

Nevertheless, Quarrel wanted to be prepared. Alone in his hotel room after dinner, he set out to ensure his own safety. He tucked the handgun he had checked out of CIB under the pillow on the bed and waved to the hidden cameras that were planted throughout the room.

The hotel was of the standard business/economy/travelling salesman variety: a single bedroom with a desk, two chairs, and a twin bed. The desk was one long piece of furniture running the length of one wall, doubling as a stand for the 30-inch TV across from the foot of the bed. The washroom was small and right next to the door. He was on the seventh floor of a ten storey building, a height that he knew would not discourage any would-be assassins should they decide to enter via the balcony.

He checked for messages on both of his cell phones. One of the numbers had been in the information packet given to the suspects. The other was known only to Thorpe and Milton. There were no messages or missed calls on either of them. He decided to call CIA's witness protection service, to check on the status of Maggie Reville. He couldn't get Maggie on the line, but the agents assured him that she was in transit to a comfortable and secret location.

Finally, there was a knock at the door. Quarrel approached the door quietly. He made sure not to block the light so that his shadow would not be seen by anyone watching the crack at the floor. Leaning to the peephole, he strained to make out who it was that had come to see him.

It was Swift. Right on time.

"Come on in," said Quarrel as he opened the door.

Swift entered cautiously, taking in the surroundings. She eyed Quarrel up and down, likely checking to see if he had any concealed weapons. She seemed, on the surface at least, to be intimidated by Quarrel. But then, with agents this talented, you could never trust the surface. Quarrel had to expect Swift to game him, to trick him, and to fool him. He had to expect these agents to be false, or else he'd wind up walking into a trap. That was all good in theory, but in the real world Quarrel was banking on allies making themselves clear. How could he bring himself to separate friend from foe if he was too busy worrying that he was being played?

"So how's this work?" asked Swift. "Is this an interrogation, can I leave whenever . . . ?"

"I'm not sure. For the others I was putting on a front. A cover story to get close to them and see how they behave. But I never got a chance to meet you."

"It would have been obvious if you did. The Academy has never sent me a partner or a handler. Or anyone, for that matter. They just gave me a cell phone and told me to do what Jupiter orders."

"The Academy?"

"Where they made me."

"Your file just calls it a CIA rehabilitation program. How about you tell me about it?"

Quarrel sat in one of the chairs. He had placed both the desk chair and puffy lounge chair, into the small clearing between the bed and the balcony door. He sat in the one by the windows, so his back was to the glass, reminding himself that the curtains were closed and any would-be snipers couldn't see him. Swift surprised him by ignoring the desk chair and opting to sit on the edge of the bed. He wondered if she could tell there was a gun under the pillow.

#

Jessica Swift noticed her interrogator's eyes flinch toward the head of the bed, then pull back to face her. Why would he care about that? Then she got it. Gun under one of the pillows. Whoever this Quarrel was, he was either completely paranoid or trying to play mind games. He would have read her file and seen her record. He would be aware of her problem with violence and fear of being around death. And here he was making a show of his firearm. Her shoulders sagged towards a point between her feet as her fingers intertwined between her knees. She didn't like to think about her past. It always brought back the image of burned bodies in black bags.

"I never killed anyone. I never even hurt anyone. I just stole some things. In this country people get ten years for murder sometimes, you know? But I got twenty-five for theft, no parole at all for the first twenty years. So when they came and told me I could change my fate if I wanted to . . . 'Serve My Country . . . ' "

"You ever think the charges were trumped up just so they could pressure you to work for them?"

"Of course they were." When she said it, Swift wasn't angry. It was just a sad fact of life that she had long since accepted.

Quarrel nodded. "Some would see that as a good reason to strike back against the people that forced you into this life."

"Some people. You mean yourself. You would say that. Not Some People."

"OK," said Quarrel. "I might say that you must have a real grudge against the U.S. intelligence world for taking your life away."

"You don't get it. I'm not angry. I didn't have a life for them to steal. When the Academy came along, I took a real shine to it. I wanted to help. And for a good while there, I couldn't wait for the next mission Jupiter sent my way."

"But not anymore?"

"No." She studied his face. Quarrel was too young for his job. He was a stranger and he was obviously in over his head. Even if she could trust him with the things she knew, he would almost certainly blab them to the wrong person. She couldn't risk it.

"What changed?" he insisted.

"Ask again after you spend five years in the field, Mr. Quarrel."

Quarrel stood up. "You could at least make something up. Tell me that it's too much or tell me what Jupiter's terrible sin made you do. Lie to me, for god's sake. Don't just come in and dodge questions."

Swift sighed. She didn't want to come, and now that she was here it was clear that Quarrel was too inexperienced to fill the shoes of a senior agent. "I'm done here, Mr. Quarrel. You're welcome to have me followed."

"Sam Boswell should handle that for me, I'd think."

"Meaning what?" she felt herself getting red.

"There are maybe three people in the world who are capable of learning where Saleb was held, and then

172

breaking him out. One was in New York and the other was sitting next to you this morning. Pretty narrow suspect pool."

"Now that's where you're wrong, Mr. Quarrel. You think the information on Saleb was kept that quiet? That kind of facility would have guards who rotate in and out. The guards would have friends and families who would know their hours and have an idea of where they worked. They would have food deliveries and someone would have to pay the bills. There would be dozens of people who know about a place like that and hundreds who they might talk to."

"Your defence against breaking into a safe house is that you know a lot about stealing information on safe houses? Not the best rhetorical strategy."

She was getting angry now. She stood up too, face-to-face with Quarrel.

"As I understand it, your whole deal is to find out how that Crowe guy got killed. Look at my file. I wouldn't have taken that job, because I can't stand the sight of blood. Bombing a building full of people? Stealing nuclear components? Isn't it getting kind of insane to think I'd have anything to do with that kind of violence?" She was breathing hard, her passion a little too obvious, her defence a little too vehement. She felt that she had tipped her cards, and Quarrel knew everything. Like she'd be arrested for assisting Saleb at any second. She needed to leave.

Quarrel didn't stop her from heading for the door, but just as she was turning the knob, he called out.

"I never asked you about those jobs. I asked about Saleb. And you didn't offer an alibi." She ignored him and opened the door, and as she stepped through, he

173

continued, "I find it interesting that Saleb's escape was the only time in this whole mess where the traitor made sure not to hurt anybody."

The door shut behind her and she bolted to the stairs.

20

In the room next door to Chris Quarrel, William Thorpe was watching several camera angles displayed on his laptop. There were four cameras hidden in Quarrel's room, and Thorpe was watching through all of them. He was Quarrel's back-up plan, his protector. Quarrel's meeting with the suspects had done one thing: it made Quarrel into a piece of cheese, and this hotel into a mouse trap. With several loaded guns spread out on top of the bed, William Thorpe was ready to trigger the trap.

Thorpe was so busy watching the cameras in Quarrel's room that he didn't see four small capsules slide along the floor inside his own room. Someone, armed with a very small air-powered gun, had just forced the tiny, penny-sized pucks under the door, sliding them across the room. All at once, these tiny devices exploded, and the bright white light they created blinded Thorpe long enough for someone to get the door open and get inside. Thorpe had his pistol in hand and ready to fire as soon as it happened, but he couldn't see a thing and the attacker was silent as a ghost.

A second later, his vision fading back in, Thorpe detected a shape coming at him, and turned the gun at the presence, but then a cool, noxious wind sprayed his face and he knew he'd been gassed. He stopped breathing, rolled to his left, and fired. The pistol had a suppressor on it, so his shot was a quiet *thwip* that made a small hole in the closet door.

"Now, now, Willy. Is that any way to treat an old friend?" He knew the voice even if he couldn't make out her face. The girl from New York, Mercier's assassin. Quarrel's bomber. The one they set this whole trap for, but she had seen their play and countered it. She jabbed a syringe into his neck.

Fatale came into focus for a moment, before Thorpe's hand went so numb the gun fell away. She smiled and was viciously beautiful. She was having fun. She whispered to him, "My hotel was nicer."

#

Quarrel was wondering what to make of Jessica Swift's dramatic exit when the floor of his hotel room lit up with blinding flashes. Someone, somehow, had set of a series of flashbangs. He dove to the bed, hand reaching for the gun concealed under the pillow, but he landed diagonally across the bed, and by the time he had his bearings the gun was gone. He opened bleary eyes to the sight of his old colleague, the girl he'd had such a crush on, aiming his pistol at his face.

"Hey Chris," she said.

"Erica?"

"It's Fatale. Just Fatale. And you knew that. After all, you did invite me."

He found himself, somehow, smiling. "I mentioned you to a roomful of trusted American agents. That's not an invitation."

"You ought to remember all those training courses, Chris. I beat you at every strategy game. So stop playing."

Quarrel's plan had worked. She took the bait. It was unfortunate that she got his gun, but Quarrel was sure that Thorpe could take her down—and keep her alive for questioning—even if she was armed.

"Mr. Thorpe won't be joining us, if that's what you're thinking," she said with a grin. Quarrel's smile

176

faded as he realized that she really was better at this game. He had set her up to walk into a trap, and now he was alone with a killer and she had every advantage.

"Did you get orders to kill me?" he asked. She eased into the armchair, still aiming Quarrel's gun at him, and crossed her legs. She was dressed in black spandex from her neck to her black leather boots. Her hands were covered in small black gloves, her hair in a loose ponytail. Fatale was an entirely different person from the modest girl-next-door good looks of Erica Gibbons.

"Of course. You're causing problems."

"Finishing what you started at CSIS-2?" He sat up on the bed, but she waved the gun at him.

"Keep your feet on the bed, legs stretched out." He laid back, leaning on the wall. She continued, "Would you believe I didn't know about the bomb? No, you probably won't. Either way, you have to die this time."

"Who gives the orders? Mercier? Or do they come direct from your mole?"

She smiled and waved around the room with her left hand. "I know the room's filled with cameras and bugs. Why would I tell you anything like that?"

"Last request?" he said sheepishly.

"Sorry. If you'd requested something else, maybe . . . " she crossed her legs on the other side, slowly, "then maybe I could have obliged. But telling all my secrets isn't part of the plan."

"So just kill me then. Kill me like you killed the rest."

"Actually," she said, almost purring "I have questions for *you*."

"Which is?"

"Why was there no funeral for Hershey? Is he alive too? Where are they keeping him?"

Quarrel was stunned. He hadn't kept up with the memorial services, but one thing he knew for sure was that Hershey was dead. He had been standing so close to the bomb that he would have been turned into pink vapour. And what the hell did she care, anyway? She was the one who killed him.

He was about to tell her that, when something behind her caught his eye. The curtains were still closed, but a space behind the curtains got darker; there seemed to be something blocking the streetlights. Something moving on the balcony. Thorpe!

Realizing that there was still a faint hope to survive, and maybe to even take Fatale alive, he decided to taunt her, to draw out the answer. Maybe he could get her distracted.

"Why, it wasn't enough to kill everything he ever loved, you want to rub it in his face, too?"

She sneered. "What do you know? I loved the guy."

"He was someone you screwed on the side while you planned to kill him the whole time. You don't bomb people you love."

"Did you see him at CSIS or not?" she said, aiming the gun at his head.

"He's dead. Before I got out of the building he was just taking a smoke break. He was standing about three feet from your friendly fertilizer truck. If they didn't bury him it's because there was nothing left to bury. Thanks to you."

Amazingly, she seemed hurt by his anger. She lost the angry sneer and looked distressed. She shifted awkwardly in her seat, and for just a moment, the gun was pointed away from Quarrel. That's when the curtains burst open and Jessica Swift jumped out, holding in her hand something that looked like a laser pointer. But it was much more than that, and when she aimed it at Fatale, the assassin's hand was sliced open and she dropped the gun. Jumping to her feet, Fatale was shocked to see the other woman in the room.

"Who the fu—" she didn't get the words out before Chris Quarrel jumped from the bed, wrapping his arms around her. Fatale turned his momentum against him, dropping her shoulder and judo-flipping him into Swift. They both tumbled to the floor by the sliding balcony doors while Fatale ran for the other door.

She was pulling the heavy door open and about to make it into the hallway when Quarrel smashed into her from behind, the force of the impact throwing them against the door and pushing it shut. He heard her gasp when his shoulder hit her and knew she was at least a little bit winded. He grabbed her right arm and pinned it behind her back, and realized he didn't have anything to bind her with.

Suddenly Swift shouted from behind him, "Knife!" and Quarrel pulled back just in time to feel a blade across his thigh, cutting through the cotton and drawing blood as it scratched his skin. Fatale kicked at him, stomping on his ankle, and he fell to the side. He hit the wall awkwardly, bracing himself to avoid falling, and then her right arm was free again. She turned on him, switching the knife to her good hand, and Quarrel let well-practiced self-defence moves take over as he grabbed her forearm and attempted to strip the knife from her hand. She fought him at first, but after a few seconds he got her wrist to buckle backwards and she dropped the knife rather than suffer a broken wrist.

Still nervous, (in fact he was terrified) Quarrel called to Swift. "Help Me!"

But Swift was still near the sliding doors, crouched and watching the fight, her face a mask of nervous tension. Quarrel couldn't understand why she wasn't helping him now, after having just saved his life.

The woman, who looked so little like the Erica he knew, turned up the intensity now. Without her weapon there was no easy, elegant way to hurt Quarrel and escape, so she went for brute violence. She broke his grasp, her arms flying outward for a second, before coming at him in a ferocious flurry of kicks, punches, even scratches. He blocked what he could and counter-punched her hard in the ribs twice, but pinned in the corner between the wall and the door, Quarrel felt like he was being mauled. She drove a knee hard into his testicles and he felt himself sink lower to the ground, but stayed on his feet. That's when she followed up with a hard elbow to the jaw, and Quarrel started to fade.

Then he inhaled the nose-curling smell of burning hair and Fatale screamed, turning toward Swift. For just an instant, the beam of that cutting laser touched his bicep and Quarrel was jolted out of his haze. Fatale had turned her head and shoulders to face Swift, while dodging the cutting beam, and she was wide open.

Quarrel threw a hard right cross to her chin, and Fatale crumpled to the floor, knocked out cold.

Quarrel rolled her face-down and moved her arms behind her back. He looked around for something to tie her up with but couldn't see anything. He turned to Swift, his eyes wide, hoping for help. Swift was still holding the laser pointer in front of herself, but her face was frozen in tension, her mouth hanging open.

"Little help?" he shouted.

Swift snapped out of her daze, shook her head, and started to laugh. It was a rough, racking exhale that hardly made a sound, but shook her body as it escaped. Finally, her mouth curled into a grin.

"Did you see that?" she asked, amazed.

"Yeah I was the one she was murdering over here. Can you help me before she wakes up?"

Swift seemed confused. "No, I mean . . . " she didn't finish the thought. As if a fog was finally lifting off Swift's brain, she snapped back to reality and into action. Tearing a lamp off the desk, she ripped the cord out of the wall socket before jerking it from the base of the lamp, and took over from Quarrel, tying the wire around Fatale's wrists.

"Bring me a big towel for her ankles," she said.

Quarrel nodded and followed the order. As Swift was working on wrapping the towel around Fatale, she told Quarrel to go next door. "Your friend over there needs some help."

Entering Thorpe's room, Quarrel found the older spy passed out on the floor, handcuffed but alive. Opening the adjoining door to get back to his own room, Quarrel found Fatale squirming against her binds at the foot of the bed. Swift was gone.

#

Quarrel put in a call to CIB to arrange a transport for Fatale. She would be kept in a holding cell in Harry Milton's underground headquarters. However, before the

181

team arrived, Thorpe and Quarrel had ten minutes alone with her. They tossed her onto the bed and stood on either side, taking turns asking questions.

"Why did you blow up my office?" Quarrel demanded, pacing back and forth.

"You mean *our* office. I worked there too," she said.

"Who killed the man in the Russian Embassy in London?" asked Thorpe.

"There's an embassy in London?"

"What's the plan for the stolen computer?" Thorpe asked, his voice rising.

"I don't own a computer. Just a smartphone." Her taunts were getting to Thorpe, and Quarrel was getting worried.

"You said you didn't blow up the office. So who did?"

She smiled again. "Now that's the question, isn't it? I'd sure like to know."

Quarrel stepped closer. "You think it was Hershey? Was he another fake like you?"

She repeated, "I'm just wondering why nobody seemed to mourn him."

Quarrel had a hunch, and decided to test her reaction. "You saw me scanning that book, you left, and then the bomb came in. That was it, wasn't it? You couldn't let us crack that book cipher."

She didn't try to deny it, instead she nodded. That could be a lie, accepting whatever premise her captors offered up. But it played into what Quarrel wanted to hear, and he wearily continued down that line of questioning.

"How did it work? Calling in the bomb?"

"I told you. I didn't. I was asked to look out for a Jekyll and Hyde with a yellow cover. When I saw it, I texted my contact. He wrote back with the 'get out' signal, so I left. I thought it meant my job was over. Honestly, I thought they were playing you. I assumed the book was a lie they planted for you, and they wanted to be sure you believed it. But then they blew everything up. Every*one* up." She was looking down, into the pattern on the comforter.

"Including Hershey," said Quarrel.

She nodded. "I just keep hoping I didn't kill him." There were tears in her eyes, but Quarrel had to assume this was all a show. "I loved him," she said.

The thought lingered in the air, and there was silence between the three of them. Thorpe was studying Fatale, Quarrel was thinking over her answers, looking for the lie, and Fatale was still playing it remorseful, as if she actually felt bad about killing people. Maybe she had real feelings for Hershey after all, and whoever she texted had taken him from her. Maybe they could use that to turn her against her handlers. The 'maybes' were piling up, but Quarrel still felt like she was lying. He realized he was starting to doubt and mistrust everything, just like the jaded agents he was investigating. *That must be a good thing*, he thought, *since those jaded agents are still alive*.

Even on the seventh floor, they heard the sound as several car doors slammed shut outside in the parking lot. The collection team was here.

"How long have you worked for Martin Mercier? Where has he been hiding all these years?" Thorpe blurted.

"I've been around long enough to learn a few things," she said.

"What's that supposed to mean?"

"How's Julia?"

Thorpe backhand slapped her across the mouth. Her eyes went wild with hatred, and for a tense, silent second Thorpe and Fatale stared at each other with pure loathing, until three knocks at the door interrupted the scene. Quarrel went to let the team in.

The team was Harry's best. Former military, guys who graduated from the Navy SEALs, Army Rangers, and Marine Force Recon into the world of top-secret clearance levels and underground HQs. There were four of them, all male, and all professionals. They showed Quarrel their ID badges and he stepped aside to let them in.

Within a minute they had replaced the knotted wire and towel with cuffs and shackles, gagged Fatale, and knocked her out with an injection. She was thrown over a team member's shoulder, and they carried her out to one of the big black SUVs parked outside. Before they pulled away, one of them turned to Quarrel and asked if he wanted to ride back to base with them.

"Milton says you're the point man on this," he said.

"No I've got some digging to do. Milton has a list of people I've asked to investigate this. If any of them come to see her, let them interrogate her through glass, but nobody gets inside the room with her, nobody gives her anything. And tape everything."

The team leader nodded. "Understood."

He climbed into the driver's seat, and the pair of SUVs took Fatale away.

Left alone, Quarrel turned to Thorpe. "Who's Julia?" he asked.

Thorpe shook his head a little, his voice fading to almost silence. "Julia," he said, "was the last person Mercier killed before he disappeared. Not that I could ever prove it."

Thorpe shook Quarrel's hand, apologized for not being there to save him from Fatale, and then he left as well, saying he was going to go find a drink. Thorpe hadn't even cleaned up after himself, so Quarrel was left with the job of collecting the hidden cameras, and the laptop that they fed their video to. The only thing Thorpe had taken with him was his bar-in-a-briefcase.

#

This hotel was far too dangerous now, so he decided he needed to relocate. Quarrel transferred to a much more expensive place on Pennsylvania Avenue, tossed his suitcase on the floor, and picked up the phone. It was after midnight now, but he didn't care about the time. He needed answers.

He called the CSIS switchboard. "I'll need Mr. Thompson, MM28." She asked who was calling, and Quarrel identified himself as four-zero-four-two. It was less than a minute before a groggy Thompson picked up the line.

"Thompson, it's Quarrel."

"Quarrel?" He paused, possibly because he didn't remember the name straight away, or more likely to shake out the cobwebs of interrupted sleep. "What do you want? One day you were there and the next you were gone. They wouldn't even tell me where you went."

"I guess you could call it a field promotion. Listen, Thompson, I need you to connect me to someone far

185

enough up the ladder that they can give me classified information."

"Like how high? It's not like the director takes my calls."

"Just pick someone who you think knows where I got shipped out to, and call that person's boss, OK? Tell them to check me out with the Americans and call me back at this number. It's urgent."

"OK, fine, whatever," said Thompson through a yawn, "but don't hold your breath."

They hung up. It sounded like Thompson was a little put out that the junior agent he had been babysitting was now involved in something top secret, but he was a good man and he'd do as asked.

Ten minutes later, Quarrel's cellphone rang.

"Hello?"

"Identify."

"Four-zero-four-two. Whiskey Oscar Sierra." The spoken ident number would be matched to a sample of Quarrel's voice.

"This is Avril Standing, CSIS Deputy Director of field operations. I was in one of your, um, debriefings not long ago." Quarrel remembered her. A short, thick woman with glasses. She had been one of the people who saw Quarrel's survival as suspicious. She had likely blamed him for the bombing.

"Yes, ma'am. I remember."

"You called up one of our men in the middle of the night and demanded some attention. So here it is. What do you want?"

"You know the nature of my assignment with the Americans?"

"I know enough."

"Before the bombing, there was a book cipher. A copy of Jekyll and Hyde. You remember that from my debrief?"

"Yes."

"I need both the book and the message that we were going to decode. It had to have come from one of our contacts outside the office, so somewhere in the CSIS world there is still a record of that sequence of numbers. Not to mention that I need to know who was sending the message and who was reading it. If I can decode that message, I can find your bomber."

"How's that?" she sounded irritated.

"Because I just had a chitchat with another survivor. Erica Gibbons. She's playing for the other team now, and always had been. She's a known assassin called Fatale. I didn't understand why they would blow up the building but I get it now. They weren't blowing up the office to kill the *people*. They were trying to destroy the *book*. Erica must have reported that I was scanning it into the servers, so the only way to suppress the book—"

"—Would be to blow up the whole thing. Kill the servers, burn the book, and anyone who might have read the message, all in one fell swoop."

"So can you get me that message?'

"Believe it or not, Mr. Quarrel, but CSIS does its job even when you aren't here to leak intelligence to random agents you meet in the hallway. We've got the number sequence in the office and we've compared it to every printing of Jekyll and Hyde we could find. So far, it's not working. A jumbled mess of words with no meaning behind them. If you want the number sequence I can arrange that, but you'll have to find that rare printing all on your own."

187

"Send the sequence to this phone. It's secure. Nobody will see it but me."

She sighed. "Yes, OK. After all, the people who might want to kill you would probably know these numbers already." She was gone for over a minute, and then Quarrel's phone vibrated as the email came in. Ms. Standing came back on the line. "One more thing, Mr. Quarrel. We also know the source of the message, but not its intended reader."

"Who sent it?"

"A former KGB agent turned Russian oil tycoon. Vladimir Plunov. He was killed the day the last message was sent, and no more transmissions were intercepted, so he was likely the only person on the other end who knew the cipher. We didn't know at the time that Plunov was the target of an American assassin. I believe you are already familiar with Mr. Crowe."

"So if Plunov's dead, I guess your source has dried up," Quarrel said with a sigh.

"Actually, no. Someone else took over posting for a little while. They sent more numbers through a website—"

"Which you'll give me," he said.

"Fine. It's a bird watching website. Sometimes someone uploads a picture of a dodo bird, and the number sequence is the file name on the picture."

"Isn't the dodo extinct?"

"Exactly. Makes it easy to tell communiques from random posts."

"Yeah. Yeah I get the idea." Quarrel said, "And Ms. Standing, I have a question for you: Is Pete Hershey dead?"

She stuttered. "Why do you ask?"

"Because the woman who blew up my office seemed to think he was alive."

"There were no remains, but that close to a bomb there wouldn't be. The only account of his death was *yours*, Mr. Quarrel. You testified that he was killed, and we have no evidence to dispute that. Now if you're done, I'd like to go back to bed."

They traded emotionless goodbyes and hung up.

The number sequence had been sent by the same man Matthew Crowe had been impersonating, on the same day that he died. And Harry had insisted that Crowe didn't kill Plunov. It had been his second-in-command. Another Russian, what was his name? Quarrel pulled the file for his luggage and found the name: Maslov. Alex Maslov. So was this guy, Maslov, a friend, because he killed Plunov, or an enemy because he was mixed up with Crowe's death? It was a moot point now, since Maslov was dead.

Quarrel stared at his phone's screen, reading over the series of numerals. Ten minutes ago, this number code was a loose end. A detail that Quarrel couldn't tie to anything else.

Now it was the one piece of evidence that tied the case together. Quarrel's office had this information before it blew up. That connected the office bombing directly to Crowe's murder. There was no doubt now that this was all the work of the same mole, the same group plotting something around the world. Digamma.

Quarrel set about memorizing the entire sequence. He set the numbers to a musical tune inside his head; a mnemonic that would help him remember the sequence later. Behind that thought was another, one which he repeated over and over just as often as the mnemonic: *I have to find that book.*

21

Helping to save Quarrel's life had been a revelation for Jessica Swift. She hadn't been able to actually jump in and help him fight her off, but staying at a distance, using the laser to save Quarrel, Jessica had actually contributed to a physical fight in a way she hadn't thought possible before. She had hurt someone, when it needed to be done, and even though it made her nauseous, she knew that it had been the right thing. It also helped her realize that there were other things that needed to be done, and she wanted to do them as soon as possible, before she lost her nerve.

She slipped away from Thorpe and Quarrel, back to her own hideaway inside a stolen van which she parked in a forest before she slept. She spent the next day getting in touch with a few of her contacts—there weren't many friends left but luckily the ones she still counted on lived on the eastern seaboard—and gathered the supplies she needed. She put together a new utility belt—the old one was in Europe—and loaded it with ropes, tools, a tranquilizer dart gun, spare darts, and two small pellets of gas that would induce unconsciousness within three seconds. She also treated a cloth with a chemical to neutralize the gas, sewed it into the inside of a painter's mask, and folded it into one of the belt's many pockets. She also went to one of her old dead drops—a loose brick in the basement of a D.C. church—and collected her favourite watch and a couple of hair pins.

By the time she had assembled all the gear and prepared as well as she could, the sun was going down and it was time for her to make a move.

She didn't know the building's layout, or its security systems, but assumed the worst. She was most likely going to be caught before she got where she needed to be, but the risk was worth it. She needed to locate Jupiter, and there was no time to waste.

To the outside world, the bank in Virginia had been closed for hours. Of course, underneath that bank there was a facility that never closed. She was going to break in.

During her first trip to CIB, Swift had studied the environment, looking to see how safe it was. Or, as a professional infiltrator might look at things, to see how vulnerable it was.

The elevator room from the bank seemed to be the only access, but that was a lie. There was no way a place like CIB didn't have at least one emergency exit, and given the depth below ground, they also needed to pump in fresh air.

Down one of the many corridors she had detected the sound of a large fan. Her well-honed sense of direction told her when she heard it that she was about twenty metres north of the elevator, and that the fan was around thirty metres west of her current location.

Now, only a day and a half later, she walked there on the ground level. It was another building, across the street from the bank: a fast-food restaurant. Dressed all in black, hair pulled back, face painted black, she climbed to the roof of the burger joint and headed for the peak. There were a few basic chimney pipes like any building, but there was also something else. A section of the roof that looked like shingles but wasn't. It was a fabric covering dyed to look just like the shingles. She wouldn't have noticed it if not for the small but noticeable suction coming from that patch of roof.

Cutting through the fabric, she found a four-foot-square air duct heading straight down, through the restaurant, below ground level, and into darkness. She pulled out her rope.

The fan was only disabled for about ten seconds while she climbed between the blades. Nobody in CIB would notice.

Once she was past the fan, CIB belonged to Swift. It was a network of tunnels, bending and turning, and very few wide-open spaces because open spaces underground needed a lot of support to keep from caving in. That meant that CIB was sprawling, confusing, and unusual. The air vents were just as tangled as the rest of the facility, which was both good and bad. Swift could get just about anywhere because they needed breathable air pumped into every room, but it took a while to figure out where she was going. Finally, she started to follow the cold.

The server room was chilled to keep the computers from overheating, which meant that it would be the coldest room in CIB. Once she found it, the real challenge began. The ducts went to vents in the ceiling of the server room, but the vent covers were too small for a body to fit through, and there was no way to open them. The ceiling itself seemed to be one huge metal grate, designed to stop anyone who might be inside the ducts.

And then there were the lasers. A spray of aerosol revealed a network of criss-crossing green lines. The lasers ran in perfectly horizontal lines, spaced only about two inches apart, in four places. They divided the room up like a tic-tac-toe game, with the access console at the center square. You wouldn't be able to slide out a screen or keyboard to access information while the laser system was on, which meant that Swift would have to shut the lasers down.

There was a usable air vent in the hallway outside the server room. Before exiting the vent, she wanted to make sure the coast was clear. Snaking a fibre-optic camera out of the vent, she spotted a security camera pointed at the server room door. There were no other visible cameras in the area. She climbed out of the vent.

Quickly analyzing the camera's shot of the door, she created a solution. The security camera was three feet left of the door, and it's shot would only show the door and the security console in the wall next to the door. Jessica stood in the same spot—but to the right of the door instead of the left—and took a small gadget from her bag.

It was a still camera, of sorts, and by jumping into the air she took a still of the door from an angle that was very similar to the one the security camera was seeing. Of course, it was from the wrong side, a mirror image. With a swipe of her finger on the touchscreen, she flipped the image. Now it looked like she had taken a photo from the left of the door. But in this one, the security panel was on the wrong side of the door. She drew a square around the panel and another around the empty spot on the wall on the other side of the door. The image automatically swapped the two squares, placing the console back where it belonged. It was a decent-enough duplicate of what the security camera was seeing. Another button made the gadget spit out a high-res print of the photo, which Jessica snapped into a flexible plastic frame.

Shooting a small magnet at the side of camera made the image fuzzy—the same trick she had used when breaking Saleb out of custody. While the camera was down, she ran at it, jumped, and hooked the frame in front of the lens. When the camera stopped malfunctioning it was aimed at a photo that showed the server room door, rather than at the actual door. Now she could open it. But that would require a retinal scan, and she didn't have the right eyes.

Back inside the vent, she searched around until she found someone who would have access to the servers. He was a lanky, t-shirt-wearing techie fiddling with the inside of a computer tower at the side of one of the offices. She had never met him, but Swift assumed that this was their in-house computer guru, codenamed Kilo. Now, she needed to get him alone so she could use his eye.

Gently tapping a screwdriver on the side of the duct got his attention. He looked around, confused, and eventually looked up at the duct over the office. Swift had him on the hook, and now it was time to reel him in. Retreating to the vent over the corridor, she tapped again, urging him to follow.

He came out into the hallway, looked up again, but instead of following her back to the server room he jogged away. Swift retreated to the vent above the server room door. Maybe he would go get a guard and try to investigate. She could handle that. At least, she hoped so.

Kilo did what she had hoped for, but not like Swift had wanted. When Kilo came jogging back toward the server room door, he didn't bring a guard, but Samantha Boswell. The most lethal agent in CIB.

"If anyone's inside the walls, this would be what they're after," he said to Boswell.

"Sure. Now that that Quarrel kid blew the mole, they have to break in to steal secrets."

Swift rolled her screwdriver to the grate over the server room. It just barely squeezed between the metal bars and fell eight feet to the floor below. When it hit the concrete, it was loud.

"They're already inside," said Kilo nervously.

"Open it," demanded Boswell. Kilo typed a code into the security console, then leaned in to let it scan his eye. The door clicked and opened.

That's when Swift shot Boswell in the neck with a tranq dart. Boswell started to curse, and collapsed. Kilo made a quiet yelp, but shut up when Swift opened the vent and dropped to the floor, Boswell's body between them. She saw his eyes flicker to the security camera, and when he noticed the plastic frame blocking the lens his shoulders slumped.

"Epic fail," was all he said before Swift shot a dart into his chest.

She took the time to disassemble Boswell's sidearm before she went into the chilly server room. Once she was inside the door closed automatically to keep the cold inside. She used the security console to lock the door. She should have dragged the unconscious bodies inside—any passerby could see them—but this room was a meat locker and they'd be unconscious for at least a half hour. Leaving them here would possibly kill them.

There was another security camera in here. They might be watching her, right now. But there was nothing to do about that now. She'd get the file and the file would prove she was innocent. Even if they came to bust her now, she'd have the proof on Jupiter before she was arrested. It would only take a little cyber-sleuthing.

There were firewalls; they didn't last long. The computer requested passwords; she got through without them. Even if "Jupiter" was just a computer program, she could still find out who it was that wanted Saleb's file destroyed. All she needed to do was find out who had accessed the Jupiter program on that day, and she'd have the traitor. It took a while to look through everything, because she really didn't know what a Jupiter-type program would look like, but eventually she found it: a list of login codes and timestamps.

She popped a thumb drive into a USB port and copied the file to her own drive.

She had it.

"On your knees, bitch." The voice was like ice on the back of her neck. Samantha Boswell was standing behind her, holding a Glock, aiming for Swift's head. She felt Boswell jerk the dart gun out of her belt and toss it back through the closing server room door, before stepping back to a safer distance. "I mean 'on your knees, *right now.*' "

Boswell had somehow resisted a powerful tranquilizer. This was not good.

The file finished copying. She didn't move to reach for it, but she was about to. Boswell spoke again. "I just put this gun back together and trust me, it *will* fire."

Swift let out a ragged breath and her stomach dropped. Boswell had her. She slowly got down on her knees.

"How the hell did you break in?" Boswell demanded.

"It's a secret." Swift put her hands atop her head without being asked.

Boswell kept her distance. "What the hell are you doing in here? Stealing more information to give to your terrorist buddies?"

"I really need this information."

"You're helping Saleb. You broke him free. Because I sure as hell didn't."

"Listen to me, Boswell. You're a good agent so just trust me on this. I need that file."

Boswell's gun was still aimed at Swift's head. "Tell me where Saleb is and you get to leave this room alive."

"Saleb isn't a traitor. He was set up and that file can prove it."

"If we had that kind of info on file, don't you think someone would have noticed?"

"I'm asking you to help me—"

"Did you know I've never missed when I pulled the trigger? At this range you'd have a closed casket."

Swift realized that this tactic wasn't working. There was no reasoning with Samantha Boswell. There was no give. Boswell was too jaded, too untrusting, or potentially even worse: Boswell could be the Jupiter who had sent her to destroy Saleb's file. Either way, Swift was out of options. She needed to escape this room and get back to Saleb. Back to Europe. Back to her own mission to find the mole. She needed a way past Sam Boswell. And the file she'd read at the briefing made it sound like nobody in history had ever gotten past Boswell.

But Jessica Swift was no slouch, either. She hadn't planned a perfect infiltration of America's sixth-best-defended structure without a Plan C. Placing her hands on her head had been the first step. A tiny RFID tag in one of her hairpins had sent a signal once it was within two inches of her watch. As long as that signal was on, the watch was counting down. And that had been not-quite-exactly one minute ago. She shifted her weight, a whole-body movement that masked the imperceptible shift of her wrist to angle the watch face at Boswell.

"You have three seconds," said Boswell, "before I—"

Swift's watch fired two hundred small beams of light into Boswell's eyes. The instant she saw the "blinder" strike Boswell's face, Swift dove to the left, rolling around the server tower. Boswell screamed, her eyes temporarily blinded. She squeezed the trigger at the spot where she expected Swift to be, and the bullets passed within inches of the rolling intruder.

Now Swift had the advantage. Boswell might have had some kind of freakish ability to make any shot, but nobody could take a close-range blast from that watch without at least ten minutes of complete visual impairment. Boswell wouldn't completely see right again until she's had a long sleep. Swift knew that Boswell would be relying on her other senses now, and that played to Swift's advantage. She was used to moving in total silence. The cold of the server room would throw Boswell's sense of air movement way off. Swift eased the painter's mask from her belt, slipped it on, and drew the knockout gas capsules.

She slinked around the room, one capsule in each hand, and threw them. One exploded off the server tower near Boswell's head, the other on the wall behind her. Boswell would not be able to tell where they had been thrown from. Swift eased a pair of goggles over her eyes as Boswell tried not to breathe, felt for the door, and finally collapsed, her gun clicking against the concrete.

Swift circled back around and silently removed the USB drive. She'd have to read the file later. Right now she had to get back out, which meant climbing over Boswell, getting back into the vent, and getting out through the restaurant before they could capture her. As she stepped over Boswell, Swift realized that Boswell wasn't immune to just one form of tranquilizer. Sam Boswell wasn't knocked out at all, but rather she'd been playing possum in order to lure Swift close enough to hear her, and as soon as Swift stepped into a vulnerable position, Boswell grabbed her leg, took her hard to the ground, and picked up the gun.

"Neat trick with the watch, bitch. But I won't miss when I'm holding you in front of the gun, now will I?" Boswell coughed. "Y-B gas. I worked up an immunity years ago."

With her one free leg, Swift kicked the gun, surprising the still-blind Boswell and knocking the gun to the floor. Boswell raised an arm to protect her face, so Swift kicked her in the side of the head, her heel hitting Boswell's ear.

Boswell shrieked and her grip lessened. Swift pulled free and jumped to her feet. Boswell felt along the floor for the gun, which gave Swift enough time to hit the red button on the console beside the door. Boswell wasn't going to let Swift get out of this, so she was left with only one other option—get arrested with the Jupiter data and prove Saleb's innocence from a holding cell. The alarm went off. Swift jumped silently behind the central console, keeping it between herself and Boswell.

Swift heard a whirr of rubbing fabric as Boswell rolled over and drew down on her. Even blind, Boswell's gun was perfectly aimed at Swift. Swift pulled away, leaving no part of herself showing behind the cover of the server tower.

Seconds later, a team of military security arrived, opening the door behind Boswell.

Jessica Swift stood up to surrender, and before she could speak, a man's elbow was in her sternum. They strapped her wrists in cable ties behind her back and searched her. They took everything in her pockets, including the USB stick. They removed her watch, her belt, her hair pins, and her shoes. And then they locked her in an interrogation cell down the hall from Fatale.

It was over. The only goal in this whole thing was to quietly identify the Jupiter who had set up Saleb, and instead she was trapped, cuffed, and since she hadn't had a chance to read the file, she still knew nothing. If Jupiter was here, they'd know what she was after. They would cover their tracks, and if that wasn't possible, they would disappear. Jessica Swift had tried a very risky gambit in breaking into CIB. And now the mole was going to get away.

And it was all her fault. She had fooled herself into thinking she could handle herself among these violent, dangerous people. But she was no match for someone like Boswell, not even when Boswell was blind. Jessica Swift was a weak, pathetic criminal and now she'd pay for it.

She'd blown it, and now she was alone, shivering and terrified. A million fears swirled in her head. The mole was out there, covering his tracks. And there would be more dead people. More murder. More bombing.

More blood she was responsible for because if she'd only been stronger, she could have stopped it. Why the hell hadn't she been straight with Quarrel? She could have told him what information she needed, gone about it his way instead of this insane risk. Why had she tried this foolish plan alone? Who would be the next to die because Jessica couldn't do what needed to be done?

All her fault.

All her fault.

At first it was only tears, but after a few minutes alone with herself and the cycle of self-hatred, she was sobbing uncontrollably. With her hands cuffed behind her back, Swift couldn't wipe her eyes, so she lay her face on the steel table and let the tears form a puddle beneath her cheek.

22

"We had to expect that one of those women would arrest the other."

Chris Quarrel stood while Harry Milton sat, and both of them waited.

The elevator from the bogus bank and into the heart of CIB moved slower each time Quarrel had to ride it down. Or maybe things were just more urgent each time. Maybe his sense of time ticking away was synching up with that of Jack Hall, the man without patience. Anyway, he was standing on that ugly carpet, watching the gouges and scrapes in the wall scroll past his feet to above his head at a snail's pace, waiting for that first crack of light at the floor that would mean they had finally reached the bottom.

He had little to go on so far, and was impatient at the thought that the information was waiting for him at the bottom of this ridiculously long elevator shaft. Swift broke into CIB. Tried to steal information. Boswell was there. The alarm sounded. All hands on deck. And now here he was, stranded alongside Milton for the ride back into the pit.

"We locked it down. More guards, nobody allowed to leave. Cut off all our computers from the outside world. Nobody in here is getting information out."

Quarrel didn't care about Milton's security measures. He cared about the fact that the same woman who'd saved his life was also arrested for treason.

"Relax, kid," said the old man. "This place has dozen of the country's best soldiers on duty. There's no way those ladies are going to kill each other before we get in there."

"I." Said Quarrel.

"What's that?"

"Before I get in there. This is my case, and I'll be asking the questions. Alone."

Milton snorted out a sigh.

Finally, there was a line of light at the floor.

Quarrel speedwalked through the gathered guards, his CIB identification card held out with a straight arm, staring ahead. Avoid eye contact, and they won't ask questions. In the viewing room outside the interrogation room, a red-eyed, pissed-off Boswell jumped to her feet when he came in.

"Finally! Can we—"

"Wait outside," he said, casting his eyes to the one-way glass and the sight of Swift, who sat slumped over, looking pathetically broken.

"Excuse me?" Boswell stepped uncomfortably close and Quarrel felt compelled to meet her eyes. They were bloodshot from whatever she'd been exposed to, which only added the fire behind them, and Quarrel was reminded that despite her usually professional demeanour, Boswell was the most lethal woman in the country. She got so close he could feel her breath. Close enough that it would only take her a second to kill him if she so chose.

He almost caved to Boswell's imposing posture. If not for Swift saving him the previous night, he probably would have. He even managed not to stutter when he finally spoke.

"I need to interrogate her. And I need you outside so you don't hear her side of the story. Then when I'm done, I'll get to you."

"Oh you'll get to me?" Those vicious eyes narrowed and Boswell took a half-step back. "I'm the one who caught her stealing intelligence while you were twiddling your thumbs. You took away my house, my family, you force me to spend my nights in this underground hell and 'you'll get to me?' Between me and you, I'm the only one actually doing anything about the leak. And you come in and tell me to take a time-out? Do you know who the fu—"

Quarrel flicked his eyes to the nearest guard. "Get her out of here and don't let her back in until I say so."

Boswell started to yell, but the soldier placed his hand on her arm. The second soldier moved to her other side. She calmed down. Still looking Quarrel in the eye, she spoke slowly and calmly. "I don't want to hear your second-hand report of what she says. I want to hear it directly. I want to solve this goddamn thing before someone nukes my kids."

"Good," said Quarrel. "Then you'll respect my need for some privacy and wait your turn." He nodded to the first soldier again, and they escorted Boswell out of the room. Before another guard could come inside to replace the others, Quarrel put his thumb on the flat screen next to the door. The scanner registered his identity, and he flicked the door lock.

When he entered the interview room, Swift lifted her head off the table. Her hair fell in limp strands across her face, matted down on her cheeks by streaks of tears.

Quarrel turned his back to Swift and faced the wall. Above the mirror/window there was a small black security camera. He punched it with the side of his fist, knocking it to face the nearest corner. Then he picked up the microphone from the center of the table, ripped the cord out its back, and threw it into the other corner. He pulled the only other chair in the room out from its spot at the opposite end from where Swift was sitting, and pulled it up beside her. Sitting down, he was practically touching her knee with his own.

"So . . . "

She sniffed. "So, what?"

"You broke in. You might want to give me a reason why."

"Doesn't matter now."

"Can I ask you something?"

She didn't answer, just stared at the floor.

"You don't look like the same girl I saw yesterday."

Again, she did nothing. Swift was bordering on catatonic.

"Yesterday I saw someone who was willing to break into my room and take on an assassin, just based on a hunch that I was in trouble. Yesterday I saw someone who was willing to take on a very dangerous woman to save me, even though I made it damn clear that I think you're lying to me about pretty much everything." Quarrel waited, but she didn't move. Her intermittent blinking was all she had to offer. "And today I hear you orchestrated a plan to break into what I have to assume is one of the most secure rooms in one of America's most secure buildings, and that you actually got inside, and well . . . here you are. Crying and sobbing."

"Here I am." She croaked the words out, her voice hoarse.

"And you're putting on the crybaby face why? Either I gave you way too much credit yesterday, or you're not giving me enough today. Because I don't buy this."

"Doesn't matter."

"You said that before."

She shrugged. "Because it doesn't."

"Boswell's chomping at the bit to come in here and beat the information out of you. You want me to let that happen or do you want to talk to me?"

"Doesn't matter."

Quarrel remembered Thorpe slapping Fatale when she taunted him during questioning. That might have been Thorpe's way, but it wasn't Quarrel's. He'd have to talk her out of this funk.

"What did you want? What information was so valuable to you?"

Swift spoke in a loopy, spaced-out voice that made him think she was having a psychotic break. "Well I'd tell you go check, Christopher, but it ain't gonna matter anyway by now, 'cause by now they've got it all sewn up. So charge me with treason and let Boswell beat me and let Hall torture me and lock me in a cabin in the desert until the firing squad's ready because it ain't gonna matter after the nukes kill us all and it's all my fault so I might as well be dead by then . . ."

Quarrel couldn't take her rambling any more. Throwing himself forward he wrapped his hand over her mouth and leaned in until he was eye-to-eye with her, practically daring her to look at him. She shut up, and her watery grey eyes finally looked up from the floor, partially hidden behind the limp brown hair draped over her face. He lifted his hand from her mouth, and used it to tuck her hair behind her ear.

"What is your fault?"

207

"Everything, it's all—"

"Be specific here. I'm the new one here. I'm the outsider. If you want to confess to someone you can trust, confess to me. I'll cover it with Boswell and everyone else. But you have to tell me the truth."

"People are going to die."

"Why? Who do you work for?"

She almost laughed, and in closing her eyes to suppress the laugh, she squeezed out fresh tears. "I work for Jupiter. I'm not CIB or CIA or C-I-Anything. I just follow orders."

"And Jupiter gave you orders that are going to hurt people? What did you do?" Quarrel wiped the tears from her cheeks and she started to seem almost lucid again.

"It's not what I did. It's what I failed to do. I could have ended this if I had that list."

"OK, what list?"

"You know I got a bunch of people killed a few years back? Was that in my file? Perfectly innocent people."

"Jessica." She was starting to look to the floor again. "Jessica." He touched her chin and made her look him in the eye. "Is that your real name?"

"Yeah. My codename's Io. You know who Io is? Zeus screws her and then turns her into a cow so he won't get caught cheating on Hera. That's me."

"My real name's Chris Quarrel. So we're just two people investigating a case right now. And I owe you a lot so I really want to help you, but you have to tell me what you broke in here for."

"It's not really treason. I have clearance to access that server. I just didn't want to ask."

"What do you mean?"

208

"I could have requested access. But then they'd know. They'd change the file. Like they have by now. They'd erase what I need before I got a look at it. So I had to break in. I had to. Nobody could know what I was looking for until after I had it."

"What did you want?"

She smiled at him. "I was gonna bring Jupiter down. Prove that one of those Jupiters ordered me to help him destroy evidence of his crime. I just needed to know who accessed the Jupiter program on a specific date and time. But now's too late. If Jupiter is really Boswell or Milton or whoever else is here now then they've changed the file already. Hell, they might have changed it when they first used the program. Might have changed it when I asked questions at your big meeting. But now it's gone for sure."

"What did Jupiter order you to do?"

She leaned in close and whispered in his ear. "They made me steal the proof that the so-called traitor, Khalid Saleb, wasn't even in the same city the night his wife was murdered. They wanted me to burn the file. So now I know. Saleb's the good guy. Jupiter's the bad guy."

"And there's a record every time Jupiter calls you?"

"Supposed to be. They told me, back at the Academy, that the commands all came from a central command centre and that Jupiter used a special computer to hide his voice and his location so nobody could track him. But then they also told me that Jupiter was just one guy. But I thought about it and the central computer made sense. And since it's CIB pulling my strings, it had to be here. And I was right. I found a file on there called 'Io Contact Log.' Except for some reason Boswell was having a sleep-over here and my tranquilizers did nothing to stop her."

"She's probably built up an immunity to that particular drug."

"Didn't know she would be here. I was just trying to lure in the science geek to open the door."

"Just wait a second, OK?" Quarrel said, standing up. "I'm going to find that file."

"It's too late, I told you."

"I'm checking it anyway."

He was at the door when she spoke again, a little louder than before.

"Then I'd better tell you what to look for."

Quarrel stopped and went back to listen as Swift became cooperative and functional for the first time since his arrival.

#

Quarrel barged out into the hallway, where Boswell, Milton and a dozen soldiers were waiting.

"You destroyed my recording equipment." Said a stern Milton, pointing a finger like a second-grade teacher.

"Can we get this over with?" interrupted Boswell, cracking her knuckles.

"Not now," said Quarrel. Then, turning to the same guard that he had spoken to before, he said, "I want to see the file she came here to steal."

"It's in my office," said Milton. "I've got her data stick."

"What about on the server itself? Has anyone been in there since the alarm?"

"Not in the room with it, we locked down after we dragged Swift out of there," said the guard.

"But it's still in use. People inside the office are accessing that server all the time?"

Milton answered: "Yes. But what she was after was highly encrypted. You'd have to be granted special access and I haven't granted any."

"I want to see both files."

Three minutes later they were in the ice-cold server vault, with Quarrel reading the same document twice. One was a paper hard copy printed from Swift's USB drive. The other was on the server console screen. They were identical.

Jupiter seemed to call on Io every few weeks. There was a pattern. The first message told her a place and a date. The next, delivered on the preset date, would give instructions. The third was a confirmation that the job was done. This cycle repeated for a few years. The most recent entry was a month prior, in Milan. No Zurich mission. Nothing since Matthew Crowe was murdered. Nothing in the days before Swift broke Saleb out of his private prison. Nothing about a safe deposit box, or the specific date Swift had told him to look for.

Quarrel stood alone near the console—nobody reading over his shoulder—but there were a dozen people gathered in the small server room. Their breath filled the cold air with a constant cloud.

"When was the last time anyone legally accessed this file?" Quarrel asked Milton; Milton looked to Kilo.

"Nobody as long as I can remember."

"Is this where you'd need to be to become Jupiter?"

"No."

"Then where is it? She said there's a central hub that her orders come from."

Boswell answered, in a surprisingly neutral voice. "Not true. You call in and the switchboard connects you. Then you chose which graduate from the Academy you want to use. It's all automated. I've been Jupiter from three continents. We just tell them Jupiter's some central figure to make them feel like they're working for someone at the top."

Quarrel compared the documents again, scanning the list of people who had used the Jupiter system. Boswell had indeed been Jupiter on many occasions, but there was no record of where the calls came from. But as Swift had pointed out, that was the point. Jupiter had no real face, no real location. He was untraceable by design. Hall had used Jupiter a few times. Milton took up the bulk of the list. Quarrel scanned both the screen and the paper. He could feel the eyes of ten onlookers waiting for him to explain himself. The problem was, he couldn't explain. So he said nothing. Dropping the printout to the floor, he started to click through other records. He could feel the onlookers shifting their weight as he dropped the pages, but nobody tried to stop him. Quarrel was wearing his game face, and so far the real spies were buying it. He really was running the show, and everybody was waiting for him to act.

He locked himself in with Swift again. But this time, he untied her hands.

"I'm going to tell them not to charge you with anything."

"You mean you found it?"

"No. There's no record of a call sending you to Zurich. The last mission is Milan."

"So why believe me?"

"Because whoever hacked this thing didn't cover their tracks well enough."

"What do you mean?"

"Read the list of names."

He laid the printout in front of her and her eyes hungrily sized it up, flipping through the pages. "I don't—"

"When we were at my briefing, and you asked the room about Jupiter, what did they say?"

"Most of them had been Jupiter. Milton, Hall, Boswell . . . "

"And Smith. He told us outright."

Swift scanned the pages again, and although she was too sullen to smile, her eyes smiled brightly.

"His name's not on the list."

"Almost like someone deleted him. Or he deleted himself."

#

The next time Quarrel opened the door to the hallway, the crowd was smaller, but Boswell was still there. Her face twisted in frustration at the sight of Swift standing behind Quarrel.

"You let her out?"

"Agent Boswell, you did a great job tonight. But Swift had a damn good reason for wanting that file and it gave me a genuine suspect. So thanks for your help, and I'm taking it from here."

"Like hell."

Swift had not only regained her senses, she had also regrown her backbone. From behind Quarrel, she interjected, "No offense, lady, but we have work to do."

"So you're back to playing the tough chick after you had a good cry?"

Quarrel was getting impatient again. "Sam, go have a cupcake."

He reached behind himself, and in a gesture he immediately realized was far too personal for the moment, he took Swift's hand and led her past the guards.

"Shouldn't we tell someone what we know?" she asked.

"Sure, just name someone we can trust."

"Welcome to my world."

They met no resistance on the way to the bank office elevator, which was currently just an empty shaft since the fake office was back at ground level. Once Quarrel hit the call button, Milton rounded the corner behind them. "That woman broke into my office, shot two people with a tranquilizer, and you're making off with her?"

Quarrel let go of Swift's hand as the elder walked past them, planting himself between Quarrel and the exit.

"I need her help right now. I can't tell you about it until I know more but this girl came up with a genuine lead and I'm going to bring in a suspect right now."

"Sure. Who?"

"You know I can't tell you. You had access to that file. You could have altered it. Can't trust anyone in this building right now."

"But you'll take the word of a street rat who we just caught stealing from the very server that contained Matt Crowe's mission."

"For now, yeah."

Milton lingered between Quarrel and the elevator. The fake bank office lowered into view. Quarrel took a single step forward, never looking away from Milton's eyes. The old man gave him a silent nod and stepped aside.

"I hope you realize," he said as Quarrel and Swift stepped onto the carpet, "just how big the stakes are."

Quarrel nodded in response and pressed the UP button. They watched Milton disappear beneath them

#

"We should call the CIA or somebody. Get a Navy SEAL team to take down Smith or something." Swift was in the passenger seat of Quarrel's rental, fixing her hair in the mirror.

"Can't count on anyone else. Until we have some real intel on this Digamma thing we have to assume everyone's a suspect."

"So how do you get to Smith?"

"I'm running this operation, remember?"

Quarrel pulled out a cell phone and found Smith's number. The phone automatically connected to the hands free system in the car and the ring came through the car stereo. Smith answered on the first ring.

"Smith."

"This is Chris Quarrel. I'd like a status update."

"On what subject?"

"Everything. The mole, GX, anything you got."

"Is this line secure?"

"We're not talking on the phone. I'm coming to you, just tell me where you are."

"At my apartment in Langley."

"I have the address. Stay there until I arrive."

"Understood."

Smith disconnected.

Swift put her feet on the dash, reminding Quarrel of just how tiny she was. "He sounds friendly," she said.

23

Jack Hall walking into the Pentagon was a fairly typical activity. The guards made sure to follow their basic entry procedures, but Hall was one of the few allowed to keep his sidearm as he entered. He nodded politely, yet brusquely, to a few familiar faces passing in the hallway. To the Pentagon Force Protection Agency agents who were monitoring the security camera footage, Jack Hall was his typical self: focused, calm, but impatient and in a hurry. He moved with purpose, never stopping to chit-chat or wavering from his path. The Pentagon has a number of fast-food offerings, but Jack Hall wasn't interested in Subway or Starbucks. He headed straight for the elevators to the underground levels.

The CIA, DOD, and DHS agents who would later review the tapes saw him calmly swipe his ID in the elevator's console and direct the lift to Level SB4—the fourth subbasement. He moved calmly and seemed perfectly at home, even as he entered the offices of Maj. Herman Slater, an Army officer who was also tasked with providing protection for nuclear decommission programs. Maj. Slater was the lowest-ranking person with intimate knowledge about which of America's nukes were to be decommissioned, as well as when and where the dismantling would take place. Using Slater's computer, and a sophisticated hacking program, Hall was able to access a server which provided this information.

A red flag went up at DOD when Hall opened a document pertaining to the recent decommission of several 1980s nuclear weapons. Part of the decommissioned bombs had been stolen recently, so the DOD was closely monitoring the flow of information.

When Hall-as-Slater specifically sought out the location of the fissionable materials, official efforts were made to contact Slater and see why he needed this information.

Slater was three states to the south.

Hall left the Pentagon before the alert went up to stop him.

To the agents of the PFOA, CIA, DOD, and DHS, Jack Hall soon became a high priority target to track down before he could intercept any nuclear materials.

The CIB, whose job was to track down traitors in America's covert agencies, were told that Hall had stolen information, but the exact nature of what he stole wasn't revealed to Harry Milton, or anyone else at CIB. They were simply ordered to find Jack Hall and bring him in.

They knew Jack Hall had been America's best agent in the 1990s. They knew his skill-set and his devotion to getting the job done, so they took precautions when preparing a team to arrest Hall. They could not have known, however, that every agent on the team sent to arrest him would end up dead.

#

While most of CIB turned its attention to hunting down Hall, William Thorpe was in the viewing room of Interrogation Room 3, staring through glass at Fatale. The assassin sat upright, her posture confident, hair draped over her shoulders. Even after a day locked in this room, she looked gorgeous.

Boswell had left shortly after Quarrel and Swift ran off, and Thorpe didn't care where any of them went. Fatale was the story here, nothing else mattered. Fatale was the link to Mercier, and once he had something concrete on Mercier, something the Ringmaster would accept, Thorpe could finally bring Mercier to justice.

Fatale had resisted questioning at the hotel, and Thorpe'sfirst round of interrogation this morning. But it was late at night now, there had been some noisy commotion with Boswell and Swift, and Fatale looked tired. Thorpe was about to take his third crack at the freelancer. Picking up a bottle of water, he went inside.

He threw the water at her, and since her hands were cuffed in front of her body, she caught it. She drank about a third of the bottle and recapped it.

"Thank you," she said. "I'll have breakfast at eight. Pancakes would be nice."

"You'll have a bucket to piss in."

Fatale smiled again. "It's been a year since anyone tried to question me. I missed it. All that time in Canada was just so mundane, you know?"

"You were there for over six months. How'd you manage to get into such a secret agency?"

"I have very good people skills."

Thorpe sat down across from her. "And this man Hershey, who you were so worried about? What's his story?"

She looked away. "He did what most men do, which is whatever I ask."

"Oh, I think he was more than that," Thorpe said. "I think that particular honeypot got a little too sticky for you. You'd have saved him if you could. You would have blown your cover for him. And Mercier knew it, which is why he didn't tell you they were going to bomb the building."

"Who said anything about Mercier? I just texted an anonymous number. Who knows who it was . . . " And then, looking confused, she asked, "Wha-why did I say that? What did you—"

"Just a small truth agent in the water." Thorpe placed his hands open on the table, like he was laying out his cards. "I got sick of your games, so I changed the rules."

Fatale was a little stoned now, swaying left and right in her chair. "That's no fair."

"What do you know about Julia?" he asked, knowing that the microphones were off and he could mention her safely.

"Your wife. You married her. She got shot and you blame Mercier."

"What else?"

"She didn't really die. You hid her somewhere, didn't you?"

At least they didn't know where Julia lived. Thorpe said a silent prayer of thanks for that.

"Who shot my wife?" he asked.

"You know who."

"Martin Mercier."

Fatale winked at him. "Mayyyybe."

"How did you end up infiltrating CSIS-2?" he asked, still keeping his voice down.

"It was just a job he gave me."

"Who? Mercier?"

She slumped her head forward, nodding limply.

"He gives you your orders directly?" Thorpe was getting excited now. He could feel his heart racing. "Can you set up a meeting with him? Perhaps you want to explain why you didn't kill Quarrel?"

She shook her head. "He'd see through that. I don't ask to meet. He calls me."

Thorpe wondered aloud, "So, if he were to call your phone sometime soon, you might want to agree to meet with him . . . "

"So you can trap him?" Fatale shook her head, blinking hard in an attempt to make her eyes focus. "I want immunity. For everything I've ever done. When you get Mercier, I walk out the door no questions asked, and my record is wiped out."

Thorpe nodded. "I can't guarantee that from the Americans, or the Canadians. But if you get me Mercier I'll cut you loose on the spot. All I want is to get my hands on the bastard."

Fatale was silent for a while, eyes closed, until suddenly she turned to face him and smiled.

"Go work it out with Harry. Then we have a deal."

24

Mr. Smith lived in a tremendously ugly apartment complex in an unincorporated town called Tyson's Corner, which is a little southwest of Langley; an area where frugal government employees live so they can commute to Washington or Langley or Pentagon City. Where Langley is tree-lined and largely suburban, Tyson's Corner is paved over and filled with mid-rise buildings like the one where Smith passed his time. The building was one of a half-dozen identical buildings in the complex, each as bland as the next. It was a rectangle made of concrete, rising twelve stories. Each floor was the same as the one below. It had no penthouse, no balconies, no distinctive or memorable architectural features. Much like Smith himself, the building was boring, functional, and someone in the seventies had thought it was a good idea.

Inside, the lobby was just an empty square, where on both the right and left walls there were two elevators and a stairway door. Other hallways ran to first-floor apartments, and somewhere to the left there was a laundry room that could be heard but not seen from the lobby. The floors were an ugly laminate roll-on made to look like blond wood. There was no furniture in the lobby. No flowers. No art on the walls. Just elevator call buttons and the sound of an off-balance load in the dryer.

The front door had been propped open with a cinderblock, so Quarrel didn't need to buzz Smith. Instead, he and Swift just walked in and he pressed for an elevator.

Inside the elevator, Quarrel started to say, "We should—"

And Swift finished, "—I bet he bugged the elevators."

So they rode in silence.

Quarrel's heart beat faster with every floor they passed. From the file he'd read, it seemed like Smith was some sort of perfect killing machine. Hall and Boswell had some impressive resumes, and people still whispered that Boswell had never fired a bullet that didn't hurt someone, but Smith was something else. Boswell had kids, a husband, and bake sales to attend. Hall had a son somewhere and a heap of psychological evaluations indicating that the trauma of a life spent killing weighed on him. Thorpe had the bottle. Shark was a bitter loner who smoked like a chimney. But Smith had none of those; no telltale weakness, no relationships, no life beyond the job. No sign of any humanity beneath the career assassin. Smith was sent out to kill people, follow people, and extract information. He had no family, no personal history, and no crises of conscience. He just killed whoever needed killing, and then came back to the world's blandest apartment complex to await further orders. And now Quarrel and Swift were going to . . . to what? Confront him? Arrest him? To discover the secrets that he'd kept buried inside that emotionless head for so long? This wouldn't end well. And the fact that Swift was hard-wired against hurting anyone, even to defend herself, made her seem pretty useless as backup. It was great to have an ally, to finally have someone who Quarrel felt he could trust, but Swift would fall apart again if this went bad.

But it was too late to turn back now. Quarrel had risked everything by believing Swift's story that Jupiter was the mole, and the evidence said Smith was Jupiter. Quarrel had turned against Harry Milton, who pulled all the strings, and pissed off Boswell, who was America's best agent. If Quarrel couldn't bag Smith, he could find himself with no allies at CIB.

Smith opened his door just as they reached it. He was bigger than Quarrel remembered. The first time they had met, in the cab in New York, Smith had worn a black suit. He still wore the suit pants, but on top he just had a white t-shirt, neatly tucked in. The sight of Smith's bare arms was surprising, because they seemed thinner and less muscular than Quarrel had guessed they would be when Smith was dressed in the suit.

The apartment smelled like bacon. Somehow, Quarrel hadn't expected that. He had an image of Smith eating bran cereal while reading mission briefings. Bacon and eggs made sense, though. He was a big guy. He'd want his protein. For Quarrel and Swift this was a very late night, but for Smith it was breakfast time, and he waved an arm toward the living room.

It was a small apartment. They entered into the living room, and off it were three doorways. The first door was clearly the kitchen, and the others would have to be the bathroom and bedroom. The walls were white, and held no pictures or artwork of any kind. Smith had two bookshelves, both of which were neat but full. He also had a desk, beyond which were a couch, an armchair, and on the opposite wall an old TV. Several documents and folders were stacked on the desk, with a folded newspaper page on top of the stack, likely placed there after Quarrel announced that he was coming.

"I didn't expect you to bring Ms. Swift," said Smith in his unpleasant, monotone voice.

"Guess you didn't need to know," responded Quarrel.

"Sit down, please. I'm just going to get my bacon off the pan. Juice or coffee?"

"Coffee." Swift said bluntly. Quarrel nodded in agreement.

They casually walked to the couch area, both of them taking their time, studying the apartment. Swift seemed to be checking the angles—escape routes, hiding spots, places you could hide if there was a sniper out the window. Quarrel was happy to let her look. He had given the place a similar scan but still didn't trust his instincts when it came to being a field agent. He always felt as if he was play-acting the part. It was better if Swift knew what to do if things went wrong, so he could follow her lead.

Obviously satisfied that she knew the layout, Swift plunked herself into the big armchair. Quarrel was taking his time looking through the bookshelf, refusing to admit to himself that he was looking for the book. After all, if Smith was actually in possession of the old Jekyll & Hyde, he wouldn't leave it sitting around for the lone survivor of the Ottawa bombing to see. Still, he took his time looking at each row on the shelves, and then he saw a yellow cover and crouched down.

Reaching with one index finger, he pulled the skinny old book from between two large hardcovers. The Strange Case of Dr. Jekyll and Mr. Hyde. Yellow paperback, same cover.

"What are you looking at?" asked Smith, who had reappeared from the kitchen holding two mugs. His voice was a little too loud when he said it, a little irritated. It was the first time Quarrel had heard any real emotion from Smith, and something in that strange voice set Quarrel on edge.

Suddenly, Quarrel dropped the book, reached behind his back to grab his pistol while he stood upright, and drew down on Smith.

"On your knees, Smith."

"What is this?"

"ON YOUR KNEES!"

Swift jumped to her feet. She had a gun too. It wasn't loaded, but she pulled it out and aimed for Smith as a show of strength, and Quarrel appreciated the solidarity since Swift would have no real clue what the book meant. Smith's head tilted just a little, trying to see the book on the floor behind Quarrel's foot, then he slowly started to kneel. Once on the floor, he carefully set the steaming mugs on the floor before raising his hands.

"So I'm the mole, am I?"

"You're damn right you are." Quarrel almost shouted.

"He's Jupiter? For sure?" Swift waved her gun when she talked.

"He's got the same book that got my office blown up. It's him."

"You son of a bitch," she said so quietly Quarrel almost didn't hear it.

Smith squinted quizzically at Quarrel. "What book?"

"You know damn well. My office in Ottawa was decoding a book cipher, then someone blew up the whole building. Because destroying the book wasn't enough. They had to kill the book, the database, and everyone who had seen what it looked like. And I'll bet that book cipher they intercepted was really meant for—"

"You killed that woman then? You killed Saleb's wife? You sent me to cover your tracks so you could get away with murder?" Swift interrupted Quarrel, shouting and punctuating her words by jabbing her unloaded gun toward Smith.

Smith shifted his gaze to her. "So I guess that means you're the one who broke out Saleb." She was so enraged now that she went back to shouting at him, but Quarrel had picked up on something Swift hadn't heard. Quarrel was piecing it together now. Smith's voice was different. When he asked about Saleb, his gravelly, monotonous tones were gone, replaced by a different voice, a thoughtful-sounding man who had a genuine curiosity about Saleb.

"Don't you even—" she started to shout before Quarrel cut her off and put a hand on her gun. He pushed the gun down and she let her arms drop.

"It's not him," he said.

"You just said—"

"—that Smith is the traitor. And he is." Quarrel turned his attention back to Smith. "Smith was decoding messages from Russian tycoons with that book. But you left it sitting on the shelf. The real Smith would have known to hide the book when I called to say I was coming. But you didn't hide it. Because you didn't know which book to hide."

"What are you saying?" Swift asked, as Smith knelt there, his grim visage relaxing into a smile.

Quarrel finished his realization only now, recognizing the smile on the kneeling man's face from a photo in Harry's office. "Smith was a traitor. But he was also the victim. The headless body at the embassy? That was Smith. And this man in here with us—"

The man in the white t-shirt spoke in the new voice and smiled. "Matt Crowe, master of disguise. It's nice to meet you."

25

Although he was still dressed in the Smith costume, Matthew Crowe was now a completely different person. Quarrel had read Crowe's file and heard some stories from Milton, but to see the transformation was incredible. It wasn't just the make-up, either. The foam-latex nose and chin applications were seamlessly attached to Crowe's face, and more conventional make-up blended it all together so that Crowe's face was physically identical to Smith, even from only inches away.

However, the thing that made the transformation whole was Crowe himself. His voice, his vocabulary, the way he carried himself, even the shape of his body was different when he stopped playing Smith. His shoulders were smaller now than they had seemed minutes before. His voice was warm, engaging, and brimming with an easy confidence. Crowe seemed quite proud of himself for pulling off the deception and Quarrel guessed that for a man whose job is to be invisible, getting to pull back the curtain was a bit of a treat.

Swift was still dumbfounded that Smith wasn't really Smith. In her confusion she had gone to the window and pulled the curtains shut, as if someone spying from the opposite building would see the change from Smith to Crowe even though his face was still the same.

Crowe had moved from his spot kneeling on the floor. Since he wasn't really Smith, he also wasn't really Jupiter. If anything, the fact that he had left the code book sitting out so casually meant that he knew nothing of Smith's conspiracy. Crowe sat in the armchair and Quarrel sat on the near-side of the couch, while Swift stood by the window, leaning against one of the bookcases.

"Smith came to kill you," Quarrel said.

"Yes. It was a surprise that somebody knew I wasn't Plunov, since I was working alone. It was a bigger shock that the man they sent to kill me was an American agent."

"You put him in the Plunov suit so everyone would think you were dead. But you can't fake dental records . . . " Quarrel trailed off but Swift picked it up, her voice quiet yet forceful.

"You cut his head off to hide your identity."

"I had to, yes. I decided to become Smith, to see if I could draw out the people he works for. But in order to make my mask I needed to mold his face, which meant I had to . . . take it with me. Plus, I know that CIB keeps their agents' DNA and fingerprints out of all law enforcement databases so they have total deniability. Without prints, DNA or a head, they'd have no way to prove it wasn't me."

"So you think CIB sent Smith?"

"Not necessarily. I knew CIB would get the case if they thought I was dead, and it was reasonable to assume that they wouldn't be able to tell the difference if I played Smith for a little while. So long as 'Smith' came back alive and the man in the Plunov suit was dead, they wouldn't know."

"But what about the people who sent him after you, how could you be sure they didn't have your prints on file?" Quarrel was still astonished by Crowe, and was eager to hear the details.

"I don't know much about Smith. I've encountered him before, knew he was Milton's little science project.

230

Beyond that, who else he might answer to, I couldn't say. The whole reason I became Smith was to hope that whoever was pulling the strings would try to contact me. But so far, nothing."

"They spoke to him with a book cipher. The series of numbers could have been anywhere online, or broadcast, it could have been a dead drop somewhere ..."

"None of which I could possibly know about. In the end I resigned myself to living as Smith until one of Milton's agents got fed up that "Smith" wasn't cooperating and came to see me. No offense, kid, but I had been hoping to hear from just about anyone other than you."

Quarrel shrugged. Across the room, Swift was starting to rat-a-tat-tap her fingers along a shelf, nervously fidgeting. "So what's up with the symbol? The digamma on the wall?" she asked.

"It was a stupid risk. I was still freaked out from Smith kicking my ass. The adrenaline was still kicking through my veins. I decided to leave a big message to steer the investigation in the right direction. So far it hasn't helped much, though. All I accomplished was pissing off Smith's handlers, who didn't exactly want their secret painted on the wall." Crowe looked to the floor for a moment, and Quarrel could see how the agent regretted the decision.

"So what is it? Digamma? You wanted someone to investigate, so what do you know?"

"I've been knee-deep in the Russian underworld for the last three years. A lot of the big money players are ex-KGB. Oil barons, arms dealers, drug smugglers, some government figures, they all tie back to the Cold War in one way or another, and a lot of top guys, legitimate and

231

otherwise, worked together back then. Eventually I broke into the office of a man who was looking to blackmail some of his former KGB friends. Whatever dirty secret he had on them, I wanted it. Turns out it was a document, but the copy I found was mostly redacted information."

Crowe got up from his seat and pulled a folder from Smith's desk drawer. Inside was a print of a photograph of a document.

"It's a record of one of their first meetings. No names on it, just codenames. There were six of them. Digamma is the Greek numeral for six."

Quarrel read the document. The date was blacked out. There was no listing of a location. But there was a list of attendees, their names also blotted out:

Alpha (KGB)
Beta (KGB)
Gamma (CIA)
Delta (USA)
Epsilon (GBR)
Digamma

Quarrel turned to Swift, who was still keeping her distance, and summarized. "Digamma was the name of the group. Two Russian spies, an American spy, a Brit, someone from the US government but not CIA, and one with no affiliation."

She nodded. "Private sector? Freelancer?"

"Assassin," said Crowe. "Digamma was a notorious freelancer in the eighties. Worked for KGB, MI-6, and the CIA, not to mention certain private interests. But he made too many enemies, ended up working for Russia almost exclusively, and after the USSR collapsed, he was cornered. So he brokered a deal.

His contacts, the people on this list, would erase him. They got rid of his files, his fingerprints, his photos, whatever."

"That's gotta be Mercier." Quarrel said, "Thorpe and Milton remembered him but nobody else had even heard of the guy. It's because according to CIA documents, he doesn't exist."

Crowe nodded. "They made it so Martin Mercier never existed, and I'll bet he paid them pretty well to do it. Enough for Plunov to start his oil company, anyway.

"Far as I can tell," Crowe continued, "the original document was at least twenty years old. This is a meeting from the early nineties. That means Smith wasn't there—too young. And that means that the real traitor, the one who helped Mercier all those years ago, is still out there. Maybe Thorpe's Epsilon. Maybe Delta's Scarret, since he still would have been Special Forces at the time—USA but not CIA. Or Gamma could be Milton, or Hall. I don't know if Boswell would have had enough access back then to delete Mercier from the records, so she's probably not Gamma.

"I know that Plunov was one of the Russians. That's why this was being used to blackmail him. The other KGB could be anyone. I'm crossing my fingers it was an old-timer and he's long dead.

Crowe sounded like the pursuit of this information was weighing on him. "I sent that letter to Kimura because I needed someone from outside the American and British spy world to solve this thing. Not that it helped. But now all I have to bank on is that you two were too young to be there so maybe you aren't a part of whatever Mercier's doing."

"It's the three of us, then." said Swift. "Four, really. With Khalid. Four against five. Not so bad, considering that not all five of them can be bad."

"I'm not trusting a traitor like Saleb," Crowe said dismissively. "We'll follow the book cipher, that's it."

Swift jumped to Saleb's defence. "He didn't kill his wife. He was in a different city. One person shot him, another shot his wife. Maybe one of the shooters was Smith, and that leaves Jupiter as the other. Fifty-fifty odds that Khalid saw the traitor. We just need a way to make him remember," she pleaded for Crowe to believe her.

"Maybe your traitor shot him. And maybe Saleb saw the shooter, but if there's one memory that man will never get back it's what happened in the hours before the bullet went into his brain. He probably won't remember that day at all for the rest of his life. And just not being a killer doesn't make him innocent of everything else he was accused of."

"Khalid's too young to have been in Digamma."

"So was Smith. This thing is bigger than just cold war agents. This Digamma guy is up to something and he's got people everywhere. Our best bet is to track Mercier." Crowe turned to Quarrel. "Can you crack the book cipher?" asked Crowe.

"I memorized it the other night," answered Quarrel.

"Get to it," said Crowe. "I'm gonna go touch up the makeup, in case anyone else decides to follow you here."

Crowe headed into the farthest door—the bedroom—leaving Quarrel and Swift alone. Quarrel sat down at Smith's desk, found a pad of paper and a pen,

234

and started to write down the number sequences he had memorized the other day. Swift wandered off, poking around the apartment.

The sequence began with 070512,080104 . . .

The twelfth word on the fifth line of the seventh page was "bird."

Then it was a simple, yet tedious matter of flipping back and forth through Jekyll and Hyde, tracing a finger along the page, and counting out line and word numbers. Soon enough, the first message was decoded:

bird in London in disguise already kill him at party

Obviously "bird" meant "Crowe." Smith had been sent to kill Crowe, that much Quarrel already knew. What was more concerning was that the message didn't have to explain that Crowe would be dressed as Plunov. Obviously, Maslov and Smith both knew that Crowe was on Plunov's case and knew which party he would attend. This message confirmed Milton's fear that the mole had intel from the heart of CIB. It wasn't really anything new, but it was also the earliest intercepted message. Quarrel wondered if Maslov had told Smith the details of Crowe's disguise, or if it had been the other way around. It would be comforting to think that once Smith was dead, so was the leak, but the theft of the nuclear components weeks later suggested that information was still getting out. There was another leak, still alive inside America's covert underworld.

Quarrel sorted out the next message:

need papers from array deliver to drop box in two days

Quarrel double checked the combination for the fourth word. It was correct. The sender had requested that Smith get papers from an "array." That was a strange choice of words, but with an antiquated book it was possible the word had a double meaning. Array could mean a collection, an antenna, a group of numbers, or as a verb it could refer to troop deployment. "Papers" was equally troublesome. It could refer to emails, stolen files, security codes, or . . .

Quarrel sat back and sighed. "Blueprints," he said to himself. "Weird blueprints that I couldn't understand." Smith's contact, Maggie Reville, had brought him some very odd-looking blueprints. She thought she was blowing the whistle, but maybe she had actually been unwittingly feeding Smith information that his masters needed. She thought someone at Globection was stealing information from the CIA, but by giving her "evidence" to Smith, Maggie might have actually been stealing information for Digamma to use.

Thankfully this message would have been posted after Smith was dead, which suggested that the "array," whatever that was, was still safe.

He was about to start work on the third of his memorized sequences when Quarrel realized that he should check the bird watching website to see if there were any newer messages. He flipped open the laptop on the desk, not knowing if it was Smith's or Crowe's. It asked for a password. "Hey . . . Matt . . . " he shouted, suddenly unsure what to call Crowe, "I need to get online."

Crowe shouted from the other room. "Call me Smith, and just click 'login,' I hacked that laptop last week."

Quarrel did as he was told, and after a little bit of rerouting through various proxy servers, he was on the bird watcher site. Sure enough, there was a picture of a dodo, uploaded that morning at five, roughly the same time that Quarrel had been interrogating Swift.

"There's a new message," he said, writing down the numbers in the file name. "Posted this morning!"

Swift came back from the kitchen, where she had been opening all the cupboards and snooping around. Crowe emerged from the bedroom, but he was back in Smith-mode now, dressed in a suit and tie, walking stiffly and speaking in the Smith-voice.

"What's it say?" he asked. Quarrel was already flipping through the book to find out.

Letter six requests meet Edward Street at Henry Avenue Noon

"Where's that intersection?" Quarrel asked as soon as he had it decoded.

"Not far. This side of the river," said Swift, surprising Quarrel with her knowledge of the DC area.

"It's still a few hours away. We can make that meeting," said Quarrel. "Or more accurately, you can make that meeting."

Crowe/Smith smiled. "If Mr. Digamma himself wants a meeting, I think we should attend."

"Can we trust Milton with this?" asked Quarrel. He looked to Swift. "I thought someone in CIB altered the file you stole, but if Smith isn't Smith then there's no reason his name would have been on it. Maybe Milton and Boswell are trustworthy?"

"No way," she said. "Maybe Smith was never Jupiter but someone was. And Milton, Boswell, and your pal Thorpe were all in CIB this morning. Anyone could have altered that file before you arrived. We can't let anyone at CIB tell Mercier that we're coming for him."

"Alright," Quarrel said. "We'll do it alone."

"Smith" adjusted his tie. "We'll need some equipment."

26

The building that the book cipher referred to was a four-level parking garage. When they surveyed the area from inside Smith's car, Quarrel wondered which level the handler would want to meet on. "Second," said Crowe in his creepy Smith voice. "Ground level's too exposed, and so is the roof level, which narrows it to two or three. This guy will want a quick escape and the second level's closer to the road, so that'll be it." Swift nodded in agreement.

It was two hours before Smith's meeting with "Digamma," who they believed to be Martin Mercier, the assassin who had disappeared twenty years earlier. Smith's car was a big black Oldsmobile, with plenty of room for all three of them. Quarrel and Crowe were in the front, while Swift was in the back, constantly moving around to look out both sides of the car and study the area.

"Over there," she said suddenly. "That apartment had the best view of the second level of the garage. We can set up in there." She was pointing to a four-storey building across the street from the parking structure, specifically at the corner apartment on the second floor.

"And if it's occupied?" Quarrel asked.

She shrugged. "Then we go next door to the second best view."

"We could always just tie up the people who live there," offered Crowe.

"No," Swift said emphatically. "I won't hurt innocent people just to make my job a little easier."

#

239

It turned out to be a moot point anyway, since nobody answered when they knocked on the door of the second-floor apartment that Swift had picked out. Swift quietly picked the lock and let herself in, leaving the men out in the corridor. Quarrel and Crowe waited around in silence for a minute before she returned to usher them in.

"Nobody home," she whispered. "And the photos suggest the people who live here are young professionals. No kids to come home for lunch and interrupt us. We should be good to set up."

It was a fairly plain one-bedroom apartment. Most of the floor space was reserved for the large living room with the corner windows. A bedroom was next to it, with more windows, and behind that there was a bathroom and a small kitchen. It was actually a lot like Smith's apartment, but brighter, more lived-in, and with art on the walls. It was like seeing what Smith's place could have been if Smith wasn't an emotionless robot.

They set up a tripod to hold a video camera with a lens the size of a travel mug and plugged it into the wall to make sure it didn't run out of power. They also set up a recorder, which would pick up the signal from Crowe's microphone and capture it on both digital audio and analog tape. They had a parabolic microphone as well, which they might need if Mercier was using anything to detect or dampen the bug that Crowe would be wearing. The parabolic mic was a big plastic device, shaped like a massive cup, which would have to be held out an open window in order to pick up the sound from the parking garage. They would only take the risk of opening a window if they needed to.

In addition to the equipment for documenting Digamma's meeting, they also had rifles and ammunition in case Quarrel needed to protect Crowe. Quarrel insisted he was trained to hit a moving target from this distance, but training is not the same as firing a live round at a live person, so he was worried. He knew from the firefight on the highway that he was capable of shooting at someone when he needed to, but he was unsure whether he'd be a good shot when he had to be. Quarrel kept his self-doubts out of the conversation, knowing it wouldn't do any good to make Crowe doubt him.

As noon approached, Crowe went to his car, circled back a few blocks, and drove up to the second level of the garage. He reversed into a spot facing the entrance ramp and waited. Quarrel and Swift turned on the recording devices. Quarrel held the rifle while Swift worked the camera, which was currently zoomed in (with hi-res detail) on Smith's car.

At exactly noon, a Lincoln Navigator with tinted windows pulled into the building, and a moment later it climbed to the second level and stopped in the middle of the lane. Crowe, looking perfectly Smith, got out of his car. The man he was meeting got out of the back of the Navigator. Through the recorder, they heard the door open and close. Crowe's bug was working perfectly. Quarrel raised the rifle, squinting into the scope to see the face of Digamma.

"Long time no see, Mr. Smith," said the man, who wore a handsome blue suit. "Where have you been?"

"Milton's got me jumping through hoops," said Crowe in his Smith impression. "Have to put up with some kid they brought in to look for leaks."

"I heard about this kid. Quarrel. Survived the bomb in Canada," said the man. Quarrel knew that the mole would have immediately gone back to Digamma to warn him about the investigation, but it was still worrying to hear that such a dangerous man knew his name.

"In fact," the man continued, "that's why we're here. I wanted to make sure that the kid isn't getting too close."

"OK," said Crowe, "what do you want me to do?"

"I was hoping," said Digamma, "that you would get the code phrase right and prove that you're not under duress. But you already got it wrong."

Suddenly the side of Crowe's head exploded open in a bloody exit wound, and he collapsed to the floor. "Sniper!" Swift shouted, kicking over the tripod. A moment later, shots shattered the large window and Swift grabbed Quarrel by the shirt as she dove out of the living room.

There was a steady stream of bullets, fired one at a time from a powerful semi-automatic somewhere outside. There may have been multiple shooters since there seemed to be a lot of bullets coming very quickly. Even with the glass window gone, Quarrel heard no shots, only the sounds of impacts as the bullets buried themselves in the wall and furniture.

Quarrel wanted to run from the apartment, but the door to the hallway was in sight of the window. The sniper would have a great shot at anyone trying to open the door. Staying in the kitchen was safe for now, since it had no windows for the sniper to use, but staying here long would only get them killed. Quarrel knew that there would be more than one shooter. A strike team would be on its way, attacking them either from the hallway or by rappelling into the now-shattered living room window.

"This is Milton or Boswell. They must have followed us from CIB," whispered Swift, who hunched down below the counter, even though no bullets had penetrated through the bedroom and bathroom walls to reach the kitchen.

"This meeting was on the website before I came to CIB this morning. They couldn't have known that we'd be with Smith."

"Not until Boswell or Milton called to them that we'd gone to Smith's apartment. They must have figured it out eventually. Plus, how hard can it be to fake a timestamp on that website?"

Quarrel accepted her logic. "We have to get out of this apartment. They're closing in right now."

Swift whispered back, "No way. That door's exposed to the window. They'll shoot—"

Quarrel cut her off, raising his voice: "I know! You're the expert here, get us out!"

Swift shook her head. "The door's the only out. Window's too high to jump without breaking something and they're watching it anyway."

Quarrel looked around the kitchen, praying for a solution. Then he found one: "The fridge. Drag it in front of us. No way a sniper can shoot through that before we make it to the hallway."

Swift looked at the fridge, sizing it up, and he was sure she'd agree. But they never got the chance to try the plan anyway. With a shockingly loud thump, the apartment door was kicked inward. Swift instinctively stood up and tucked herself into the narrow gap between the doorway and the counter. Quarrel knew that it was only a split second before the attackers came into the apartment and spotted him, but luckily they were moving slowly and cautiously, giving him a chance to scamper onto the countertop on the other side of the door. Tucked in as they were, they were in prime position to jump the attackers as they entered the kitchen, but the invaders would be armed and armoured. That was a huge advantage for the invaders, since Quarrel had dropped the rifle in the frantic dive for cover, and Swift was unarmed. All they had was Quarrel's sidearm, which he quietly pulled out and cocked.

Cocking it made a sound. It was a quiet click, but it was enough to get the strike team's attention.

"Kitchen!" shouted a male voice.

Quarrel saw that Swift had nothing to use to defend herself. She was pressing her body against the wall, shrinking as much as possible, but she looked helpless. Quarrel spotted a spice rack next to Swift. He nodded to it, then made a gesture of forcing his eyes shut, as if in pain. Swift understood. She grabbed a bottle of red powder, spun off the top, and dumped spice into the palm of her right hand.

A moment later, before the spillover powder had even reached the floor, the barrel of an automatic rifle stuck through the doorway. The intruder spotted Quarrel, awkwardly sitting on the counter as he was, and the gun barrel swung toward him. Just then, Swift swung her arm out, smacking a handful of cayenne pepper into the attacker's eyes. He screamed and reflexed to rub his eyes. The gun barrel jerked up, and that's when Quarrel swung himself down from the counter.

Using the first man as a human shield, Quarrel lowered his pistol at the man who was still in the living room. The other man fired first, his bullet striking the first attacker in the back of his bulletproof vest. Quarrel lined up his sights and pulled the trigger. The man in the living room took the bullet in the cheek and collapsed next to the tripod. Meanwhile, Swift had grabbed the first man's gun and pointed it at the empty space between herself and Quarrel. The impact of the shot in his back made the blinded man grab for the rifle again, but Swift twisted the gun and he couldn't find the trigger.

Quarrel used his left hand to grab the man by his collar and leaned out of the kitchen with the man's body as cover. A third attacker was standing in the doorway out to the hall, and Quarrel fired two quick shots to the man's vest, which made him wince. The third man fired a burst from his automatic, spraying up the back of the cayenne-blinded man, who screamed for a moment. The last shot must have taken him in the back of the head, because the blinded man went limp and Quarrel couldn't hold him upright with just his left hand, so the human shield fell away. The man in the doorway had a clear shot at Quarrel now, but Quarrel had recovered from missing his first shots and the man in the doorway was winded from the shots to his vest. In the instant where the gunman sucked in a deep breath, Quarrel put two careful shots into the man's forehead. And for a moment, there was silence as the gunpowder hung in the air.

"Clear!" he said to Swift, who had turned white from the sight of three men dying.

"Jesus Christ . . . " she gasped.

For a second they looked at each other and they both felt nauseous. Quarrel had just killed three men, and Swift looked disgusted at having a part in it. Quarrel had trained for this, mastering his grip, his aim, practicing in

245

war games and playing at being a real spy. Now he had gunpowder on his hands and blood on the floor, and the knowledge that he had killed surprised him as much as it nauseated. He inhaled the gunshot smell and wanted to throw up.

Swift sprinted into the living room and picked up the camera, still attached to the tripod, and threw the whole unwieldy thing toward Quarrel. Then she snatched up the digital recorder, rolled behind the loveseat so any snipers out the window couldn't see her, and called to Quarrel.

"You make sure the hallway's clear. I'll carry this."

Quarrel nodded, unscrewed the tripod from under the camera, then he ran straight from the kitchen to the open doorway, rushing into the hallway before any possible remaining sniper could hit him. It was a big risk, since there could have been an attacker waiting in the hallway in either direction. It turned out that there was nobody else in the hallway, so Quarrel lowered his gun and whispered that it was all clear. A moment later, Swift somersaulted across the room and out into the hall.

"That street's side will be covered by the sniper. We'll never make it to Smith's car. We have to get out the south side and make it out of here on foot," Swift told him in a rush. Quarrel got the sense that she planned these back-up escape routes constantly; that Jessica Swift was never at rest, and her frantic instructions were a glimpse into her fever-pitch brain. She was still talking: "Best bet is to take the nearest stairwell, since they'll probably expect us to take one at one of the far ends of the building. Once we get to the ground floor, use one of the apartments to escape out a window, don't exit through the main doors or fire escapes. And never stop running."

Quarrel followed Swift as she sprinted to the stairs, and rushed downward, taking the entire ten-step staircase with only a step in the middle before hitting the landing, turning one-eighty and doing it again. Quarrel tried to do the same jump but felt that the time it took him to recover was too long. After that, he hit every second stair while Swift continued hopping around like a water bug. They got to the ground floor before anybody else joined them in the stairs. When they pushed out of the stairs into the main floor corridor, they emerged into a rush of sounds. A dryer was humming in a laundry room, someone was playing music that came through the walls as a deep thumping, and there were police sirens approaching. Someone had heard Quarrel's gunshots and called 911.

Swift didn't miss a step, sprinting down the hallway without a moment's hesitation, working out the details of the escape on the fly while Quarrel followed and struggled to keep pace. She was trying every door on her left. The fifth door opened and she charged in. Quarrel, lagging several steps behind, followed her.

Inside, a mother was eating breakfast with a girl of about ten years old. They both screamed, but Swift just ran around the table, pulled their sliding door open and hurdled the three-foot concrete fence of their tiny patio. Quarrel ran by, gasping for breath, the gun in his hand making the woman scream. Quarrel caught the woman's eye and coughed out "sorry" before hurdling the wall and following Swift across the pavement that circled the building.

Behind him, the mother ran out onto the patio and screamed at him, "You leave that woman alone!"

That scream was enough to draw out the attackers who had been stationed at the exit at the far end of the building. Two men came around the corner, saw Swift, and opened fire. Swift took cover behind a dumpster, and their attention turned to Quarrel. He fired four shots at them, clicked empty, and made it to the dumpster before they returned fire. The man in the suit and the Navigator were nowhere to be seen, no doubt fleeing the sound of sirens, which were blaring now.

The police were on the street around the building, their cruisers coming to a stop. Quarrel had only a quick glimpse of the area, but back here behind the apartment building there was no cover other than the dumpsters. They were very, very exposed here. There was a grassy field about the size of a soccer pitch, and then another identical apartment building. Quarrel poked his gun out to the side of the dumpster as a distraction for any potential snipers, then peeked over the top to see what was happening. The gunmen were gone, and there were flashing red lights washing across the pavement at that end of the building. Quarrel tucked his gun out of sight under his shirt.

"Cops went straight to the shooters," he said.

"Never stop running," she whispered, while her eyes told him which way to go.

Swift took off without any further instruction. In the tract of grass between the two buildings she was completely exposed, but neither the cops nor the attackers spotted her. Apparently, the cops and attackers were busy with each other. Quarrel came running a few seconds behind her, letting her lead him around to the front of the neighbouring apartment building. They made it to a road on the far side of that building, which was busy enough for a weekday at lunchtime. Swift ran straight out into traffic and into the middle of the first lane. An approaching car screeched to a stop and honked at her. Swift glared at the driver.

The driver leaned out her window and started to say something, but before she could get the words out, Swift pulled out her pistol and shouted "Get out of the car!"

Quarrel saw what was happening and pulled his gun. "She means business, lady. Get out of the car!"

The driver saw the guns and obediently got out of the car. Swift jumped into the driver's seat and Quarrel opened the passenger's door. He had to shove the woman's purse off the passenger seat before he could get in, and Swift was pulling away before his door was even shut.

"People saw that. People see things, then they get on their cellphones, then the police show up. They'll know which car we're in in a couple minutes." She was driving faster and faster, weaving through the traffic. "We have to get a few blocks away and quietly ditch this thing. Take the lady's cash if she has any."

Quarrel was surprised at Swift's cold efficiency, but then he realized that her training had kicked in. In the same way that Quarrel was able to kill those men in a matter of seconds because muscle memory programmed him to aim and shoot, Swift was able to escape from a sticky situation without needing time to stop and think. It was automatic to her. In under a minute she was parking in front of a plaza with a convenience store, a dentist's office, and a few other shops. She found an unlocked blue Honda Civic in seconds and had it running by the time Quarrel was in the passenger seat.

Five minutes later, they were just another car in the morning commute.

Quarrel's cell phone rang. Swift shot him an angry look. "You should have ditched that."

Quarrel checked the display. "It's Milton."

Swift pushed the button to lower the passenger's side window. Quarrel stared at the phone, considered that Harry Milton was either trying to kill him or to save him, and chose to throw the phone out the window. He heard it shatter on the road.

"We're on our own now," he said as he rolled his window closed. "At least until we know who's trying to kill us."

"No we're not," she said confidently, "we just have to get back to Khalid. We have to get back to Europe."

27

Quarrel and Swift drove out of Virginia and into the city of Washington, D.C. The little blue Honda hadn't attracted any attention, but they both knew they weren't out of danger. Neither of them needed to say it, but they could still be followed. They didn't know who sent the strike team to Smith's apartment, but it was either a team sent by "Digamma" or a CIB team that could have answered to either Boswell or Milton. If Milton was against them, then the full resources of CIB, including satellite tracking, would be deployed to hunt them down. And if their attackers had been sent courtesy of Mercier, there was no telling how much power "Digamma" did or didn't have.

"We'll head downtown. Park indoors. Walk indoors. Change what colours we're wearing before we head outside again." Swift was talking, but Quarrel wasn't sure if she was talking to him or just repeating her training. She stopped to take a breath. "I just don't know where we're going to go now."

Entering the city, Quarrel snapped his fingers and sat up. "I know where."

An hour later, they stood in the entrance of a four-storey, red brick building on Q Street. Quarrel scanned the list of names next to the door, smiled, and pressed the buzzer.

"Where are we?" Swift inquired.

"Edwin Brown's apartment."

"Who's Edwin Brown?"

"Don't know. Never met him." Quarrel cleared his throat. "Well, technically he doesn't exist." There was no answer from the apartment. " . . . Which is why he's not home. Pick the lock, OK?"

They rode up to the third floor and found Mr. Brown's apartment, where Swift once again worked her magic on the locks so they could slip inside. There was a staleness to the air, dusty and very dry. Mr. Brown hadn't been home in weeks, and the windows hadn't been open in months.

"So how'd you pull this place out of your ass?" Swift asked.

"My job in Canada was paying the rent on this place. It's one of three apartments our man in Washington used. I wasn't sure whether he'd be here. Figured after my office got blown up, the agents would either switch over to CSIS or just fade away. Still not sure either way, but at least he's not here. If I had to introduce myself, and explain our situation, I might not have been sure what to say."

Quarrel dropped the yellow-covered book and Crowe's digamma file on the table. Swift sat down, looked for an instant like she was going to start reading, then she slumped back into her chair and sighed. The tension and adrenaline of their morning was finally draining away, leaving her sleepy. She yawned and stretched, looking almost feline, before turning back to Quarrel to ask, "So can you read the book cipher?"

"Yeah. It'll just take a little while to do it."

Quarrel opened a few of Mr. Brown's cupboards, looking for anything they could use. Whoever Mr. Brown was, he had a telltale Canadian love of rye whiskey. He had several varieties. Quarrel grabbed a bottle.

"Drink?"

Swift shook her head, trying to look nonchalant, but Quarrel saw the way her hands tightened into fists. "I don't drink."

"The Academy's rules?"

"Mine."

"Why?" he asked, deciding to put the bottle away and not drink in front of her.

She realized she was clenching fists and shook her hands loose. "It's one thing in my life I actually control."

#

Swift finally gave in to sleep. She had been awake for almost two days and she was unconscious the moment she settled into Edwin Brown's bed. While she slept, Quarrel decided to play back the video to get a better look at Digamma. If Crowe's theory was right, the reason no photos of Mercier existed was because the members of the Digamma conspiracy had deliberately erased him. That meant Quarrel had nothing to compare him to, to ensure that Digamma really was Mercier. The voice had no trace of a French accent, but then again Mercier had stopped being French decades earlier.

Quarrel hooked up the camera to Brown's flatscreen TV and started playback. When the Lincoln pulled up, Swift had done a perfect job of aiming the camera at the passenger side of the car, so Quarrel could watch Digamma climb out. He had short, neatly combed hair and a perfectly tailored blue suit. He was obviously very wealthy and looked about the right age to be Mercier. Quarrel hadn't bothered to sync up the audio to the video, so he was watching in silence now, as Digamma smiled and made chit-chat with Crowe.

253

Quarrel felt sick to his stomach watching it, knowing that those opening statements by Mercier had actually been a test, one that Crowe had failed. Quarrel paused it before the sniper took his shot at Crowe. He stared at the paused image, captured in HD through a great zoom lens, studying the man called Digamma.

And realized that Digamma looked familiar. Quarrel had seen that face before. It took a moment to scan his memory to figure out where he was getting this feeling of déjà vu, but then Quarrel figure it out. The last time he'd been spying through windows. But that was too big to even think about. He had to turn on Brown's computer and do a quick internet search to be sure. Had to see a photo to confirm his gut feeling. Once he saw the photo, there was no doubt.

He had spent an evening with Thorpe, spying in the windows of Globection's head office. Watching for any sign of Fatale in the CEO's office. They hadn't seen her that night, but they saw plenty of the CEO. Hugo Zoeli, the President's golf buddy; the nation's second-largest military contractor. Quarrel opened a recent photo of Zoeli on the computer, and turned back to face the TV.

Martin Mercier hadn't just disappeared twenty years ago. He hadn't just erased his old identity. He had started a new life, a telecommunications company that had grown quickly and expanded into weapons and mercenaries. Martin Mercier, Digamma, the linchpin of whatever was happening, had become Hugo Zoeli.

Zoeli had an army of private military contractors. He had UAVs, satellites, and a mole in CIB. Chris Quarrel was up against the most powerful unelected man in the country. He decided he needed that drink after all.

#

It made no sense to call the CIB. Someone from that office had set up the trap that Mercier had sprung. Someone, likely to be either Milton or Boswell, was trying to get Quarrel killed. Calling them meant risking that they could track his location. But he had to tell them. There were still good people in CIB. People Quarrel knew wanted to do the right thing and stop whatever catastrophe Mercier was orchestrating. They deserved to know just who and what they were up against. He turned on Brown's computer, attached the camcorder to it, and called Milton using a voice over internet service.

"Where are you?" he shouted as a greeting when Quarrel's call finally made it through.

"I'm in hiding. Now, we're going to do this as a video call and I want to see that there are several agents in the room."

"Why should I do that?" Milton demanded.

"Because I want to know that other people will hear this. If you don't put me on speaker, I'm sure Hinkston at the CIA would love to know what I've got."

Milton swore and went away. While Milton was distant, Quarrel switched to a video call and set the camera on a shelf, pointed at himself. He was careful not to show any windows, since they would betray his location. After a while, the monitor lit up with a video image of several people standing in the large "command centre" at CIB, the room where Milton barked orders. There was Gig, the gun guy; Meg, the mad scientist; Kilo, the computer tech; as well as an assortment of people who identified themselves as analysts or guards. Quarrel thought they must have wired him through a laptop webcam, since they all looked below frame as they talked to him.

"So what was so important?" Milton asked.

"I just met Matthew Crowe. And Martin Mercier."

"Crowe's alive? And with Mercier?"

Quarrel ignored that. "Twenty years ago, a man called Digamma paid top agents at the CIA, KGB and MI-6 to erase him. They removed his files, his photos, his fingerprints. They let him start a new life. That's why Martin Mercier disappeared so long ago. He became a new man."

"Thorpe came to America because someone matched his prints. So your case falls apart," said Milton. "You're wasting my time."

"The Brits still had his prints because the mole at MI-6 screwed up. That's why they found his prints when they recovered stolen documents from Globection. But they never realized why his prints were on it: Martin Mercier is Hugo Zoeli."

A few of the analysts behind Milton gasped.

"That's absurd. There's no way a man like that could—" Milton started.

"Hugo Zoeli is an Italian citizen and after the Digamma plot, nobody had his records on file. The only things we know about Hugo are the things his false papers tell us."

"OK, we'll look into Zoeli," said Milton. "But where the hell did you go this morning?"

Quarrel told them all the story of the morning's events. Smith's betrayal, Crowe's theft of the Smith identity, the meeting at the parking garage, everything. By the time he was done, several of the analysts were talking to each other, shaking their heads in confusion.

Milton was turning to face some other agents, no doubt ordering them to steal the parking garage investigation from the local police. When he turned back to the screen, he said, "Anything else, Mr. Quarrel?"

Quarrel leaned in toward the camera. He was pissed off and he wanted everyone listening to know it. "Someone tried to kill me today. Someone who knew where I was this morning. Someone at CIB. My money's on either you or Boswell, so where is she?"

"She left after you ran off with her suspect."

"Thorpe?" he asked, knowing that Thorpe had been interrogating Fatale that morning.

"He ran off with your suspect."

"Fatale?"

"He told me she would set up a meeting with Mercier. I guess we'll see how that goes now, huh?"

Quarrel tapped the keyboard and ended the video call. He pulled the other phone from his pocket; the cheap disposable phone he used to keep in touch with Thorpe. He dialed Thorpe's number, since he didn't keep anything programmed into the phone's memory, and waited. After eight rings, there was no answer. He hung up and tried again, making sure he was dialing each number correctly. There was still no answer.

Thorpe was gone, most likely to the same sort of meeting Matthew Crowe had just walked into, and Fatale was leading him right into it. If it went anything like Crowe's meeting, Thorpe was doomed.

28

After Quarrel and Swift had run off in the early hours of the morning, leaving Boswell to scream at Milton, William Thorpe had plenty of time alone with Fatale. Under the effects of the truth agent, she was very cooperative, and Thorpe learned so many things. He learned about her boss, Martin Mercier; he learned about how Mercier had been hiding out in South America for years; he learned about how Mercier trained people to be assassins and double-agents for profit. She gave him everything he would need for MI-7 to give him permission to kill Mercier, and all he needed now was to actually find the bastard.

All of the other players in Quarrel's big meeting the other day had been caught up catching a leak at CIB and in pointing fingers at each other. None of that mattered to Thorpe. He had been in the espionage game long enough to realize that there would always be leaks, doubles, and traitors, and when they were revealed, Thorpe would hunt them down. But until then, he had a score to settle with Martin Mercier.

The other agents were so concerned with leaks and stolen computers and other distractions that they didn't realize how monumental it was for Mercier's fingerprints to show up again. They didn't realize that Mercier, active in the espionage world, was more dangerous than some anonymous group called Digamma. It didn't matter to the others that years ago, when he was known simply as The Whisper, Mercier had been the best freelance assassin in Europe.

It didn't matter to the others that when The Whisper killed an American general in 1986, the CIA stopped giving him work, and so The Whisper started working almost exclusively for the KGB. It didn't matter that after the fall of the USSR, Thorpe's investigation proved that The Whisper was a French national named Martin Mercier, or that Mercier had tried to kill Thorpe.

It didn't matter to them that The Whisper had fired a long-range sniper rifle at Thorpe, who was on his honeymoon in Jamaica.

It didn't matter that the bullet missed Thorpe by inches and hit Julia in the head.

It didn't matter that Thorpe's wife's brain took so much damage she would never walk or speak or take care of herself again.

It mattered to Thorpe.

And Thorpe was ready for a fight.

The other agents at Chris Quarrel's meeting had been concerned with chasing each other, but doing so only ignored the bigger issue. They didn't know where the leak started, but they did know where it ended: an assassin killing Matthew Crowe, inside a well-guarded embassy, during a party. If anyone could do that, it was Mercier. Thorpe was the only one on the case who realized that it would be easier to track the leak from that end: start with Mercier and work back to the mole. Thorpe worked alone anyway, so it was easy to stay away from the others and set out to solve this thing without them.

He wanted to be at the heart of this thing; he wanted to be the man who brought Mercier down. When it was clear that Mercier was involved with this Digamma group, that he was The Whisper, and when MI-7 had their proof, Thorpe could finally have his revenge. Sometimes over the years, Thorpe had wondered if he only kept the license to kill so he could use it on Mercier. Now, he'd have the chance.

Thorpe thought it was somewhat ironic that it was Quarrel who had helped him stick to this path. Because while Quarrel was off chasing phantom intelligence and duplicitous agents, he was ignoring the biggest piece of evidence in the whole plot: Erica Gibbons.

Fatale was a mysterious figure, much like The Whisper had been. Barely photographed, hard to pin down. But Thorpe knew human nature, and anyone who risked their cover to ask about a former lover had a soft spot, and soft spots were useful. It only took a few hours of pointed, drug-induced interrogation, with none of the torture that you so often heard about in American black sites such as CIB. She had given him the schedule that her interactions with Mercier went by, which suggested he would call her this morning. So he made sure her phone would still receive calls deep down inside the CIB, and they waited. Sure enough, at a little before noon, the phone rang. Thorpe was listening in through a connection they attached to the phone, and he knew Mercier's voice immediately even though he hadn't heard it in over twenty years. Mercier was calling to find out what happened when Fatale went to Quarrel's hotel. She lied, wonderfully, and told Mercier that Jessica Swift had saved Quarrel's life, and that Fatale had been forced to run away. She also added, with her eyes staring bitterly at the British agent, that "Thorpe was even easier to take down than you said. I just wish I had killed him."

Thorpe ignored that and tapped his watch. Fatale nodded to say she understood and told Mercier she needed to see him in person to hand over some files she had stolen from Quarrel. Mercier told her he would find a quiet spot to meet and let her know. He called back several hours later and gave the address where he wanted to meet, and a quick check showed that this was an abandoned farm a little north of Baltimore.

While Milton ran around screaming about his investigation, about Quarrel and Swift and something about Jack Hall and the Pentagon, Thorpe was busy going over his plan with Fatale. She would be the bait to lure Mercier into the open. Then Thorpe would swoop in to take Mercier down, alive if possible. Thorpe wanted to squeeze Mercier for information before he killed him. He wanted Mercier to know that it was William Thorpe who killed him. And when the time came, Thorpe would kill Mercier in the only appropriate way: with a bullet to the brain.

Thorpe managed to convince Milton to let him take Fatale out of CIB, in order to lure Mercier into a trap. Milton didn't trust anyone, so he had forced Thorpe to take three tactical agents with him. They were former Marines, good in a fight but likely to get in the way if Thorpe needed to bend the rules at any point.

Fatale drove a silver SUV the CIB provided for her, with two of the agents in the back seat. Thorpe had stressed repeatedly that if Fatale ever needed them to duck down and get out of sight, they were to do so. He didn't trust them to listen.

Thorpe followed in a red Porsche Cayman, customized by MI-7 to suit Thorpe's needs. It wasn't subtle, but it was fast. He hoped he wouldn't need to use the car's speed, or any of MI-7's little treats for that matter. They drove out of Virginia and into Maryland without incident.

Fatale pulled into the lot of an abandoned farm, circling the turn-around and putting the SUV in park. Thorpe pulled in after her and was relieved to note that he couldn't see the agents in the back seat. He drove into the old barn, pulled out of sight, and turned off the Porsche. Milton's third agent, a big guy called Brannock, looked over from the passenger seat.

"I'm gonna get out and set up upstairs. I saw a window," Brannock said.

"Fine, stay out of sight. And if you have to fire, shoot for the knee. I want this guy alive," said Thorpe. Brannock nodded and climbed out of the car.

Once the hulking agent was gone, Thorpe turned up his earpiece. "It's your show, Ms. Gibbons."

The woman's voice was calm and silky in the earpiece. "Five minutes, he'll show."

Thorpe spoke again, "Agents Charles and Fengen, are you are out of sight?" he asked in a mocking voice, like the stern old English schoolteacher. He expected a chuckle, or an annoyed swear, but got no answer.

"Agents, report."

Static.

"Fatale, what the hell is—"

Her voice was still calm and smooth. "Sorry, Billy-boy, your friends didn't make it."

"God dam—"

"They're still in the car, but I don't think they can talk right now. Or ever." She laughed a little.

Thorpe fired up the Porsche, the engine roaring to life. "Brannock!" he shouted.

Brannock, watching the road from his heightened vantage point, shouted through the earpiece. "We've got cars coming from both directions. Jesus, I'm picking up men on my thermals—"

Brannock's body fell from the loft, crunching against the concrete behind Thorpe's car.

"Sorry, Billy," Fatale teased over the earpiece, "the only one getting taken alive today is you. Your old friend Sidorov would like to finish what he started. What was it? Tarred and feathered?"

A hulking SUV pulled into the barn behind Thorpe, blocking the way he had entered. It was black, not Fatale's silver, so whatever backup she had managed to call in was already here. There was no other way out of the barn.

The doors opened and a team of men in black body armour climbed out, raising machine guns. Thorpe could tell in a glance that they were professional killers. Before they could get far from the SUV, Thorpe flicked open a panel on the dash and accessed the weapon controls. A heads-up display projected on the touch-screen control panel, which Thorpe aimed by dragging a finger. Then he fired.

A rocket launched out of the rear left turn signal light, impacting the black SUV and blowing the whole hitman crew straight to hell. Thorpe launched another rocket, this time through the front left headlight, and blasted a hole in the barn in front of him. He stomped on the gas and the Porsche roared outside. He was circling back to the road as soon as his tires touched the field.

"Where are you going?" Fatale taunted over the earpiece. "You think I only had one truck full of guys?"

Thorpe's Cayman raced past her silver SUV and fishtailed onto the paved country road. Another black SUV tried to turn sideways to block him, but Thorpe's car was too fast, and he only had to pull half-way onto the shoulder to avoid it. Now the SUV was only blocking Fatale's vehicle from the pursuit. He could hear her swearing in his ear.

As he rounded a corner, Thorpe hit the button to release a series of caltrops from the back bumper. A few seconds later he watched in his rear-view mirror as Fatale's silver SUV popped its tires on the multi-pointed metal spikes and slid off the road, and then the black SUV followed, ramming into Fatale's truck from behind. He saw fatale's door open, knew that he had the advantage back again, and did a quick one-eighty.

Roaring back toward the crashed SUVs, he saw Fatale dive for the gutter just as he launched the front right rocket, which blasted the black truck. The explosion also devastated Fatale's CIB-issue silver truck.

He pulled to a stop and immediately Fatale popped up, a gun in hand, and fired a shot at Thorpe's driver's side window. The bulletproof glass stopped it.

"Fine bit of acting you did," he told her through the headset.

"It's amazing what people will tell you if they think you're under a truth agent. All I had to do was agree with your questions and you told me so much." She smiled at him through the window. "I don't meet with Mercier. I do, however, have standing plans to get busted out of custody should I ever need a hand. You were so kind to help out."

Thorpe sighed, knowing that the shred of hope he had for getting to take down Mercier today was fading. At least he could take Fatale back to CIB. "Drop the gun and surrender. This car still has machine guns and you can't kill me from out there. Your little game didn't work."

"Sure it did. We killed Milton's men and you got me out of CIB."

"And now I'm taking you back in."

He heard a cell phone ring and watched Fatale calmly tuck the gun away and answer a phone he had never seen before from her front pocket. Where the hell had she gotten that phone?

She walked right up to the side of the Porsche, and held out the phone toward his window. He was tired of her games.

"Toss the phone, lie on the ground, and surrender," he ordered.

"You don't want me throw this phone, William." She said with a malicious look on her face.

"Why? Will it explode?"

"No, silly. It's for you."

"Tell Martin we'll talk sooner than he thinks. I know that was his voice on the line this morning, and I will bring him down."

"It's not Mercier," she said, giving the phone a little shake. She took a few steps toward the car, until she was actually tapping the phone against the bulletproof window. "You should have left me alone. Gone after that mole that my old friend Chris is looking for."

"Your friend Chris thinks you blew up his building. You're going down for terrorism."

"Maybe. After you take this call, you won't be so sure."

"You must be joking."

"It's just a phone, William. You don't even have to hold it. Just take a look at the screen." She pressed it against the glass. Thorpe didn't want to give in and look, knowing it was a trap. He expected that the screen would likely flash a blinding light the moment he looked, but even if it did, he also felt very secure in the MI-7-issued car.

She grinned. "It's a video call from Jolly Old England."

Finally, Thorpe gave in and looked down to the screen, and his heart almost stopped. The screen showed a shaky image. "It's Saint Michael's, William. It's your wife."

He couldn't ignore it now, his eyes reflexively focused on the screen. And there she was, lying in bed, her eyes open and teary, as someone recorded her. She had bruises on her face. Her lip was swelling. She was helpless, barely able to move on her own, completely unable to cry out, and someone had come to the room where she slept and beaten her. Thorpe felt all his control, his composure, all the walls he built around himself and dared to call "Triple-Eight," breaking inside himself. His hands shook and he gripped the steering wheel so hard he thought he'd break it off.

They had Julia. The bastards had Julia.

"I told you, you should have left me alone," said the smirking Fatale. "If you'd just gone after the mole like Quarrel wanted, well then maybe the mole wouldn't still be free to beat the piss out of old Missus Thorpe. But you had to have me. You had to have Mercier." She was trying to open the door now, but it was locked.

"Well now we've got you, instead of CIB having me. And unless you want someone to finish the job on the old lady, you're working for us now."

Tears gliding down his cheeks, Thorpe opened the car door. "OK. I surrender." He held out his pistol for Fatale to take. She was still smirking.

"Get in the other seat, William," she said. "I'm driving now."

#

Thorpe needed a drink so bad he was practically shaking. The woman, Erica or Fatale or whatever she called herself, was strutting around with such arrogance that Thorpe fought to suppress the urge to slap her. He resented that she hadn't even bothered to tie him down, so instead of fighting against bonds he had only to fight his own rage, to swallow his frustration.

There were two other men, posted on either side of the open garage door. The hanger was mostly empty except for the chair Thorpe sat in, a folding table, and a few boxes that sat on the table. One of the men was holding a video camera that was connected to a laptop computer that sat on the floor next to him. They were transmitting video of Thorpe's capture to someone, probably Martin Mercier.

Fatale's cellphone beeped. She answered, listened for a second, and hung up. After capturing Thorpe, she had changed into a black dress, styled her hair, and applied makeup. She had changed from a defeated prisoner into a domineering femme fatale, and every facial expression she made drove Thorpe further into his rage because there was no denying that she was in charge now.

"Let's put on a show," she purred through her bright red lips.

267

She strutted over to the table, opened a box, and pulled out a white shirt and a black dinner jacket.

"You'll wear these. I'm sure you'll notice that one of the buttons on the shirt is a microphone and one of the buttons on the jacket is a camera. If you tamper with either the sound or the picture—"

"I know, I know," Thorpe interrupted.

She sneered at him, ran her tongue over her upper lip, and continued her speech. "If you tamper with either the sound or the picture, my associate in England will cut your wife's left arm off and cauterize the wound with a blowtorch. And don't interrupt me again, or I'll tell them to give old Julia some free dental work." Fatale paused, tilted her head as if thinking deep thoughts, and taunted him. "You think she would even feel it if they did? From I understand, you married a brain-dead vegetable."

Thorpe balled up his fists so tight his arms shook. His voice cracked when he spoke. "She feels everything. She feels every little thing you do to her. Don't you feel the slightest guilt for abusing and taking advantage of a defenceless woman?"

Fatale brought the shirt over and laid it in his lap. Her fingers found the top button on the shirt Thorpe was wearing, and started to strip him. "Oh, I've been taking advantage of defenceless men for so long, this is just a change of pace."

She got him changed into the new shirt and jacket, and the men watched him while she went to her new car—a black BMW that had been waiting inside the hanger but was now parked outside—to check the feeds from the camera and microphone. "Get him to say something!" she yelled.

268

"When this is over, I'm going to bury your head and leave your body for the birds." He spoke in a voice that tried to sound defiant, but only betrayed how afraid he was.

"Excellent! Coming in loud and clear!" she called from outside.

She walked back slowly, taking her time. It was clear that Fatale was enjoying her momentary triumph over Thorpe. No doubt she had strutted like this after she left him in a room with a dead body and the police on their way, but that trap hadn't worked. Nor had her attack at Quarrel's hotel. Thorpe tried to convince himself that this trap wouldn't work either, but for the first time in decades, his confidence was gone.

They had his wife, on another continent, a world away. It would take him at least nine hours to reach her, whereas they could send the order to kill Julia in an instant.

"So I'm a walking camera crew. Who am I to spy on?"

"We'll get to that. But first you're going to call Harry Milton and give him a message."

"And what's that?"

She smiled. "You're going to call in a team to arrest Jack Hall."

"Arrest Jack? Nobody can even find him."

She pulled out a satellite phone and started dialing. "Oh that's easy. He's in Carolina committing treason."

PART FOUR:
WE HAVE WAYS
OF MAKING YOU TALK

29

Jack Hall didn't reach the facility until the late afternoon. He had spent the day driving here, which on its own was a six-hour journey, but he also took pains to avoid major highways or anywhere that he might be seen by a security camera. Breaking into the Pentagon files would bring a half-dozen federal and military agencies after him, so he had to be careful. Once he found some proof of what was going on, once he caught the terrorists who were going after the nuclear materials, he would let the authorities know. And one thing he was sure about was that once they knew where he was, they'd come running.

He had a line on CIA chatter, thanks to his old pals from the Navy who were working on some other high-clearance-level jobs and who still trusted that Jack was acting in the country's best interest. According to the chatter, the word was out that Jack was snooping into nuclear secrets, that Jack was the leak who had caused the attack on the convoy. He didn't much care. If they send extra guards to watch the bombs being decommissioned and to escort the materials off-site, all the better. More security was more security, no matter the reason. That was all that mattered.

He parked a mile away from the secure location that he had discovered in the Pentagon's files, and hiked in from there. The facility was in the middle of nowhere, North Carolina, surrounded by forest. There was only one road in, which came in from the county road to the east. Jack parked on a road to the north and hiked through the woods.

The nuclear storage site was a fairly boring place. A chain-link fence surrounded the building, which looked like it was a cheap steel-walled warehouse or a sort of square Quonset hut. The facility's cover story was that it was a factory space for an artist who made large metal sculptures. The artist actually did work there, recycling old steel into metal absurdities for towns that wanted abstract statues, but beneath the floor there was a repository for retired nuclear weapons. Whether they were being dismantled or just shelved, Hall didn't know.

There were no soldiers patrolling the outside of the building, but the security cameras were obvious. Somewhere inside the steel building were highly-trained guards, and they were watching those cameras. There may have been cameras in the trees as well, but Hall would never spot them if they existed, and the fact that he had made it so close told him he hadn't been noticed; if they had seen him coming, he'd have been attacked or arrested by now. A helicopter sounded in the distance, but Jack knew not to be paranoid. The helo would pass.

There was a glint of light to Jack's left. Just one little flash as something shiny moved in the distant trees. Someone was out there.

Hall moved straight toward the target, never quite breaking out into a run. When he reached the area where the flash had come from, Jack spotted a small black

271

duffel bag resting next to a tree trunk. He studied the area carefully. There was no sign of another person, and the ground looked free of traps. He ran to the bag and opened it.

There was a black nylon rope on top. Below that, wire cutters, pliers, screwdrivers. There were two Sig pistols and six spare clips, as well as a small black packet of various tools and useful gadgets. He recognized that package. This was his own gear.

Suddenly Jack realized that the helicopter in the air still hadn't passed, but was hovering or landing somewhere nearby. He turned to read the horizon and saw a group of soldiers in camouflage body armour approaching with their rifles aimed straight at him. Turning to face the north, where he had come from, he saw a second squad. They had circled behind him to spring the trap. Unless he wanted to kill American soldiers, he was caught.

Jack was searched, disarmed, had his hands cuffed in front of his body in order to have them visible in the car, and had shackles locked to his ankles. Once he was fully prepared for the road, Hall was loaded into the back of a Hummer. Agents got in the back on either side of him, one Caucasian and one Asian, both men. Another agent drove, and the passenger seat was empty. They drove between two other vehicles—a Jeep in front and a Mercedes sedan behind. All three were different colours; the Jeep was black, Hummer green, and the Mercedes was silver. It was less conspicuous that way, as opposed to the mythical black SUVs that people seemed to think the CIA used for everything.

Jack asked just one question, "Who set me up?"

He got the response he expected, which was silence.

"Call the President," he said. "The President trusts me. He owes me one. You're arresting the wrong man. Whoever called in my location is the one who planted that packsack full of my gear." Jack knew he sounded crazy now. His excuses were flimsy, his evidence non-existent. Someone had known he would try to stop the theft of nuclear materials from this site, and they had known exactly when to plant the incriminating evidence. Digamma, whatever they were, were good.

The agents said nothing, and their faces revealed less. If they were from the government, they were a top CIA extraction team; if they were soldiers from the storage site, they were probably among the best of the best. Hall could risk taking them on, but with his handcuffs chained to his ankle shackles, he'd have narrow odds of winning the fight. Twenty years earlier, or even ten, he'd have been foolish enough to try it anyway, and strong enough to survive. But Jack Hall was in his fifties now, and he wasn't likely to defeat three armed men while shackled and surrounded. Still, the itch was there. The nagging feeling at the base of his skull that told him You don't have time for this. Do something. It was a feeling he hated, but rarely ignored. He swallowed hard and tried to push the feeling out of his thoughts.

After about twenty minutes of riding in tense silence, the three vehicles pulled onto interstate 85 going east. It was past dinnertime on a weekday so the traffic wasn't bad. The convoy picked up speed and Hall leaned

273

back in the seat and let out a sigh through his nose. It was a deliberate test to see how the agents would respond. The one on his right, a short white guy with a crewcut, responded to Hall's sigh by letting his guard down. His eyes looked out the side window and his shoulders slumped a little. For that instant, he wasn't on edge, and wasn't protecting his weapon.

It was enough.

Hall threw his body up and to the right, whipping his head sideways at the short man. His headbutt snapped the agent's nose to the side. That kind of jolting pain would flood his eyes with tears and distract him. As the agent screamed, Hall was already grabbing the gun from the agent's shoulder holster. A small Sig.

Sensing the other soldier, the Asian man, going for his own weapon, Hall pulled his feet up, leaning his whole weight on the short man, and kicked at the Asian guy with both feet. The chain between his shackles took the Asian in the front teeth, breaking them. Without hesitation, Hall raked the chain down the man's chin to the hand at his chest. When the chain hit his knuckles, the agent dropped his gun, which clattered the floor between his feet.

"Don't you dare reach!" screamed Hall, who now had the short man's sidearm aimed at the Asian man's bloody face. "Hands on your knees! Lean your head toward me."

The agent slowly complied, tilting his head toward Hall. Hall raised the gun and hammed it down, cracking the top of the agent's head and knocking him out cold. That was where Hall had made his mistake. Because he had leaned over, the Asian man's body had nowhere to go but straight down into Hall's lap. That was enough of a burden and distraction that the short man was able to get his hands around Hall's throat. The agent was cutting off his air, but so far he hadn't cinched the choke hold enough to cut off the arteries and knock Hall unconscious. He didn't want to kill any of these guys, but as the panic of choking started to take over, he raised the gun, angling it backward at the short man.

The black Jeep at the front of the convoy exploded.

The green Hummer hit the wreckage at full speed.

For a second Hall felt that he was free from the short guy's choke hold, and for another moment he was weightless.

Then there was just pain.

Hall had crashed cars before, but generally he was in the driver's seat, hitting an airbag. This time he was in the back, laid out across the seat and entangled with two other men. When the hummer rolled—and he couldn't count how many times it rolled—Hall was bombarded with impacts from every direction. The Asian man's head and arms pummelled his torso. The short man's arms cracked against Hall's skull. The roof of the Hummer hit him like a wrecking ball.

When it was over, Hall had lost the gun. His wrists and ankles were bleeding where the steel restraints had dug into him. He was pretty sure he had a broken rib, and his head was incredibly heavy. The whole right side of his head felt like it expanded to double size, and his ears were ringing so loud that no other sound could be heard. He freed himself from the other men's bodies and felt for the window. He felt only air, crawled forward with his hand outstretched, and the feeling of empty air continued for a distance that seemed too far, as if he

275

should have found the Hummer's door already. He had to make an effort to lift his head to look, since just tilting it upward sent jolts of pain through his whole body. His hand was sticking out through the hole where the window had been. Shaking off cobwebs, he felt along the bottom of the window frame for a door handle and couldn't find it. It took a moment to realize that in an upside-down car the handle would be above the window, not below. He was vaguely, distantly aware that he was thinking too slowly, his mind not understanding what his eyes were showing him. In a very dreamlike way, he knew that his brain wasn't working right.

Crawling out, he was surprised that the Hummer was still on the pavement. In the roll he was sure they must have gone off the side and down the embankment. The team from the silver Mercedes were hiding behind their car, popping out occasionally to return fire at whoever were inside a maroon plumbing van parked two car-lengths away. Unable to hear anything and with blurry vision, Hall didn't realize the implications of the flashing light coming from the van's windows. The windows were a constant flash of muzzle flare from a machine gun, but Jack just stared at it, trying to figure out why the van was flickering like that. Once he clued into the fact that the van was full of enemies who had attacked the convoy, and that someone was attacking the CIA team, his instinct was to crawl toward the silver Mercedes and join the fight. He struggled to crawl, pain flashing though his numbness with each movement, and saw a flicker of recognition from the nearest member of the Mercedes team when they saw him coming.

Then the plumbing van moved, cutting him off from the Mercedes. The side door slid open and two men in black ski masks jumped out to pick him up and pull him into the van. Once he was in, the van took off. He saw the thick barrel of an RPG launcher sticking out from under the seat and understood what had blown up the Jeep.

Someone stuck a needle in Hall's arm. The stinging made him turn to look, and there he saw a familiar-looking man with a face that was half-melted. Of course it was him. Who else could lead an attack against a CIA kill team and win so easily?

"You've always been a traitor . . ." he managed to say, still trying to focus his eyes on his captor.

"Go to sleep, Jack," the man said in that gruff, familiar voice.

#

Jack woke up in a bed, shirtless, his head and ribs bandaged. He was tied to the bedposts at hands and ankles, although the captors had been kind enough to wrap gauze around those areas before they tied him up.

"Hello?" he called out, grateful that he could still hear.

His voice triggered the sound of movement and a man stood up from a chair in the corner. He was a big man, muscular and square-jawed, but his grey hair and deep wrinkles showed his age. Jack was familiar with him, having chased him around the Mediterranean for most of the nineties. Anton Sidorov. Former KGB, but since the fall of the USSR he was extending his talents in all manner of illegal trades. Killer for hire. Drug smuggler. Some informants called him the king of the Russian underground, others said he was just a trained dog whom

277

the real shot-callers turned to when times were tough. Either way, Jack hadn't wanted his first face-to-face to happen like this.

"Sidorov."

"Jack Hall." Sidorov smirked. "It's insulting to meet an adversary like you under such circumstances, but sometimes these games are necessary."

"Games?"

"Distraction. Misdirection. You were arrested for treason, Jack. But you broke out of custody. Cameras in the truck saw you fight the guards just before the kill squad came to free you. Lots of dead Americans, Jack."

Then there was the gruff voice again, the hard, hateful American who had killed the CIA team on the highway and stuck a needle in Jack's arm. He stood in the doorway, smoking a cigar and squinting at Jack.

"It's your turn to be public enemy number one now, Jack," said Shark Scarret. "Let's see how you like it."

30

Chris Quarrel was lingering at a railing, looking down at one of the best looking rooms in Washington. The reading room in the Library of Congress, with tables proportioned to form concentric rings inside the round room, was something Quarrel hadn't expected to be so impressed by. It was simultaneously historic and modern, busy but not crowded. It felt like a building that was important both historically and right now. And Quarrel was waiting for the CIA to escort him to a private room to show off some documents that were definitely not housed here.

After he had been unable to call Thorpe and warn him that Fatale was tricking him, Quarrel had called the number from Hinkston's business card. The card only listed the name "Hinkston" and a phone number, and Quarrel felt foolish that he didn't even know the guy's first name.

"Central Intelligence Agency," answered a pleasant-sounding woman.

"Director Hinkston, please."

"Authorization?"

"I don't have one. Just tell him it's Quarrel from Canada. Regarding a Ms. Reville."

"Hold the line, sir."

Quarrel waited for five minutes before the telephone clicked repeatedly. Quarrel was still standing in the kitchen of the CSIS-2 safe house belonging to Edwin Brown, while Swift slept in the bedroom with the door open. Finally, Hinkston's voice came on, sarcastic and angry. "Mr. Quarrel, so nice of you to think of me. I hear you killed a bunch of men in my back yard this morning."

"I don't know what you mean, but if a bunch of people were dead, would you be able to tell me who they were working for?"

"The guys you killed were Americans, actually. And don't play games with me when you shoot up an apartment down the highway from Langley."

"What?" Quarrel shouted, his voice a little too loud. Swift stirred in the bedroom. She walked into the kitchen, stretching and yawning. She opened up Mr. Brown's fridge. It was mostly empty, but there were a few unopened bottles of Gatorade, so she took one. She sat on the counter and sipped it, her eyes alert as she watched Quarrel cautiously.

Hinkston continued, and seemed to delight in layout the dangers that Quarrel faced. "They were Americans. Born here, trained here. Former Marines who went pro about six years back. We've seen their work before, mostly in South America. These are the guys the drug cartels use when their own soldiers can't get it done. Honestly, I'm surprised you got out alive. These guys don't mess around."

"They shot the other guy first. Gave me a chance to hide."

"Of course they did. After all, someone was impersonating Agent Smith. But you knew that, didn't you, Mr. Quarrel?"

Quarrel wondered if Hinkston could identify Matthew Crowe but chose to ignore that for now. "And who did they work for?"

"Anyone who pays the bills."

"So I still can't tell who to trust in this mess."

"Never trust, Mr. Quarrel. Only use people as long as you need them. And I hear you want to use my witness."

"My witness," Quarrel corrected, "she had some documents, they were some kind of blueprints or schematics. Per your request, I didn't make a copy for myself and now I need them back. I've got evidence of something big and I need to piece it together."

Hinkston's end of the conversation went totally silent, and Quarrel knew he'd been placed on hold. Hinkston was talking to someone else and didn't want Quarrel to hear. Swift knew it too and interjected.

"Who the hell are you talking to?" Quarrel waved her off as Hinkston came back on the line. "Sorry, Mr. Q, but the information on those pages was very sensitive. We're not in the business of handing out state secrets."

"Tell me about the array, Mr. Hinkston."

"Array?"

"That's what's on those plans, isn't it? Some kind of high-tech machine you guys cooked up. Funny how GX had that data on their server and how an international terrorist group is sending coded messages about it."

"Which group is that?"

"I'm not in the business of giving away my information for free, Mr. Hinkston. By the way, did you know GX is run by a KGB assassin?"

Hinkston blustered that he was "tired of games," but then the line went silent. Someone else had pushed the hold button and cut off Hinkston in mid-sentence. There was another silent wait where Quarrel could practically feel Swift's eyes poking him. Hinkston returned, sounding deflated. "OK, Quarrel, you have a deal. I'll show you mine if you show me yours. We'll meet tonight. You're calling from D.C. so how about we give you a nice tourist destination. Library of Congress, twenty-hundred hours. Got it?"

"Got it. And Mr. Hinkston?"

"Yes?"

"Do you have a first name?"

Hinkston hung up.

Quarrel had instructed Swift to use whatever resources she had available to plan a trip back to Zurich. She swore she could arrange passports, and other IDs, good enough to get them through an airport without Harry Milton or CIB knowing about it. While she went out to manage that, Quarrel came to the Library to see what Hinkston had to share.

His pocket vibrated. Quarrel had ditched the cell phone he usually carried; the one whose number he had given out to Milton and everyone involved in the investigation. But he had kept the second phone, the one only Thorpe knew about. It was a relief to finally hear from Thorpe, although it was worrying that he had been alone with Fatale for so long.

It was a text: I have photos of the traitor. Will deliver to you. Where?

Quarrel typed back: What happened with Fatale?

Thorpe: I will explain it all tonight. On my way to see Milton right now. Meet tonight?

Quarrel wondered if he could trust Thorpe, but remembered Hinkston's advice. OK. Meet me at Library of Congress, 1 hour.

Quarrel deleted the messages.

A man in a navy blue suit approached Quarrel. "Mr. Quarrel? Director Hinkston is waiting. I'll take that cell phone."

Quarrel didn't bother to ask Navy Blue's name. He was one of the CIA-types who wouldn't even bother to use an alias. He would just smirk and not respond, as if his name was an unpronounceable look of contempt. It was no wonder that Milton had trusted an impossible-to-read robot like Smith, considering how common such men were in various roles within the intelligence world. Guys who had maybe been military, or perhaps trained somewhere off-the-grid, who believed that showing an emotion—any emotion—would betray state secrets. Quarrel had once believed that Hershey would eventually become one of these drones, but the person who drove a fertilizer bomb into CSIS-2 had guaranteed that Hershey's career ended as a functionary in lower-middle-management.

God, Quarrel thought, I actually miss that brown-nosing asshole.

Quarrel allowed the navy blue spook to lead him down a hallway and into a private reading room where Hinkston's hulking figure waited, leaning over a small chestnut table. Quarrel was still impressed by the American's imposing size. For someone who seemed like a desk job type, Hinkston sure was huge. Once Quarrel was inside the room, Navy Blue nodded to his superior and left the room, closing and locking the door behind him. No doubt he would also block the wooden door with his impressive frame while Quarrel saw what he came to see.

"Where's my information?" Hinkston demanded without so much as a greeting.

283

Quarrel untucked his shirt and pulled the folder out of the back of his pants, where it had been resting against his back.

"How clever, Mr. Quarrel. If someone decided to chase you, you could have had my government's secrets falling out of your ass."

"The group is called Digamma. Archaic letter F. As in archaic number six. As in six people who once had a purpose, but now exist with no defined meaning or allegiance. There were six members in the early nineties, founded after the USSR fell. Two Americans, Two Ruskies, a Brit and a private interest. The group's founder, also called Digamma, was Martin Mercier."

"Who?"

"Exactly. He was an assassin. Ended up mostly aligned with KGB. This group got together to erase him from your files so he could slip away anonymously. The only people who even had his prints on file were the Brits."

Hinkston grabbed the folder from Quarrel with one of his massive gorilla hands and flipped through it so fast it was hard to believe he was reading anything. "Where did you get these? Most names are redacted. Not much information to be found in black sharpie marks."

"I got them from a dead American. Matt Crowe. He didn't die after all. Well, he's dead now . . . "

"In that parking garage." Hinkston paused, thinking of the right words to use in front of an unknown like Quarrel. "He was disguised as Smith. So Smith was the mole then?"

"Smith was the tip of the iceberg. Crowe was the one who finger-painted that symbol on the wall and he was the one who mailed it to my office in Ottawa, too.

Trying to start an investigation outside of England or the US. Hoping to shine a light on Mercier before any of the moles could stop him."

Hinkston closed the file, exhaled hard. He squinted at Quarrel, as if scanning him, sizing him up. "CIB's purview was specifically related to finding Crowe's killer. If he wasn't murdered in London, you have no right to see anything from me."

Quarrel didn't speak louder, but his voice took a harsher edge. "CIB's job was to find a mole. I haven't, yet. And I'm pretty damn sure that I got Senator Anderson killed when I kicked this thing into motion, so shut up and show me the array."

Hinkston looked at the screen on his phone and Quarrel wondered if it was possible a third party was listening in, guiding Hinkston's actions. After a moment's grumbling, Hinkston unrolled a blueprint on the large table. This was the same thing Quarrel had seen from Maggie, but while she only had letter-sized photocopies of sections of it, this blueprint had everything.

"So what the hell is it and what does Digamma want with it?"

"It's not so much an 'array' as a single unit. A number of emitters linked together, in order to multiply their effect."

"Emitters?"

"Microwaves. In the eighties there was a project to try and control the weather with a targeted microwave beam."

Quarrel knew that, but not from his spy experience. He had seen a special on TV about it: "HAARP. In Alaska. So this is it?"

"No. HAARP was fairly public. I mean, it is basically an acre full of big metal things pointed at the sky; pretty hard to hide. People know where it is, and we've barely even lied about what it was built for. To be blunt, it doesn't work and never has. The idea was that if you could heat water in the atmosphere in very specific locations, you could bounce the molecules together and make it rain. Cure drought. Or if an area was flooding you could make it rain somewhere nearby, spread the water over a large area to avoid flood damage."

"But it doesn't work?"

Hinkston shrugged. "Before my time. But as far as anyone at the CIA will tell me, this thing was a huge waste of money. DOD and DARPA took a run at weaponizing it, but the damn thing's in Alaska. Even if it did work, you'd only be able to hit the U.S., Canada, and the emptiest parts of Russia, and flooding Canada's not really in our mandate. Moot point anyway, since it doesn't do jack shit."

Quarrel tapped the paper. "But this blueprint isn't HAARP? This is something else?"

"Like I said, it's a very large grouping of microwave emitters. HAARP times ten. And built to be angled, targeted toward where we needed it. They call it TCPE. Targeted Charged Particle Emitter." Hinkston pronounced the acronym as "teacup". "I honestly don't know what kind of radiation or particles or whatever this thing was supposed to shoot out, but it all falls into the category of 'microwaves' as far as I know."

"And this thing was actually built? In the eighties?"

"Yeah. DARPA was stubborn about HAARP, so they built a bigger one. I guess they had something to prove."

Quarrel snapped his fingers, realization dawning. " . . . And if this thing was built expressly as a weapon, not just a scientific experiment, I'm betting that there were some safeguards in place, weren't there?"

Hinkston shrugged. "I'd assume so. But again, it's before my time."

"And if you were going to build a big-ass weapon in the eighties, you'd use the best safeguards you had. Nuclear safeguards. Nuclear bomb control computers."

"The shipment that got hijacked!" Hinkston said, eyes widening. "They didn't go for the fissionable materials. They didn't try to steal a nuke."

Quarrel nodded. "They only went for the computers."

"Because with one of those things, you could turn Teacup back on."

Hinkston pulled out his phone. "I'm putting a satellite over that place, right now. And I'm calling in a team. I want to lock this thing down. I want to own it."

Quarrel studied the blueprints. "So where is this thing?"

"Ask your government," Hinkston said, dialing. "It's in the Yukon."

Before Hinkston could even get someone on the line, Quarrel interrupted him. It was something he had meant to ask, and he wanted to get it out there before Hinkston ran off chasing teacups. "I need the rest of Maggie Reville's files."

"You said you wanted to see the array. You have."

"She didn't start out with this. She turned whistleblower when she saw some unusual billing practices. I want to see what got her so spooked."

"A very big company overcharged us. They all do it. Not exactly enough to charge the CEO of said company with high treason."

"It is when that CEO is Martin Mercier."

Hinkston's fingers stopped tapping the phone. "What?"

"After Digamma gave him a fresh identity, Mercier became Hugo Zoeli."

"You can prove that?"

"I watched him kill Matt Crowe this afternoon. And now I want to know what he's up to."

Quarrel had nothing left to say. He just held out his hand and waited for Hinkston. Hinkston hung up the call and tilted the screen and looked like he was waiting for something. After the cell phone gave him some kind of a message, Hinkston sighed, opened his briefcase and pulled out a small stack of photocopies.

"Keep them. Just invoices, really. A reporter with a freedom of information request could get those. But if you find something, I want to know."

Hinkston was about to dial his phone when it surprised him by ringing. "Hinkston," he said in lieu of a greeting. As he listened, his face turned red. "Jesus jumping Christ . . . you tell them to bring him to me, goddammit! Not to Milton. Bring him to Langley. To me!"

Hinkston was jerking the door open, waving at Navy Blue.

"What's happening?" Quarrel called.

Hinkston didn't really answer, he just shouted, "Jack goddamn Hall is a goddamn traitor."

As Hinkston and his muscular accomplice ran away, Quarrel muttered to himself. "I guess Thorpe really did have some interesting photos."

#

When Quarrel exited the historic building, William Thorpe was waiting. Thorpe was dressed in his typical dinner jacket, although this one didn't fit him quite as perfectly as his others. It must have been off-the-rack rather than custom tailored. As they descended the large grey staircase to street level, Thorpe handed Quarrel a large envelope.

"Photos. What of?"

"Your old pal Jack trying to steal nuclear components."

Considering that only a few minutes earlier, Quarrel and Hinkston had deduced that there wasn't a nuclear threat, it was a bit of a surprise. Combined with Thorpe miraculously returning from his trip with Fatale, Quarrel realized that he couldn't trust the old agent anymore.

"Really?" is all he could muster.

"Coffee. This way." Thorpe pointed and Quarrel followed. It was a warm spring night and Washington looked good for once. After the grey, slushy winter, it was nice to walk around outside again.

They ended up at a nearby café, sipping overpriced coffees. Quarrel took his time with each photo, soaking each one in. They looked unaltered, but Quarrel was no real expert. They clearly showed Jack Hall in some sort of a deal with a number of people Quarrel didn't recognize.

"So who are they?"

"Don't know. I took Fatale to see if she'd lead me to Mercier, but the bastard cancelled the meeting. Fatale guessed that Mercier must have been waiting for Hall, so we went to him instead. This is where she took me. I got the photos, called in CIB, and Hall was arrested. After that, I decided to head back to CIB and hand over my photos and give Milton a heads-up. Unfortunately, the story doesn't end there."

Quarrel wasn't sure where this was going, so he waited for Thorpe to continue.

"The team that arrested Jack put him in an armoured truck for transport back to a black site. The truck was hit before it could bring him back. Jack was rescued by a team of very efficient operators. They killed the whole CIB crew. I suppose I might have stopped him escaping, if I had been there, but I could just as likely have died in the crash, or been killed in the firefight."

Thorpe raised his coffee to his mouth, and Quarrel thought he saw a quiver in the British agent's hand. Thorpe saw Quarrel seeing it. "Bloody shakes. Been cutting back on the martinis."

"Oh." Quarrel found himself re-evaluating his trust in Thorpe. He was acting differently, suspiciously. "And Fatale?"

"She did right by me. It's not Mercier but it's close. I'm keeping her in a secure location of my own. Don't worry, I won't let her out. I know what she did to your office."

Quarrel was doing his best to keep his poker face, but nothing Thorpe said rang true. There was no way Fatale had ever set up a meeting with Mercier, when Hugo Zoeli was in that parking garage around the same time. Nor was it likely that Thorpe would leave a threat like Fatale alone in an unguarded room somewhere, considering her talent for disappearing.

"Milton already knew Jack was a bad egg." Thorpe said, "That Pentagon break-in proved it, and all those agents getting gunned down in the street proved it again. My photos only added fuel to the fire. He's about ready to go to war against Jack, and he practically screamed when I said I was bringing this to you. I guess you're not in Harry's good books anymore?"

"A team tried to kill me this afternoon. Not sure who sent them, but someone at CIB tipped them off. So Milton's not exactly in my good books, either."

Thorpe nodded. His eyes dipped to the floor and for a second, Quarrel saw a mask of sorrow settle on the older man's visage. Then Thorpe shook it off and had another sip of his latte.

"So what's new in the Library of Congress?"

Quarrel stuttered, tried to say something, and came up blank. It was the biggest rookie mistake you could make. He didn't want to tell Thorpe what he had been up to, since all this talk about nuclear components and Thorpe's skittish behaviour had Quarrel spooked. He knew he couldn't trust Thorpe with the information on TCPE, and rather than think of a believable lie, he had blown it completely with a rambling stutter and an awkward silence. Finally, he managed "Just meeting a contact. From Canada. I've never been inside the library before, so I thought it was a good place to have our meeting."

Thorpe's eyes narrowed and he nodded. "I see."

Thorpe leaned in, crossing his arms and resting both of his elbows on the table. This pose seemed somehow unnatural. It took Quarrel a moment to realize that there was something in Thorpe's right hand. A pen.

He was staring straight at Quarrel, but tucked under his left armpit, his right hand was writing on the empty envelope the photos had been in. "Listen, Chris. I know you really want to trust Jack, but in this game there is no trust. There's betrayal and there's photographic evidence. You need to muster whatever resources you have and track down Jack. You hear me, kid? Find Jack Hall. Stop wasting time with progress reports and sightseeing tours, understand? Track the fugitive."

His hand quietly flipped the envelope over, and he leaned back, uncrossing his arms. Quarrel realized that this was a show. Someone was listening. He didn't look at the message on the envelope. Instead he picked up one of the photos of Hall.

"I lost a lot of friends in the bombing," he said, looking Thorpe in the eyes. "And I know first hand that Jack Hall was in Canada less than twenty-four hours before that bomb went off. My priorities are straight."

"Good. I'll be in touch." Thorpe picked up his coffee and left. After a few seconds alone, Quarrel exhaled hard, his stomach churning like a cement mixer. Unsure if he was still being watched, Quarrel picked up the photos on the table, tapped them against the tabletop to line them up, then reached for the envelope to tuck them away. He tried to look nonchalant as he tucked the pictures into the paper sleeve, reading the message scribbled in rough, almost illegible cursive.

ALL LIES. FATALE HAS MY WIFE.

Quarrel froze as the information sunk in. Thorpe was being controlled. Hall was posing for staged photos, which meant they had him, too. Fatale—Erica—was back on the street, likely waiting to finish the job on Quarrel. He felt his stomach tighten, his throat seemed to want to close up and choke him. He chugged his coffee and realized that he was so tense his hands shook. His long-time goal was finally happening: he was an agent in the field, alone, with no older agents to guide him. It was his dream come true. He was terrified.

#

Quarrel returned to Edwin Brown's apartment with the Maggie's file on GX and Thorpe's envelope of photos tucked under his arm. He walked in, tossed the file on the table and went to the cabinet. The apartment was empty and quiet. Finding a bottle of Crown Royal, he pulled the cork and took a long swig, not even bothering to get a glass. He corked it as the whisky-burn filled his throat, and tucked it back into the cupboard. When he shut the cupboard door, revealing the other half of the room again, Swift had materialized at the table, having slipped in silently when he wasn't looking.

"Good meeting?" she asked, poking at the file but not opening it.

Quarrel shrugged. "You get the new IDs?"

Swift nodded. "Passports, driver's licences, and I dug up an old bank account I had five grand in. I just need to know if you want to fly on the four a.m. or wait 'til tomorrow afternoon."

Quarrel nodded, a little relieved. "Take the four. I want you to get out-of-country as soon as possible."

"What do you mean?" she stepped closer. "You're not coming with me?"

"Everything here's screwed right now. It all went to hell." He could still taste the booze and for a moment he wanted to go back for another swig, but he knew that he still had much to do. "I blew it."

"What happened?" She got up from the table and came to Chris, standing close enough he could smell her shampoo, which was actually Mr. Brown's but was still nice.

"Our big plan," he said, "me and Thorpe, thinking we're geniuses. The plan worked. We thought we were pulling everyone in to help us. But we were just drawing them into a trap."

She came closer, putting a hand on his shoulder. "Chris," she said, leaning in, "what happened?"

"Fatale got free somehow. She's controlling both Hall and Thorpe. Seems like they're working for her now. Crowe's dead. Shark disappeared, probably scared of actually having to stick his neck out for something. Then there's Milton and Boswell, one of whom must have ordered the hit on Smith's apartment, which means we can't trust either. There's nobody left to trust. I doomed us."

She wrapped her arms around him, leaning in to talk into his ear. "We can get out. Find the evidence Jupiter's still hiding in Zurich. Saleb's ready and waiting. It can be our leverage. Protection. We can disappear."

"No we can't. We can't just run away from this."

"I can disappear." She was whispering in an almost silent voice, but it didn't waver. She meant it, believed it. "And I can show you how to disappear with me."

Quarrel closed his eyes, longing. He leaned his head down to rest his forehead on hers. "They have a weapon. Something called a 'teacup.' It's a microwave beam—basically a death ray. They have the plans, and they have the computer that's the key to turn the whole thing on. If this thing really works, they could kill so many . . . " he wasn't even sure he could finish it. After he trailed off they just stood like that, leaning on each other. Quarrel felt his heart thumping and knew she could feel it. She slid her hand from his shoulder to his chest, nodding gently as she thought of what to say.

"You know I can't let them kill anyone. I won't. If they haven't fired it yet then they still need something. And whatever that thing is, we'll find it first." Swift still sounded confident. He wasn't sure how she vacillated so quickly and easily between confidence and despair, but he was glad she was back to believing in herself again. He leaned into her embrace, relieved to have someone to lean on. "We'll find it first," she repeated.

They stumbled to the bedroom, still wrapped around each other. It was only after they fell into the bed that they finally looked each other in the eyes, and when their lips met and their eyes closed, their despair didn't matter for a little while.

#

When Quarrel left her, he tucked his phone, the one that only Thorpe knew about, in her hand while she slept. He set the alarm clock for only a few hours later, when she would have to go to the airport.

The spring night had cooled to almost freezing. Quarrel pulled his hood up as he walked out onto the empty sidewalk. He thought about Swift, hoped that her search would find something that would break the case open. He sighed, and in the cold he saw a faint cloud of his own breath which faded into the night air until it disappeared, and he walked alone into the night.

31

Quarrel spent the night tucked into a study carrel in the quiet study area on the second floor of Lauinger Library at Georgetown University. It was open all night as students prepared for the coming exam season and Quarrel only needed to pickpocket a swipe card from a sleeping student in a cafeteria in order to get into the library at such a late hour. It was also quiet and seemed like a good place to hide out until he figured out some kind of a plan to stop Digamma, Fatale, and whatever else he would have to face. He wondered how far William Thorpe would go to protect his wife, and shuddered at the thought of having to fight against deadly agents like Thorpe and Jack Hall.

He spread Maggie's GX files around the desk, staring into page after page of seemingly pointless lists and numbers. Globection was good about their bookkeeping, and the files here detailed a lot of expenses from GX's military projects. Some of it seemed totally pointless: lists of expenses from technicians in the field, such as hotels and dinners; lists of components going into a new wi-fi router designed for use in Afghanistan's mobile bases; a note that four researchers were due for their annual $1000 pay increase that had to be approved by some supervisor. Quarrel stared at the data for hours trying to understand why Maggie had bothered printing it. Sure, some of the invoices to the Army or to the DOD seemed to be a little costly, but there was no sign of a proverbial $10,000 toilet seat.

The sun was rising when Quarrel wondered why Maggie had printed the same sheet twice. There was a list of costs associated with a new communications satellite.

Something to do with the Army communicating with their troops in the Middle East. It all seemed pretty straightforward, as least as far as Quarrel knew. Students were starting to file into the library in greater numbers now, getting in some cramming before tests or finishing homework that was due that morning. And with the movement of students came the attention of a security guard. One library employee, an African American woman dressed casually, but obviously there to serve as more of a guard than a librarian, spotted Quarrel and started toward him. Quarrel sighed and thought to himself guess you look too old to be here, which was a little disappointing since Quarrel was still well shy of thirty.

The woman was approaching, so Quarrel pulled out his stolen swipe card, but also decided to get ready to leave if he had to. He pulled all the leaves of paper into a stack, with the identical satellite invoices on top. As they slid in place, one aligned to the other, and that's when he saw it.

"Excuse me, son," said the library woman, standing right next to Chris, "swipe your GO-card here, please."

"Uh huh," he said absent-mindedly, pulling the two pages away and holding them side-by-side.

"You realize that before eight in the morning this is a student-only building?"

"Uh huh," he said again, his eyes tracing a line between one page and the other. There was just one line that was different from the original GX internal invoice and the one that was sent to the CIA.

"You are required to swipe your GO-card when asked by library staff," she said, thrusting a handheld card

298

reader at his face. Finally, Quarrel stood up, speaking softly in an exaggerated Quiet Library Voice.

"I gotta go. You're great at your job. I'm going to leave now." He picked up the papers and stuffed them back into the folder. The woman looked at him in a disbelieving, condescending way and jerked her thumb toward the door. "And by the way," he asked, "how old do I look? I'm really so old that you single me out?"

#

After he was escorted out into the magic-hour light of a predawn spring morning, Quarrel took another look at the pages, folding them over at the line that they changed. In the internal GX invoice, the company listed a large, extremely expensive reflector as one of the satellite components. In the invoice they sent to the CIA, the reflector was replaced with "transmission dish" and cost much less than what the GX invoice said it was worth.

Maggie had become a whistleblower thinking that GX was over-billing the government, but the reverse was true. They were doing the opposite: hiding expensive components on a cheap satellite. The satellite was built with features the government didn't know were there. The CIA wouldn't have their own engineers combing over the satellite, so they wouldn't know what GX was up to. And the guys that actually loaded the satellite onto a rocket and launched it would have no idea what was or was not supposed to be attached to the CIA's new toy. So GX could essentially launch whatever they wanted into orbit and hide the launch under cover of the CIA. As long as the Afghan bases still got their high-speed internet, nobody would know the difference.

Quarrel had left his cell phone with Swift, so he walked to a gas station and bought a cheap disposable. He was still realizing the implications as he called.

"Hinkston," answered Hinkston, sounding distant. He was on a speakerphone.

"It's Quarrel."

"I'm busy, kid."

"You said if I found anything in Maggie's files—"

Hinkston suddenly picked up the phone, the background noise vanishing. "What did you find?"

"Globection hid a huge reflector on one of the CIA's satellites and changed the books to hide it."

"Reflector?"

Quarrel waved for a taxi. "You said yourself, HAARP could only hit the area above it, not around the world. But if you have a targeted emitter . . . "

Hinkston picked up the thought. "You can bounce your big death ray off a satellite and hit any target within two-thirds of the Earth's surface."

"This proves everything. That GX is in league with the crew who stole the control computer, that they've been planning to hijack the TCPE. You need to lock that thing down and arrest Hugo Zoeli."

"Whoa, slow down, kid. You don't arrest the President's golf buddy based on some unverified stolen invoices. As for the Teacup, I have a CIA Ops team assembled at an airfield in Washington State. Once we clear the red tape about crossing the border, I'll have that thing locked down tight."

"You can't just let Zoeli off the hook! For god's sake he's a mass murderer with his own private army!"

"I know that, kid!" Hinkston bellowed. "Unlike you, this is not my first week on the job. I'll call you later at the phone you're calling from. We'll meet up, you'll show me the evidence, we'll talk to some Canadian officials about getting my team into your country. But right now, the CIA is dealing with the mess you left in Tyson's Corner, a pile of dead agents that Jack Hall killed, and figuring out what the hell Thorpe did with that Fatale woman. So you'll excuse me if dealing with jurisdictional red tape takes a back seat to cleaning up Harry Milton's mess!"

Hinkston hung up. It was hours before he called Quarrel to set up a meeting at a CIA safe house in the area.

Quarrel knocked on the door of a small, plain-looking house in the suburbs. It was early evening and the weak orange sunlight made the beige paneling look dark, striped with shadows where each panel overlapped. Within three seconds of Quarrel knocking, a fit young woman answered, dressed in jeans and a t-shirt that showed off her very muscular arms. The casual clothes made her look like a normal suburbanite relaxing after work, but her intense fitness level revealed the truth. She was the house agent who lived here full-time and was most likely former military. She ran the safe house, which meant guarding captives, protecting assets who were hiding out, or in this case, hosting a secret meeting. She didn't offer her name.

"Come on in, Chris," she said like they were old friends.

She did such a good job playing the welcoming hostess that when Quarrel got inside he had the urge to

301

take his shoes off, and had to consciously remind himself that this wasn't really her home. He shook off the feeling of visiting someone's home and looked to the agent for direction. The house looked ordinary in every way. They were in the main hallway, with a living room to the right and a kitchen straight ahead. On the left there was a closet, a bathroom, and a closed door that must have went to the basement. This is the door the woman pointed to. "Basement. Hinkston and his guest are already here," she said in a welcoming tone.

Quarrel went to the doorway, and the agent flipped open the plastic cover around a light switch, revealing a small keypad. After typing a quick code into this secret security measure, there was a clicking sound from the basement door and the door opened automatically. Quarrel stepped through to the landing at the top of the stairs, and the house agent closed and locked the door behind him. There was no back door in the stairwell, and there were no windows at all. The stairway was drywalled and painted beige, looking quite ordinary, but Quarrel knew the drywall would contain soundproofing, fireproofing, and maybe a few hidden compartments of guns or gadgets.

The stairway led to a typical suburban rec. room, with a couch, chairs, a TV mounted to a wall, and a large table covered in extremely high-tech equipment and various screens. Other than this table, it would look to any observer like a completely normal house. It took Quarrel a moment to realize that the high-tech touchscreen table was actually a pool table, with the surface flipped to reveal the gadgets inside. There were only two men waiting for Quarrel. One was Hinkston, and the other was a pudgy man with red hair that was more grey than red, who looked like a child next to Hinkston's bulk. Quarrel recognized the Canadian official immediately.

"Thompson! I didn't expect I'd see you here."

Mr. Thompson smiled. "Nor did I, Mr. Quarrel."

"I didn't know they sent level-fours on international trips. You must have been higher up than just a four."

Thompson's lip twitched and he reddened a bit. Quarrel realized that Thompson had been in the intelligence business much longer than himself, but was now reduced to answering Quarrel's summons. Thompson was obviously irritated, and Quarrel regretted his comment immediately. "I am a level-four. They sent me because you know me. And I didn't really like having to fly down here on a half-hour's notice, so let's just get on with it, OK?"

Hinkston chuckled and intervened. "Well, anyway it's nice that we all know each other. If you'll come here and let us run a scan, Mr. Quarrel." Quarrel nodded and stepped closer to the table, holding his arms out like he was passing through airport security.

Hinkston picked up a device from the table and waved it around Quarrel. After a while he decided he had done enough of that and sat the device down again. "Well, you're not broadcasting anything right now, but if you've been bugged they could turn it on again in a few minutes."

"I haven't been bugged."

Thompson patted Quarrel on the shoulder, almost reassuringly. "Very likely you've lost whoever it was that tried to kill you, but we want to be safe. Are you carrying anything, anything at all, that anyone has given you since you arrived in the USA? Or even something you took without permission? Equipment, clothing, pens, weapons, even notepads could have a tracker in the cover."

Quarrel was wearing all new clothing and he had ditched both of his old cell phones. There was only one thing he had that could be traced back to anyone else.

"I have a gun. Signed it out of CI—" he stuttered, not wanting to reveal the existence of CIB to Thompson, who probably didn't know it existed "—CIA." He pulled the weapon from the pocket of his hoodie and handed it to Hinkston. Hinkston ran a couple of small handheld scanners over it, shrugged, and set it on the table.

"Well it's not singing either," he said. "Let's get to it." He leaned over the table, the middle of which was a big touchscreen monitor. He tapped the screen and it brought up a topographical map.

"This side's Alaska. This side's the Yukon," he pointed. "There's Whitehorse." He moved his finger northwest, toward the border. "And right in here, is the TCPE. Targeted Charged Particle Emitter. Now, as far as I or the CIA know, this thing doesn't do jack. If it had ever worked, I think I would know. But nonetheless, it seems that someone stole the plans for this thing, and the one device that can turn it on was recently stolen."

"You've confirmed that?" Quarrel asked. "The control computer works on this thing?"

Hinkston nodded. "The exact same model that was stolen." He zoomed in on a spot on the map. "We need to make sure this thing doesn't work, and never will."

His finger touched the map in what seemed to be an empty section of the Yukon Plateau, an area with very little population. It seemed unlikely that anything that big

304

could stay secret, but almost nobody lived up there. And if they had provided a decent cover story in the eighties, maybe the locals would just accept it.

"So you want to send in a team to destroy this thing? Or you want to sit on it and arrest whoever shows up?" Thompson asked.

"Destroy it," said Quarrel.

"Sit on it," said Hinkston at the same time. They looked to each other and both men smiled.

"I don't want another building full of dead people. Not when I could stop it from happening," said Quarrel, his eyes moving to Thompson.

"And I want to plug a leak. If we don't get them now we might not have another chance. We send a team to sit on it and catch the mole when they show up."

Thompson scratched his chin. It was late and his stubble was showing. He gave it another rub and shrugged. "The one thing I was told when I came here tonight was that I can't allow American troops over the border. Canada can handle this."

Hinkston started to say something, but Thompson held up a hand. "Canada can't be seen relying on Americans to solve domestic problems, and we sure as hell can't have anything that looks like U.S. troops invading the Yukon. You give me the location, and I'll let CSIS make the call. We'll either have an army team stake out the area, or our air force will blow it sky high."

Hinkston shook his head. "I already put together a strike team, real black ops guys, and they're on standby in Washington State. They can be in Yellowknife before dawn and nobody will know they're there."

Thompson exhaled hard. "This team, do they know their target already?"

Hinkston shook his head, "These guys work need-to-know. I have satellite surveillance on the Teacup, but it's not a very clear shot since it's all the way up north. I'd rather have eyes on the ground."

"But at least you didn't send a team into my country without permission."

Hinkston frowned at the suggestion and picked at the edge of his phone with a fingernail. "I wish I could have."

"Good." Thompson snatched Quarrel's gun off the table, used his left hand to cock it and flick the safety, and in the same impossibly quick movement shot Hinkston in the forehead.

Quarrel twitched reflexively toward Hinkston, as if to catch the larger man, then when he saw the spray of blood his sense took over and Quarrel dove behind the pool table. Hinkston's phone fell from his hand and hit the floor an instant before his body; the phone popped open and lost its battery, which slid past Quarrel. Hinkston's body fell toward the wall to Quarrel's left, and there wasn't quite enough open space for him to fall, so his head clunked into the concrete wall with a sickening shuk sound a split second before his body hit the floor.

Thompson turned, stepping away, and aimed the gun at Quarrel. "On your knees!" he shouted. "There's nowhere to hide in here, so give it up!"

Quarrel stuck his hands up, then peeked over the top of the table and stared hard into the eyes of the man who he had seen as a dull, functionary office drone until that moment.

"Kneel down now. If you try to run I'll kneecap you and if you come at me I'll kill you."

Quarrel was already down in a crouch so he just shifted his weight and sat on his knees. Thompson slowly eased himself around the corner of the table to get a clear shot at Quarrel.

"Good. Now I have a simple question. Who else knows?" Thompson was starting to sweat, and he was making sure to keep the stairs in sight just in case someone came down the steps. The house agent hadn't come running when the shot was fired, and Quarrel wasn't sure what to make of that. Quarrel assumed she was watching through some kind of security feed, so the fact that she wasn't doing anything meant she was either dead or complicit in Thompson's plot. Or maybe, the room really was totally soundproof and private and the house agent had no idea what was happening. But Quarrel doubted that. It was prudent to assume she was in on it.

"I know you've spoken to the girl Swift," Thompson said. Something about the way he said her name was meant to be a threat. Quarrel was trying to piece together how much Thompson knew, how he had managed to get the drop on Quarrel so completely. "You used one of our own spies' apartments, of course I knew everything you've been up to," Thompson gloated. "But who else? Who have you been spilling secrets to, kid?"

Quarrel kept his voice calm, even though he wanted to scream. "No one. Everyone. Some people. Your momma."

Thompson shook his head. "I guess we'll just have to torture you. We have a guy for that." Thompson reached into his jacket and pulled a second gun. Then he pulled the magazine from Quarrel's gun and ejected the bullet from the chamber. He pulled on gloves, wiped

Quarrel's gun with his shirt, then held it out for Quarrel to take.

"Grip it tight and pull the trigger."

Quarrel didn't move. Thompson aimed the second gun for Quarrel's leg. "Grip it and pull the trigger or the torture starts right now." Quarrel did what he was told, leaving his hand and fingerprints on the murder weapon. Satisfied, Thompson took the gun back and slapped the magazine back in. Then he tossed the gun under the table, sliding it across the room.

"I want you to know that there's no point in an escape. So don't try it. Before I came here, I buried you. Most of your records were destroyed in the bombing, but the few that remained at CSIS have been red-flagged. You've been labeled as a potential mole, someone to keep tabs on. I've added a few back-dated notes from CSIS-2 to our database, just little inconsistencies that your peers noticed. When they find your prints on this gun it'll all add up. Even if you got free and called for help, they'd arrest you for murder, maybe even for the bombing."

Quarrel had nothing to say. Thompson had been such a surprise that he still couldn't fathom it. All he managed as a response was "Why?"

"You've been a problem. The people I work for are everywhere. They've been positioning Digamma agents in various roles for years so that this operation could proceed without obstruction. Yet somehow, even with all our people in place, you get thrown in the middle of everything. And not just on some loose end, something we could just brush over. You come right into the damn CIB. And then you get Milton to follow your orders to introduce all his top agents and get them all chasing each other around the world. Do you have any idea how hard it is to manage an operation like this when you let all those spies loose on each other? It's chaos.

"You messed with the wrong people, and now you're going to tell those people exactly what you know and who you told it to." He waved the gun, "Get up."

Quarrel rose, and Thompson pointed to the bottom of the stairs. Thompson kept his distance as he marched Quarrel up the stairs.

"Have you thought about the agent who'll be waiting for us? Won't she wonder why you have a gun drawn and her boss is dead?" Quarrel asked, as he slowly walked with his hands in the air.

"This building is soundproof, so you didn't hear when my partner killed her five seconds after she closed the basement door."

Quarrel, seeing a chance to get inside Thompson's head, kept talking. "You sure your partner is that good? What if the timing's off and they're not here yet? Or if that agent was as tough as she looked and all you did was piss her off? She could be waiting outside this door, ready to blow you away with your dead partner's gun."

Thompson pressed a button on the wall to unlock the door. "If she's waiting, then I guess she'll shoot you once that door opens. Move."

Quarrel took a deep breath as the door opened in front of him. The hallway smelled of gunpowder, and there was no sign of the house agent. As Quarrel stepped into the hallway, he saw the agent's denim-clad leg sticking out from the living room. She was laying face-up on the floor, unmoving. Thompson's partner had been good.

"Front door," said Thompson, still keeping a safe distance. Quarrel started down the hallway and heard Thompson emerge from the stairway behind him, when there was suddenly a second set of footsteps coming from the darkened kitchen.

"She's dead," said the partner in the darkness. "But killing the cameras alerted Langley. We have to move."

Quarrel turned, the partner's voice sending a chill up his spine.

"Did CIA send anyone to the Teacup?" asked the partner.

"No, all he did was put satellite surveillance on it," Thompson said. "How long do we have?"

The partner's voice was monotonous, emotionless. "Oh, not much time at all."

There was a muzzle flash from the darkness, and Thompson took the bullet in his forehead. He went limp and fell straight down, a tangle of limbs. His partner stepped out of the kitchen, silenced pistol aimed at Quarrel. He was dressed all in black, including black face paint, but Quarrel recognized him all the same.

"Hershey."

Thompson's partner smiled, his white teeth standing out from his darkened face. "Hiya, Chris. I'm alive." Pete Hershey fired a shot into the floor behind Quarrel's feet. "Move it, or you won't be."

"I saw you die."

Hershey kept smiling, but his voice was still heartless. "You weren't supposed to be outside, but then you were such a great witness to convince everyone that I was dead. I really should thank you for that."

Hershey shot another bullet into the floor. "Outside. Get in the back of the SUV. You don't want to keep Sidorov waiting."

32

"Sometimes, when I'm torturing somebody," said Anton Sidorov, a cigar shoved into the corner of his mouth, "the men I pay to do the torture say to me, 'Anton, why not just kill him? Why make it so slow?' And do you know what I tell them?"

Jack Hall shivered and exhaled hard through gritted teeth. Frustrated, Sidorov picked up a plastic bag full of ice with his right hand and swung it at Hall's shoulder. The bag was heavy, the impact knocking Hall against the steel arm of the chair he was bound to. Hall grunted. "You tell them," Hall said, teeth chattering, "that you're a sadist."

"Not so, Mr. Hall. I tell them I do it because death should hurt. You should feel it filling your body, weighing you down and pulling you to hell. You should spend your last hours knowing that you are already dead and that I'm the one who killed you. The last hour of your life, your thoughts should be nothing but pain and regret and fear of my name. Because if I can do that to my enemies, no one will get in my way."

Hall was shirtless, his feet bare, tied to a steel chair in a corner of a basement somewhere. The walls were concrete; the only window was at the top of a wall looking out onto a window well and some brown grass. His feet were in a bucket of ice and water, his chair surrounded by bags of ice. There were a car battery and some jumper cables sitting on a folding table against the wall, but so far Hall had not been electrocuted. There was a red metal toolbox sitting below the table, which they hadn't opened yet. Sidorov liked to mix up his tortures, make his enemies die for days. There were stories of

Sidorov pulling out defibrillators or adrenaline shots to revive dead victims, just so he could kill them again a few hours later.

For the last twenty-four hours, Hall had been through two of Sidorov's tortures. The first was a set of headphones taped to his head playing a loud high-pitched screech, accompanied by randomly timed sandpaper swipes against his skin. The sound was worse than the scraping. Nevertheless, Hall had been grateful for it. The car crash he had survived while Sidorov and Scarret framed him had knocked him out cold. He had a severe concussion, and he knew that if he blacked out again, he could likely lapse into a coma. The high-pitched tone, while maddening, had the effect of keeping him awake. He wasn't sure how long that torture had lasted, but Sidorov was wearing a different shirt when he returned to the basement and ordered his men, in Russian, to "Switch to cold."

The goons were two young men, early twenties, with muscled arms and eyes that never showed any emotion but sorrow. They worked in shifts, one watching Hall at all times, the other resting or eating. It was rare that Hall had more than one man in the room with him. Hall figured they were street criminals who had earned Sidorov's interest through a combination of brutality and loyalty. Sidorov's network was filled with this sort of man; impressionable, violent, able to completely suppress their humanity when Sidorov ordered it. Hall knew he would get no sympathy from men like them.

Now Sidorov had returned, holding a blowtorch in one hand and a drink in the other, a thick Cuban cigar in his mouth. He had told the guard to leave, and now Sidorov was alone with Hall, indulging in a rant about the joys of slow death, sipping his vodka on ice and snorting out smoke.

"I was going to hook up that chair to the car battery. It's so much fun to watch Americans lose their bowels and twitch and scream. It reminds me that I'm better than them." He sipped his drink, put the cigar back in his mouth, and continued. "But your old friend Shark told me the story of how you burned his face, and made me promise to use fire."

Hall couldn't feel his feet in the tub of water, and he had given up fighting to suppress the teeth chattering, but he was far from broken. He had tested the ropes that tied him down; they were good, tight lines and well tied. He would need to find something to cut himself free. His legs had been bound during the first torture, but the guards had cut them free in order to put them in the ice tub. The tub was as tall as the seat of the chair, and once his feet were submerged, the goon had tied his thighs down to the seat so he couldn't lift his legs out of the water. The chair was heavy and solid, but Hall was sure he could at least tip himself over if he needed to. Beyond that, there was little a concussed, hypothermic, bound man could do to escape from this situation. If Hall was going to survive, Sidorov would have to make a mistake.

"So the question is," Sidorov put the cigar down on the table and opened the gas on the blowtorch, "what part of you do I burn? I was thinking I'd see if I could remove your pants with nothing but the flame, but seeing as your pants are soaked with water that would be tricky." Sidorov lit a match and used it to fire up the torch. He dialed in the propane until he had a solid blue flame. "Perhaps I could burn the hair off your head. That would be fun. It should make quite the smell. And then

314

tomorrow when I really get you screaming, every movement of that face will make your burned scalp shift and bleed and shoot pain all through your body."

The look in his eyes was hunger, and betrayed that the oncoming torture filled a need that Sidorov couldn't appease any other way. His was gleeful. "Yes. I think that would be fun. Hair it is."

Sidorov set his glass on the table and approached Hall with the blowtorch. It was a typical torch you might see a plumber use, with a blue propane tank beneath the blowtorch itself. He held it in his right hand—his dominant hand—but as he neared Hall he steadied it with his left. Sidorov came around Hall's right side, between the chair and the cement wall. He had to walk a wide path around the chair since there were still bags of ice piled under and all around Hall.

As the searing blue flame came down toward his head, Hall waited through the first jolts of pain, not tilting his head away from the flame until he could smell his own hair burning, then he flinched hard to the left.

"Ahh, so you thought you were tough. Nobody is tough when it comes to fire. Not even you."

Sidorov leaned over the ice toward Hall, shoving the blue fire toward his victim's scalp. That was when Hall snapped his head and shoulders to the right, toward the blowtorch. His skin shoved through that searing flame until his skull clunked off the metal nozzle on the blowtorch, and caught Sidorov off guard enough that the force of the headbutt knocked the blowtorch out of his hands. The blowtorch bounced off Hall's shoulder, then fell to the top of a bag of ice, which served as a landing ramp and rolled it straight at Sidorov's feet. The Russian jumped and the blowtorch passed under his left foot and

315

settled, still burning blue-hot, against the wall. The puddle of melted ice sizzled around the flame.

Sidorov scoffed and punched Hall in the face, a weak punch with his left hand, while he was looking at the blowtorch on the floor. It was a punch Hall could have shrugged off normally, but in his concussed state it sent a jolt of pain thundering through his skull, and sent a wave of nausea through him that was so strong he nearly vomited. Sidorov placed his right hand on the back of the chair and leaned to pick up the blowtorch with his left.

Hall did his best to brace his useless feet against the side of the ice tub. It may have been the guards' one mistake that they filled the tub so full, and made it heavy enough for Hall to push off of it. He put everything he could muster into forcing his weight as hard to the right as he could, and he felt the chair tip. Sidorov felt the impact of Hall's weight, but he was half-bent-over, with one foot standing on a chunk of melting ice. When he tried to shove Hall's chair back into its upright position, his twisted body fell with it, landing face-down on the wet cement. The piled ice beside the chair acted as a brace, a pivot point, and Hall turned upright as the chair came down hard. Hall's weight and the weight of the chair hit the ground at one single point—the seatback over his right shoulder, precisely where Sidorov's hand had been clutching. The impact mashed the hand with a wet crunch like the sound of tearing a head of lettuce. The ice bucket tipped with his legs, dumping ice water over both men, and Hall's body weight pulled him down until a second point of contact—his right knee on Sidorov's right thigh—took most of his weight.

Hall was upside-down, balanced for the moment on a small stack of ice, his own weight pinning Sidorov to the floor. Sidorov's body was more or less pinned between Hall's chair and the wall, with Sidorov's left arm jammed between himself and the wall, only inches from the still-blazing blowtorch.

Sidorov moaned in pain, first from the crushing blow to his hand, and again when he realized the heat of the flame was inches from both his fingers and his face. With a grunt, Sidorov pulled his left arm free, stretching it out above the burning torch for a moment, before awkwardly reaching down to fish at the blowtorch. He managed to get a grip on the top of the propane tank and pulled the blowtorch up and away from his face.

Sidorov swung his arm backward until he was flailing the blowtorch over his own lower back in an attempt to catch Hall with the flame. It was a fruitless effort, since Sidorov couldn't see what he was doing but Hall had a clear view. Hall waited for Sidorov's weapon to come close enough to his own hand to snatch at it. Hall was bound to the chair, but Sidorov was awkwardly twisting his arm behind himself. It didn't take much effort for Hall to pull the blowtorch away from Sidorov's grip. Then it was only a quick shake of the wrist to turn the torch upside-down and angle the flame toward the ropes that bound his left hand.

Sidorov braced his now-free left hand against the wall and shoved. The bags of ice shifted and Hall's chair tilted away from Sidorov, lessening the weight that pinned the Russian. Sidorov twisted his legs and got his left foot against the wall as well and braced for another shove that would knock Hall away and free himself.

Hall took his time on the ropes, burning each almost completely, but not all the way because he didn't want the flame to touch his bare skin. If he burned himself he could involuntarily flinch and drop the blowtorch, so he had to be patient, his eyes flicking from Sidorov to the ropes on his own forearm, and back. Just as Sidorov started to shove again, Jack snapped his arm free of the bonds, and with this freedom he shoved the flame at Sidorov. He jammed the tip of the blowtorch at Sidorov's left hand until the Russian flinched and pulled his arm away, ending the attempt to push off the wall.

Hall went to work on freeing his right arm, his eyes always watching Sidorov for any move. The painful tingling in his feet told him that feeling was slowly returning, and he knew that tingling would become agony as the blood flow returned to his feet. He ignored it and kept the flame steady against the ropes.

"I'm going to make you die for a month!" screamed Sidorov, and he jammed his left foot and hand on the wall in a last-ditch effort to scramble free. Sidorov shoved hard, and Hall fell away, freeing Sidorov. Hall was still tied firmly to the chair by the ropes around his right arm and his thighs, so he could do little as the chair slipped away from Sidorov. Sidorov quickly rolled over, facing Hall and scrambling to find his footing. As he turned to face Hall, his face was a grimace of pure rage, nostrils flaring, mouth gasping for air. In that instant, Hall jammed the blowtorch away from his effort to free himself and jabbed the blue flame straight at Sidorov's hate-filled eyes. Sidorov jerked back and away, recoiling in shock and horror and pain, toward the wall.

Hall screamed in effort as he pulled his right arm against the weakened lines that held it. One of the sections of the rope broke, and that loosened the rest of the loops enough that he squirmed his right arm free. He was still tied to the heavy chair, and his legs were useless, but at least he had two arms and a weapon.

Sidorov, blinded at least temporarily by the bright flame, waved his hands in the space between himself and Hall. Sidorov's right hand was useless—crushed at the knuckles, the fingers hung by the skin, with trails of runny blood and ice water trailing down Sidorov's arm. The left was still a useable hand even though Hall had given it a bit of a burn. Hall used his own left hand to grab Sidorov's by the first two fingers, wrenching them out of the way with a snap, while his right hand held the blowtorch out toward the torturer's face.

When the flame hit his lips they melted on contact, and Sidorov's involuntary scream was enough for Hall to shove the flame inside Sidorov's mouth. He held it there as the Russian screamed and shook, his left hand fighting so hard to get at the blowtorch that he broke both of his own fingers in Hall's grip. The right banged uselessly against Hall's forearm, the dangling broken fingers slapping weakly on his skin. After twenty agonizing seconds of holding the torch in his enemy's mouth, Hall heard Sidorov take a breath. It would have been involuntary, his body's last effort to acquire oxygen when there was none to be inhaled. It was the same sort of dying gasp that invites water into a drowning person's lungs when their body can't go on any longer, and with that sharp intake of breath, Anton Sidorov inhaled fire into both of his lungs. His arms dropped and his head went limp.

Hall removed the torch but kept it burning since he still needed to get his legs free. While Hall tended to the careful business of cutting himself off the chair, Sidorov twitched, opened his eyes, and died.

Hall managed to cut himself free, lying awkwardly in the sideways chair until he pulled the lines away from his tingling legs. The henchmen hadn't come down the stairs despite Sidorov's screams, so Hall hoped that they had left the building. Hall rolled off the arm of the chair, over the bags of ice, into a puddle of ice water and bumped into Sidorov's legs. He crawled, mostly on the strength of his arms, to the table and out of the puddle. He was directly under the fluorescent light here, the brightest part of the room, and he took the time to study his legs.

When he poked at his foot, he could feel it, but his flesh was soft and he got jolts of pain. He flexed his toes and winced as the figurative pins and needles stabbed him. He reached for the button of the fly of his jeans and found his fingers shaking. He took a slow breath and tried again. He popped the button and pulled at the zipper. Sliding out of the wet pants took a few seconds but was relatively easy. Still crawling, the nearly-naked Hall searched the basement for clothes. Near the stairs there was a hallway, and Jack crawled along until he found the next room. Jack had assumed from the looks of the basement that this building was a house, and discovering the laundry room confirmed it. There was a pile of men's dirty clothes on top of a washing machine, and Jack recognized a red shirt that one of the goons had worn the day before. There was a laundry chute above the pile. The chute was the sort of thing a younger Jack might have used to climb up to the top floor, but in his current state he was just glad to drag the pile of clothes down to the floor.

There were some pants in a size larger than Jack's, all of them dirty. He pulled on a pair of black chinos that smelled like sweat and grass, then found a baggy pair of sweats to pull on top of them. One pair of socks was wet with someone's sweat, but Jack dug through the pile until he found two dry socks for his feet, which had thawed from pale blue to a shade of deathly grey.

He pulled a t-shirt on before slipping one of Sidorov's expensive dress shirts over his arms. He didn't bother trying the buttons. Gripping the side of the washer, Hall pulled himself up to a vertical position that was almost standing. He kept most of his weight on the washer while he tested the strength of his right leg, then his left. Satisfied that the pain was bearable, he tried putting his full weight on his feet. He stood for a moment before his knees felt rubbery and he had to lean back to the washer again.

He took the time to study the room. There was nothing really here, just some shelves of towels and detergent. It was all too domestic to be Sidorov's, likely some cottage or country home they had found empty near that military base where Hall had been arrested.

But the laundry room did have another window well, and it was right above the dryer. It was fairly easy to climb onto the dryer and swing his legs up, but standing on top of it long enough to get the window open was tricky. His right leg completely buckled, sending him careening to the side, where his shoulder punched into the drywall. His head screamed and he tasted vomit. He stood there with his shoulder embedded in the wall until his vision cleared, he took three quick breaths, and stood up to the window again. His uncoordinated hands made opening the window harder than it had any right to be, but after about a minute he had managed to slide the glass to the side and pull the screen off.

He turned backward, reached both arms up and out, bracing the wall, and used his upper body and back to haul himself about a third of the way out. The back of his neck touched the cool metal of the window well and the top of his ass rested on the edge of the window. He rested again, legs dangling, head pounding, until he reached out of the well, felt grass, and grabbed the metal. He pulled himself to a proper sitting position, his legs from the knees down still inside the house, the rest of him outdoors. He was indeed at an isolated house in the woods, just as he suspected. There was no sign of a neighbouring house, just woods on the three sides he could see. It was light out now. The window well in the room where he had been locked up had let some light in, so he knew that it had been dark not long ago. Even the pale morning sunlight hurt his eyes and spikes of pain shot through his head like the worst hangover Jack had ever had. Thankfully the sun was still below the trees so he was spared further pain.

Once he was out in the yard, Hall stumble-walked, leaning on the cedar siding as he made it to the northern corner of the house. The corner led to a small barbeque and picnic area, where everything was tarped over for the season. Past the picnic table there was another building, a three-car detached garage. The unpaved driveway ran from the garage and away from the house, into the woods, where it turned to the left and faded into the trees. Hall headed for the garage. There were no cars in sight. There might only have been a single vehicle, the big van they had captured Hall with, but he was betting Sidorov had something of his own to drive. Even if the henchmen had taken one, Hall was banking on there being a second vehicle.

The garage wasn't locked. The first bay was being used as a workshop, the floor filled with a table saw and a lathe, counters of tools along two walls. The middle bay was empty, and the far end of the garage housed the black van that Hall vaguely remembered from his kidnapping. Hall searched the workbenches until he found a pair of needle-nose pliers.

He climbed into the driver's seat, knocked plastic off the steering column with his knee and set to work hotwiring the van. Thankfully for Hall's dimwitted legs, the van was an automatic.

Hall pulled out onto the unpaved driveway, which took a curve around some marshland before straightening and heading for the local highway. It was reasonably flat and well-maintained, surrounded by a mix of trees on either side. Just as Hall made it to the straightaway, another vehicle turned off the road and blocked the way. It was a silver SUV, and Hall saw that there were two men in the front, and probably more in the back. He stomped on the gas pedal and headed straight for them.

He knew, somewhere in a more sensible part of his brain, that another head-on collision would finish the brain damage that the first crash started. He'd either knock himself into a coma or die on impact. Still, he sped straight toward the advancing SUV, which hadn't slowed down. The road was only wide enough for one vehicle, and soon enough they'd collide. Hall decided that the van was a little higher from the ground than the SUV, so he would at least crush the SUV's drivers with his engine block. That might be enough. That might be worth dying over.

When the van and the SUV were close enough for Jack to recognize that the driver was one of the men who had tortured him, he made up his mind. Jack would not lose this game of chicken, even if it killed him. He let go of the steering wheel and tried to go limp, hoping the airbag wouldn't kill him when it went off.

Then suddenly a man in the back seat of the SUV leaped around the driver's seat and grabbed the steering wheel, jerking the SUV off the road. Jack's van punched through the very edge of the SUV's rear bumper as he passed it, and the SUV struck a thick old oak tree with a sound like the tree had been split by lightning.

Jack let out a yelp of surprise and elation and grabbed the wheel again as he pulled to a stop. He reversed the van back past the SUV to see if there were survivors. As soon as the van pulled to a stop next to the crumpled wreck of the SUV, the rear passenger-side door opened and someone stumbled out, hiding behind the SUV, and then ran off into the woods. In his condition, Jack would never be able to catch him, so he let the guy run off.

The two in the front, the guards who had stacked the ice under Jack's legs, were crushed by the impact. Through the shattered windshield, Jack could see them both, slumped over and bloody. That left one more—the guy who had grabbed for the wheel. Jack had to assume the guy was in pretty bad shape after the crash, so he took the risk of climbing out of the van and walking over to the SUV. He tried the back driver's-side door and found it jammed shut, but with a strong yank it pulled open.

A bloody man, hands bound together by plastic cuffs, was laid out on the floor between the front and back seats. The man muttered something that sounded like gibberish.

"What you say?" shouted Jack.

"I said he's getting away!" came the response. The guy on the floor rolled over, and Jack was stunned to see Chris Quarrel, who had a bleeding wound somewhere above his left ear but seemed OK otherwise. "Jack?" said Quarrel, who was just as confused.

"Kid?"

"Stop that guy! He's the one who set off the bomb in my office. He's getting away." Quarrel tried to sit up, but just winced and lay back down. Quarrel let out a shuddering sob. "Hershey! He's gone."

33

Jessica Swift left Khalid Saleb in a van parked around the corner, which was farther away than she would have liked. They were back in Zurich, where there isn't a lot of space to park on the roads, so Saleb was a good hundred metres away from Swift as she strolled in her best false-confidence walk into the Douxieme Banque Suisse. For this job to work, she'd have to go in alone. It was the same sort of job she had done before— stealing from a bank—but this was an entirely new way of doing it. She had broken into banks before, of course, but never during operating hours. Never with an appointment.

It was the same bank she had planned to break into before she was called to Quarrel's briefing, which was only days ago but seemed so much longer. While she had been in America, Saleb had done his best to lay low, since he didn't have any contacts or friends in Zurich to call up to help plan a break-in. None that he remembered, anyway. The job of actually planning the break-in was all on Swift, but now that she was back, she had no time. They needed to identify Jupiter, but with the threat of some kind of giant microwave beam hanging over her head, she had to get into that safe deposit box immediately.

This led Swift and Saleb to abandon the late-night break-in in favour of the gambit they were about to play. She was dressed stylishly, in a form-fitting but not immodest skirted suit. Her hair hung loose, slightly curled and styled. She wore lipstick, and wondered how many years it had been since she'd even owned a tube of lipstick before today. She had spent the last day and a half practicing the signature of Mrs. Roux, the probably-fictional woman whose probably-fictional husband had opened a very real safe deposit box here.

Mr. Roux was also the owner of the original box, where she first stole the truth about Saleb, and Swift's hopes were pinned to the idea that there would be another cache of secrets here, in Box 222. If this panned out, the new information could be compared to what they knew of their small pool of suspects, and they would find Jupiter.

Jupiter had been complicit in setting up Saleb for his wife's murder, and had been covering his or her tracks ever since. It was a safe bet that the same traitor who had two fellow agents framed and shot in France was also behind the new threat that had taken Crowe's life in that parking garage. She even wondered if the marksman who had put a bullet in Saleb's brain was the same person who had put one through Matthew Crowe's head, but they would likely never prove that. Whatever was going on went back much farther than the few months ago when Jessica Jordan had died in France, but it was all connected. This mole was a poison inside the CIB, and Swift had to believe that whatever was inside that box would be the antidote.

She had no idea what "Helena Roux" looked like, or if anyone at this bank would know either. As she rode the escalator to the second floor, she ran through escape routes in her mind. The box had been rented only a few months previously, and it was very likely that the same person who had met "Mrs. Roux" back then was also going to be here today. All it would take is one employee with a good memory for faces and Swift would have to get back to the van as quickly as possible.

At the desk, she introduced herself as Helena Roux and waited for someone to come and greet her. Roux was a French name, and she spoke it much better than she spoke German, so that was what she went with. The bank associate replied in French and asked her to wait.

A chubby young man in his late twenties came out from behind a frosted glass door and greeted her, also in French. Swift's French was strong, but her accent was a bit rusty. She went with it anyway, shaking his hand.

"What can I help you with today?" asked the man, who called himself Michel.

"I would like to drop something off in my safe deposit box."

"Very good," said Michel, "follow me through."

He led her through the glass door, into the interior of the bank. The tellers were out front, but behind the glass there was a wide open room with small offices honeycombing off the sides. There were two large vault doors on the wall in front of her, to the left and the right. Michel led her to the left. In front of the open vault there were two uniformed guards, both in good shape, and there were two more at the other vault. Swift gave them a friendly nod and sized them up. They had guns, but she doubted they would shoot her for having a questionable signature.

Michel stepped around a short counter where a computer faced him but was angled so that she could not see the screen. A security checkpoint.

"I liked your husband very much, Mrs. Roux." He smiled, clicking his mouse. Damn, Swift tensed and fought the urge to run. If Michel knew the Mister, then he likely would have met the Missus. He was likely clicking some security command to bring in more guards. She smiled at him.

"He is very busy," she said.

"He didn't say how he makes his living."

Swift forced herself to keep talking. Do. Not. Panic. You can do this. "The beauty of a Swiss bank," she said in English, "is that you don't have to."

Michel reached under the counter. Swift kept her breathing steady, but her eyes flicked to one of the guards. She hoped she wasn't betraying the lie. He brought his hand back up, holding a small touch-screen keypad. He laid it on the counter, spinning it to face her. He offered her a stylus.

"We scanned the signature card your husband brought in. Please sign in the box and the computer will verify." That was a relief. If Mr. Roux had to bring in a card, it meant Mrs. Roux had never been here to sign it in person. Swift could actually pass herself off as Mrs. Roux and nobody would know any better. At least, as long as Mrs. Roux hadn't made any visits to this box in the past four months.

She held the stylus to the screen. "I don't usually sign computer screens," she said, sounding nervous.

"Don't worry. The computer knows that you can't have identical signatures each time, and I do a visual match."

She touched the screen and dragged the point. The signature on file had been large and ornate. Huge, cursive H and R, carefully printed O U X. The last line of the X cut back under the other letters, underlining the signature. Swift repeated the motion she had practiced for hours.

Michel looked to the screen and gave a slight nod. "And now the PIN."

The touch screen changed to a number keypad. Swift typed six digits and the enter key. Another wait. The guards looked her over, but that might have been because of the form-flattering clothes. Or because they knew she was a fraud.

Michel pulled the pin-pad and stylus away. "Mrs. Roux," he smiled his well-practiced smile again, "you have your key?"

"Of course." She did not have a key.

Michel led her past the guards, through the vault door. Inside there was a small space before a door made of steel bars. Michel fished a key ring from his inside pocket and opened the door.

Inside that door was a room lined with safe deposit boxes of various sizes. "Box 222," she said, wondering if he would expect her to know where it was. Michel pointed to a box about knee-high from the floor.

"Your key?" He held out his hand.

"I'll be holding onto it. Thank you very much, Michel. I can manage from here."

Michel's shoulders seemed to stiffen beneath his suit jacket. "It is customary to escort you to a private room."

"No need. I only need privacy long enough to grab something and drop something off." Michel nodded, his smile fading. "Privacy, Michel." She said his name with a hint of anger. The young banker nodded and went back outside the steel bars.

Swift reached into her purse and rattled a keychain, before pulling her hand out, holding lock-picks the way one might handle keys. With Michel standing only a few feet away, she crouched to the box, slipped in the picks as discretely as possible, and tried to look as if she was turning the key with both hands when in fact she was fooling around for the tumblers.

The small lock inside the box was easy enough to pick for a practiced hand, and Swift had it open in a couple seconds. She slid the box out of its slot in the wall and opened the lid. There was a stack of papers inside, and she calmly packed them into her large purse. She knew that she should leave, that she should get out before she was caught, but the curiosity was too strong. This was probably the evidence of what really happened to Saleb and his wife, and "Jupiter" had tried very hard to have it destroyed. She pulled a few pages out of the folder and looked through it.

It was a printout of an email conversation with Jessica Jordan. It provided an excuse for Jordan to stay in Paris and meet with a contact on a night when Saleb had orders to be in Lyon. This was the set-up that had gotten Jordan killed.

The emails came from someone Jordan was working with to bring down the mole.

They came from Samantha Boswell.

#

Getting out of the bank offered no sense of relief. Walking as fast as she dared, Swift was sweating from the thought that Boswell was Jupiter. Boswell, the most lethal marksman in the world, the woman who never fired a shot that didn't hit its target, was the one hunting her down. Suddenly, Swift realized that even crossing the ocean wasn't enough protection from someone like

331

Boswell. There was nowhere you could hide from an agent that deadly. All Swift wanted now was to get to a safe place, read through Box 222's paperwork, and see if she could get Boswell arrested.

She made it back to the van, which was painted to look like it came from a foundation repair company, and knocked three times on the back door. Before entering the bank, she had worked out a safe-code with Saleb. If everything was fine, Saleb would knock four times in response, then slide open the side door. If something was wrong, he would do anything else.

After a second of delay, the person inside the van unlocked the back door. Without hesitation, Swift grabbed the back corner of the van, put a foot on the bumper, and launched herself onto the van's roof. She guided herself down onto the roof with her arms, so that when her knees settled onto the metal roof there was no sound whatsoever. She set the bulky purse aside, and waited to see what would happen.

A second later, the back door opened, and a female police officer climbed out. The blonde-headed cop had a pistol drawn, which was pointed back inside the van, likely to keep Saleb in line. What was she doing there? How had anyone known to come to this van, and why was she inside? Swift decided she didn't care. All that mattered was securing the files, and getting Saleb out of danger. Her heart was pounding at the thought of having to fight someone. It was one thing to fire a laser or a tranquilizer at a dangerous assassin, but this cop was just doing her job, protecting people. Swift felt nauseous thinking about the possibility of hurting someone who didn't deserve it.

Finally, she made her mind that she could disarm the officer without doing any real damage. Feeling sick to her stomach, she threw herself off the roof. Wrapping her legs around the cop's arm as she fell, she flipped the female officer hard onto the road, twisting the gun out of the officer's hand. As she sprang to her feet, Swift tossed the gun into the road, across the tram tracks and safely out of reach. Behind her, Saleb shouted from inside the van. "She's not a cop!"

As the woman in the police uniform climbed to her feet, Swift had to look past the blonde wig to see that the cop was actually Sam Boswell. Boswell dusted herself off, cracked her knuckles, and settled into a martial arts stance. She had a bloody lip and some road rash on her temple that was slowly oozing blood down her cheek.

"We both know you won't kill me, not that you even could," she said to Swift. Inside the van, Saleb rustled around in the equipment before climbing out to stand next to Swift. He had a handgun, which he cocked and aimed at Boswell.

"She won't kill you," Saleb said, "but me? I'm very dangerous."

Swift pulled the purse from the van's roof and pulled out one of the many pages. "It was you. You're the one who wanted these boxes destroyed because they prove you're the traitor."

"What?" Boswell sounded genuinely confused.

"You sent me to destroy the files about Khalid. You were the one who set him up."

Saleb aimed the gun for Boswell's face. "You killed my wife?"

Boswell kept her hands raised, realizing she was screwed. Saleb was screaming. It seemed that even though Saleb couldn't remember his wife, he could still feel the hurt from her death. He screamed again and again, repeating the question, "Did you kill my wife?"

Boswell shook her head. "Listen—"

Swift shook the papers. "You and your accomplice set up Khalid and his wife to be apart so you could kill them, but your accomplice kept evidence to blackmail you so you tried to make me destroy it. You're the mole."

Boswell only looked at Saleb, deliberately ignoring Swift. "I wasn't the one trying to destroy the evidence. I was the one saving it. That was my safe deposit box in there. And I didn't kill your wife."

"You expect me to believe that?" Saleb felt his face tightening into a grimace of rage and hate. He fought to keep the gun from shaking. "You killed my wife."

"No, I didn't," Boswell insisted. She took a softer tone. "I didn't kill your wife. I couldn't have possibly been there. Because I was the one who shot you."

"What?"

"You were in separate cities. That means two shooters. Someone else got Jessica, but I was assigned to kill you. You know my reputation? I kill what I aim at. Every time I wanted someone dead, they ended up dead. You understand? I shot you and you lived."

Bystanders were watching this happen on the streets of Zurich—an Arab man aiming a gun at a white police officer in the middle of the street. Sirens were coming.

"Let's get out of here and I can explain it," Boswell said. "You're alive because I deliberately didn't hit anything vital in your brain. I let you live because I thought you were innocent."

The part about her reputation was true. They said that Boswell had literally never missed. If she had shot Saleb, he should have died.

"Then why have me destroy the files?" asked Swift.

"Think it through, girl. I didn't. Would I need to send a thief to access my own box? I was keeping those files for my own investigation. My own suspicions that something was wrong inside CIB. And someone found out and sent you to steal from me. That was my evidence that you stole, get it? I'm not your Jupiter."

"Then who is?"

"Best guess? Harry Milton. He's the one who ordered the hit." She still stared in Saleb's eyes. "It was Milton who ordered your wife to be killed. Milton who sent me to kill you. Milton who had you locked in the desert without a trial when you inconvenienced him by living. Milton is the rotten egg here, not me."

"Why did you follow us to Zurich?"

The sirens were on the same street now, closing fast. "We don't have time."

"Answer the question!" Saleb shouted. "Why are you trying to arrest me if you think I'm not guilty?"

"Because Milton has to believe that I fell for it. Because I need to arrest you. Because this bitch was dumb enough to break you out of the safety of secure custody and put you in grave danger out in the real world."

"She's lying to save her own ass," said Swift, moving to the driver's door. "We have to get out of here, and she's not coming with us."

Boswell ignored her. "Take me with you, we can talk this over—"

335

"No chance I'm confining myself in a van with you." Swift shouted, as she got in and started the engine. She leaned back to shout through the rear door. "Leave her and get in, we have what we came for!"

Saleb stared down the sights of the gun, lined up to the face of the woman who had either shot him or killed his wife, depending on which story he believed. Part of Swift prayed he wouldn't shoot her but she was mostly praying that he'd get back in the van before the real cops boxed them in. The thought of going back into captivity with so much on the line made her sweat. A police car roared down the road behind Boswell.

Saleb shouted another question, not shouting out of anger but because the sirens were so loud. "Was my wife a traitor?"

Boswell's eyes watered. She was either telling the truth or a hell of a good actress. "I don't know."

Saleb lowered the gun, climbed in the van, and shut the door. Swift was already pulling into the street before he had the door shut. Saleb slumped to the floor, ejected the magazine, popped the bullet from the chamber and then pulled the trigger over and over, shooting imaginary rounds at the back door as if he could take out all of his frustrations on Boswell then and there.

Swift pulled over in a parking lot, looking to steal a new vehicle. When she pulled the van's door open to get Saleb, she saw that he was still sitting there, his cheeks streaked by tears.

#

After abandoning their stolen car, Swift and Saleb used the city's tram service to travel back to the small hotel where they were staying. They were sharing a room, under the pretense that they were a couple of American tourists. Once back in the room, Swift gave Saleb the files to read over to see if anything jogged his memory, and called Quarrel on his new cell number. Earlier, just after she landed in Zurich, Quarrel had called to tell her that he was with Hall, that his CIA contact was dead, and that Hall swore Shark Scarret was the traitor. Now she called him back to let him know that Scarret wasn't the only one.

"How did it go?" Quarrel said as soon as he answered.

"Got in and out," she said. "And then Boswell was waiting for me."

"Boswell? She followed you?"

"It was her safe deposit box."

Quarrel sighed into the phone. "Damn. Boswell and Shark both?"

"She swears she's not Jupiter. Says the file was her evidence against Milton. I don't know what to believe."

Quarrel said nothing, so Swift kept talking. "How are you?" she asked.

"I'm OK. Better than Jack. He got beat up pretty bad in a car wreck, then Sidorov tortured him for more than a day. He's sleeping right now."

"But you're . . . ?"

"I'll live. Hershey took me captive but the only injuries were the ones I gave myself when I crashed the truck into a tree."

"You did what?"

"I'm fine," he said with a little chuckle. After another pause, he offered, "I think Boswell's the mole. I think she lied to you today."

337

"How do you know?"

"Thorpe. I told you he's answering to Fatale, but I didn't tell you why. The mole kidnapped his wife."

"His wife!?" she said the latter word too loud, and Saleb shot her a look, suddenly more interested in her conversation than the file of documents. She shook a hand at him reassuringly, trying to make him go back to reading. "I didn't know he had a wife. It wasn't in your briefing."

"I didn't know. He's kept her secret all this time. Officially, his wife died on his honeymoon. I think she must be in England, somewhere in the London area. So if our mole is on that side of the Atlantic, and Shark is still in the USA as of this morning . . . "

" . . . then Boswell's the mole," she said, completing his sentence. "If she's on this side of the ocean, then she's the mole."

Quarrel agreed. "And, the other thought I had was that we need to know if we can trust Harry Milton. I'm going to call him and tell him Jack's story about Shark. I'll give him Sidorov's location as proof. If he moves on Shark, he's a good guy. If he leaves Shark free to roam the world, he's not so good."

"Sounds like a plan, I guess." She wanted to say more to him, something more personal, but it was awkward and Khalid was sitting right there. "What do we do? Now, I mean?"

"Find Boswell. Follow her back to Mrs. Thorpe. We need to get Thorpe off the other team and back on our side. Think you can do that?"

She watched Saleb turn the pages and decided that they could. "Yeah. We'll watch the airport for anything bound for London. She'll be on one of them, and we'll follow."

"OK," Quarrel said, "I'll see you soon."

"See ya," she said casually, maybe too casually since Saleb raised his eyebrows.

They hung up.

Saleb looked up at her from his position lying across the bed with the files spread in front of him. "Flying to London?"

"We're gonna follow Boswell. Quarrel thinks she kidnapped another agent's wife."

"This Quarrel seems pretty sure of himself."

"He's the man in charge of the whole thing."

Saleb nodded. "OK. But I don't think you'll find her there."

"Why not?"

"Because I believe her. I think Boswell was on my side. What evidence do you have that she's this kidnapper?"

Swift wished that Saleb had been with her throughout her ordeal in America. He would have seen how Boswell threatened her at their meeting—attacked her so savagely when she broke into CIB. Of all the agents on Quarrel's list of suspects, Swift had more reason to hate Boswell than any of the others. It was her box, her fake passports, and she had just coincidentally flown across the Atlantic on the same day that Mrs. Thorpe was kidnapped in England. Swift explained it all, and Saleb, still doubting, nodded.

"We'll go to the airport. But I really think you're wrong about this."

"This is what the evidence gave us. We put everything into finding that safe deposit box. We have to follow up." She didn't want to force him to come along. She wanted him to be fully on-board. There was only one way to earn that. They had to find Boswell at the airport.

34

Chris Quarrel entered the bank first, followed by Jack Hall. The agent who normally greeted people under the guise of offering banking services recognized them immediately, and she just stepped aside and let them enter the office that held the hidden elevator. Nobody made any move to stop them. If anything, the faces of the greeter and the various tellers showed a look of shock and something close to fear. Jack Hall was number one on the federal Most Wanted list. In their eyes, he had killed an entire CIA team when the team interfered with Jack's theft of nuclear materials. He was a terrorist, a traitor, and an unrepentant killer. Their retreat meant that they felt safer staying out of the way and pressing the alarm. Quarrel didn't like to induce fear in everyone, but at least he didn't have to draw his gun and force his way to the elevator.

As soon as Quarrel and Hall were in the office, the drop-away floor hidden in the carpet started to lower into the hidden elevator shaft, and both men had to hop down to catch it before it got too far.

"They'll have the Marines waiting for us," said Hall.

"Guaranteed," agreed Quarrel. "Better disarm now."

Hall nodded. Both men pulled out pistols and ejected the magazines. They both pulled back the slides to eject the bullets from their respective chambers, then set the guns and magazines on the floor, close to where the door would be once they reached the bottom.

"You ever think," asked Quarrel, "that maybe this thing stops half way down and they'll just gas us?"

Hall smiled. It was the first time Quarrel had seen that since the training exercise in the Ontario woods. Despite his concussion, possible cracked skull, badly burned scalp, and generally tortured condition, Jack still seemed to find amusement in Quarrel's inexperience.

"It's a base that happens to be underground, kid. Not a magical underground lair."

"I was just sort of, you know," Quarrel said, suddenly unsure what he had meant, "just half-joking."

Hall nodded a little. "It's OK to be cautious. But trust me, Harry will want to talk and talk means we'll both be wide awake." The elevator was low enough that the first inch of the doorway cracked above the floor now, a line of light in the dark shaft.

"Best to get against the back wall, hands up," said Jack. Both men followed that advice, raising their hands and standing with their feet shoulder-width apart. As the elevator settled to the floor they saw that the entire doorway was filled with Marine guards, dressed in their black suits and ties with white shirts. There were six of them here, each with an automatic rifle aimed at Quarrel and Hall. They were waiting for orders, or for Jack to make a move. For a little while, nothing happened.

"All you, boss," said Jack without turning his head.

Quarrel swallowed hard, worked up some courage, and spoke sternly at the Marines, as if giving them orders. "I brought him in. This is still my case," said Quarrel. "Jack Hall is my witness, let us through."

"Your jurisdiction ended when you murdered Agent Hinkston, Mr. Quarrel." The voice was Harry Milton, who must have been standing somewhere behind the guards, out of sight.

"That was not me. I was there, I put my prints on the gun. But it was the Canadian agent, Thompson. And the house agent was killed by Pete Hershey."

"Yet another survivor of your bombing?" Milton's voice asked. "Seems a lot of untrustworthy people walked away from that one." He was caustic, spiteful. Quarrel had turned his organization inside out; Hall was seen as a traitor. It was no wonder Milton sounded like he was about to order the Marines to fire.

"Yeah," shouted Quarrel, trying to talk past the wall of Marines. "Hershey pulled the trigger on the bomb. He bragged about it."

"And I presume Jack's also innocent of his crimes?" asked Milton, adding a heap of sarcasm onto the word 'innocent.'

"Yes," shouted Jack. "That was all Scarret. He's your goddamn rat."

There was a long pause. Quarrel felt one of the Marines staring at him. Most were focused on Jack, but the Marine directly in front of Quarrel was staring right at him, challenging him, and almost daring him to move. Quarrel felt more afraid of that guard than he had been of the men he killed in the apartment.

Finally, Milton's voice came back. "Escort them to the interrogation cells. Keep them separate."

Quarrel and Hall were marched down the corridor in a column of soldiers. Milton was nowhere to be seen, and Quarrel realized that Milton was talking to them over the speakers from the safety of his office. Jack was placed in the first interrogation room, the same one where Swift had been held, while Quarrel was taken a little farther, room 2.

Quarrel had to wait over an hour before Milton came to see him. He must have spoken to Hall first. When he came, Harry was alone. He wore suit pants and an untucked, wrinkled dress shirt. He looked like he hadn't slept in days, with pale skin and dark circles under his eyes. He looked old. Milton sat across from Quarrel, who was cuffed and shackled to a metal chair at one end of a bolted-down steel table.

"So let's have it. Everything from the safe house where Hinkston died to walking into my office uninvited. I want to hear it all."

So Quarrel told him. He told him about the Teacup, about Hinkston's team waiting in Washington state, about Hershey and the long drive south to Sidorov's hideout. He told him about meeting Jack on that long, narrow driveway in the forest, and gave a vague account of Swift leaving the country to follow a lead. All the while, Milton just listened. He didn't ask questions or need clarification. He just sat and took it all in, his face revealing nothing. The only thing that got a response from Milton was when Quarrel mentioned that Fatale had gotten to Thorpe's wife.

"His wife?"

"That's what he wrote."

"Officially, they were never married. And even among those who knew about her, Julia died twenty years ago."

"I don't know anything about—" Quarrel started to say.

"You wouldn't. Only a handful of people in the world knew that Julia was still alive. And William Thorpe wouldn't tell you she existed at all unless it was true. Fatale has Julia. Son of a bitch . . . " Milton trailed off,

344

lost in thought. After almost thirty seconds of silence, he told Quarrel to continue with the story, so Quarrel told him some more, staying vague about Swift but being very clear that he believed Hall that Shark Scarret was the traitor who killed that CIA team. When the story was done, Milton asked no follow-up questions, instead he just stood up and left the room without a word.

Harry Milton had spent an hour alone with both Hall and Quarrel, evaluating the stories they told, and dammit if Milton didn't believe it. Too much of what they said fit with evidence that had been puzzling him until now. Quarrel swore that Thompson had killed Hinkston, and the crime scene report had already told him that Thompson was covered in gunshot residue. The team on the highway had recovered Jack's toolkit, which had seemed like slam-dunk proof except that the bag was still neatly packed. If Jack was going to break into a nuclear storage depot, wouldn't he have packed the tools onto his body for the mission, not left them neatly packed in a backpack? And the highway attack itself had been so sloppy. Van exploding on public highways, Jack's SUV rolled over so violently. It wasn't Jack's usual sneaky style. But it did fit Shark Scarret's explosive tactics to a T.

And the address they had given of Sidorov's hideout had turned out to be real. Sidorov was still rotting in the basement, in a puddle of water that had once been a pile of ice. Milton had a team searching the place for any sign that Shark had ever been there.

After working his way back to his office, Milton poured a tall scotch from his decanter, took a long gulp,

345

and sighed. He paced around the room, taking a few smaller sips, and moved behind the desk. He stared at the phone, and within a few seconds, it rang. Answering it, he got the confirmation he needed: they had Scarret's fingerprints all over Sidorov's hideout. Hall was telling the truth.

He wiped a layer of dust off his computer monitor and booted it up. The machine was top-of-the-line, upgraded more often than Milton actually used it. It was connected to the satellite network within thirty seconds. Milton brought up Scarret's file, and the satellite tracked him down right away. He checked that the satellite was in position to send a signal to Shark's implanted bomb. It was.

A small window popped up, asking for the password. This was a code only Milton knew; a random series of numbers that he used as a password on some of his more "unorthodox" projects. He typed it from memory and it appeared onscreen as ten asterisks.

Now it was just a matter of choice. Click on "Execute," or click on "Cancel."

"Execute" was an appropriate word for what this program would do. He clicked it. The signal would be sent after a one-second delay, and a second after that, Shark Scarret would be dead.

Another window popped up. Signal sent.

There was no third window. Milton had used these devices before, and there should have been another message. One that says, "Target detonated." It never came.

He reached for the phone on his desk to call Kilo and find out what was wrong with the system, but the phone rang before his hand reached it.

"Milton," he said as he picked it up.

"Hi, Harry," said a taunting, spiteful voice. "It's about time you tried to blow me up," Shark Scarret teased.

"How?" Milton couldn't understand how Shark was still talking to him. The signal should have killed him already.

"Oh that bomb you had them wrap around my spine? I had that taken out a year after you put it in. Bet you thought that was impossible, eh? Tamper-proof? Not with the people I know, Harry." Shark chuckled, but it was forced, taunting. "I took it out and took it apart. I kept the GPS tracker in my neck, so that when you scanned for it, you'd still think you had me. You'd still think I was on your leash. But the explosive? That fun little nugget of plastic explosive you wanted to use to blow my head off? That, I kept safe."

Milton saw red, the anger, frustration and futility of the moment washing over him. For over ten years he had thought Shark was leashed, contained, that the traitorous bastard would never risk betraying CIB. All that time, he had been wrong. Shark kept taunting.

"The real question is, were you stupid enough to use the same password on my bomb as you were on this big ol' particle emitter? Just let me see . . . "

Milton felt numb. Shark was typing something, then he came back on the line with a smile in his voice. "Ahh, yes. Well, that just about wraps things up. Thanks, Hare. You've been a real treat. I guess I'll be going. Oh, and Harry? If you were wondering what I did with that little remote-activated bomb after I took it out of my neck . . . "

Milton had never been so defeated, so useless, so defenceless. For the first time in a forty-year career, he didn't know what to do next. Shark continued: " . . . I reprogrammed it and put it in a pacemaker. Bye, Harry."

Milton dropped the phone. If it was all true, if Scarret had outsmarted him, strung him along for all those years . . . no, Harry didn't have time left to think about that. He had to check the GPS. See if Scarret really was where Milton suspected him to be. He might not have much time left, but he could still help Jack, help Quarrel, tell them where Scarret was hiding now. He closed the extra windows on his screen and told the satellite to zoom in, all the while reaching for the dropped phone with his left hand, but never finding it.

The left side of his chest exploded outward as if someone inside his chest had swung a sledgehammer into his ribs. Broken bone jabbed and tore the fabric of his shirt, and the force of the internal explosion forced blood into Milton's brain so fast he died before he even knew that it had happened. He slumped backward in his chair, both his eyes turning red with burst blood vessels.

Harry Milton was dead, sitting in the office where he spent most of his life, bloodshot eyes still open and looking toward the monitor. On the screen a window popped up.

TARGET DETONATED.

PART FIVE:
I EXPECT YOU TO DIE

35

William Thorpe was pulled from the trunk of a car after a two-hour drive. The stops and starts near the end made it clear that he was in a city, and given where they'd started, it was obvious that city was New York. The mercenaries who pulled him out of the car—his arms were bound with a loop of metal ribbon that had cut him on both wrists—were not the same goons who had loaded him into the car. They hadn't made the trip. From what he had heard through the car, those guys were all going "to the project."

The new goons were dressed in suits, but underneath they were carved from stone. They were clearly former military, the sort of guys Globection liked to hire as contractors. They were in a parking garage. It was just Thorpe, the two suited men, and the car's driver, Fatale.

"You're doin' so good, Willy." She said with a smirk, pulling at the elastic that held her hair and letting her tresses fall over her shoulders. She was dressed down today, in a pair of black yoga pants and a long sweater. Even without makeup her looks were enchanting, dangerous. She was letting the hair down for someone else's sake. That and the parking garage were all Thorpe needed to be sure.

"You're giving me to Mercier."

"I always give gifts to boys on naughty lists," she said with a sarcastic smirk before turning her attention to the pair of gigantic thugs. "Heel, boys," she mocked, snapping her fingers and pointing toward an elevator ten metres away.

One mercenary grabbed Thorpe's arm and marched him behind Fatale. The second man opened the back door of the car and pulled out Thorpe's briefcase from the back seat.

They rode the elevator without speaking, although the superior smirk on Fatale's face had triggered the urge to insult her. Just a little pithy comment to remind her who she was dealing with, but somehow, he couldn't think of anything to say.

There was a churning in his gut, tightness in his chest, a buzz behind his eyes.

He was about to be in a room with Mercier.

Oh, how Thorpe had waited. His adrenaline was rising as fast as the elevator.

The doors parted as Thorpe was ushered into a large sitting room. Mercier had the entire top floor of the building, and his actual office was only in one corner of it. The rest was opulent meeting and sitting space, something to wow clients and politicians. You could see all of Central Park almost as soon as you got off the elevator. The chairs were leather, the wood on the counters a warm brown. The wall with the elevator was surely concrete, but it had been covered in old wood that looked like something you'd see in a century-old gentlemen's club. "Hugo Zoeli" was nouveau riche, but he did it well.

There was even a well-stocked bar along the right wall. Thorpe looked at the half-full bottles and felt his hands quiver.

The mercenary pushed Thorpe toward a cushy leather armchair and shoved him into it, his wrists still bound. The other laid Thorpe's briefcase on the coffee table, then placed Thorpe's cell phone on top. The two thugs moved to positions standing behind Thorpe's chair, no doubt to hold him down if he tried to attack Mercier. Fatale stretched languidly across a loveseat, each of her movements deliberate and slow. She watched Thorpe, an eyebrow cocked, and smiled. "Don't worry, Willy. You did good for us. Mrs. Willy even got to have her breakfast shake this morning."

Thorpe finally found the will to speak, but it wasn't a pithy pun or a swaggering taunt like he usually offered up. He was too angry, too broken, for that sort of thing now. Instead, he looked her in the eyes and told her, "When I kill you, it'll hurt."

"William Thorpe: the very definition of class," said a slightly accented voice from behind him. Martin Mercier had done well to adopt an American accent, but an experienced ear could still hear the continental French underneath the phoney New York Italian.

"Martin Mercier."

Mercier came around the chair, dressed in a tailored suit, hair slicked back, holding a cell phone. "The name's Zoeli. Please, don't get up." He lifted fatale's legs off the arm of the loveseat, tucked himself under them, and sat back down, letting her drop her legs back over his lap. "So, Thorpe, we meet again. What's it been?"

"Twenty-three years."

"Oh that's right. Your honeymoon." Mercier's phone beeped. He looked at it briefly, then set it on the side table. "Sorry, business is booming." Mercier shifted uncomfortably, as if something was poking at him. He reached behind himself and when his hand came back he was holding a Glock pistol, which he absentmindedly placed next to the phone. "Damn things always get in the way," he said with a toothless smile.

"Twenty-three years," Thorpe almost growled as he repeated it.

Mercier still smiled. "I want to clear something up. I know you think I tried to kill you and accidentally shot your wife."

"Don't try to deny it!"

"OK. OK." He held up a hand and tried to look contrite, but his face was still viciously playful. "I did fire that bullet. But here's the thing. You think I was hired to kill you, and I took my shot, and it missed. And your wife's brain-dead because of me. That's what you think happened."

Mercier turned to Fatale, "My dear, I'm sorry you have to hear this part." Back to Thorpe: "I shot the bitch on purpose. You think your wife was an angel, but she was a snake. A Judas. I paid that bitch—"

"Julia!" Thorpe screamed, jolting forward so hard he almost jumped out of the chair, but the hulking guards shoved him back into his seat. Mercier looked pleased.

"—I paid Julia some very good money to make sure I disappeared from MI-6's database. But she let me down. So she had to go."

"She wasn't a spy," said Thorpe. She had been a secretary in a corporation Thorpe had investigated. Julia had been just another well-placed woman whom Thorpe

352

used to get close to a powerful and dangerous man. But then she had been so much more than that. She could touch his heart in ways no other woman could, and his heart still beat a little faster whenever he saw her, even after all these years in the hospital. She hadn't been a spy. That was his life, not hers. She had been another victim of William Thorpe's lifestyle, another woman who suffered for Queen and Country and Agent Triple-Eight.

"She was a better agent than you, Thorpe. You're a drunken, womanizing sexist and you always were. But Julia was the real thing. She could get close to any man and make him feel like he was the most important person in the world. Make him feel real, genuine love for her. She did that for you, didn't she?"

Thorpe's face twisted as he fought to think of anything to say. Julia wasn't a spy. His life with her wasn't a lie. She was his wife.

"She played you and you bought it, but you never even knew that while you were working her for MI-6, she was conning you for MI-7." Mercier rubbed his hand along Fatale's leg. "I know because she did it to me first."

Thorpe couldn't look at Mercier anymore. He had to let his eyes sink to the floor while Mercier kept talking. "I thought I had tamed her, just like you did. I thought she would betray England for me, erase my photos and my fingerprints, get my name out of all the files. But she backed out, she left some of my information intact. She took my money, broke my heart, and betrayed me."

Thorpe lifted his head again. "We found your prints on those documents, even after the Digamma plot should have erased them from our records," he said, knowing that he shouldn't say it. He knew that once he started matching the real facts with Mercier's fiction, he'd

353

never get it out of his head, but the story fit. He had been a sucker, thinking that Julia was an innocent victim, when she had been a higher-level agent the whole time.

"It was unfortunate that you fell so hard for her. If only you had known what a duplicitous bitch she really was, you wouldn't have spent all those years visiting the hospital."

"So what do you want with me?" Thorpe asked, his voice quiet and resigned.

"I want you to move on. Show that lying bitch that she can't ruin your life anymore. Take her place in my organization. Destroy my files at MI-7, and you can live out your days sleeping around in Jamaica like God intended."

Thorpe shook his head, tears welling in his eyes. "You want me to betray the Service."

"I want you to be free of it. Free of her. Be your own man for once."

The tears squeezed out when Thorpe closed his eyes. He let out a shuddering breath and looked Mercier in the eyes. "So she betrayed you. She betrayed you and then she married me," responded Thorpe. "She was loyal to her country, and to me. What she did was lie to a murderer and a fool to keep her country safe. And thanks to Julia's choice, you can't go on pretending to be Hugo Zoeli any longer. You want me to be a traitor, because Julia was a patriot." Thorpe's eyes cleared as he stared into Mercier, and the tears stopped flowing. "I'll never betray England. Arresting you will mean finishing her work."

Mercier shrugged. "We both killed people for a living, but let's face it, Thorpe, I did it better. I made better friends. Friends," he waved, gesturing to the opulent setting, "in high places. You only made enemies and got women killed. Once you and that Canadian kid are dead, Martin Mercier returns to the ether and Hugo Zoeli carries on. I have other friends who will make sure of that."

Thorpe still stared hard into his enemy, his determination growing with each poisonous word Mercier spoke. "I don't need friends," said Thorpe. "I'll kill you myself." Mercier's fake smile finally slipped, and he picked up the gun without ever looking away from Thorpe's staring eyes.

Fatale interrupted the stare-down, flipping her long legs off Hugo's lap, momentarily blocking his eyes to break up the staring contest between the men, before spinning out of the loveseat and standing up. She put her hands on her hips and talked down at Mercier. "OK, you got your British boy-toy. Now give me what you promised."

Zoeli rolled his shoulders, his face relaxing out of the tense, coiled posture it had taken in his talk with Thorpe. "The money's already been transferred to your account. Now show me what's in the case." Fatale sighed, and marched over to where the bodyguard had set Thorpe's metal case on the counter. She moved the cellphone to the countertop and tossed the case onto the sofa next to Mercier, where she had just been sitting.

"That case is all he had with him in the car when he thought he was going to arrest you. Just some booze for the old boozehound. He had no evidence."

Mercier flipped open the case to find the bottles, glasses, and martini shakers. He shook his head and made a disappointed tut-tut sound before examining around the edges of the case for hidden compartments.

Eventually he was satisfied, so he caught Fatale's eye and then nodded toward the elevator doors. "Just call the right-hand elevator down from the roof."

Fatale trotted over to the wall and called the second elevator, and it descended just slowly enough for everyone to watch as she awkwardly fidgeted, not sure of what to do with her hands. When the doors opened, she rushed toward someone, wrapping her arms around him.

"I knew I'd see you again," she said.

"Just had to lay low for a while," said the man.

She slipped her arms off him and down his body, so that they ended up holding hands like high-schoolers when they walked back toward Mercier.

Mercier smiled for them. The smile was just as fake as the rest of Hugo Zoeli's life, and Thorpe only hated him more for it. "Now," Mercier said to Fatale, "you have been paid in full. I'll be in touch if I ever need to hire you again, but for now the job's done. The project will be ready soon, Scarret has the password, and Harry Milton's dead. You're free and clear."

Fatale nodded and headed back toward the elevator, pulling her boyfriend's hand as she went, but the man lingered. "I'm not done with Mr. Hershey yet," said Mercier. Fatale stopped and turned.

"What do you mean?"

"He still owes me for saving his life. You're done, but he has one more job to do. Head on down to the lobby, he'll meet you there."

Fatale looked disappointed and disheartened, her entire posture sagging, but she obeyed the order and dutifully walked into an elevator and closed the doors. Mercier waited for the elevator to move down before waving for the man to speak.

356

"So what now?" asked the boyfriend. Thorpe had never met him, but from the name it was clear that this was Pete Hershey, another traitor from Quarrel's office.

"Now you finish what you started in Ottawa. And when it's done I want you at the Teacup. It'll be up and running soon."

"Understood," said Hershey, who seemed to have no emotion about any of this. Hershey walked over to the second elevator and followed Fatale down to the lobby, never once looking back or saying anything to Thorpe.

"Finish what he started?" asked Thorpe.

"Sure," said Mercier, standing up and walking over to the seat where the guards held Thorpe. "Quarrel still hasn't been taken care of, and Fatale knows too much about me. I didn't get to be Hugo Zoeli by leaving loose ends."

Once Mercier was close enough, Thorpe spat in his face. Mercier wiped the spittle away with his cuff and pointed the gun at Thorpe's chest. "One in the heart and one in the head. I'm sure you've seen my methodology before?"

The guards pinned Thorpe down. His arms were still bound in the steel restraints. He tried to shake and fight it, but the goons gave him no room to move. He had no way to fight it when Martin Mercier leaned in and held the gun only a metre from Thorpe's chest. Thorpe closed his eyes so he wouldn't have to watch as Mercier pulled the trigger.

36

"Jesus," said Quarrel as he stepped into Milton's office.

Many of the top CIB staff were already gathered inside the office, or huddled outside the door. Quarrel had to push past analysts, technical experts, and even a few of the muscle-bound guards, all of whom had gathered around Milton in a collective state of shock. Inside, he found Hall, Meg, Kilo, and Gig waiting for him.

And, of course, Harry Milton, slumped backward in his chair, his rumpled dress shirt stained with blood.

"What happened?" said Quarrel, after everyone else looked to him.

"His ribs are poking outward," said Meg, the resident expert on novel ways to kill a man. "I'd say something inside his body blew up."

"You mean . . . " Quarrel started to say, before he was sure what he even intended to ask, "you mean he ate a bomb?"

She shook her head. "I'd say it was implanted. Anything that could create this kind of force would have been too big to slip into his food. I've X-rayed Harry before. He had a pacemaker. I'd say it was hiding a small plastic explosive."

"Jesus," Quarrel said again.

"And I know what triggered it," said Gig, who was standing beside Harry's desk, the closest of any of them to Harry's body. Gig had Milton's computer screen turned sideways so he could see what Harry had been working on. "Harry never used this thing. He kept his mission files on paper, got his briefings in hard copy. He only turned the computer on if he absolutely had to. And today, he was using a program that I've never seen him use."

"Which was what, exactly?" demanded Hall, his patience wearing thin. Hall, like Quarrel, had only just been released from custody only to find that their boss was dead. For a man with Hall's short fuse, it was agonizing to stand around waiting for answers. Gig turned the big old computer monitor to face Hall.

"Harry was using his satellite tracker program. This is designed for detonating a small explosive implanted inside a GPS-linked tracking implant."

"Oh, shit," said Meg, realizing what he meant.

"What?" asked Quarrel.

Meg answered him: "As far as I know, there's only one man alive with a bomb inside a tracker: Shark Scarret. It's the threat that Harry used to keep Shark in line."

"The bomb in Shark's neck," said Quarrel. "Harry triggered it, and his pacemaker exploded."

"Dammit!" shouted Jack. "I'm the one who told him to take Shark out. He could have killed him ten years ago!" Hall turned away, shaking his head. Quarrel thought Hall may have wiped his eyes, but he made sure nobody could see it happen.

Quarrel looked to Harry again. The old spymaster's head was tipped way back, his bloodshot eyes still open. Quarrel walked past the techies to reach Milton, and closed the old man's eyes. He looked to the others to see that they were all looking to the floor, in an unspoken, impromptu moment of silence. Quarrel took a deep breath and let the silence linger for just a few seconds before he interrupted it.

"Can we at least see where Shark was?" he asked Gig.

"Actually, yeah. I guess Shark's tracker was still implanted. Must be how he could fool Harry for all these years . . ."

"So where was Scarret?"

"The Yukon. I've got it coordinated right here onscreen." Gig pointed to the corner of the satellite image.

Hall turned back to face everyone, his face red but his anger less. "Write it down, find me a plane. This ends tonight."

Meg nodded. "I'll get a plane, but if you want a pilot, I'm coming with you."

Hall shook his head. "Not a chance. You're not a field agent."

Meg stepped closer to Hall, her petite frame dwarfed by his massive, linebacker-sized body. "Oh, I'm sorry, do you know how to disarm a gigantic microwave gun? Of all the people here, which one is a scientist whose entire job is building crazy weapons?"

"You can come," said Quarrel. He turned to Hall, "We need her."

"No we don't need her," Hall snapped. "Because I'm not disarming it, I'm blowing it sky high. Kilo, get me as much C-4 as we've got."

"Then fly your own damn plane," responded Meg. "Oh, that's right, you don't know how."

Finally, Hall caved. "I don't have time for this. Load up and let's get to the plane."

#

While Hall loaded up on guns, bombs, and ammo, and Meg packed a bag with electronic gadgets, Quarrel got on the phone. He knew that while Hall's plan to blow the Teacup to pieces was the best way to ensure it was never activated, there were no guarantees that they would succeed. Quarrel needed to know that even if the Teacup was fired, it would never hurt anyone. He needed to know that there wouldn't be another building full of people dying for whatever insanity plagued Mercier, Shark, and Boswell.

So Quarrel imagined a plan, happening one step at a time, like falling dominoes:

Swift tracks down Mrs. Thorpe, and rescues her from Boswell.

Swift finds a way to tell Thorpe that his wife is free.

Thorpe escapes from Fatale and Mercier, and shuts down the satellite.

The Teacup becomes useless without the reflector to point it down at the Earth.

It was a perfect redundancy: Quarrel and Hall's mission set out to the Yukon to stop the TCPE, while Swift and Thorpe work on killing the satellite from the other side of the world. When he had been an office drone back in Ottawa, he had dreamed of the spy life. He had imagined himself as a solo operative, working alone, needing no help. Now, he was praying for the success of a plan that he wouldn't even be involved in. A plan where he was counting on Swift, Saleh, and Thorpe to come through. It wasn't what he had imagined. It was the real world, and he finally understood that.

He called Thorpe's cell.

#

In the penthouse of the GX building, William Thorpe squeezed his eyes shut so he wouldn't have to watch as Mercier pulled the trigger.

And then his phone rang.

"What's that?" said Mercier to one of the goons.

"It's his phone," said the guard.

Thorpe's phone had been brought in for Mercier to examine, along with his briefcase. Mercier had left the case sitting on the loveseat, but the phone was still on a side counter, chiming out an urgent ring. Sensing that the phone call might keep him alive a minute longer, Thorpe spoke up.

"Only Quarrel has that number. If he's calling, he's got something important to say."

Mercier's nostrils flared and he lowered his gun. "Bring the phone," he said to one of the guards. One of the two former-military bodyguards went and retrieved the phone from the counter and placed it in Mercier's free hand. "Answer it, on speaker, and do be discreet."

Thorpe nodded and reached for the phone. Thorpe knew what Mercier didn't, that he had already tipped his hand to Quarrel. Quarrel knew that Thorpe was being blackmailed, so both ends of the conversation would be lying. He only hoped that Quarrel knew which lies to tell.

"Thorpe," said Thorpe, answering the call.

"It's me," said Quarrel.

"What's up?"

"Milton's dead. Shark Scarret's still alive. The bomb implant, it was . . . "

"I see," said Thorpe. Quarrel was doing well, thought Thorpe. Tell them truths that they already know so they don't see the lies. "Where does that leave you?"

362

"There's no one left to run CIB so Jack's calling the shots now. We're going all-out on the weapon in the Yukon. I need you to get everything you can out of Fatale and take down the satellite that GX is using to aim the beam. Between the two of us, we should be able to stop this thing."

Mercier nodded. Quarrel had just revealed his own plan, to attack the weapon in the north, which Mercier would now counter-attack with a plan of his own. However, Quarrel had also been clever enough to keep up the lie that Thorpe was in hiding with Fatale, which is what he wanted Mercier to hear. The bit about Thorpe taking the satellite down was clearly an instruction for Thorpe, but Mercier was so confident that Thorpe was beaten, he only smiled at that part. When Quarrel paused, Mercier whispered, "The girl?"

"Where's your new friend? Swift?" Thorpe asked into the phone.

"Overseas," said Quarrel. "Retrieving some important messages, files, photographs. She'll be safe. Once she had what she needed, she was going to disappear for good."

"OK. I'll do what I can on the satellite. Stay in touch."

"I will," said Quarrel. They both hung up.

Mercier grinned. "So, they're about to leave CIB, heading for the Teacup. I should have an army around the place before they arrive. You've been very useful, Mr. Thorpe."

"Obliged," responded Thorpe.

"We'll keep him alive for now, in case Quarrel decides to check in with more insights into his brilliant plan of attack," Mercier said to one of the guards. "Take him upstairs and lock him up. And make sure that phone stays charged!"

The goons jerked Thorpe out of the chair and marched him to a stairway leading up into a hidden level between the penthouse and the roof. Thorpe didn't fight them. He was too inspired by Quarrel's hidden message. "Messages, files, photographs. She'll be safe." Thorpe had told Quarrel about his wife's kidnapping by writing a message on the file that held photographs. Swift was overseas, and she would be safe.

There was still hope for Julia. And that was a reason to live.

It was a reason to keep fighting.

#

After Quarrel hung up, he looked at Gig. "Did we get it?"

Gig grinned. "Thorpe's cell went through this cell tower," he said, pointing at the screen on his workstation computer. Both men were crammed inside Gig's surprisingly small office while Hall, Kilo and Meg were gearing up for their mission. "Thorpe answered that call from the GX building, Manhattan."

It was Quarrel's turn to grin. "He's with Mercier. That's where Mercier will control the satellite from." Which meant that as long as Thorpe could stay alive, all it would take is word that his wife was safe and Thorpe would be able to take out the satellite. "He's exactly where we want him to be."

There was a knock on the door frame, and Hall was standing there. "We're set. Let's roll," he was already heading for the elevator before he finished saying it.

364

Quarrel shook Gig's hand and ran after Hall. They reached the elevator shaft and called for it to descend, and Meg caught up to them just before the bank-office-elevator reached them.

"What took you so long?" demanded Hall.

"Sorry, sorry," she said. "It just occurred that maybe I should pack warm clothes."

They climbed onto the elevator and started to rise, three people about to fly across the continent to take on God-knows-how-many GX contractors, Shark Scarret, and a giant ray gun.

"Don't worry," said Quarrel. "Canada's beautiful in the spring."

#

Erica Gibbons and Peter Hershey found the nearest hotel and booked a room. After weeks apart, weeks where she wasn't even sure that Mercier had kept his promise to keep Pete alive, she had her man back. With him, she didn't have to be Fatale, the ruthless bitch that she played with Thorpe. She could just be Erica, and now that they were reunited she realized how much she had missed being Erica.

They were making out in the elevator, holding hands in the hallway, and somehow managed to get the door open with their hands all over each other. They fell into the bed, already with clothes loosened, buttons open. His kiss was the same, maybe a little more aggressive, a little hungrier, but they had been apart for weeks and she felt the same way. She needed him.

Ottawa had started as just a job. Infiltrate the CSIS-2 office. Cultivate useful relationships with higher-ranked agents in order to get at classified intelligence. Watch out for certain red flags, like the Jekyll and Hyde book. It was easy work for someone as skilled as Fatale. But it was also a long con, and she had ever been a quick-and-dirty sort of agent.

And over time, Fatale had settled into the role so well that she felt comfortable there. CSIS was small compared to the American or British Services. The agents there watched out for terrorism and protected people. It was good work, with a minimum of politics or personal games or bullshit. It was easy to do that work and feel good about it. It was easy to be Erica and feel good about it.

And the agent she seduced, Pete Hershey, was a good guy. He had enough ambition and drive to keep him distracted from her deception, and was a good enough man to make her feel loved. It was easy enough to fall for Erica's man and feel good about it.

And when she did hear from Zoeli, whom she didn't know was actually Mercier, it was almost jarring to think about having to call in a hit against the office, to disrupt all their good work, to kill them. To kill Hershey.

It was only a week before the bombing that she had bargained for his life, telling Zoeli that she wouldn't call in red flags if Zoeli didn't guarantee Peter's safety. After Zoeli agreed, they went on the training course together, and spent every night together in that motel, living as openly as a couple as they had ever dared. For Fatale, this would have been a deception, a game she played to fool a man into feeling something. But when she was with Hershey, she wasn't Fatale, she was Erica, and Erica was in love.

She had given five years of service to Hugo Zoeli's organization, and each year was a two million dollar payday. She now had ten million dollars, the man of her dreams, and no obligations. It was time for "Fatale" to go away, and she had a feeling that wherever they ended up living, her new identity would be named Erica.

The first time they made love in that New York hotel was rough, fierce, almost violent. Hershey had betrayed his nation, his office, he had let people die for her. All that aggression, all the emotional hell of the last few weeks came out of them both in rough, passionate, angry love.

The second time was slower, more like the old them. He was only alive because of her. And the more she thought about it, the more she felt she was only living for him. Her entire adult life had been a series of crimes, of short-term stays among people she couldn't stand. And then Hershey had come along and she suddenly had a home. He still smelled like the old Pete, even if he had spent a few weeks locked up wherever Mercier was hiding him. When the second session was over, they rolled onto their backs, side-by-side, catching their breath.

"I guess you got over it," she said.

"Over what?"

"That I'm not who you thought I was." She rolled to face him, looking deep into his eyes, and she realized that she wanted forgiveness from him. She had lied, betrayed him, she had called in the bomb that killed his entire office. She had ruined his life. Looking at him, she realized that she could never make up for the pain she had caused him.

After the bombing she had tried to be heartless about it. She had treated Thorpe like garbage, attempting to dehumanize him in her mind because she knew that Mercier would kill both Thorpe and his wife, which was another cross to bear. She had tried to bury guilt, to be as cold as Mercier, but now that Peter was back, she started to feel the weight of the last month. She realized now just how horrible it all was that for once in her career she couldn't justify a kill. She was the bad guy on this, and she had made Peter Hershey her victim. Lying in bed with him, she was more than naked, she was hollow. His forgiveness would do a lot to fill that hole in her heart.

"They explained it," he said. He reached to squeeze her hand between his.

"How did they do it?" she asked.

"Explain it?" he said, "Explain you?"

"No," she said, "how did they keep you from dying in the bomb?"

"Oh," he looked away from her, and she knew she shouldn't have brought it up. Pete sat up, turned away, and reached to find his underwear on the floor. "They waited for me to come down for my smoke break," he said, his back to her. "Then a couple guys threw me into a car and drove away, and as soon as we hit the safe distance the building exploded."

"And then they told you why you lived," she said, ashamed. "They told you I bargained to keep you alive."

"Basically," he said as he leaned over the side of the bed to pick up his pants.

She pulled a sheet over her body as he climbed to his knees on the bed, still holding his slacks in front of his body. He walked to her on his knees, his right hand digging in one of the pants pockets. She stretched out, contented, and smiled up at him.

Hershey pulled a knife from the pocket and tossed the pants over her face.

She swung her left arm up to block the pants from landing over her eyes, and the arm consequently blocked the first stab from the switchblade as Hershey swung it down hard for her throat. The blade cut into her forearm instead of her throat, but Hershey had put his weight behind the thrust and the knife continued down, stabbing Erica in the left shoulder. She screamed and rolled as the knife pushed her left side into the soft hotel bed, so her right arm came up and around Hershey, grabbing at his free arm before he could use it to steady himself. She hooked her right arm around his left, grabbing his t-shirt at the shoulder, and with a turn of her hips she tossed them both off the side of the bed.

In a different situation, this move would have allowed Fatale to land with her attacker in an incredibly painful arm-bar. But as it was, she hit the ground on her left side, where the knife was still buried in her shoulder, and with a shriek of pain she let him go and Hershey rolled away, taking the blade with him.

"Peter," she said, her eyes flooding with tears. Hershey didn't acknowledge her voice. All of his tenderness, his affection, his very personality was gone. All Hershey did to acknowledge that the woman who loved him was calling his name was adjust his knife in his hand and go for another killing blow.

But the first stab had woken her up. She wasn't Erica now. She was back to what she had always been before—Fatale—and Fatale would defend herself. She was figuring out his style now, all recklessness, going for a quick, hard kill, and she was ready for him. She called his name again, in her gentlest, kindest voice, pleading for him to snap out of it, but underneath it she was preparing to move. Peter had been playing her, stringing her along and now that she was done working for Zoeli—or Mercier, now that she knew who he was—Peter was going to get rid of her. She hoped he would interpret her pleas as weakness and go for another foolish stab, and that's exactly what he did.

While Fatale was still lying beside the bed, he dove at her, knife first, throwing everything into a desperate attempt to kill her with one good shot. She exploded from the floor, letting his blade catch in the hotel carpet. His hand punched hard into the bed's metal frame and he grunted in pain, but by then it was too late. As Hershey landed on the ground, his sore hand searching for the knife beneath him, Fatale landed on top of him, pinning him face-down on the floor. Her hands went to his throat and pulled back hard, strangling him. He stopped feeling around for the knife, which she could see was beside his body, and instead he held his hands up, as if surrendering. She kept choking him. He bucked around, tried to turn his hips, but she adjusted and stayed in control.

"Why?" she asked. "I gave up everything for you, so we could be together."

Hershey choked out a sound. She relaxed her grip to let him breathe and speak.

"Did you think you were his only mole? When you came along they told me to keep you in line." She cut him off by pulling back hard, choking him again.

"By lying to me? Sleeping with me? You could have just sent me to seduce another agent. You didn't have to..." she trailed off, because now the tears weren't caused by the pain in her shoulder.

"I could see you were drawn to Quarrel. He was so low-level he'd be useless to Digamma, not to mention he's such a boy scout—ch—ackk"

She squeezed his windpipe hard. "So rather than tell me who you were, you decided to manipulate me until, what?" She stared into his eyes. "Until it was time to murder me?"

Hershey choked again. She held his throat hard for a count of twenty before she let him answer. His voice was raspy, and she knew how much it must hurt to talk. "Mercier cultivated your skills for more than one mission. We couldn't risk you falling for some kid and blowing the whole thing. And he warned me to never trust you."

Her fingers were wet, and she realized that Hershey was crying and drooling all over himself.

"I trusted you," she said. "You were the only one in my whole life I ever trusted. In my whole life . . . "

He gasped for air and afterward, in an instant where she was readjusting her hands, he said, "I'm so—"

She reset her grip, one hand on his jaw and one on the back of his head, and she jerked her hands around like she was turning a giant screw, and snapped Peter Hershey's neck in one stroke. His hands dropped to the floor, and when she let go, his head thumped to the carpet like she had dropped a bowling ball. She stood up, naked except her own blood and tears, her first love between her feet, and all her dreams about the rest of her life were just as dead as Hershey.

"Not as sorry as I am."

37

Jessica Swift watched through binoculars as Sam Boswell entered a warehouse on the outskirts of London. It wasn't some run-down abandoned old building, but rather a fully operational and extremely busy place of business. Large trucks pulled in and out on a regular basis, and men could be seen gathered by a side door, having a smoke on their break. Beside Swift, Khalid Saleb was taking apart the remote control of a toy car they had bought from a nearby store.

"How's it coming?" she asked, her eyes still in the binoculars.

"It'll work. You sure this is the place?"

"She's been here three times. It has to be the place."

Saleb stopped working on the remote. "If you were going to stash a hostage, would you bring her to a place full of a hundred potential witnesses?"

"Best hiding place is plain sight. Boswell's the only one of Milton's suspects who came across the pond, and to the very city where Thorpe lived. We need to see what she's doing in there. Quarrel's counting on us to get Mrs. T out of there tonight."

"Technically," said Saleb, "you were one of Milton's suspects. Or me, for that matter."

"Actually Milton ruled you out. You were unconscious or in prison for all the good stuff."

"It's nice to be trusted," he said with a shake of his head, before going back to work on the remote.

"You can remember how to do all that, but you can't remember . . . " she started to say but stopped herself.

"I still have skills. I remember languages, electronics, the alphabet . . . " he carefully set a screw aside, maybe to be used later. "But I have no real clue about who I was or what my wife was like. Some things give me flashes, sort of like a faint smell, if you know what I mean. Like, you think you smell something but you can't quite tell what it is until you get closer? That's what my memory's like, only I can never get any closer. I can tell certain things once had meaning, but I can't recall why. It's floating in front of me, but I can't place it."

She set the binocs aside to look over at him. "You'll have time to remember her. Once her killer's been brought to justice, you'll have all the time in the world."

Khalid smiled. "That's the problem. When this is done, I'll have nothing to do. Catching Jupiter is all I have."

She put a hand on his shoulder and gave a reassuring squeeze. "You can always work as a toy car repairman." Saleb chuckled and Swift pulled away from the window to look at the tools she had on the table. There wasn't much here, but she was working under such a tight timeline that it would have to do. She picked up the small, pocket-covered belt she wore whenever she was infiltrating a target, and began the familiar, comforting routine of packing her kit.

"What do we do if the plan doesn't work?" asked Saleb.

Swift grunted. "I won't let Mrs. Thorpe die. Or any of those workers caught in the crossfire. So if the plan doesn't work," she tucked a packet of folded paper into one of the pockets, "I guess she'll kill me. But I'll dial 911 first."

"It's 999 here," he said. "See, memory."

She chuckled. "Good to know."

"If we die, Mrs. Thorpe dies with us," said Saleb. "So if it comes down to it, I'll kill Boswell. Even if you can't."

Swift shuddered. Saleb knew the truth, even if she pretended not to hear him. They were in a kill-or-be-killed situation, and Swift would never kill. As she tucked her tranquilizer darts into the belt, she made sure to get the positioning just right, since this was likely the last time she'd ever do it.

"I'll take her alive," she said finally. "I have to."

After the sun had settled below the horizon, Swift was on the roof of the warehouse. She was tucked behind the air conditioning unit for the warehouse's offices, using the toy car's remote while staring into the screen of a tablet computer. On the screen she saw the output from the camera that they had mounted to the car, which was now driving through the office's vents. The air vents in the warehouse were big enough for Swift to climb through, but she assumed that there were too many workers in the warehouse for Mrs. Thorpe to be kept there. It was more likely she was tucked away in an office, where only a handful of people might pass by on any given day. In the office, the vents were big enough for the toy car, but far too small for even a person as small as swift to fit into.

Swift turned the car toward a vent that looked down on an office, then touched the tablet's screen to zoom the camera through the opening. This was one of the only offices with lights still on, but there was no hostage here. A couple of men, likely employees from the warehouse, were talking. One was leaning on a desk. Swift wished she had a microphone to listen in on their conversation, but the car only sent back visuals.

She zoomed back out, ready to drive on toward the next vent, when a woman entered the office. It was Boswell. She spoke brusquely to the two men, then all three went into the hallway, with Boswell leading the men. Swift turned the car and began to follow them, running above the offices while the trio walked down the hallway that ran a parallel course to that of the vent. She quickly checked each office she passed, making sure that they hadn't stopped in each one, but after a minute there was no sign of the trio and the vent came to a fork.

Straight ahead there was a vertical drop. She knew the layout enough to know that this was a drop down from the office to the warehouse level, which meant that if she committed the car to that course, she would never be able to backtrack to the office. It would be stuck down there for good. The other option was to turn left and circle around to the offices on the other side of the hallway, which seemed safer. Ultimately, she decided to keep the car on the same level simply to avoid the noise that it would make when it fell down the vertical shaft.

Rounding a couple of corners, she saw there weren't just downward-facing vents on this side. There was also a single vent that looked out to the side, and there was light coming in through this one. The camera on the car, which was a small wireless device sold in a surveillance shop, was mounted so that it faced forward and down, allowing Swift to see into vents but also drive the car. But now that she was looking out this unexpected sideways vent, she had to run the car's front tires up the grille a bit, to tip the camera upward to see what was outside. It took a few tries, and Swift silently cursed as she wondered how much noise the toy was making.

Finally, Swift got the camera to look out, and the vent faced the warehouse floor. She watched as Boswell led the men to one of the loading bays, and kicked the door of the truck that was backed up there. The door lifted upward and revealed two more men standing in what appeared to be an empty trailer. The men exchanged a few words, and then Boswell's pair climbed into the trailer and the other two got out. Swift realized that there was a faint glow of light inside the trailer, coming from a source that was far enough into the empty trailer that she couldn't see it. Swift tried to turn the toy car so she could see more of the area in front of the loading door, but the view was limited. From what she could see, there were no warehouse employees around, only Boswell and her cronies.

"I found her," said Swift.

"Where?" asked Saleb through his earpiece.

"Inside a parked tractor trailer," she studied the screen. "Bay twenty. At least two armed men inside, two more plus Boswell are heading back to the office."

"I'll reposition."

"Get inside the warehouse by the southeastern loading docks. I'm taking the truck from the outside," she said, already pulling the toy car away from the grate and setting down the tablet.

"When are you moving in?" he asked.

Swift pulled on a pair of leather gloves. "Right now."

376

She kept her head down and ran to the edge of the roof, looking down at the truck parked in bay twenty. It was the only truck parked on this side of the building. There were no people outside the truck. She looked along the wall and saw no cameras watching. She grabbed the edge of the roof, hopped over, and hung against the wall with her back against the cold brick. She bent her knees, pressed the soles of her shoes and the palm of her left hand against the brick, and let go. She slid down the wall, kicking off at the last instant so she hit the ground rolling and came up on her fingers and toes. She cautiously looked around to see if anyone was moving before rising to a crouch and moving to the sliding side door on the trailer.

The truck was completely ordinary, with a plain white semi-trailer. Swift took off the gloves and tucked them into her belt, retrieving both her lock picks and her tranquilizer gun. She checked that the gun was loaded with a clip of tranq darts and a fresh canister of compressed air, then set to work on the sliding door's lock. The lock was high enough above her head that she had to stand on her toes to pick it, but it opened without any problems.

"Wait," said Saleb, "I'm not in position yet."

Swift was too close to the truck to make a sound now, and too close to Mrs. Thorpe to wait any longer. All it would take now was to tranq the two guards, cut Mrs. Thorpe's bonds, and they could run away without Boswell even noticing. She passed the tranq gun to her right hand, aimed it toward the door, and slid the door open.

As soon as the door opened, one of the guards yelled for help. She hit him with the first shot. The tranq gun was manual, so she had to cock it again, and by then the second guard had his handgun drawn. He fired a shot at Swift, but she had ducked below the door to reload, so his shot missed. If he had been smarter he would have aimed the gun at Mrs. Thorpe, but he wasn't smart. Swift popped up for just a moment to shoot a dart into his thigh and ducked out of sight again. She heard him hit the floor of the semi-trailer with a thud, and that's when she popped up again and climbed into the trailer.

The guards were down, nobody was hurt. The noise was bad, but Swift had hoped to be gone before Boswell could react. It was only when she turned to Thorpe's wife that she realized that that wasn't going to happen.

Mrs. Thorpe was in a wheelchair, and she wasn't moving. Swift could see the older woman's eyes were watching her, saw a hint of pleasure on Mrs. Thorpe's face, but beyond that there was no sign that this hostage was going to be any help in her own escape.

"Are you Mrs. Thorpe?" she asked.

"Ool-ya," said the woman. It was like her tongue didn't really work.

"Is that a yes?"

The woman nodded.

Swift looked over the wheelchair and saw no ropes, chains, or bonds of any kind. Boswell must have taken Mrs. Thorpe's condition for granted, since there was nothing stopping Swift from taking her away. "I just hope I can lift you," she said.

That's when the truck's rear door flew open, and Samantha Boswell stepped inside, a handgun aimed straight at them. "Oh, it's you," she said. "I figured maybe Quarrel finally grew a pair."

"I'm taking Mrs. Thorpe out of this," said Swift.

"Another tranquilizer gun?" Boswell taunted when she saw the weapon Swift carried. "When are you going to learn I'm immune to those things? If you want to have a chance, bring a real gun."

"How could you do this?" asked Swift.

"How could I not?"

Swift screamed at her. "You have little daughters! I read your file! How can you possibly kidnap a helpless woman like this?"

"You answered your own question," said Boswell. "Is it horrible to take old Julia hostage? Yes. But you do horrible things to protect your kids."

"Your kids are in a safe house, protected from all of this. You don't see me pointing a gun at them."

Boswell moved her arm a little so the gun was aimed at Julia Thorpe instead of at Swift. "A safe house in the USA. There's no such thing as a safe house in a country that doesn't protect its people."

"You are goddamn crazy, lady."

"I'm a patriot. I signed on for CIA training when I was eighteen and spent my best years protecting that country. And what did we end up with? Fifty different intelligence agencies, each with its own jurisdictional pissing contests. Each one putting itself above the good of the nation. The safety of the nation. There have been terrorist attacks on our own soil. Assassinations of high-ranking diplomats, American children taken hostage, and every one of them could have been prevented if we didn't have a million goddamn agencies getting in each other's way. Withholding evidence, blocking investigations, protecting their own. This country is protected by a

379

shattered, broken shield. And I'm going to replace it with a new one."

"By kidnapping Thorpe's wife?" Swift stepped in front of Julia, so that the gun was once again pointed at Swift's chest. "By firing a giant microwave beam at your own country?"

Boswell didn't seem fazed by the fact that Swift knew about the Teacup. "I'm showing the world how broken the old system is. Think about it. Shark, one of CIB's guys detonates a DARPA-DOD weapon, built with the pentagon's knowledge and armed forces tech, which should have been guarded by the CIA. So many agencies are tied to the Teacup, and they'll all be torn down when the media learns what happened. No more CIA, bye-bye DHS, no more DOD or armed forces spy agencies. My friends in high places will ensure we replace them with a single, powerful new intelligence agency to keep America safe. We'll end all this nonsense and get back to protecting the nation."

"And you'll just happen to run this new agency? You kill Americans to get the big chair and the high pay grade?" Swift reached behind her back to touch something that was sticking out of her belt. "You say you're protecting your kids, but you're just another power-hungry asshole trying to manipulate everyone else, just like I've been dealing with my entire life."

"My daughters will grow up safe," said Boswell. "They won't be street trash that steal for a living."

There was a quiet thump inside the large air ducts that hung over the warehouse. It wasn't much, barely perceptible above the sound of Boswell's voice, but it was enough to catch her attention. Boswell turned, studied the vent that ran toward bay twenty. "Oh, is that

Saleb?" she asked causally before turning to face the warehouse, raising her gun, and firing five shots into the vent in a zigzag pattern.

A second later, several of the bullet holes in the vent started to drool strings of thick red blood. Boswell turned back to Swift, and Swift prayed that she hadn't noticed the object Swift pulled out of her pocket while Boswell's back was turned. "Looks like Khalid won't get his payback. I told you I never miss."

The blood from inside the vent was hitting the floor in sporadic drops, and gradually formed a small puddle before the bleeding stopped. Swift tried not to stare at the vent, but her hands were shaking now.

"Oh, you don't like blood, right? See, I read your file too." Boswell stepped into the trailer and moved toward Swift. "And you seem to break down when people around you die. Like Saleb up there just did." Boswell pointed the gun at Julia. "Step aside or I'll kill the crippled hag. I barely need her anymore, anyway."

Boswell walked right up to Julia and pressed the tip of her handgun to Julia's temple. Swift heard footsteps and saw that the two other guards were running down from the offices, each holding a handgun. Boswell stared into Swift's eyes, and Swift saw an insane calm. Boswell was a true believer. She thought that Mercier's plan was the morally right thing to do, and she'd do anything, including shooting Julia in the head, if it helped her accomplish that goal.

"I'm gonna kill this woman," said Boswell. "And I'm gonna warn Shark that you know about the Teacup so he'll be ready when your pal Quarrel shows up. And then he'll die, too. And when that thing goes off, some random oil workers in Texas are gonna die, too. And you know what? You could have stopped it if you had just brought a real gun. You think not killing people makes you noble? This is kill or be killed. Every one of those deaths is on you." Boswell aimed the gun at Swift again. "So would you like me to make you live through it, or would you prefer to die?"

Swift stared right back into Boswell's crazed eyes and felt something wonderful. It was the same crazy calm of when her training took over, but she was still in control. She knew exactly what she was doing. "I'd prefer to be smarter than you."

Swift nodded her head to the side, urging Boswell to look over her shoulder, to the end of the semi, where the two replacement guards suddenly collapsed and fell face-first to the ground.

"What? . . . " muttered Boswell, and just as Swift was about to say something clever, Julia Thorpe lunged forward and sank her teeth into Boswell's forearm. Boswell screamed and tried to pull away, but Julia grabbed at her with her one good arm, and Boswell lost her grip on the handgun before she managed to pull away.

And then Swift was on her. With punches and kicks practiced for years at The Academy, Jessica Swift let loose on Boswell, letting her fury power the punches. She backed Boswell into the wall and prepared for a judo throw takedown, but Boswell grabbed a handful of her hair and jerked her head to the side. Swift screamed and was pulled off balance, which was all that Boswell needed to take over the fight. Boswell wasn't emotional like Swift. She was a perfectly trained, efficient killer and she set to work chopping pressure points and elbowing Swift repeatedly in the jaw. Swift felt herself fading, knew that one or two more solid hits would knock her out cold, and that's when she opened her hand and let her thumb find the trigger button on her laser pointer.

Just as Boswell pulled back for a knockout punch, Swift clicked on the cutting blade and the light burned a jagged line on Boswell's forehead. Boswell screamed and flailed, stumbling backward. The smell of burnt hair hit Swift's nostrils as she pushed off the wall, raised a foot and booted Boswell backward, hoping to kick her right out the side door of the truck. But Boswell found her footing before the door, and stood up straight again in front of Julia, grinning with a look of grudging admiration. Boswell must have liked a good fight. Swift raised the laser cutter, ready for another rush from Boswell, but before they could clash again a gunshot rang out.

Boswell's pistol had landed in Julia's lap, and the older woman had managed to turn it around so it pointed straight at Boswell, and pulled the trigger. Boswell took the bullet in the thigh where it shattered on her femur. She doubled over in pain, barely standing, and muttered something that Swift couldn't make out. Swift later imagined that maybe Boswell had said, "So that's what it feels like."

And while Boswell was leaning forward, off-balance and in brutal pain, Swift stepped forward and threw a straight jab at Boswell's chin. The most dangerous woman in CIA history was knocked backward, out the door, and hit the pavement several feet below.

Swift and Julia looked at each other for a moment before Julia shoved the gun to the floor. Swift offered a handshake. "Jessica," she said.

"Ool-ya." Julia moved a shaky hand toward Swift, but when Swift shook the hand, she felt that Julia only really controlled the movement of a few squeezing fingers.

A moment later they heard footsteps and Swift turned to see Khalid Saleb walking up with his tranquilizer rifle raised. He walked right through the puddle of red corn syrup that had poured down from the vent that Boswell shot.

Saleb paused to cuff the unconscious guards and eventually joined Swift and Mrs. Thorpe at the side door of the semi, looking down on Boswell, who was laying helpless on the pavement, awake now but bleeding badly.

"I killed you," she said when she saw Saleb.

"You killed a toy car with a bag of fake blood on it," Swift said.

"But I never miss . . . " she said, her voice trailing off now as the pain and loss of blood were sending her into shock.

"We really taking her alive?" asked Saleb.

Swift patted him on the shoulder. "She left you alive to get arrested for treason. You get to return the favour."

Swift and Saleb hugged, and when they pulled apart, Boswell was unconscious. They pulled the earpieces from their ears and then they both pulled out cellular phones. "You call for an ambulance, and MI-6," she told him. "I'll call Mr. Thorpe."

She turned back to Julia as the phone dialed overseas. "Julia, it's time we let your husband do what he does best."

Julia might not have had much for fine motor skills, but her smile was absolutely gorgeous.

38

Thorpe woke inside a control room of some sort. There was a long black desk on which three computers sat side-by-side, and on the wall above them, a huge monitor displayed a fourth image. It was a satellite camera, pointed down at a body of water. Mercier sat at the desk, his rolling chair in front of the left-side computer, where he was clicking away at a screen which Thorpe couldn't see since Mercier's body blocked his view. Mercier was whistling. Thorpe craned his head to the sides, looking behind himself, and saw the same two guards from the penthouse had joined them in the control room. Thorpe supposed that made sense, since Mercier would only share his crimes with the smallest circle of trusted employees. It made it easier to kill the witnesses.

Thorpe was tied to a heavy chair. His arms were still cuffed together by the steel band, but now there was also a nylon rope looped around his waist several times to tie him to the simple, steel, four-legged desk chair.

"Where are we?"

"Oh, Thorpe," Mercier said with a smile. "I thought you'd sleep through it."

"Through what?"

"The end," Mercier said, waving to the screens, as if their displays would mean something to Thorpe.

"What are you going to do?"

"I'm going to use America's weapon against them. Don't you see the brilliance in it?"

Thorpe shrugged. "Murder's murder."

"A machine, built by the defence department, triggered by a control computer the army and air force intelligence agencies were supposed to be guarding. A weapon that the CIA and the CIB knew about, but didn't destroy. A weapon bounced off a Department of Homeland Security satellite. Do you see it yet?"

"You're going to kill all those people, just to stick it to the intelligence community? Why, because they stopped hiring you in eighty-seven?"

"To replace them. Once it all comes out, and it will, can you imagine the fallout. When the public learns that Shark Scarret—a convicted traitor who the CIA continued to let out in public, free to travel the world and plan his attack, with access to top secret files—was the one who pushed the button? Heads will roll. Entire agencies disbanded and merged together. The impractical system of dozens of agencies will end, and a new all-powerful agency will take over. And when power concentrates in a new, single intelligence service, who do you think they'll turn to?"

"To the company that's already running everything."

"Globection. I have enough senators in my pocket to guarantee it will come my way. A new, single espionage service, run for private interests, running the government and turning a profit all at the same time. I'll be America's god."

Thorpe snorted. "You think Shark will let you sell him out? Once his name leaks, he'll hunt you down."

"Don't think so. At first I had planned on ordering my men to kill him, but now I think your pals, Hall and Quarrel, will do it for me. And if Shark survives, I always have more contractors to send after him."

Thorpe's cell phone, sitting on top of a filing cabinet to Mercier's left, started to ring. Mercier held up the display for Thorpe to see. "Who's calling? Quarrel?"

"That's one of his old numbers."

Mercier put the call on speakerphone.

"This is Thorpe," he said.

"It's Jessica Swift."

"Oh, hello, Swift. You're on speaker with a few analysts."

Mercier shot him a look for that, but Thorpe only smiled.

"What have you got to report, Swift?"

"I'm in Zurich," she said. "I found out the truth about Khalid Saleb. He's dead now."

"Did you do that, Swift?" Thorpe asked, shocked at what she was saying.

"I found the files Jupiter was protecting, but they contradicted Saleb. It was the details that caught him in the lie. Proved he was in on his wife's killing after all. When he went on missions, he always gave her his wedding ring. She wore it on her necklace. But not that time. So that proves he was in on it; kept his memento since he knew he'd never see it again. You see what I mean, Thorpe?"

Thorpe nodded for a second, before realizing he needed to say something.

"Understood, Swift. I don't know who you report to now, Harry Milton's dead."

"I heard."

"I'd tell you to disappear, but I bet you're doing that anyway. Have a better life, Swift."

"I will. And Thorpe," she paused, "stop whatever's happening."

She hung up. Mercier ended the call and smiled.

"Poor thing. 'Stop whatever's happening!'" he mocked. "Broke her own rules about killing and Saleb wasn't even in on it. I think when this is over I'll track her down and let her know she killed an innocent man. In her mental state I bet she'd have a real meltdown. You think she'd kill herself or beg me to do it?" Mercier put the phone down and walked back toward his computers. "And well done, Thorpe. I like having you for a pet. You say all the right things."

He slid the rolling chair to the center computer and brought its display up on the big screen for Thorpe to see. It was a sort of schematic of the satellite. As Mercier ordered a command, the machine began to change. Thorpe realized that this was the program that controlled the satellite, and the visual was a computer model showing what was happening to the real satellite in orbit. What looked like wings began to unfold out the sides of the module. Once they were straight out, the arms began to rotate, unfolding as they did, forming a circular ring around the front of the satellite. A giant reflective dish in space.

"It's a Homeland Security satellite. The irony's the best part." Mercier waved his arm theatrically and pressed the enter key. "There. It's locked in. Even if you got loose and killed me, there's nothing you could do to stop it."

He brought up the other image, the satellite's camera. It had moved, no longer pointed at water, it was aiming for a dry patch of land with some kind of industrial buildings in the crosshairs.

"What are you aiming at?" asked Thorpe.

"My Russian friends put a lot of money into this. You see, we need to attack an American target to get the politicians in line, but the exact target doesn't matter much to me. The Russians have requested that we microwave a few oil refineries. It'll give their new pipelines some added value."

"So you'll get to take over the intelligence world and your pals in Moscow take over the oil business."

"Finally, you see the beauty of the plan."

"But your friends are killing each other. Maslov, Plunov. They're not even in charge of those companies anymore."

Mercier shrugged. "I still have to keep my friends friendly. The Russians know a lot more about my past than your side do."

Mercier pointed to the refinery on the screen. "You ever put metal in the microwave? I wonder what'll happen when we do it to an entire building. All that metal, all those flammable liquids. Should be quite a show."

Thorpe slumped in his chair. "If it's over, then kill me," said Thorpe, deflated.

"Giving up so easily?" mocked Mercier. "You don't want to stay alive while the public reacts? When they know that dozens of intelligence agencies failed them? Don't you want to live long enough to see me crowned as America's new intelligence czar?"

Thorpe shed a tear. "I'd like a drink."

"You always were a drunk."

"My briefcase," said Thorpe, "is just a travelling bar. A testament to my weakness. It's holding my favourite vodka and vermouth. If you don't mind."

"A cigarette before the firing squad, eh?" Mercier nodded to a guard and told him to get the case. The muscular guard popped open the case and held it in front of Mercier, the contents on display: vodka, vermouth, a jar of olives, two metal glasses, and two martini shakers.

"Good stuff," said Mercier. "Is that martini shaker solid gold?"

"Of course. I took it from your old employer, Hans Midas. Although I confess I've never used it. I thought that the ice cubes would dent the gold, so I've always used the steel shaker."

"Hans was a strange man. Gold everything. He even paid me in gold when I shot his wife." Mercier opened the vodka and sniffed it. "But since we have no ice cubes . . . " he pulled the gold shaker from the case and set it on the desk. As he opened the vermouth, Thorpe made a request.

"Martin, this is the last drink I'll ever have," he said staring his enemy in the eyes. "Don't skimp."

Mercier laughed and picked up a bottle in each hand, pouring both into the shaker, more than enough to fill a glass. He seemed to relish the moment. The satellite reflector open and waiting on the screens, his worst enemy begging for a last drink, the moment made even sweeter by having a few minutes to spend taunting Thorpe before the main event got started. Mercier whistled again, making exaggerated flourishes as he placed the other half of the shaker on top, twisting it to make sure it was tight.

And with just as much exaggerated gusto as he had displayed in pouring the bottles, he began to shake the golden shaker. The one that Thorpe had avoided shaking for all these years, even though he carried it with him all the time. Thorpe counted the shakes, up and down.

Up and down.

Five shakes, six, seven . . .

And Martin Mercier became a red spray that painted the walls and ceiling. The explosion from the gold shaker launched the guard with the case backward, but it completely destroyed Mercier.

As soon as the bomb went off, Thorpe was on his feet. In all the conversation, he had distracted the guards from the fact that he was using the saw in his watch to cut the rope around his waist. One guard was down from the force of the explosion, his face sliced in a few spots by golden shrapnel, and the other guard was too stunned to react when Thorpe jumped from the chair and ripped the gun from his hands. Thorpe's wrists were still bound by the metal cuff, so he had to turn all the way around to fire three shots into the other guard, who was still on the floor, dazed by the explosion. The other guard recovered from losing his gun and grabbed Thorpe in a bear hug, forcing him to lower the gun and stopping him from turning back around.

Thorpe aimed down, between his feet, and fired a shot into the guard's toes. He screamed and let go, and Thorpe spun away, creating enough space to raise the gun at the guard.

"Can you shut that satellite off?"

The guard was bewildered. "I don't . . . I—"

Thorpe shot him between the eyes.

He turned back to Mercier—or the red splash that remained of him. The gold shaker had accelerometers and plastic explosives in each end. After eight good shakes in rapid succession, the bomb was triggered.

391

Thorpe had kept the shaker around for all those years for just this occasion, disguising a last-resort weapon behind his reputation as an unrepentant drunk. Thorpe had been in tough situations before, but never so completely defeated that the enemy would pick up that tempting shaker and make him a drink. Mercier had been the first to have Thorpe so helpless, but he had also been so confident that he didn't realize the solid gold shaker was a trap.

The explosion had completely obliterated Mercier's forearms and much of his torso. His remains had blown backward, into the computer desk, crushing the center-most monitor. His blood covered the walls, floor, and ceiling. Most of his head was intact, but had been snapped backward so hard it was barely attached to his neck, and jagged chunks of gold shrapnel stuck out from what remained of his arms and torso.

Thorpe spat on his body. "Waste of good vodka."

He searched the floor for his cell phone and called the number Swift had used. Even if Julia couldn't say anything to him, he had to talk to her. He had to at least let her hear that he was OK. Once that was done, he would get to work on freeing his hands and trying to get in touch with someone who could evacuate that refinery in Texas. Even if Quarrel failed to stop the weapon, Thorpe could try to save some lives.

But hopefully, hopefully, Quarrel could shut the damn thing down.

The phone rang once and Swift answered. "Hold out the phone for Julia," he said, the tears on his cheeks surprising him as much as the croak in his voice. "And thank you." He finally broke down sobbing.

He heard Julia's breath and broke down crying. "It's alright now, hon. We made it."

39

Quarrel was freezing cold as the helicopter flew over the coniferous Yukon forest below. Quarrel and Hall were in the back of the chopper, with Meg in the pilot's seat. The roar of the rotors was loud enough that they could only speak to each other through their headsets. Quarrel was holdings his arms around himself, trying to stay warm, but Hall was busy sorting through the gear he had brought.

"We're getting close," said Meg through her radio.

"OK. Don't get too close," said Hall. "They might shoot us down. Find a road or a clearing and land." The trees below were sporadic, with many open spaces where Meg could have landed, but she saw that there were two roads nearby intersecting near the TCPE location, and opted to set the chopper down on the pavement.

Within a couple minutes, Meg had settled the helicopter down on a road south of the TCPE. As she killed the engine, Hall threw the door open and started to unpack. It was below freezing outside, but Jack didn't seem to notice. "Grab that," he said, pointing to a backpack. Hall took two packs for himself and jogged for the tree line at the side of the road. Quarrel noted that Jack was keeping his sidearm in his right hand, ready to fire at any moment, even as he carried two backpacks and had his assault rifle slung over his shoulder. The helicopter was loud, and Shark would know that they were close. Quarrel pulled out his own gun, grabbed the backpack and climbed out, ducking under the spinning blades. Meg hopped out too, and together they ran after Jack, into the forest.

Jack had already run up a small rise in the land, seeking high ground to survey the TCPE. Meg and Quarrel caught up after Jack found a spot he liked and lay down. The spruces that covered the landscape as far as Quarrel could see were spaced quite far apart, with several feet between trees, so the forest wasn't great cover. Fortunately, the ground was already sprouting thick grass, so once they were able to lie down, Quarrel felt like they were well concealed. Jack already had his binoculars up to his face by the time Quarrel and Meg lay down next to him.

"How's it look?" asked Quarrel.

"Well guarded," said Hall, passing the binoculars.

Quarrel crawled to the edge of the hill and looked down and saw the TCPE for the first time. The facility was roughly square-shaped, encircled by four straight walls of concrete. The walls looked about ten-feet high, but then there was a chain-link fence on top of the wall, and that fence was topped with barbed wire. From this vantage point, it looked like the only way in was through a single gate that accessed the road. The gate was guarded by a team of eight armed GX men who looked like soldiers. Quarrel knew that these guys would be loyal GX contractors who Mercier or Shark had chosen specifically for this job. On one hand, it was good to see professionals like this, since they were guys you reason with, as opposed to a gang of criminal thugs who would just kill you outright. On the other hand, Jack Hall could take down criminals and thugs but up against professional soldiers, their little group was severely outmatched.

Inside the Teacup's walls, there were two prominent features. One was the bunker, a chunky cement building with few windows, which housed the power supply, control room, and living quarters for the people who worked on the array. It would have been designed to hold soldiers if it had worked, but since it was deemed a failure, Quarrel reckoned the only people who had ever lived in that bunker were the Defence Advanced Research Projects Agency construction team who built it. The bunker was in the southwest corner of the square complex, leaving most of the area open. In this open field was the other feature, the array of microwave emitters. These looked to Quarrel like huge antennae; hundreds of giant metal objects pointing at the sky. The emitters were laid out in concentric circles, with the tallest of the emitters on the outermost ring. The result was that the array looked a bit like a cup, and the bunker looked a bit like a handle, so the Teacup name wasn't just a convenient acronym but actually represented the shape of the facility in an abstract way. Quarrel knew from the blueprints that each emitter could be angled and controlled by the consoles in the bunker, and that collectively they created a beam that was supposed to be strong enough to cook an area the size of half a football field.

"There are hundreds of those things," Quarrel said. "There's no way we have enough detonators to take them all out."

"I was thinking the same thing," Jack replied, "but we have more than enough to blow the control room to hell."

In addition to the team guarding the gate, there were other hired killers patrolling the yard, and a handful were lingering around the bunker. There had to be twenty of them. Mercier had spared no expense.

"OK, but how are we supposed to get past all them?" asked Meg.

"Hell if I know," growled Hall. "I figured it would just be Scarret and a handful of men, keeping the circle of people who knew about this thing small. Didn't expect a goddamn platoon."

Quarrel dug into his pack and pulled out a walkie-talkie. He flipped it on and started scrolling through frequencies. "What are you doing?" Meg asked.

"Finding their frequency," he responded.

Hall took the binoculars back and studied the TCPE while Quarrel listened to static. It took a while, but eventually Quarrel caught a snippet of a voice and was able to dial in the right frequency.

"—landed to the south," said one man.

"Well there's no sign of 'em. Probably circling north," replied another.

At least they hadn't been spotted yet.

Hall put the lens caps on his binoculars and set them down beside his pack. The second pack, he tossed toward Meg. "I think we can take them. I once had to take down a compound in Afghanistan that was a lot like this. Meg, can you shoot?"

As Jack was about to get rolling on some crazy plan where the three of them charge dozens of mercenaries and survive, Quarrel cut him off by pressing the transmit button on the walkie and joining the mercenaries' conversation.

"Attention Globection contractors," he began, "you can all go home."

Hall's eyes widened with shock, but he held his tongue.

"I repeat, you can all go home ASAP," Quarrel continued, before letting go of the transmit button.

"What the hell are—" Hall started, but then a man's voice came over the walkie.

"Who the hell are you?" asked the man.

"I am an agent of the Canadian government, and every last one of you is committing treason against the United States by being here. Your company is working against your country, and any man who does not leave immediately will be charged with terrorism, murder, and high treason. If you fire that weapon, you will all be facing the death penalty.

"Your employer, Hugo Zoeli, was actually a known terrorist named Martin Mercier. Mercier has already been executed for his crimes. Globection no longer exists. You will not be paid, you will not be rewarded. Leave now and you might escape charges, or stay at your posts and die by lethal injection."

He let go of the button again, waiting for someone to respond, but there was nothing.

"You expect that to work?" Hall asked.

"They're not a bunch of evil henchmen. A lot of those guys are former soldiers just following orders."

They watched as the guards at the gate talked to each other. One man seemed to be visibly angry, and another threw his rifle to the ground. They yelled at each other. Finally, radio silence was broken by a familiar voice.

"He's lying," said Shark Scarret's raspy, cigar-ravaged voice. "We are here to protect America's secret weapon from the terrorist traitor, Jack Hall. Every man who leaves his post will answer to me."

398

Quarrel raised his own walkie. "I'm not Jack Hall. My name is Christopher Quarrel. Don't believe me? Call GX headquarters in New York. Try to get Zoeli on the phone. I bet the FBI answers your call. Or call up the Canadian Security Intelligence Service and ask about me. You are all being lied to. Peter Scarret is here to use the weapon, not to protect it." Quarrel turned off the walkie and tucked it into a pocket on his pack.

"Oh, great plan," said Jack, watching as the guard at the gate picked up his rifle.

"Hey, it was worth a shot. They already knew we landed nearby, but now they have a reason to desert this place and let us in. Even if they all stay put, we haven't lost anything for trying."

"Yeah, I like the idea of talking better than the idea of charging in there and getting shot to death," added Meg.

"You notice anything about those emitters?" asked Hall.

"Like what?" she asked. "They all seem pretty well preserved for being almost thirty years old."

"What I notice is that there are no nerds like you out there working on them. When Thorpe called he said the satellite reflector is open and ready. So if they're not prepping that array, then it must already be prepped. So I'd say we have the next couple minutes to shut that thing down or a lot of lives and America's economy are about to get cooked."

Meg nodded and said nothing.

"So," Hall continued, "when I propose that we assault that place and take those guards down, I don't say it because I want to die; I say it because we have no

399

choice. This is what it's like in the field. You can't solve anything with a goddamn conference call."

"OK," she said. "I get it. And I can shoot, if I have to. I'm a good shot."

"Wait," said Quarrel, who was still facing toward the TCPE facility. A Hummer had driven out from behind the bunker and was at the gate. After a discussion with the driver, the gate guards let the Hummer leave. It got on the road, headed west, and took off at high speed. A few of the gate guards watched the Hummer go, and then all eight of them ran toward the bunker. They disappeared behind the building, and a moment later another large SUV pulled out, headed for the road, and took off west.

"They're leaving," said Quarrel. "The guards are all leaving."

Hall and Meg watched in rapt silence as another two vehicles left down the road, and after five minutes, the facility looked empty.

"They left," said Meg. "I can't believe that worked."

"Or they want us to walk into a trap," said Hall.

"Then we'd better walk into it quick," said Quarrel, "so we'll have time to plant some bombs before they get back."

Hall grunted approval, and the three of them picked up their packs and started down the hill toward the facility. Hall and Quarrel holstered their side arms and readied their rifles. Meg only had the handgun. As they jogged, Hall offered advice on how to plant the bombs. Meg already knew all this, since she was the weapons expert, but Quarrel was glad to hear it.

"In your pack, you have two components. One is the plastic explosive, the stuff that looks like putty. Put a golf-ball sized clump on every computer or electrical panel you see. The other component is the detonator. You switch each one to the on position and stab it into the putty, and make sure it's secured in place by both prongs. Got it?"

"Yeah."

"I'll plant mine on support structures to bring the building down. We each have a remote trigger, so if I don't make it, you can still blow this place," said Hall. "And one more thing. Those detonators are small explosives. Make sure you only turn them on as you plant them. If any of the detonators in your pack are turned on when you push the button, you'll blow your own ass off."

"Got it," said Quarrel. As they ran, with adrenalin flowing in his veins, he barely felt the weight of his pack, although he was unusually attuned to the feel of the gun in his hand. He understood the weight and texture of the rifle more now than he had ever felt another weapon. He knew that he was going to go in there to kill at least one man—Shark—and it was the first time in his life he'd had time to think about killing beforehand. He thumbed the safety off as they reached the east-west road in front of the facility and headed for the gate.

Once they were inside the walls, Hall headed for the building, checking inside the door before waving for Quarrel and Meg to follow him inside.

While he waited for Hall's all-clear, Quarrel tried to ignore the fact that the emitters were quietly humming.

#

Jack slipped into the bunker first, checked that the hallway was clear, then opened the door for Meg and Quarrel to join him. He looked to Quarrel once all three were inside.

"Do you know where the control room is?" he asked.

Quarrel had seen the blueprint for this bunker, so he would have the best idea of the layout. "Downstairs," he said, "it's underground."

"Then that's where Shark will be. That's where I'm going. You clear the upper level. Plant bombs wherever you find electrical or computer systems. And we don't know how many guards they had. I don't want them sneaking up behind me so make sure this place is empty."

Quarrel nodded and said, "That thing outside was ready to fire. Be quick." Then he raised his weapon and took off around the corner.

Jack looked at Meg, who was fidgeting, running her thumb along the textured grip of her handgun. She was terrified, which meant Jack couldn't take her with him. "I'm going after Shark. I need you to stay out of sight until the coast is clear. Once I secure the control room I'll need you to shut this thing down," he said.

"I can come with you," she said, "I told you, I can shoot."

"What's better, your technical skill or your combat experience?"

She snorted.

"Exactly. We need you alive to kill this damn thing, so hide in here," he opened a door and found a small kitchen with a few empty tables, "and stay quiet."

Meg rolled her eyes, and went into the kitchen. "We don't have much time. Kill Shark and get back here."

"I will. Keep your safety off and watch this door. Just don't shoot me when I come back."

Meg nodded. She walked behind the table closest to the door and knelt down, supporting her hands on the tabletop, her gun aimed at the door, exactly where Jack was standing. "I'll be fine," she said, looking down the sights.

Jack smiled reassuringly and pulled the door shut.

From the main door of the bunker, there were two corridors. The one Jack was in right now had a few doors and ended with a door that was labeled as a stairway. The other was the corridor that Quarrel was working through. Jack headed for the stairs.

The stairwell was just cement with fluorescent lights in the corners. He ran down the first flight of stairs in a rush, jumped a one-eighty spin, and settled on the landing with his gun raised. The gentle impact of his back against the concrete wall, which he normally wouldn't have noticed, sent a spike of pain through his head that left him seeing double. He squinted hard, opened his eyes slowly, and let them focus again. His concussion was still overwhelming, but the mission didn't allow him time to take a few weeks off to get better. He had a man to kill and no head injury would stop him. Once he was seeing clearly, but still feeling a headache and powerful nausea, he crept slowly and carefully down the rest of the stairs. At the bottom of the steps he slipped off his backpack and tucked it into the corner. He could come back for it when he came for Meg. First, he had to kill Shark, and weighing himself down with explosives would only make that job harder.

He worked his way down a hallway, and saw only two doors: one at the very end of the hall, and one on the left. He opened the one on the left and found a small closet full of ancient cleaning supplies. That meant the one at the end of the hall was the control room. Kicking the door open, he scanned the room beyond the doorway, his eyes and gun-sights always pointed in the same direction. Inside the door was a room lined with hulking metal consoles covered in an assortment of buttons and dials; the computers of an earlier age. Mounted at eye level were several monitors, most of which were very old, except for one modern flatscreen that displayed a satellite's point of view of the Earth. The others were displaying security camera feeds from all over the TCPE facility. There was no sign of Scarret. Jack stepped toward the door, about to step inside, when a small black ball bounced off the door frame and exploded.

The flashbang sent a jolt of pain through Jack's head like he'd never experienced before. Sidorov's tortures were nothing compared to the blinding, all-encompassing pain of having that little grenade explode less than a foot from his concussion-rattled head. Before he could even comprehend where the sudden pain had come from, he felt the rifle stripped from his hands. An instant after that, something hit him hard in the jaw.

Jack slipped into unconsciousness just long enough to wake on the floor, his ears ringing and his mouth full of vomit. As he spat he felt a combat boot kick him hard in the ribs, and for a second he was choking. Strong hands grabbed his wrists, forced them above his head, and then steel cuffs squeezed around his right wrist, then his left. He coughed out the last of the vomit and forced his eyes open, but the flashbang had essentially blinded him. He saw a shape that he knew was a man, but for that moment he couldn't even remember who the man was. He pulled against the cuffs, but he had been locked to something secure and all he did was bruise his wrists. The strong hands stole the side arm from Jack's hip, then felt around his body until they found the remote trigger he had been keeping in a chest pocket.

"There we go," said Shark Scarret's voice.

Jack tried opening his eyes again and was able to see the shape of the traitor standing above him.

"Hey there, Jack, nice of ya to drop by." Shark slipped Jack's detonator into his own pocket. "I saw on the security camera that you guys brought Milton's little techie with you. How about you just tell me where you stashed her?"

Jack spat thick, foul-smelling saliva toward the traitor, but it fell short and landed on Jack's leg.

"Try to be nice, Jack. You don't want your legacy to be that you died in a pool of blood and puke, now do ya?"

Jack stared at his enemy until the ugly, burn-melted face came into focus. Slowly, the fog over Jack's brain cleared away. "This is insane, Scarret."

"Yeah," he replied. "You tend to go a little nutty when your own country puts a bomb in your neck."

Shark walked over to one of the consoles and started inputting commands. Jack's eyes focused enough to see the shape of the stolen control computer resting on the console, connected by a rope of multi-coloured wires. "I heard Quarrel's little speech on the radio. I

405

guess old Thorpe managed to take down Mercier, huh? Good riddance."

The image on the screen above Shark's head changed. The satellite was moving to a new target, but Jack's eyes couldn't see what it was.

"Now, if Thorpe's still at GX, and he's got a whole bunch of Feds with him like Quarrel said, then they probably know about me. And since Mercier's plan was shot once Thorpe evacuated the refineries, I think I'll just use this here giant laser gun to get rid of all those witnesses."

"You're pointing it at Globection's head office?"

"You guys forced my hand. I was happy blowing up refineries in Texas, but a man's gotta do what he's gotta do."

"You're gonna microwave New York City," said Jack, his voice both disgusted and defeated. "So many innocent people . . . "

Shark finished typing on the controls and made a show of pushing one last button. The console that Jack's hands were cuffed to started to hum, as if there was suddenly so much electricity flowing that the pipe might burst. Shark strutted over to Jack, leaned over his fallen enemy, and smiled.

"New York is nothing but a bunch of assholes living in the world's biggest target. The only thing that protects that target is a bunch of guys like us, Jack. Guys willing to die for the country. And when that country forces you into slavery with a goddamn bomb in your vertebrae, well then that target kinda deserves to take a shot, don't you think?"

Shark looked back at his various displays. "Looks like the reflector won't be in position to get New York

406

for another five minutes." He picked up Jack's rifle. "But I think maybe we should try a test run."

#

Quarrel was inside a room that was intended to be an office, sticking a blob of explosive to a fusebox on a wall next to a picture of President Bush One. He was flipping a switch on a detonator when his walkie crackled.

"Quarrel, buddy. Long-time no see. How ya like my place?"

It was Shark Scarret's voice on a frequency that only Jack and Meg's walkies were programmed for. Quarrel hated to think what that meant.

"No response?" asked Shark. "Nothing? Now I realize it's a fixer-upper but it does have cable TV. So wherever you are, you should switch one of the CCTVs to channel four."

Quarrel reached for the rifle that was hanging off his shoulder, but then he thought about the detonator in his hand. If he blew up the handful of bombs he had planted, it wouldn't be enough to bring the bunker down. He felt the weight of the brick of explosives in his bag and wondered if he put the whole brick on the floor above the control room, would that be enough to cave it in on Shark's head?

The radio crackled again, and Shark's voice returned. "Hope you're watching. I was really worried that this wouldn't work, even after Mercier's engineers said it was good to go."

Suddenly the entire building seemed to vibrate. Quarrel ran to a TV that was mounted to the wall in this office and turned it on. He was shocked to see a security camera feed showing the array of emitters. Shocked because Jack Hall was on his knees, his hands cuffed to one of the metal towers. Shark was standing about ten feet away, holding the walkie and an assault rifle.

"Any last words? Jack?" he taunted, then held the radio toward Hall.

Jack Hall shouted at the walkie, "It's aimed at New York! Blow it up now!"

On the screen, Shark ran away from the array, disappearing from the frame. Then Quarrel heard the humming get louder and louder, higher in pitch. He dropped his pack and ran out of the office, hoping that he could make it to Jack in time. When he made it to the door, there was a glowing red light bulb above the door, which was locked by an automatic system designed to stop people from foolishly killing themselves by walking outside when the array was active. Quarrel looked out through the small window in the door and saw Jack convulsing.

His skin was turning red as blisters formed all over his body. Jack's entire body was stiff as if he was having a seizure, jerking against the cuffs that held his ankles and wrists to the tower. Quarrel couldn't hear any sound from Jack over the throbbing hum of the field, but the open mouth betrayed that Jack Hall was screaming. And he was bleeding from everywhere. Fingernails, eyes, ears, nose, mouth. Jack's blood was boiling in his veins, the pressure bursting blood vessels from the inside out. After thirty seconds, the noise settled back to a deep hum, and Jack slumped closer to the ground, but the cuffs held his body in a sickening imitation of kneeling. His skin was bright red, his cheeks stained pink where blood mixed with what remained of his eyeballs. The field of emitters had cooked him alive.

If that radiation had bounced off the dish and hit New York, there could be thousands of people in the same condition.

Quarrel wanted to go out there and see if there was anything he could do, but he knew that he needed to get back to his explosives and find a way to bring the building down on top of Shark. Then he heard Meg's scream echo from the stairway down the hall.

Shark's voice came back again. "And now we know it works. I still have one hostage. Bring me your explosives in the next sixty seconds or I put a bullet in her heart."

40

When Quarrel got to the bottom of the stairs, the door to the control room was still open. Through the door, he could see a puddle of vomit on the ground, with drag marks passing through it.

"Come on in," said Shark from somewhere inside the room.

Quarrel slid his rifle into the room, then he tossed the heavy object that he was holding in his right hand. The grey brick, topped with small metal objects, landed in the middle of the room with a thump.

"I just stuck every detonator I have into ten pounds of plastic explosive and I have my finger on the trigger. If you shoot me, this whole place comes down," Quarrel called into the room. He walked through the door with his hands raised so Shark could see the remote trigger.

Inside, Shark was standing against the far wall, Meg standing a few feet in front of him, her hands on head, her face lined with tears. "I'm sorry," she said. "Jack said to watch the door but there was another way into the room and he got behind me . . . "

"It's OK," Quarrel reassured her.

The brick of grey putty had landed a few feet from both Shark and Meg. The control room wasn't all that big, maybe fifteen by fifteen feet, and in this underground location the walls would have no give. If Quarrel blew up the plastique, the explosion would leave nothing alive in this room.

Shark took a second to look at the explosive, and Quarrel glanced at the monitor that showed what was clearly a satellite view of a city.

"It's already revving back up to fire, you can't stop it now." Shark sounded almost giddy, as if it was Christmas morning.

"I can blow it up."

"Then we all die. You ready for that?"

Meg's tears still streamed. "Blow it up. It'll kill thousands of people."

Shark screamed at her. "Shut up!" and then he was calm again as he faced back to Quarrel. "You slide me your detonator, and I let her go."

"And then what?"

"And then the two of us watch that building burn and then I kill you. But I promise lil' Meg here can live."

Shark waved the rifle at Quarrel, gesturing for him to walk to the corner of the room where Jack's puke stained the floor. "You stand in that corner and I'll let her walk to the doorway. Then you just give me the detonator and she can go. Come on, you don't really want to watch this girl die. Her only crime was that she wanted to get out of the office and help you out."

Quarrel walked to the corner. Meg shook her head at him to say she didn't want this, but when Shark told her to walk to the door, she did what he wanted. She was only a step from the doorway when he told her to stop. "Now, the detonator."

Quarrel's handgun was tucked into the back of his pants. He had been careful to keep it hidden. He extended his left hand, holding the detonator in front of himself, and started to slowly walk toward Shark.

"I said slide it to me," Shark snapped. Quarrel kept walking, slowly, toward Shark. "Stop moving!"

Quarrel stopped, but now he was so close, Shark could reach out and grab the detonator from his hand if

411

he wanted. "She leaves before I take my thumb off the trigger. Then you can take it."

Shark sneered, which was a particularly ugly expression considering that half of his face looked like Freddy Kruger. Finally, Shark decided that Quarrel's terms were acceptable, and he turned so that the rifle pointed at Quarrel instead of at Meg. "Get out of here," he called. Meg was gone in an instant, and then Shark clamped his hand over the detonator. For a second, Quarrel's thumb was still on the trigger. With only the two of them in the room, they stared into each other's eyes, and Quarrel relaxed his fingers, letting Shark take the trigger from his hand. Shark leaned over to set the detonator down next to two identical devices—Jack and Meg's—while at the same time, Quarrel's right hand slipped behind his back to grab the gun.

Shark saw him make the move.

Shark's finger twitched on his rifle's trigger and Quarrel ducked to the right. The three-round burst missed by inches, and then Quarrel lunged at Shark, knocking he older man off balance. Quarrel pulled his own gun, but Shark slapped at it, raking the butt of his rifle over Quarrel's right hand. The blow to his knuckles knocked the sidearm from Quarrel's grip, and the gun landed on the floor. Quarrel shoved past Shark, reaching for one of the detonators, but Shark grabbed him and pulled him back. They wrestled over Shark's gun, Quarrel trying to keep it pointed away while Shark tried to line up a shot. Shark squeezed the trigger and bullets hit the cement between Quarrel's feet. Quarrel head-butted Shark in the nose and tried to wrench the gun free, but Shark countered with a hard kick to the side of Quarrel's knee. Quarrel stumbled, and Shark got behind him, wrapping his arms around Quarrel's throat. Quarrel tried to grab Shark's hand, hoping to pull the gun free and get himself out of the choke hold, but it was hopeless. Shark squeezed tighter and Quarrel felt lightheaded as the blood flow to his brain was cut off. He felt weak.

"Let him go!" commanded a woman from the doorway. It was very hard to hear over the ever-increasing hum of the TCPE, but Quarrel didn't think that voice sounded like Meg.

Shark's grip relaxed and his arm moved away from Quarrel's neck to grab the shoulder of Quarrel's shirt. Shark pulled Quarrel in front of himself as a human shield, and Quarrel felt hot steel on his temple as Shark held a gun to his head. Quarrel wiped his eyes and saw the woman that had joined them in the control room.

"Erica?"

The woman once known as Fatale was dressed for war, in a Kevlar vest, combat boots, and military-style fatigues. She held an automatic rifle aimed straight at both Quarrel and Shark. Quarrel knew immediately that if she shot, the bullets would cut through him and go right into Shark, killing them both.

"What the hell are you doing here?" whined Shark.

Erica thought for a moment before she answered. "The right thing."

"What, did Martin's check bounce?"

Erica nodded, just a little. "Something like that."

The room was filled with humming sounds now. All of the consoles were fired up. On one of the old TV monitors, there were arcs of electricity jumping from a few of the emitters.

"Take the shot," Quarrel told her.

"Oh, shut up," Shark said. It would have been easier for Shark to hold a gun to Quarrel's head if he had a handgun. With the rifle he was forced to awkwardly hold the gun with one hand and Quarrel's shoulder with the other.

Quarrel looked Erica in the eye. "It was Hershey, right? What Mercier promised you? But he's not the guy you thought he was."

She adjusted her grip on the rifle. "He's dead."

"You do that? Or Mercier?"

"It was self-defence. Sometimes you have to defend yourself. Like in training."

Quarrel remembered this situation from Jack's training program. A hostage used as a human shield. An agent who could save the day by taking the impossible shot. Quarrel hadn't taken the shot in training, and Erica had insulted him for it. Now the situation was reversed, and she was the one who refused to shoot.

"There are two ways to win the game," she said. "You can take out the objective, or you can kill the other team."

"What the hell are you talking about?" Shark snapped at them.

And Quarrel remembered something else. He remembered that even when unarmed, Shark still had a secret weapon. A weapon the drug lord in Venezuela hadn't expected.

Quarrel and Erica looked each other in the eyes. They knew what had to be done. The machine outside was humming so loud the whole facility was vibrating.

Erica held her finger to the trigger. "Just like training."

"Defenders win."

414

Quarrel slapped Shark's gun barrel forward, away from his temple, and Shark immediately put both hands on the rifle, thinking that Quarrel was trying to steal the gun. But instead, Quarrel turned, grabbed Shark's belt buckle, and pulled. A small, razor-sharp dagger slid out of the buckle, and before Shark had a moment to recover, Quarrel buried the blade in the side of Shark's neck. Shark made a weak yelping noise and swung the gun around to point at Quarrel. Quarrel dove away as Erica opened fire, and a dozen bullets tore into Shark Scarret before he could put his finger on the trigger. Shark hit the floor in a wet heap, dead before he hit the ground.

The machine was humming at a higher pitch, cycling up. This is what it had sounded like when Quarrel reached that red-lit door, when he had watched Jack die. "Meg, get in here now!" shouted Erica.

"No time!" Quarrel shouted back.

He picked himself up off the floor as Meg ran into the room, heading for the main control console. Quarrel ran to the remote triggers. Erica's eyes went wide and she screamed at him.

"You'll kill us all!"

Quarrel grabbed one of the remotes just as the machine peaked and made a massive crackling sound. Quarrel put his thumb over the button and squeezed the trigger.

The explosion was massive. The ground shook for miles around. The foundations of the basement control room cracked wide enough for soil to spill in. The TCPE sprayed sparks, and a few of the upstairs rooms that Quarrel had planted bombs in exploded and caved in.

"What happened?" asked Erica.

"I blew up my brick of explosives," Quarrel said.

415

"I thought that was your brick of explosives?" shouted Meg, pointing at the brick in the middle of the room, while shaking uncontrollably from the damn-near-overdose of adrenaline in her veins.

"I was bluffing. That's Jack's. None of those detonators are armed."

"But you didn't have time to plant enough bombs upstairs," she said, still trying to understand.

"I studied the blueprints, remember? I realized I knew where they buried the main cable that powered all those emitters. When Shark said he had you, I just put the whole brick outside on top of the power line."

Meg's eyes went wide and for a moment she had nothing to say, and then she shuddered and a halting, hysterical laugh shook out of her. Erica joined in, her whole body shaking as the laugh escaped.

Finally, Meg found some composure again, leaning on the console to support herself. "Remind me never to play poker with you."

They found a key for the handcuffs in one of Shark's many pockets and cut Jack down from the emitter. He was a hero, and Quarrel wanted him treated like one. They loaded Jack's body into the back of the stolen pickup truck that Erica had used to get here from Whitehorse.

"How did you find us?" Quarrel asked her as they closed the hatch.

"GPS in Shark's neck. Mercier always knew where his favourite pet was."

Meg climbed into the truck's passenger seat. She called out to them. "I'm not flying in my condition. Let's just drive somewhere that's not here. Someone else can come back for the chopper."

Quarrel looked to Erica. "I just have one thing to do."

He headed back into the building, picking up Jack's brick of explosives off the control room floor. He flipped one of the detonators to the on position and set it down on the control computer, a few feet from Shark's body. He went back outside to the truck, where the two women were waiting with the truck running. He climbed into the back seat. "Jack swore to destroy that stolen computer, and now he has."

Erica was in the driver's seat, and as soon as Quarrel was in the back, she pulled out onto the road. Quarrel found the remote trigger in his pocket, and squeezed. As they drove, the sound of the second explosion erupted behind them. A few seconds later, the whole bunker caved in on itself. Meg looked back to see the roof disappear behind the outer wall.

"In your professional opinion as a weapons expert," said Quarrel. "Is that thing done?"

She nodded. "I'd say it's scrap. Still, if your air force ever wants a target to test some drones on . . . "

#

They drove for hours, finally reaching a hotel in Whitehorse. They stumbled in, exhausted and hungry, and found a table at the bar. They ordered food and drinks and soon enough the three of them were drunk, full and happy.

Quarrel excused himself to the bathroom, and while he was in there he took out his cellphone and called the authorities. He explained the situation and requested that the Canadian Army be sent to dismantle what was

417

left of the TCPE. He didn't bother calling the CIA or CIB. Finally, he dialed William Thorpe.

"I haven't heard about anyone getting fired today," Thorpe said when he answered. "And that means kudos, young man."

"One man did," Quarrel said, looking into his own bloodshot eyes in the bathroom mirror. "Jack."

"Damn shame. He deserved better."

"Are you OK?" Quarrel asked.

"Fine, fine. I'll be alright." Thorpe was talking over a lot of background noise.

"Where are you?" Quarrel asked.

"Over the Atlantic. I've someone waiting for me in England."

Quarrel smiled. "Good. I'm glad." He paused, and for a moment he just listened to the white noise. "And Swift? Is she . . . "

"Gone. I called your phone and Saleb answered. Said she's in the wind."

Quarrel suddenly felt very alone. "I'm glad," he said. "She deserves a better life."

"As do you, young man."

"Shark had that thing aimed at New York. He wanted to take you out," said Quarrel.

"Well let's be glad you stopped him. If you're ever in London, I owe you a pint."

They said their goodbyes and hung up.

When Quarrel got back to the table, Meg was drinking alone.

"Where's Erica?"

Meg shrugged. "She said you had to call the cops eventually. She's gone."

Quarrel sat down and picked up his half-empty beer. On the coaster beneath his glass, Erica had written a note: "Should old acquaintance be forgot and never thought upon."

"To Fatale," Quarrel said, raising the glass. "May she rest in peace."

EPILOGUE

The house smelled like stale air and mildew, and every surface was covered in a fine layer of dust. At some point months earlier, some relative had come and draped sheets over the upholstered furniture, but most of the house still looked like someone lived there. There was a stack of bills and torn-open envelopes on the counter, a book lying open and upside-down on the side table. The TV remote on the coffee table. All of it covered in dust, as if the people living here had simply vanished in an instant. Which, Quarrel thought, was essentially what had happened.

Quarrel held the door open for Khalid Saleb, who was carrying a large plastic bin full of personal effects and clothing. Saleb walked into the living room and dropped the bin next to a sheet-covered sofa and looked around, studying every detail.

"Welcome home," said Quarrel. "Anything familiar?"

Saleb shook his head. "It doesn't feel like it was mine, you know? Don't even know if I like this furniture."

Quarrel shut the door. "You'll get used to it. I don't think there's anything better to jog your memory than this."

Khalid Saleb had been cleared of all charges. After her arrest and the failure of the Digamma plot, Samantha Boswell faced the death penalty. She cooperated fully with the authorities, confessing to everything in order to get a reduced sentence and visitation with her daughters.

Boswell had told the truth about shooting Saleb, but she had lied about deliberately letting him live. When she put the bullet in his head, she was sure she had killed him. Saleb and his wife, Jessica Jordan, had been close to uncovering a mole in the CIB. Their investigation was into Shark, which is why Boswell was able to manipulate them into separating. Once they were apart, Boswell had moved on Saleb while Shark had murdered Jordan.

The plan cooked up by Mercier and Boswell to take over the American intelligence world counted on killing Shark as a scapegoat. Shark had figured it out and kept all the evidence of Boswell's part in Jordan's murder, intending to blackmail Boswell once she was installed as the new head of the CIA. That was why Boswell had used the Jupiter program to order Jessica Swift to destroy the files. It was only through Swift's kind heart that any of the truth came to light. Now Boswell was in maximum security, Shark was dead, and Swift hadn't been seen since that night in London.

"It's a big house," said Saleb. "I don't know how two people lived here, let alone just one."

He walked over to a cabinet in the corner and picked up a photograph. It was Saleb and his wife on their wedding day. She was in a strapless white gown, her smile showing pure joy. Saleb traced a finger around her face. "She forgot about bringing something borrowed. So right before the ceremony she traded shoes with her sister since nobody could see her feet under the dress, anyway. She got blisters walking down the aisle."

Tears welled up in his eyes. "I remember that. But then I look at her face and she's a stranger. It's like there's a hole in my life. I know she's in my head but I don't even know where to look for her."

Quarrel couldn't think of anything to say. He was realizing more every day that he felt the same way.

#

After a night at Saleb's house, Quarrel returned to Ottawa. He climbed into his own car and drove back to his own apartment, both of which were strange experiences after being away for over a month. His apartment had both a lock and a deadbolt, which had to be opened with two different keys. He had locked both when he departed for Virginia, but as he walked down the hallway toward his own front door, he noted a crack of light. His door was open.

He reached for a gun, only to realize that he had signed his weapon back into Gig's care at CIB almost a week earlier. He stayed close to the wall, sneaking up to the door, and heard the sound of music. To make things even stranger, he could smell something cooking inside his own apartment. He crept to the door and peeked inside. His apartment looked the same, but the lights were on. He pushed inside.

Creeping through the living room, he entered the kitchen where strips of chicken were sizzling in a pan. Then someone behind him spoke.

"Hungry?"

Quarrel jumped around to face her. Jessica Swift looked different. Her hair was lighter, and it framed her face in wavy layers. She was tanned, radiant even, and wearing a pale yellow dress. She was completely different from the woman who had broken into CIB in black tights, black hair, and black face paint. She was *brighter*.

But for all the changes she still had the same eyes, the same look she'd given him on their last night together.

"I tried to find you," he said. "But since you left the phone behind, I had no way to get in touch."

"I know. I had to get out of it. Away from my life. I had some issues to sort out," she was so close he could feel her breath on his neck. "I actually read that copy of Jekyll and Hyde. He thinks he's one thing, but then his bad side keeps breaking through, eventually he's always Hyde. I think maybe I'm like that. I thought I was Jupiter's secret spy, and suddenly this rebellious side just took over."

"You came back," Quarrel whispered, "from what they tried to make you. You followed me here?"

"My last ties to The Academy died with Milton. I didn't have anything to run away from, so I figured I'd run toward you."

Quarrel kissed her cheek, and pulled back a bit to look her in the eyes. "You know, this isn't the place to avoid that world. I'm still part of all that, unless they fire me."

"I know," she said. "I figured something out before I went after Boswell. With my skills, what The Academy taught me, I can do good. I don't have to break my rules; I can use my skills and still respect myself. I don't have to kill anyone. I just have to be smarter than the bad guys." She looked comfortable, confident. As if all the shattered pieces of Jessica had finally started to heal together. "And I will be."

"No more Jupiter, eh?" Quarrel asked.

"All gone. I'm a free woman." She went to the pan and stirred it with a spatula. "I suppose if I can't find work as a sneak I could work as a personal chef if someone were to offer me a place to stay."

Quarrel smiled and started to say something but his phone rang and cut him off. He answered on speaker, so Swift could hear.

"Quarrel, this is director Standing," said the authoritative woman's voice.

"What can I do for you?" he asked. He was genuinely curious what they would do with him, since his field trip to the CIA was over.

"We're been going over your report about what you were up to recently."

"OK?" he said.

"Everything seems mostly tied up except for one thing. That list you gave us, of the original members of this Digamma group who erased Mercier from the records . . . "

Quarrel had written the list from memory during his debrief at CSIS, since his original copy went with Swift when she crossed the ocean.

Alpha (KGB): Vladimir Plunov

Beta (KGB): Plunov's partner, now dead according to Crowe

Gamma (CIA): ?

Delta (USA): Shark Scarret

Epsilon (GBR): Julia Thorpe

Digamma: Martin Mercier

"We think we have a line on the one loose end. Gamma. But it's a long shot. He's a major player in the CIA's European branch. He's been in charge for decades and there's no way the CIB can touch him." Director Standing cleared her throat, and then the same woman who had once thought Quarrel was nothing but a nuisance said, "We need an experienced hand in the field on this one. With CSIS-2 in tatters, Quarrel, you're the best we've got."

Quarrel looked at Swift and she grinned. He spoke to the phone. "Director, you heard my debrief. I'm not cut out to do this sort of work alone. If you want me, I'll need to bring some backup."

Swift pulled her new brown hair back into a ponytail and moved the pan off the burner. Quarrel pulled her close. "Two tickets to London."

THIS NOVEL WILL SELF-DESTRUCT IN
3 . . .
2 . . .
1 . . .

THE END

ALSO BY SHAUN TENNANT

Blood Cell

Josh Farewell is a three-time escapee who boasts that no prison can hold him.

After the inmates take over C-Pod at Pittman Penitentiary in a brutal riot, they realize too late that they are not alone. Something is hunting the inmates.

Something hungry.

Surrounded by dangerous and untrustworthy felons, Josh must find a way to escape before the thing in the darkness kills them all.

Killing Machine

In this collection of five short stories, reformed assassin Theo Daniels takes bloody revenge on everyone who had a hand in killing his best friend.

Even if those targets are ninjas, spies, or former allies.

www.ingramcontent.com/pod-product-compliance
Lightning Source LLC
Chambersburg PA
CBHW051513250626
47156CB00001B/81